BY STEALTH

BY STEALTH

Colin Forbes

LONDON   NEW YORK   SYDNEY   TORONTO

AUTHOR'S NOTE

All the characters portrayed are creatures of the author's imagination and bear no relationship to any living person. Equally, all houses, residences, international organizations, and companies are non-existent inventions.

This edition published 1992
by BCA
by arrangement with Pan Books Ltd

First Reprint 1993

Copyright © Colin Forbes 1992

The right of Colin Forbes to be identified as the
author of this work has been asserted by him in accordance
with the Copyright, Designs and Patents Act 1988.

Grateful acknowledgement is made to A. P. Watt Ltd
on behalf of the Executors of the Estate of G. P. Wells
for permission to quote from *A Short History of th World* by H. G. Wells,
to Grafton Books, an imprint of HarperCollins Publishers Limited,
for permission to quote from *The Turn of the Tide* by Arthur Bryant,
and to The Telegraph plc for permission to quote from the edition of
November 28, 1988, © The Telegraph plc, 1988

CN 6595

Printed and bound in Great Britain by
Mackays of Chatham PLC, Chatham, Kent

FOR JANE

CONTENTS

Prologue

Paula Grey didn't notice anything sinister. At first . . .

A November sea mist trailed damp fingers across her face. She stood at the edge of the Lymington marina on the south coast of Britain, facing the invisible Isle of Wight. She was quite alone at eight in the dark of the evening. The atmosphere was creepy as the mist became fog. The only sounds were the slithering lap of waves against the stone wall below her, the muffled chug-chug of the small power-boat carrying her close friend, Harvey Boyd, further away, out into the Solent, the sea.

She calculated he was not yet a hundred yards from the marina, full of private yachts swathed in blue plastic for winter. The powerboat was moving into the main channel, no longer even a blur.

They'd had an argument over their last drink at the Ship Inn. Paula had first wanted to stop him embarking on a dangerous voyage. She had then tried to persuade him to take her with him.

'Not on your life,' Harvey had snapped.

'But you've just said there's no risk.'

'I don't know what's out there. A "ghost" ship? My pal, George, disappeared crossing to the island.'

Boyd, well built, six feet tall, dark haired, clean shaven, ex-SAS, had shaken his head. Paula persisted.

'You're contradicting yourself. No risk. Now you hint something strange is out there on the Solent.'

'I'll be back in an hour or less. Meet you here. Then a slap-up meal with Tweed at Passford House . . .'

Boyd was not only an ex-soldier of the élite force: he was an expert technician. He had erected sophisticated radar in the powerboat. So he should be all right, Paula tried to convince herself as she perched at the edge of the sea wall, pulling her windcheater closer at the neck, adjusting the scarf tied over her head. But she couldn't rid herself of some awful premonition.

Her hands touched the night binoculars looped round her neck. It was almost high tide. Larger waves slapped the base of the wall, throwing up spray. Harvey would give me hell if he knew I was standing here all alone, she mused. Then she frowned.

The swirling fog was creating nightmare shapes out over the water. She could have sworn she'd seen something large moving slowly. As the raw cold began penetrating her windcheater she raised the glasses with her gloved hands. She took off the right-hand glove to adjust the focus, heard a sound like padding footsteps behind her. Glancing round, she saw only fog. She listened. Her imagination running riot. She concentrated on focusing the binoculars.

Clouds of fog shifted, assumed weird patterns. Nothing substantial. No other vessel would be out on a night like this. Somewhere in the distance a foghorn droned its mournful dirge. The lighthouse. She could still hear the gentle chug-chug of Harvey's powerboat, moving slowly, threading a course down the channel. Then she had the first real premonition of disaster.

A muffled grinding, tearing noise. Like a steel hull bursting through wood – through the hull of a powerboat. A rending, crushing sound. She swung the glasses in the direction she thought the sound had come from, knowing the fog would distort the location of what sounded like a frightful collision. She forced herself to hold the glasses steady.

'Oh, God! No! Not Harvey . . .'

It took her seconds to realize the absence of something.

2

The chug-chug of the powerboat's engine had vanished. She breathed heavily, taking in gasps of ice-cold air. A fearful silence descended, punctuated by the crash of even larger waves hitting the sea wall. She waited.

It had seemed hours. But it was only fifteen minutes later – she had automatically checked her watch. Tweed's training jogged her even as she fought down the terror. It was only fifteen minutes later when the swift incoming tide carried a blurred shape along the wall below her. A body. She knew it was a corpse even though she couldn't see it clearly.

Her booted feet carried her slowly back along the edge of the wall, keeping pace with the floating object. Paula moved like a robot. The tide was forcing the corpse up the channel against the wall. Then a new horror gripped her. The tide was starting to go out.

But some quirk of the current continued to float the body shoreward. Beyond the end of the wall a cobbled ramp descended into the river – a ramp where craft were shoved into the water. If only the current continued to carry its hideous cargo a short distance further Paula was confident she could haul it ashore.

She quickened her pace to reach the ramp first. Stuffing the binoculars into her windcheater pocket, she ran, bent down at the foot of the ramp. Waves broke, water slushed over her boots. The corpse floated over the ramp below the waterline. She grabbed, caught hold of an arm swathed in a familiar, now sodden, pea-jacket.

It took all her strength to haul the waterlogged corpse out of the greedy sea which felt as though it was struggling to pull back its obscene catch. Despite the cold, sweat streamed down her as she heaved it clear up the ramp, then let go, fighting for breath.

Exhausted, wet through, she fumbled for her pocket torch. She hesitated before she switched it on. '*You've got*

3

to do it,' she said out loud through gritted teeth. The torch beam shone down on the upturned face of Harvey Boyd, his black hair matted to his skull. His open eyes stared up at her sightlessly. His right ear and a layer of skin had been slashed from his head.

She sucked in her breath, fought down a feeling of nausea. It was horrific. She spoke aloud again. '*Get to a phone at the Harbour Master's building. You've seen a dead body before.*' She felt rooted to the spot, not wanting to leave him exposed to the fog and the cold. And she hoped to God she could reach Tweed at Passford House.

'The body is being loaded aboard an ambulance outside. They're taking it to the mortuary at Southampton. We don't waste time round here,' said the Acting Harbour Master.

A man called Walford, heavily built with a weather-beaten face, and stubborn jaw. Tweed studied him before he replied. Deputy Director of the SIS, Tweed was a man of medium build and height. Of uncertain age, he wore horn-rimmed glasses and was the man you passed in the street without noticing him, a trait he'd found useful in his profession. But there was a certain magnetism in his personality and Walford found his stare unsettling.

'I'd like to take a look at that body now,' Tweed suggested.

'What for? Who are you? You've no authority.'

Walford's manner was aggressive. They stood in his starkly furnished office inside the big white building situated close to the ramp and the marina beyond. Tweed had taken Paula's phone call from his room in Passford House Hotel, a ten-minute drive outside Lymington.

Her teeth had chattered during her brief call and she'd admitted she was wet through. Before leaving Passford House Tweed had thrown a towel over a hot radiator, had gone to her room with the key she had left with him, opening drawers swiftly while he collected fresh under-clothes, a sweater and skirt, a lined trench coat. He had stuffed the warm towel inside a cool-bag to preserve the heat.

Bob Newman, world-famous foreign correspondent, had turned up unexpectedly just before he left Passford House. It was Newman who had driven Tweed in his Mercedes 280E to the Harbour Master's building. He was outside now, checking where the tragedy had occurred.

'I'd still appreciate a view of the body. I knew Harvey Boyd,' Tweed persisted mildly.

'A friend? You can see it at the mortuary . . .'

'I can order you to stop that ambulance. Even have it brought back here immediately over the radio.' Tweed was getting fed up with Walford. 'I'm Special Branch . . .'

He produced the folder forged in the Engine Room basement at the London SIS headquarters. Walford took the folder, gazed at it, his surly mouth tight with frustration.

'Never seen one of your lot down here before . . .'

'You're seeing one now. Hadn't you better get a move on and stop that ambulance?'

'Miss Grey has already identified the body,' Walford said half under his breath as they went out into the icy fog.

'A second identification never does any harm.'

Inside the ambulance, at Walford's request, one of the attendants pulled back the sheet covering the corpse laid out on a stretcher. Tweed gazed down on the savaged head and face with a poker expression. Inwardly he was shocked.

On leaving the SAS, Harvey Boyd had applied to join the SIS. He had passed all the severe training courses designed to break a man under pressure. Those had been physical endurance tests. Later he had sailed through the relentless psychological examinations. Now, about to serve his country again, he was going to end up on a cold mortuary slab, cut about by a pathologist.

'That's Harvey Boyd,' Tweed said tersely. 'I may wish to choose my own pathologist. Warn Southampton. I do have that power . . .'

He left the ambulance abruptly, leaving Walford to follow, went back inside the building. Paula opened a door and came in clad in the new clothes Tweed had brought, her wet things inside a plastic bag he'd given her. She rushed forward and hugged him as Newman entered a few steps ahead of Walford.

'Tweed, you're so considerate,' she gasped out. 'I was like ice. That warm towel was heaven. And the change of clothes.'

'You may be in a state of shock,' Tweed warned. 'A hot drink would help. No alcohol.'

'Mr Walford provided me with one when I asked him. A mug of steaming cocoa.'

With her back to the other two men, she lifted her head off his shoulder and Tweed caught the flash of humour in her grey-blue eyes. Only a man like Walford would serve cocoa and she hated the stuff.

'We shouldn't really have the press in here at this stage,' Walford grumbled, eyeing Newman.

'He's a close associate of mine,' Tweed said, and left it at that.

No point in explaining that Newman had been fully vetted years before, that he'd worked closely with Tweed on a number of secret missions. The Harbour Master hadn't given up. He was holding a long form while he continued gazing at the foreign correspondent.

He saw a man close to forty, five foot ten tall, clean shaven, athletic in movement, with light brown hair, alert eyes, and a face suggesting strength of character. Walford had seen photos of him in the newspapers above reports from trouble spots all over the world, but not for several years. Bob Newman had written a blockbuster international bestseller, *Kruger: The Computer That Failed*. It had made him a fortune and now he could do what he liked. Walford waved the form.

'The police will want a statement about this episode

from Miss Grey. I'll need some details myself . . .'

'The Chief Constable, Mark Stanstead, is a friend of mine,' Tweed interjected. 'She'll give her statement to him.'

'Then,' Walford plodded on, 'there's the question of informing relatives . . .'

'He was a distant cousin of Sir Gerald Andover – his only relative,' Tweed informed him. 'He also happens to be someone I know. Lives way out in the New Forest. You know his address? Good. Tell us how to get there and we'll drive to Andover's place now.'

'I'll tell you one thing, Mr Walford,' Paula said suddenly. 'Just before Harvey's – Mr Boyd's – engine stopped I saw the vague outline of a large vessel in the fog coming up the river. At least there was something . . .'

'I suppose she's overwrought with her experience,' Walford began, staring at Tweed.

'Then I'm overwrought, too. Let her finish,' Tweed snapped.

'Some vague shape, anyway,' Paula went on. 'I *did* see something.'

'Nothing else was moving on the river tonight,' Walford insisted. 'You must have imagined it.'

'Oh, really?' Paula was furious. 'You think Harvey Boyd pulled out the plug on his own boat and then sliced the side of his head off?'

'He was a bloody fool to venture out in these weather conditions . . .'

'He might have been a fool but he was a brave one,' she raged. 'He went out because a pal of his, George Stapleton, disappeared a month ago crossing to the Isle of Wight in his yacht. He just vanished. No trace of wreckage was ever found. Mind you, that *was* a month ago. Maybe you've got a short memory?'

'No need to—'

'And while we're on the subject, how many other vessels have disappeared in this area in the past year?'

7

'I'm not a computer . . .'

'So there have been other mysterious disappearances? I'd like to know how many. Please. You could check the records.'

'I suppose I could . . .'

'Then suppose you do just that. Now!' Tweed intervened.

'Five altogether.' Walford sounded reluctant to admit the fact. 'If silly stories get bandied about a lot of the yachtsmen who use our marina might look for a different anchorage. Bad for business.'

'Oh, Lord!' Newman spoke for the first time. 'Bad for the tourist trade. Here we go again – the old *Jaws* syndrome.'

'There's no sharks round here,' Walford rasped.

He reached for an old red leather-bound ledger from a shelf, began leafing through it. Newman looked grim.

'There may be no sharks but there is the odd jellyfish.'

'I'm looking up the register,' Walford growled. 'Not that I see this has anything to do with our experience tonight.'

'Just give us the statistics in detail and we'll be the judge of that,' Tweed told him.

'Mid-October,' Walford began, 'a George Stapleton took out his yacht bound for Wight in a heavy fog. Never reached Yarmouth. No wreckage ever found.' He turned back several pages. 'You should be dealing with the Harbour Master himself on a job like this.'

'So where is he?' Paula demanded.

'On holiday abroad. I'm by way of just standing in till he gets back. Here we are. Early February this year. Two youngsters sailed – separately – into the Solent with about a couple of weeks between them. Neither of them returned. No wreckage washed up.'

'The weather at that time?' Tweed queried.

'Heavy fog. The idiots . . .' He glanced up, saw Paula's expression, changed his description. 'Neither of those

8

yachtsmen enquired here about conditions. And here is number five – including your Harvey Boyd. Middle-aged chap called Benton, friend of your Sir Gerald Andover.' He looked at Tweed. 'He went out in a small powerboat beginning of February. And before you ask – again in a dense fog. No sight or sound of him or his vessel since he sailed for the River Beaulieu.'

'Five missing boats in a year?' Tweed emphasized the note of incredulity. 'Surly there's been an investigation? Questions asked?'

'Comes in cycles.' Walford closed the ledger with a snap, his expression mulish. 'In previous years you get not a single accident for ages. More youngsters can afford a yacht these days.'

'Benton wasn't a youngster,' Tweed pointed out.

'And that reminds me. Shouldn't you phone Sir Gerald Andover, seeing as he's the only relative of this Boyd?'

'You don't phone news like that when he's close enough to break the news to him face to face. You were going to show us how to get to his house. And I presume there'll be a search for any wreckage from Boyd's powerboat?'

'Coastguard's already been informed.' A gleam of triumph in Walford's eyes. 'Of course they can't go out tonight. Fog's getting worse. And I've a map here I can mark so you'll find Andover. Not easy to locate in the Forest.'

He spread out on the scrubbed wooden table an Ordnance Survey map he'd hauled off the same shelf after replacing the ledger. Holding a biro, he looked up in surprise as Paula stood beside him.

'I'm a good navigator. On land, anyway,' she explained.

'You drive back into Lymington, take the Brockenhurst road here . . .'

His biro followed the route, which was complex, warning her where she could easily go wrong. She thanked him as he handed her the map.

9

'The police . . .' he began as his visitors hurried to the door.

'I told you I'd contact the Chief Constable,' Tweed reminded him. 'Thank you for your co-operation.'

Outside the large white building a spacious car park stretched away into the grey fog. Tweed had loaned his Ford Escort to Paula to drive Boyd into Lymington. Parked next to it was Newman's Mercedes. Walford had followed them, stood in the doorway.

'Mr Tweed,' he called out, 'you said Special Branch – what was Boyd really up to?'

'That's right,' Tweed responded ambiguously. 'Must go. I'm in a hurry to let Andover know what's happened.' He lowered his voice. 'Paula, you know how to get us there. Why not take my Escort. We'll keep on your tail.'

She unlocked the door, slipped inside as Newman opened the driver's door of his Merc. and Tweed sat quickly beside him. In the distance they heard the siren of an approaching patrol car.

'That's why you were in a hurry to get clear,' Newman remarked.

Before Paula switched on the Escort's ignition she lowered her window. Despite the cold air she welcomed it to clear her mind. Near by she heard the screech of a seagull. The piercing cry, fog-muffled, sounded as mournful as the foghorn she'd heard at the end of the marina wall. A requiem for the dead.

'One thing's certain,' Newman remarked as he followed Paula's tail lights towards the car-park exit, 'whatever the rest of the night holds for us it can't be as great a shock as Paula had back there at the marina.'

It was a comment he was to regret making within the hour.

PART ONE

Kidnapped – No Ransom

1

To Paula's relief, the fog disappeared on the outskirts of Lymington. With the map open on the seat beside her, she drove at speed along the deserted A337 with desolate heath on either side. She welcomed being on her own: it gave her a chance to restore her normal resilience. Concentrating on driving pushed out of her mind the dreadful experience.

Approaching Brockenhurst, she just caught sight of the right-hand turn-off to Beaulieu in time, flashed her indicator, swung on to a twisting country road which was the B3055, leading eventually to the first place of human habitation, Beaulieu.

Walford had warned her there was a long stretch of what he'd called the wilderness – the fringe of the New Forest. In her rear-view mirror she saw the comforting headlights of Newman's Merc. tracking her a short distance behind. Now she had to be sure not to drive past *Prevent*, the home of Sir Gerald Andover, buried in the woods as Walford had described it.

In the Mercedes Newman maintained the same speed as Paula but was careful to keep a reasonable distance from her. He guessed she might have difficulty finding the house and wanted room for an emergency stop if she pulled up suddenly.

'Was it a good idea to let her drive alone out here after such a shock?' he asked.

'I did it deliberately,' Tweed replied. 'She needs to get her act together as quickly as possible. She'll want to show me she can do just that. And she'll do it much better on her own for half an hour or so.'

'If you say so. I had a look at Boyd in the ambulance.'

'And how did you manage that? They don't let just anyone examine a corpse,' Tweed remarked.

'Oh, I said, wouldn't you let his brother see him? They let me inside at once. Note I didn't say I *was* his brother. They just made the assumption.'

'One of your tricks from your foreign correspondent days. What was your impression? It wasn't a pleasant sight.'

'That a bloody great meat cleaver wielded by a Norse god had sliced away the side of his skull. No ordinary ship could have caused such a frightful clean-cut injury. It would break through the hull first, carrying some of the wreckage with it,' Newman pointed out.

'And Paula didn't hear the sound of any other vessel's engine. Only the chug-chug of Boyd's powerboat – until it stopped for ever. It's a mystery.'

'Another minor mystery is why did you come down to the Passford House Hotel? Very nice place – but you don't take holidays.'

'I had a call from Sir Gerald Andover asking me to come and stay there. He asked me to wait until he contacted me,' Tweed said.

'So you rushed down – and at the same time Paula's driving down to the same place with Boyd. What's going on?'

'I wish I knew. Another mystery.'

Newman reduced speed. The well-surfaced road, more hilly than he'd expected, was twisting and turning round sharp bends. On either side his headlights swept over bare trees, branches reaching up towards the sky like skeletal hands. A lot of oaks, and here and there a copse of dense evergreens. And mist was appearing in the Forest, curling forward between the trunks, masking his windscreen. He started the wipers going and Paula's red lights came up clearer.

'Who is this Sir Gerald Andover?'

'A near genius. For years he was research director on the main board of one of the biggest oil companies. His main job was to predict the future – how the world would develop globally. He foresaw the 1973 oil crisis long before it happened, even sent the PM of the day a report warning him the Arab sheiks would form a cartel and blackmail the West by rocketing the oil price. No one took any notice of him. Then, as you know, it all came true. I know him. Bit of an odd type.'

'Odd in what way?'

'Self-sufficient to an extreme degree. Never suffers fools gladly.'

'I can't stand stupidity myself. Draw me a picture of him.'

As they drove deeper into the Forest the grey mist thickened into a near-fog. Newman set his wipers moving at top speed. The atmosphere was becoming claustrophobic with the fog, the trees closing in to the road's edge. Not a sign of any other traffic.

'Andover is a tall, erect man in his fifties. A trim fair moustache. Slimly built. An authoritative manner. An old China hand.'

'Meaning precisely?' Newman probed.

'That was an exaggeration. He visited Hong Kong a lot but never settled there. Something strange happened about three or four months ago. At the height of his career he resigned overnight from the oil company and other directorships he held. Became a recluse. Out of character. Then this weird phone call to me.'

'What was weird about it?'

'I didn't even recognize his voice to start with – sounded as though he'd aged ten years since I talked to him five months ago in his club. He begged me to come

15

down and see him. Forbade me to call him at his house – which I've not seen so far. I asked him where he was calling from. The answer was strange.'

'Don't keep me in suspense.'

'He said from a local phone box. Why not call me from his house? I didn't ask him. He sounded agitated. Totally unlike the calm, self-controlled man I knew.'

'Give you any hint why he was so desperate to see you?'

'Not a thing. I didn't ask him. He sounded too nervous – as though he wanted to get out of the call box as quickly as he could. Something is very seriously wrong at *Prevent*.'

'Strange name for a house,' Newman commented.

'Typical of Andover. He reckons his lifetime work is to look into the future, as I explained. Hoping that by warning the people of influence and power he'll help to *prevent* a coming catastrophe. And, I emphasize, he can think in global terms.'

'What's the domestic situation? If any.'

'Divorced his wife years ago for adultery. He has one daughter, Irene. Must be about eighteen now. They get on as well together as any daughter and father do these days. Lives at *Prevent*. Mad keen on horse riding.'

'This is the right place for it . . . Now what is Paula up to?'

Ahead of them, on her own in the Escort, a small car compared with Newman's large Merc., she was feeling the sensation of claustrophobia strongly as her headlights shone through a tunnel of trees and she swung round yet another bend.

Half a minute later she slowed as quickly as she dared to warn Newman. The headlights shone on a tarred drive leading off to the left into the forest. At the entrance two large stone pillars flanked it and high wrought-iron gates stood open. She pulled up, leaned forward to see the name. *Leopard's Leap*. Wrong house.

She continued staring as Newman pulled up a few yards behind her, dipped his headlights. On top of each stone pillar was perched an extraordinarily lifelike black sculpture of a leopard leaping forward as though springing on its prey.

Paula felt sure she might have missed the entrance to *Prevent*. A short distance back out of the corner of her eye she'd seen a track leading off the road on the same side. At that point the curve of the road had angled her headlights on to the other side.

Flashing her indicator, she swung slowly through a U-turn until she faced the way she had come. Through the open window she waved her hand for Newman to follow. She drove slowly back and now the headlights showed up a cinder track leading into the trees. No gates but a squat concrete block carried the name-plate in large letters. *Prevent*. She shuddered, and wondered why.

Tweed had decided at the entrance that he would take over his Escort and drive in with Paula. He asked Newman to wait in the Mercedes, to hide the car as best he could in the undergrowth on the far side of the road facing the entrance.

'Andover may not welcome a delegation,' he explained. 'On the phone he urged me to come alone.'

'He won't object to my presence?' Paula queried.

'At times you're more persuasive than I am in coaxing men to talk. And I had the impression Andover is a frightened man . . .'

Paula found it creepy as Tweed drove the Escort slowly along the winding track out of sight of the road. On both sides massed rhododendron bushes over nine feet high formed a dense wall. They had a straggly look as though they hadn't been trimmed in years. She remarked on the fact to Tweed.

'Doesn't surprise me a bit. Andover is a man without interest in his surroundings.'

'The house confirms that,' she commented.

Rounding another bend the headlights played over a Victorian pile of no great architectural value. It was a large house with three large gables and an air of neglect. Tweed *was* surprised at the size of the place. He pulled up in front of the main entrance, his wheels crunching on the cinders.

'The front door is wide open,' Paula observed quietly. She took off her right-hand glove, delved into her shoulder-bag, extracted her .32 Browning automatic. 'I don't like the look of this.'

'What made you bring the Browning?'

'Harvey was so insistent there was something menacing on the Solent. I'd hoped I could go with him in the powerboat. I wanted to be ready for trouble. There could be some here.'

'That open door on a night like this is peculiar,' Tweed agreed. 'So, we proceed with caution . . .'

'Shall I go round the back?'

He had opened the door of the Escort and he looked at her as the courtesy light shone down on her. It gleamed on her raven-black hair, showed up her fine bone structure, the determined chin. He sensed she was making a great effort to convince him she'd thrown off the shock of her experience at the marina. Another traumatic experience tonight would be a bit much for her.

'No,' he whispered, 'we'll stick together. And we'll try the front entrance. But the minimum of talk.'

He switched off the headlights, got out, locked the car and led the way up two worn stone steps to the massive stone porch, then paused. The wide-open front door was made of heavy wood with a stained-glass window in the upper half. There appeared to be a curtain behind it and he noticed the fish-eye spyglass let into the side of the

18

door. Andover took precautions against undesirable visitors. So why leave the door wide open?

Tweed hauled on the handle of the pull-chain. Somewhere inside the brooding house a bell rang. Beyond the doorway was a large hall spread with a woodblock floor. Tweed hauled the pull-chain and again the distant bell rang. Still no one appeared.

'There's something awfully wrong here,' Paula whispered.

'I can't say I like the look of it too much myself. At this hour.'

'So what next?'

'We'll go into the hall and I'll call out for Andover. But only after we've listened for a short time. Maybe someone has broken in. Better give me the gun.'

'I can use it if I have to. It's mine,' she said firmly.

He shrugged with resignation. She was a crack shot on the range and seemed to have a grip on herself. If he insisted she'd take it as a display of a lack of confidence in her.

'Andover,' he called out as they walked quietly into the deserted hall.

He raised a hand to keep her silent. A wide old-fashioned staircase of oak mounted to a landing at the rear of the hall, then turned back on itself to climb higher. Round the first floor above them ran a railed gallery. Tweed looked up, checked it carefully. So often people forgot the danger could be at the higher level.

The hall smelt of fog which had drifted in through the open door. Paula found the atmosphere, the total lack of movement, the silence, spooky. A light shone through an open door at the rear of the hall, another from an open door to their right. No light illuminated the hall which was oak-panelled and full of disturbing shadows.

'Andover!' Tweed called out louder and waited.

When there was no response he pointed to the rear

door for Paula to explore, made a second gesture indicating he would check the right-hand room. Their rubber-soled shoes made no sound as they moved in their different directions.

Tweed, standing at the entrance, peered inside the room which had the appearance of a study and library. The illumination came from a large shaded lamp on an ancient desk. He noted the heavy ceiling to floor curtains were closed over the windows, shabby crimson velvet curtains which needed replacing.

Three walls were lined with glass-fronted bookcases and again they ran from ceiling to floor. A wooden ladder was perched against one bookcase and Tweed guessed the top had wheels so the ladder could be slid along. What was wrong with the empty room?

The desktop was neat. A blotter framed in leather, a notepad with a fountain-pen ready for note-taking. The black telephone perched at one corner within a hand's reach of a carver chair behind the desk reminded him of Andover's agonized call from a public phone box. Why?

As he walked slowly across the threadbare Axminster carpet he took off his glasses, began cleaning them on his handkerchief. A white mug with a delft design stood on a place mat on the desk full of brown liquid. He felt it with one hand and the mug was cold. In doing so he dropped his glasses.

Stuffing his handkerchief in his pocket, he stooped to retrieve them, put them on, still crouched. He was straightening up when he caught sight of something at the top of the wire frame inside the large lamp shade. He stared at the small concealed object. Like a small glass eye it was covered with a fine grille. A listening bug.

Tweed began moving with great agility. Picking up the telephone receiver, he unscrewed the speaking end.

Inside was another listening bug. It was the most advanced type and voice-activated. He searched the whole room, knowing now where to look.

Standing on a chair after lighting the central chandelier, he found a third of the devices cunningly secreted among the glass pendants. He replaced the chair, walked over to the ladder, climbed it until he could look along the rail. Nothing.

He climbed down quickly, lifted the ladder, moved it cautiously towards the door, then more swiftly when he found the wheels were well oiled, made hardly a sound. The ladder slid along the rail and was then stopped by some obstruction close to the door. Normal with such ladders.

Tweed shinned up to the top. The chandelier hanging from the high ceiling illuminated the gleaming rail. Secreted behind the block of wood acting as a stop was another bug of the same sophisticated type. Tweed's expression was grim as he climbed down and moved the ladder back to its original position. The whole place was bugged. Surely Andover must have spotted the device beneath the desk lamp? He heard a slight movement, swung round and froze. Paula was standing at the door entrance. Her facial muscles were taut, her whole stance tense.

But what particularly caught his attention was the Browning. She was holding the gun with both hands, muzzle pointed at the floor, and ready for instant firing. What the devil had she found?

Earlier Paula had walked slowly towards the lighted doorway at the back of the hall. When she got close she stopped and listened for any sound of life. The dreadful silence which reminded her of the vigil at the marina filled the old house. Made worse, more nerve-wrackingly

21

atmospheric by the smell of the fog which had penetrated, the icy cold which was as raw as it had been outside.

A very old-fashioned radiator, ugly with its separate sections, stood by the hall wall. She felt it. Barely warm. How could Andover stand living in a morgue like this?

She peered into the room and the atmosphere did not get any better. She was looking into a Victorian kitchen with a stone-flagged floor. A large and ancient kitchen range stood inside a massive alcove. It must have been there since some Victorian built this museum. She took two or three paces inside the depressing room. The cold stone flags muffled her footsteps.

The only concession to modernity was the fluorescent strip slung from the ceiling which illuminated the room clearly. That and a large chest freeezer alongside a new fridge. A scrubbed wooden table occupied the centre of the stark room. Paula frowned.

On the table were several plates. One contained a loaf with several slices cut. Another had a chunk of Cheddar cheese. A butter dish of chinaware held a rectangle of butter, the cover lying beside it. The bread knife which had sliced the loaf also lay on the table.

Everything suggested the owner had just prepared himself a spartan supper and had been interrupted before eating it. Facing her and beyond the table were windows screened with ragged net curtains, half covered with a heavy white curtain in need of a visit to the laundry.

She opened cupboards fixed to the wall, checking their contents. Next she opened a door in the wall and found herself staring into a large walk-in pantry with a tiled floor. The shelves – like the wall cupboards – were well stocked. She noticed something which contrasted with the primitive equipment: someone, presumably Andover, had arranged the items so the most recent sell-by dates were at the front.

She opened the large fridge and again it was amply

stocked. About to leave the kitchen, she paused, staring at the big chest freezer. Might as well check everything. She took hold of the lid, raised it, nearly dropped it.

Don't faint, for God's sake, she told herself. Again there was a good stock of provisions. But on top of them was a deep plastic container about two feet wide and without a lid. Inside the container was a tumble of ice cubes. And below the first layer – showing so clearly through the ice – was a human right arm severed at the elbow, a bloodstained bandage covering the stump, a woman's hand stretched out, still attached, with an emerald ring on the third finger of the hand.

She stood in the doorway to the library, holding the Browning in both hands, prepared to fire point-blank at any intruder, at whoever had committed this barbaric act.

Tweed put a finger to his lips, frowning to warn her not to speak. He walked over to her, grasping her arm, led her to the desk, showed her the bugged lamp. With a waving gesture he indicated that there were more of them everywhere.

She nodded mechanically, then it was her turn to take Tweed by the arm, holding the automatic in her right hand. Like a sleepwalker she guided him to the kitchen, raised the lid of the freezer chest. He blinked once, leaned forward briefly to examine the severed limb, closed the lid. Holding his arm again, she propelled him across the hall and out beyond the front porch before she warned him.

'The butcher is still here. Through the kitchen window I saw someone move in the back garden . . .'

2

'Go back to Newman,' Tweed told Paula. 'Tell him what has happened, briefly, then come back with him. And perhaps I'd better have the Browning.'

'We should go and find out who is roaming about behind the house now. Otherwise he'll get away . . .'

Tweed couldn't fault her logic. They couldn't afford to waste time arguing. Gesturing for her to follow, he moved off the cinder drive, stepping on to the rough-cut grass which ran round the side of the house.

There were no barriers, no side gate. Lousy security. It appeared Andover had never felt the need for it. There were no lights in the side windows to his left. On his right a wall of huge evergreens masked them from the next property.

Emerging at the back, Tweed realized *Prevent* had a sizeable estate. His night vision was coming back and a vast lawn spread away to distant trees. He paused, reaching a hand behind him to stop Paula. She had been right. In the middle of the lawn, coming closer to the house, a man was walking slowly.

'He's talking to himself,' Paula whispered.

'And I think I recognize the walk. Looks like Andover himself.'

At that moment the shadowy figure moved into the light splaying out from the kitchen window. Tweed had a clear view as the figure stood still and was appalled and shocked. In the icy cold, where drifts of fog hung motionless in the air, Andover wore only a pair of slacks and a shirt.

24

But it was his appearance which shook Tweed. Haggard, his face drawn, he had lost weight and his shoulders sagged. The phrase 'a lost soul' leapt into Tweed's mind. This bore no relationship to the crisply spoken, erect, decisive Andover he had known in London. This man was a physical wreck.

'Who is that?' He jumped as Tweed stepped into the light followed by Paula, her Browning held behind her trench coat. 'Oh, it's you, Tweed . . . What the hell are you doing here? . . . I distinctly told you to wait at Passford House until I called you . . . And to come alone . . .'

He spoke in a disjointed way, his voice hoarse. Only the last sentence was delivered in a familiar crisp tone.

'It's very cold out here,' Paula said to him quietly. 'I will fetch you a coat. I noticed a cloaks cupboard – I imagine that's what it is – in the hall.'

'Very kind of you, my dear.' His manner changed again, was polite, grateful. 'It is a cloaks cupboard.'

She turned and walked swiftly away, slipping the gun inside her shoulder-bag. Alone with their host, Tweed made his suggestion, testing Andover's reaction.

'We could go inside to talk . . .'

'No! No!' Andover grabbed Tweed by the lapels of his British warm. 'And you've been inside, haven't you? Did the two of you talk while you were poking around?'

He was very agitated, trembling as he tugged at Tweed's coat as though trying to shake a reply out of him. Tweed stood stock still, made no attempt to remove the shuddering hands.

'I'll answer you only when you get a grip on yourself.'

Paula appeared round the corner, holding a woollen scarf and a heavy coat. Andover released Tweed as though ashamed that Paula had seen his performance. Standing back, he accepted the scarf, wrapped it round his neck, slipped his arms into the sleeves of the coat Paula was holding for him.

'That really was most considerate of you,' he said in a normal voice. 'It is a bit nippy tonight.'

'Quite Siberian – or maybe you're used to the elements,' Paula continued in a conversational tone. 'And I'm Paula Grey, Mr Tweed's assistant.'

'She's more than that,' Tweed added, watching Andover closely. 'She's my deputy and acts in my stead when I'm away. A recent promotion. We're using more and more women in our organization. She knows as much as I do.'

'Women,' said Andover, 'are more meticulous. They have a greater loyalty and great powers of concentration.'

'The only reason we were inside your house – poking around as you put it – was the front door was wide open. Is that wise?'

'I've left the front door open,' Paula intervened quickly as she detected fresh signs of agitation. 'It's an easy mistake.'

'I suppose so,' Andover said in a normal tone. He fumbled under his coat and inside his trouser pocket. 'The key is here. Foolish of me. Must have my mind on my thoughts.'

'And,' Tweed went on, 'we never spoke a word to each other while we were inside. I simply called out your name twice and then tried to find you.'

'I do understand.' Andover sighed visibly with relief.

'Is your daughter Irene right-handed?' Tweed enquired suddenly.

Andover's reaction was manic. He grabbed Tweed with both hands round the throat. 'What the devil made you ask that question?' he roared. Tweed again stood his ground. He grasped Andover's wrists, squeezing hard. He had far greater strength than most people supposed. Prising the throttling hands loose, he held on to them and put his face close to Andover's. 'That is quite enough of the rough stuff.' He let go as he felt the hands go limp.

Andover was shaking like a leaf in the wind when Paula again intervened in her conversational tone.

'Driving here, Tweed and I were discussing whether more people were left-handed as opposed to right. Just idle chat to pass the time.'

'Oh, I see.' Andover ran a hand through his flaxen hair. 'Tweed, I'm dreadfully sorry. Quite unforgivable on my part. Don't know what got into me. Had a bout of neuralgia. Leaves you frightfully edgy.'

'I know it can be very painful,' Paula agreed in her soft voice.

'One of those things.' Andover was addressing Paula now as though he'd forgotten Tweed's existence. 'Irene is left-handed. Five months ago I gave her an emerald ring.' A flash of pain crossed his strong-boned clean-shaven face. 'It was her eighteenth birthday.'

'I'd like to meet her sometime,' Paula continued carefully. 'But at that age they don't spend much time at home.'

'Quite right, my dear . . . She's gone off on an extended holiday . . . with her French boy friend, Louis . . . Good chap, her Louis . . . You'd have liked him . . .'

And you're lying, Tweed thought, as he trailed off. He had the impression Andover was retreating into a world of his own and asked the question quickly.

'You asked me to come down here. May I ask why – now I'm here?'

'Of course.' Andover, normal once more, frowned. Paula studied him. About five feet ten tall, slim in build, he had a high forehead, a clever face, and almost a touch of arrogance in his manner. No, not arrogance – rather a fixity of purpose. She had the feeling that for a brief time she was seeing the Andover Tweed had known in London.

'Of course,' he repeated. 'I have a file in the house I want you to study. It's very serious. We may be facing a new enemy – far worse than Hitler or Stalin so far as Western Europe is concerned. And just when Europe thought it was safe to go to sleep. If you don't mind waiting outside at the front I'll go in and get it for you. Not the sort of thing you entrust to the post . . . Disaster, Tweed. Catastrophe might be a better word . . .'

He started to walk along the side of the house briskly, shoulders erect, when he swung on his heel, came back.

'Tweed, I really am sorry. The way I treated you. I've been pretty rotten company. Why not call in next door, have a drink with my neighbour, Brigadier Maurice Burgoyne, another old China hand. He's civilized, which is more than I've been . . .'

Before Tweed could respond Andover had disappeared and they followed him slowly. At the front of the house they waited in silence by the car, both of them shaken by their macabre experience.

Andover trotted out five minutes later by Paula's watch. He carried a large brown manila envelope under his arm. As he handed it to Tweed Paula saw it had an address scrawled on it and a first-class stamp. Andover caught her glance.

'Camouflage,' he explained to her as he handed the envelope to Tweed. 'A fictitious name and address and stamped for the post. No one will guess what it contains. You can tell the Brig. you called here.' He put his hand to his forehead. 'I've got it. Tell him I have an attack of neuralgia and sent you round for some decent company.'

During the five-minute wait Tweed had wrestled with the problem of whether to break the news about Harvey Boyd's death. It seemed quite the worst time but the police would be in touch with him anyway – and probably soon.

'Thank you,' he said, tucking the envelope inside the sports jacket underneath his trench coat. 'There is one more thing I ought to tell you before we go. And it's very bad news.'

Andover opened his mouth to say something, then clamped it shut without saying anything. Paula could have sworn his lips had formed the name *Irene*. Andover stiffened himself, nodded to Tweed.

'Well? Spit it out.'

'It concerns Harvey Boyd, who, I gather, is a distant relative of yours?'

Paula felt sure this time that a mixture of emotions had flashed across Andover's face. Relief. Then regret that he had felt that sensation. He nodded again, waited.

'Harvey Boyd is dead,' Tweed told him. He explained what had happened in as few words as possible. Watching their host, Paula saw an odd pensive expression. '. . . so soon,' Tweed concluded, 'the police will arrive to inform you.'

'*Not here!* I won't have a lot of flat-footed policemen trampling over all the place, invading my privacy.'

Andover's tone was brusque, almost rude. Staring at his visitors, he frowned.

'Tell you what,' he went on rapidly. 'The Rover is in that garage . . .' He indicated two closed wooden doors let into the side of the house. 'I'll drive over to Colonel Stanstead. He's the Chief Constable and we know each other.'

'You could do that,' Tweed agreed.

'I'll call him on the way, tell him I'm coming. Yes, that's the answer.' He paused. 'Harvey was a good chap. Just came out of the SAS a few months ago. People say the younger generation has gone soft. Don't know what they're talking about.'

'We'd better go,' Tweed decided. 'Very sorry to be the bearer of such sad tidings.'

'Sooner hear it from you than anyone else.' He reached out, took Tweed by the arm, guided him towards the house out of earshot of Paula. 'So they've got Harvey too.'

'Who are "they"?' Tweed asked quickly.

'Time for you to get round to the Brigadier's. If he's not in try Willie Fanshawe. He lives just beyond the Brig.'s place, *Leopard's Leap*. Willie's house is *The Last Haven*. Another old China hand.' He paused again, glanced to where Paula was getting into the car. He's trying to make up his mind about something, Tweed thought. Andover whispered the words.

'No ransom at all has been demanded . . .'

He turned away before Tweed could speak, walked swiftly back to the house. His head drooped, his shoulders were quivering. Tweed heard the slam of the front door closing and then he climbed in behind the wheel. Paula was waiting in the front passenger seat.

'Did you see that?' she asked. 'The poor devil was crying on his way back to the house. A strong man like that. He must be going through hell. Shouldn't we inform the police?'

'Not yet. It's obvious Irene is the victim of some hideous kidnap plot. Andover's last words to me were "No ransom at all has been demanded." I find that sinister. Plus the macabre business of her amputated arm being sent to him.'

He started the engine, anxious to get clear before Andover emerged to drive to see Colonel Stanstead. At the exit, he paused. To his right Newman appeared on the far side, waved to show his location, where he had hidden his Merc. Tweed drove right, turned off the road down what was little more than a wide path. Newman's car was parked out of sight from the road behind a copse of evergreens. He climbed into the back of the Escort as Tweed switched off the engine.

'This file isn't safe,' Tweed commented.

He extracted it from under his sports jacket. Paula said

she'd keep it in her executive case. Tweed handed it to her and she slipped the envelope inside, locked the slim case.

'Don't let that out of your hands,' Tweed warned.

'As if I would,' she chided him.

'And, Bob,' Tweed continued, 'we expect Andover to drive away soon to visit Stanstead, the Chief Constable. Keep your ear open for the sound of his car, then follow him. Stanstead has a house somewhere outside Brockenhurst.'

'You want me to make sure that's where he goes?' Newman checked.

'Partly. I don't like this set-up one little bit. Your other task is to make sure he doesn't know he's being followed, but mainly to see if anyone else *follows* him.'

He went on to give Newman a brief digest of their visit to *Prevent*, including Paula's macabre discovery inside the frezeer, his own discovery of the bugs, and their encounter with Andover.

'A severed right arm,' Newman repeated slowly. 'And you think it was Irene's?'

'No doubt about it,' Tweed said tersely. 'Andover mentioned the emerald ring he'd given her only months ago. What worries me is his comment that no ransom at all has been demanded. The kidnappers have something quite fiendish in mind.'

'So shouldn't the police be informed?' Newman pressed, echoing Paula's earlier suggestion. 'Regardless of the fact that for some crazy reason he doesn't want to let them know.'

'Definitely not. I gave him my unqualified word. We've no idea what is going on. I may know more when I've read that file he handed me. Is that the sound of a car coming?'

Newman was already climbing out of the car. He ran towards the road, looked round the end of the copse of

31

trees, ran back. On his way to the Merc. he stopped briefly where Tweed had lowered his window.

'Rover just coming out of the drive. Andover is on his way. So am I . . .'

Tweed waited until Newman had driven off, tapping his fingers on the wheel, the only sign of how disturbed he was. Paula kept quiet for a few minutes, guessing Tweed was taking a decision, before she spoke.

'What now?'

'I think we should follow up Andover's suggestion and call in on Brigadier Maurice Burgoyne, another old China hand, as he put it.'

3

Tweed was turning the Escort into the drive of *Leopard's Leap* when he stopped. Further along the wide grass verge outside the property a large pile of bricks stood next to a concrete mixer.

'The Brigadier must be having some work done,' Paula observed.

Tweed drove on between the open wrought-iron gates and along another curving drive. But this surface was newly tarred. Like sentinels, ornamental shrubs lined the borders with here and there neatly trimmed topiary.

'I smell money,' Paula remarked. 'But will the Brig. welcome strangers at this hour?'

'I'm not a stranger. I've met him several times over dinners in London. Just as I have met the neighbour further along this wilderness, Willie Fanshawe. They all belonged to a very exclusive institute and I was invited as a guest several times. Here we are . . .'

They drove round another bend and suddenly in front of them loomed a magnificent Jacobean mansion. Unlike the gloom of *Prevent*, it was illuminated powerfully with a battery of ground searchlights aimed at the frontage. A burglar alarm attached to the wall showed up prominently.

'Burgoyne's security is an improvement on Andover's,' Tweed commented.

'And I smell even more money.'

The mansion was constructed of mellow stone and its tall characteristic chimneys reared up into the night. At one corner rose a turret with a witch's hat topping it. Despite the glow of lights Paula shivered. Something about the aura of the house worried her.

'Let's hope he's in,' Tweed said as he parked the car at the foot of a flight of stone steps leading up to the imposing entrance. 'There are lights inside.'

They walked up the steps to a large porch projecting well forward from the main edifice. As Tweed rang the bell Paula looked back. At the edge of the drive was a trim lawn with well-tended flowerbeds. A strong light came on over the outside of the porch, a blinding glare. The door opened after a moment and the glaring light was switched off. A tall slim figure stood silhouetted in the glow from lights beyond.

'Tweed! Of all people. What a welcome surprise. And you've brought me an attractive lady. It's a long time since I've seen such beautiful raven-black hair.'

The man's voice was soft but Paula sensed an inner will of great strength and character. Normally she found flattery insincere but now she felt rather pleased with the description of herself.

'This is my deputy, Paula Grey,' Tweed introduced 'So, Paula, now you meet Brigadier Maurice Burgoyne.'

'Come in out of the cold,' Burgoyne responded. 'And

the fog. Expect you could both do with a good drink. Walk straight ahead while I lock the door . . .'

Tweed walked with Paula across a large hall laid with a solid-oak block floor. It was well lit with wall-sconce lights and the room beyond was tastefully furnished as a spacious living room.

A blonde-haired woman in her thirties stood up from a couch and came forward as Burgoyne followed them into the room. He waved a slim hand.

'This is Lee Holmes, my companion,' Burgoyne announced. He introduced Paula and then Tweed. 'We are drinking champagne,' he went on. He took Paula's arm. 'Fancy a glass to drive out the Arctic?'

'Arctic is the word,' the blonde woman agreed as she held Paula's hand. 'You feel frozen. Come and sit by the fire.'

Burgoyne helped her off with her coat, took Tweed's, disappeared into the hall, came back, and lifted a bottle from an ice-bucket. 'Visitors are so welcome in this back of the beyond. Especially at this time of the year . . .'

He was pouring champagne into a flute glass for Paula as he chatted, which gave her an opportunity to study him. Burgoyne had a long face like a fox, the nose strong, the chin forceful. His voice was commanding and his movements had a controlled feline grace. His thick hair was dark, well brushed, and beneath the nose was a long thin moustache.

Burgoyne wore gleaming polished riding boots with grey jodhpurs tucked inside the tops. His white polo-necked sweater was spotless. But it was the eyes which attracted her attention. Dark and alert under thick brows, they watched her closely as he served the drink. There was something almost hypnotic about his gaze.

'Thank you,' she said. 'I could just do with this.' She raised her glass. 'Cheers! Everyone.'

'Not for me,' Tweed said quickly. 'I'm driving.'

Paula had noticed a signal pass between Burgoyne and

34

Lee Holmes when they had waited to see where to sit. A brief gesture towards Tweed, an almost imperceptible nod.

His 'companion' had reacted immediately. Smiling at Tweed, she patted the seat on the couch, and he sat beside her while Paula sank into an armchair, which enveloped her. As she began talking to Tweed, Paula looked her up and down discreetly.

Lee Holmes made her feel dowdy in the clothes she was wearing. A natural blonde, her mane draped over bare and perfectly shaped shoulders. She wore a purple form-fitting dress which displayed to full advantage her excellent figure. You're a beauty, damn you, Paula thought. It was rare for her to feel such a catty reaction.

'Please call me Lee, Mr Tweed,' she was saying as she sat closer to him. She crossed her long legs, a manoeuvre which opened the long slit in her dress, exposing her left leg almost to her thigh. Clad in flesh-tinted tights, her shapely legs appeared to be bare. She took hold of Tweed's right hand.

'I like men with strong hands,' she confided.

Tweed squeezed her hand and was startled at the strength of her responding grip. He gently pulled his hand free.

'You are pretty strong yourself,' he observed. 'How do you pass the time out here?'

'A lot of riding. I can even out-race Maurice, although he doesn't like me advertising the fact,' she teased.

'Which isn't difficult for her,' Burgoyne retorted as he perched himself on the arm of Paula's chair. 'Her horse is carrying less weight.' He looked down at Paula. 'I hope you don't object to the proximity?'

'Why should I? You have a wonderful home here. Not what I'd expect to find in the New Forest.'

'Goes back into history, I gather. Mineral water for you, Tweed?'

'Maybe a little later. How did you manage to get hold of such an architectural gem?'

'I have Sir Gerald Andover to thank for that. When I was out in Hong Kong and getting ready to come home after umpteen years, we were having a drink in my favourite bar. Andover, Fanshawe – lives next door – and myself. I asked him if he heard of a likely property would he be so kind as to send details. Three months passed. Nothing. Fanshawe wanted a place, too. Then a sheaf of houses arrived from Andover – including this place. Snapped it up.'

'And lived happily ever after,' Lee interjected with a curious smile.

'Something like that.'

Tweed seized his opportunity. 'It was Andover who sent us round here. Poor chap looks as though he's had a nervous breakdown.' He waited for the reaction.

Paula glanced up at Burgoyne. The living-room was also lit by wall-sconce lights, casting a suffused glow. In the soft lighting Burgoyne's expression was saturnine. He appeared to be considering how to respond.

'Andover is a good friend – as I've just proved. But a bad neighbour. Keeps himself locked up inside that old horror of a pile. It was much better when Irene, his daughter, was around.'

'Maurice took a fancy to Irene,' Lee interjected. 'He means it was much better for Maurice when Irene was available.'

'Nonsense.' Burgoyne dismissed her observation without any sign of rancour. 'Then about three months ago Irene ups and offs to the Riviera with her French boy friend, Louis Renard. Can't say I took to the chap.'

'Maurice,' Lee intervened again, 'you only met him once.'

'Once was enough. A bit of a bounder. But some of you women seem to like the type.' He touched Paula on the

36

shoulder. 'Excluding guests. You look as though you've got your head screwed on the right way.'

'When did Andover resign from the Institute and throw up all his directorships?' Tweed persisted.

'Come to think of it, about the same time. Yes, three months or so ago. Rather foolish. His daughter goes off for a fling – the way they do these days – and her father chucks in all his interests. Told him he was bats. Wouldn't listen, of course.'

'I see you brought the East back with you,' Paula said quickly, feeling Tweed had pressed the subject enough.

She looked round the room. Perched on an Oriental chest in the large curtained bay window at the back was a small Buddha with hooded eyes, which seemed to be watching her. The walls were decorated with Chinese paintings on silk scrolls. Behind an Oriental desk angled in a corner hung a large-scale map of Hong Kong. Burgoyne smiled before he replied.

'Best years of my life were spent out there. Came back to find an England where manners had gone. You can't tell a dustman from a lord these days. The classless society has wrecked everything Britain once stood for. So I surround myself with a touch of the East. Stupid nostalgia, probably.' He looked down at Paula again. 'Can't I relieve you of that case, put it with your coats?'

Paula gripped the executive case she had perched on her knees. She smiled up at him.

'No thank you. It's stuffed with research papers I've been working on for three weeks. I feel happier with my hands on it. Then I can't forget it when we leave.'

'Do you smoke?' Lee asked Tweed.

'No. I gave it up but I still like the aroma.'

She opened a long black evening bag with a *diamanté* clasp while Paula watched her. Fiddling inside it, she brought out a long thick jewelled holder, inserted a cigarette, and then made no effort to light it, which intrigued

Paula. Lee's exposed leg leaned against Tweed's as she settled herself more comfortably.

'I never met Irene,' Tweed remarked casually. 'Did she leave suddenly?'

'I gather so,' Burgoyne replied. 'Here one night, gone the next. The young are so impatient.'

'Talking about leaving . . .' Tweed consulted his watch. 'Andover urged us to visit Willie Fanshawe while we were here. Or does he go to bed early?'

'Up half the night. I'm sure he'd be glad to see you again.'

'Tweed,' Lee said quickly, opening her bag again, 'I visit London frequently. Maybe we could have lunch together? I'd phone you first. Here is my card. I have an office in town. You're in insurance, Maurice told me. He was talking about you only the other day.'

'I'd like that,' Tweed said quickly. 'And here's my card. Best to phone first, as you suggested. I'm away from the office so much.'

He gave her a card with the legend General & Cumbria Assurance – the cover name for the SIS. The card he gave her gave only the name and the phone number. No address. He stood up, shook her hand.

'It's been a great pleasure.'

He stood for a moment, apparently admiring her. His eyes were studying the jewelled cigarette holder she held so elegantly in her left hand.

Burgoyne was standing now, hands inside the pockets of his jodhpurs. He was frowning as though his thoughts were miles away.

'I haven't seen Andover for a while. You don't think he has had a nervous breakdown – you used that phrase?'

'I'd say recovering from overwork,' Tweed replied easily. 'Thank you both for a most pleasant half hour.'

'I'll get your coats . . .'

He had gone when Paula turned to Lee. The magnetic blonde was eyeing her critically.

'It's been an experience meeting you,' Paula told her and smiled.

'I'm an experienced woman,' Lee replied.

'She's after you,' Paula said when Burgoyne had closed the outer door and they had settled themselves inside the Escort.

'There are worse fates,' Tweed teased her.

She thumped him in the ribs. Then, clutching her case, she stared ahead as Tweed drove away from the glare of the searchlights and along the drive. Passing between the gates he turned left and parked by the pile of bricks and the concrete mixer.

'What do you make of those two?' he asked.

'There's something odd about their relationship. Burgoyne has got all his marbles, is a strong character. But Lee Holmes is a strange creature. She didn't hesitate to contradict him and I wouldn't expect him to have a woman like that as a mistress. Someone with brains, yes, but more amenable. I almost had the impression I was witnessing . . .'

'A charade put on for our benefit,' Tweed completed. 'And I find it difficult to believe he hasn't been anywhere near Andover for three months or so. There's a mystery inside that mansion. Let's make one more visit, see Fanshawe. You'll find him a very different kettle of fish . . .'

The Last Haven had no gates, and a gravel drive led straight to the house which came immediately into view. Not at all what Tweed was expecting, it was a single-storey residence with a wide frontage. It reminded Tweed of houses he'd seen in Scandinavia with its small slim bricks and steeply pitched roof.

'It looks very modern,' Paula commented. 'Not a bit like a house in the New Forest . . .'

A strong light shone over the wooden front door and behind drawn curtains were more lights. Tweed and Paula had just left the car when the door opened. A heavily built man with a large head and shaggy white hair came out to meet them. In his sixties, Paula guessed, and rather like a favourite uncle. His head was craned forward and he had a broad smile as Tweed went to meet him, introducing Paula.

'This is a wonderful surprise,' Fanshawe began. 'Tweed, of all people. How are you? Not chasing kidnappers out in this neck of the woods?'

Paula nearly jumped. With a tremendous effort she kept her expression neutral. Then she realized Fanshawe must be referring to the cover Tweed used in his fictitious role as Chief Claims Investigator for General & Cumbria Assurance. With certain people he knew he gave the impression he was involved in negotiating the release of kidnap victims for an agreed ransom, which explained his frequent trips abroad.

Tweed showed no reaction at all except pleasure. Again he introduced Paula and Fanshawe obviously took an immediate liking to her.

'Come in out of the fog.' He guided her inside with an arm round her shoulders. 'Beastly night,' he went on, 'but you'll find it nice and warm inside. The Swedish central-heating system works a treat . . .'

He was helping her off with her trench coat, hung it on a hook above a slim radiator. Beyond the front door they had walked into a large L-shaped living room with Scandinavian-style furnishings.

'Swedish?' she asked as he guided her to a long couch.

'Yes, I was extremely lucky. To get this place.' He

escorted her to a comfortable couch and she sat in a corner. Fanshawe turned to Tweed who had hung his own coat alongside Paula's. 'You take that armchair facing us and then we can be cosy. A glass of sherry will go down rather well, don't you think?'

'I had too much to drink recently,' Paula said quickly.

She had observed the bottle Fanshawe was holding under his arm as he collected glasses from a shelf under the round coffee table separating them from Tweed. Cyprus sherry. Glancing round the room she saw no signs of the monied opulence of *Leopard's Leap*.

'For you then, Tweed?'

'No thanks, Willie. I'm driving. You've been here for how long? Incidentally, it was your neighbour, Brigadier Maurice Burgoyne, who suggested we drop in on you.'

'Stout fellow, Maurice. Won his MC during the Korean War as a young officer . . .'

As he chattered on, addressing Tweed, Paula studied her host. His large rounded face had a cherubic look. He had blue eyes under bushy eyebrows and radiated an air of good humour. Yes, like a favourite uncle, she thought again as he eased his bulk beside her and turned to face her.

'Sorry, I'm neglecting you. Got absorbed in what I was saying. Swedish, you enquired earlier. It was built for a Swede after they'd knocked down an old farmhouse going to seed. I said I was lucky. While I was in the East my father played the stock market, lost our old ancestral estate in Berkshire where I was brought up. This place suits my limited bill perfectly. No maintenance expenses, you see. Window frames are made of a special wood. Never needs painting. You just oil the woodwork occasionally. Do it myself.' He switched his attention to Tweed. 'Never answered your question. I expect you know Sir Gerald Andover, the brain-box, lives two doors away?'

'Yes, actually we visited him first.'

'Good chap. He was out in Hong Kong on one of his visits. We were having a drink with the Brig. and I told Gerald my time in the East was drawing to a close. He immediately offered to look for a house for me. Never dreamt he'd come up with a place on his own doorstep. Price was reasonable – some folk thought it an odd house in this part of the world and the Swede wanted to settle in the States. I've been here just over two years. The Brig. arrived about three years ago.'

'I was surprised to find three old China hands on top of each other,' Tweed commented amiably.

'So now you know why—'

He broke off as a door opened. Paula had a glimpse of a modern kitchen and then the door closed automatically.

A woman entered the room. Tall, slim, and a striking brunette, Paula estimated she'd be in her late twenties. Over her well-moulded breasts she wore a tight-fitting sunflower-patterned blouse with a mandarin collar. Swan-necked, she held herself elegantly as she moved slowly towards them. Her cream pleated skirt stopped above the knees, revealing an excellent pair of legs.

Fanshawe jumped to his feet. Like some large men, Paula noted, he was agile, swift in his reactions.

'Do come and meet our guests, Helen,' he greeted her enthusiastically. 'Helen Claybourne, my secretary and general factotum. Keeps the place in order, including myself . . .'

After introductions, he pulled up a carver chair for her next to Paula. She was holding a glass of pale liquid and her cool gaze rested on Paula as everyone sat down again. Her cultured voice was as cool as her personality.

'Mineral water,' she remarked. 'I get so thirsty in this weather. Willie, shouldn't I be serving drinks to Mr Tweed and Miss Grey?'

'Oh, I pressed them, urged them. But their resistance was implacable.'

'Perhaps they'll yield to your powers of persuasion later,' Helen suggested, then sipped her own drink.

Her penetrating grey eyes were still watching Paula, who was reminded of Burgoyne's hypnotic gaze. She found herself mentally contrasting Helen Claybourne with Lee Holmes. Lee would walk into a roomful of men and instantly be the centre of attraction. Helen would pause by the doorway, looking round. And soon all eyes would focus on her. Two most unusual women.

'Andover struck me as being under strain,' Tweed remarked. 'I gather his daughter Irene is away.'

'Andover's a good sort.' Willie beamed his cheerful smile, his tone upper crust. 'But he guards his privacy. And now I come to think of it, you're right. Irene is away. Went off on a long holiday somewhere on the Med with her current boy friend. Restless. It's the age – hers and the present day, I mean.'

'How long has she been gone?' Tweed asked in the same casual tone, his eyes half-closed.

'Must be three months or more, wouldn't you say, Helen?'

'Something like that.'

'About the same time as Andover gave up the chairmanship of INCOMSIN – the International Committee of Strategic Insight? And all his other directorships?'

Willie pouched his lips. 'Come to think of it, I suppose you're right. Had never occurred to me.'

'And from what you said a moment ago he'd become a recluse? A hermit?'

'I'm afraid he has. Helen, entertain our guests for a moment while I make a phone call . . .'

He disappeared through another doorway close to the kitchen. Helen Claybourne concentrated her attention on Tweed.

'I gather from things Willie's mentioned you're involved in a particularly dangerous form of insurance?'

'Not really. There are rare occasions when negotiations over some tricky situations become a bit tense. Nothing you could call dangerous,' he assured her.

She looked back to Paula. 'And you're working in the same outfit?'

'Yes. It's mostly poring over the fine print of policies. Really like any other executive job. What about yourself?'

'Oh, a pretty quiet life. Keeping this place going. I do get a few trips abroad with Willie. The cherry on the cake . . .'

She chatted on until Willie returned. He waved both his large hands as he settled down beside Paula again.

'Your remark about Andover becoming a recluse triggered me off. I phoned him, was going to ask him to join us. No reply.'

'I could have saved you the trouble,' Tweed said, standing up. 'He was going out when we left him.'

'At this time of night? Oh, well, he always was a law unto himself. Must you go so soon?'

'I'm afraid we must. We're staying at Passford House and I'm expecting a phone call. I see someone is having some building work done. Those bricks on the grass verge further along.'

'Burgoyne's.' Willie jumped up to fetch their coats. 'The Brig. is always having something altered. One of his main interests in life, I suspect. Very pleasant to see you again.' He was helping Paula on with her coat. 'Must keep in closer touch. I come up to town now and then. I'll give you a call before I start out next time. Lunch at Brown's would be nice . . .'

Paula said goodnight to Helen who accompanied Willie to the door and opened it for them. Tweed noticed he had two deadlocks. Better security then Andover's.

They were in the car, with Tweed driving out of the drive and turning right, back for Lymington, when Paula asked the question.

'What do you think of them? All three so close.'

4

The mobile concrete mixer appeared behind them long before they reached the main road back to Lymington.

A few minutes earlier Tweed, hands relaxed on the wheel, had enquired what she meant. The moonless night seemed to have become even darker as his headlights splayed over the wall of trees hemming them in. No sign of any other traffic. It was a lonely road to Beaulieu behind them.

'You get three old China hands,' Paula explained. 'They knew each other in Hong Kong – half-way round the other side of the world. I'm including Andover because he apparently paid frequent visits to Hong Kong. Where do they all end up, for Pete's sake? Next door to each other on the edge of the New Forest. I find it peculiar and almost sinister.'

'We were told how it came about. Find anything odd in that?'

'Yes. First, Andover never mentioned that he'd found houses for them. But he was so agitated for obvious reasons there's nothing in that. But Burgoyne said they – he and Willie Fanshawe – had a drink in Hong Kong with Andover and Burgoyne asked Andover if he could find him a property, which he eventually did. Willie told a different story. He distinctly said it was Andover who offered to find him a place.'

'So you spotted that?'

'You're impossible!' she burst out with mock anger. 'You wanted to see if I'd noticed the inconsistency too.'

'And have you noticed we have company? One of those huge mobile concrete mixers is closing on our tail.'

'I was just about to ask you the same question. I've seen it in the wing mirror. Ruddy great orange brute with its huge mixer churning round.'

'Keeps the cement ready for use. Funny vehicle to be on the road at this time of night.'

'And if he keeps up that speed he's going to come through our rear window.'

Which was true, Tweed thought grimly. The orange monster was inches from his Escort, looming over them like a huge Army tank. He pressed his foot down on the accelerator. They swung round a sharp bend far too fast, but for a brief period they left the mixer behind.

On a straight stretch Tweed rammed the accelerator down further. He thanked God there had been no rain, that the road surface wasn't slippery. The juggernaut was catching them up again. Paula watched it rushing towards them.

'The driver must be mad or drunk,' she snapped.

'Or else he has another more lethal purpose.'

'But why?' she protested.

'Let's concentrate on surviving . . .'

Tweed skidded round the next bend, regained control, and kept his foot pressed down. They passed a solitary lamp which, presumably, marked the entrance to another isolated residence. Watching in the rear-view mirror Tweed had a glimpse of the driver, wearing dark glasses, hunched over his wheel.

He was overtaking them like a rocket. Once again the juggernaut was within inches of the rear of his Escort. It was only a matter of seconds before they would feel the hammer of his massive weight smashing into them.

Tweed risked even more speed, swung round another bend. The gap had widened. But only briefly. The concrete mixer was thundering down on them yet again. Tweed thought of the weight combined with the load of cement inside that revolving drum.

'He's trying to ram us,' Paula said quietly. 'Where did we say something which so disturbed someone they set out to kill us?'

'Work that out later. Staying alive is the object of the exercise now.'

Tweed was cursing himself for bringing Paula with him. But who could have foreseen the original visit to Andover would result in a desperate life-and-death attempt to escape oblivion? He had little doubt that once the mixer reached its target they'd be crushed to pulp.

His headlights swung round yet another sharp curve and shone on a narrow side road leading off to their left. He braced himself for the manoeuvre, calculating his chances at bringing it off at fifty-fifty.

'Hang on for dear life!' he shouted.

At manic speed he swung off the main road, aiming for the side road, little more than a lane. He felt the rear of the Escort sliding away and Paula braced herself for the crash. Luckily, as Tweed had observed, on the far side of the entrance to the lane there was a level flat area covered with dead leaves.

The rear of the car slid on to the level ground as Tweed reduced speed. The Escort stabilized. He rammed his foot down again, left behind a scatter of leaves which flew up into the air. Now he was driving straight down the lane bordered with trees and undergrowth. Paula glanced in her wing mirror. The unexpected manoeuvre had taken the driver of the killer vehicle by surprise.

He had overshot the mark, was backing, turning to follow them down the lane. Tweed had caught sight of a signpost at the entrance. Too little time to read what it pointed to. Lymington, he hoped. Or it could be a dead end. In which case . . .

'Where did that signpost point to?' Paula asked, her voice still calm.

'No idea. We'll find out in due course.'

Behind them the juggernaut was building up speed. It would be on top of them again in less than a minute, Paula calculated. Where was this nightmare going to end? She glanced at Tweed. His expression was grim but his body showed no signs of tension. Frequently his eyes whipped up for a millisecond, checking the rear-view mirror.

'Let's hope we don't meet a farm tractor,' she said.

'That's what I like. An optimist,' he joked.

The lane was becoming more tunnel-like, the trees on both sides closer together. Oh, Lord! Paula thought. They had turned round a bend and left the straight stretch behind. The lane became a series of non-stop curves and blind bends, which forced Tweed to reduce speed. She glanced again in the wing mirror. The orange monster was catching up fast, sweeping round the bends with reckless abandon. He had weight on his side and knew it.

'If only we could reach a village,' Paula commented.

'Doesn't look like the sort of lane which has them. We haven't passed a single cottage so far . . .'

Another glance in the rear-view mirror revealed the concrete mixer close to their tail, its insidious sphere revolving like a clock counting down their fate. Tweed was driving as fast as he dared, bearing in mind the tortuous country lane. The headlights of the pursuing vehicle glared in his mirror. Something had to give – and damned soon.

He swung round another bend with the thunder of the cement mixer's engine and mechanism in his ears. Paula extracted the Browning from inside her shoulder-bag, reached for her safety belt to release it.

'Put that away!' Tweed snapped.

'I might get him with a shot through the rear window . . .'

'I said put it away. Travelling at this speed you will never hit him. More likely to shoot me.'

She rammed the weapon back into the bag, frustrated but seeing the sense of Tweed's objection. The Escort was now rocking from side to side as – by the grace of God – he negotiated another diabolical bend. Suddenly he leaned forward.

He had his headlights undimmed and the tunnel-like effect continued. Tweed was staring at a point ahead where two ancient thick-trunked oaks leaned from each side of the lane, forming an arch as they reached out towards each other as though in a passionate embrace. The mixer was within inches of the Escort, roaring like a thunderbolt.

Tweed pressed the accelerator down, coaxed a fraction more speed out of his engine. The gap between the two vehicles again widened for seconds. Tweed drove under the oaks, saw another straight stretch, looked in the rear-view mirror.

The juggernaut was rushing towards them at top speed. He guessed the driver was intent on finishing the job. Which is why he didn't see the arch. His machine began to pass under it but was too large to slip through as the smaller Escort had done. Tweed was still watching when he saw what happened.

'Look in your wing mirror,' he said quickly.

Paula saw the huge vehicle stopped with terrifying suddenness. The arch was too small. The mixer was trapped by the narrow vault. There was a frightful screech of tyres. A horrendous grinding of metal against solid oak. The drum continued to revolve but was twisted through a hundred and eighty degrees. An avalanche of cement descended on the cab. One oak trunk gave way, crashing

49

down on the cab roof, telescoping it. The drum was now turning slowly as though revolved by some unseen hand. Then it stopped. The sound of the machine's engine died. Tweed switched off his own engine and a silence like doom closed over the countryside.

'Give me the gun,' snapped Tweed.

It was an order. Paula obeyed without hesitation, handing him the Browning. Tweed jumped out of the car, walked slowly back towards the wrecked arch, keeping to the grass verge, to the blackness at the edge of the road, holding the gun by his side.

Paula followed at a distance. She picked up a fallen heavy branch as a weapon. Better than nothing. Tweed approached cautiously, his rubber-soled shoes making no sound on the grass. As he came close he gripped the Browning in both hands.

One headlight was out. Its mate was buckled, swivelled round by a huge branch from the fallen oak. By some freak chance it was still functioning and its glaring light shone on the battered cab. By its glow Tweed saw the driver's head, compressed into the neck, the dark glasses still in place.

The head was covered with a heavy mould of cement, exposing only the face. Tweed saw that in the cold night air the cement was solidifying quickly. The driver was entombed in a thick coating of his own cement. Tweed didn't envy the men who would have to attempt to recover the corpse.

'He's dead,' Tweed said as he heard Paula behind him.

'Obvious remark of the year, I'd have thought. Well, it was him or us,' she said coldly.

'No good trying to find some identification. It's all sealed in with the body. And no name on what's left of the machine.'

'Do we report it?' she asked.

'No. Too many awkward questions to answer. Where

we had just come from.' He looked at her, put his arm round her slim waist as she shivered. 'You know, I think you've had enough for one day. Sleep back at Passford House is what you need.'

'I am dropping,' she admitted.

5

The following morning Tweed held a 'council of war'.

They were all assembled in his large bedroom, which was practically a suite, on the first floor at the front. Room 2 overlooked a green lawn with a car park to the right and open green fields beyond. Tweed stood staring out of the window as Paula settled herself in a comfortable armchair and Newman perched himself on one of the arms.

'I like this place,' Tweed mused. 'Excellent service. That was a marvellous English breakfast. The staff is helpful, the surroundings luxurious. It's so peaceful and yet we're only a two-mile drive from Lymington.'

'I certainly appreciate it after yesterday,' Paula said with feeling.

'So when are we going to discuss the events of last evening?' Newman asked impatiently.

'Now.' Tweed snapped himself out of his reverie. He sat in another armchair, facing them. 'So tell us what happened to you, Bob. You've heard about what we experienced.'

'I followed Andover and he drove straight to the Chief Constable's house outside Brockenhurst. A patrol car was in the drive. Andover stayed exactly an hour.'

'During which he undoubtedly heard all about the death of Harvey Boyd,' Tweed ruminated. 'Since he carries clout he probably fended them off from visiting him.'

'He then drove straight back to his house. Which was when I confirmed something I'd suspected on the way out to Brockenhurst. He was also followed there and back by some character in a Land-Rover. Before you ask, no, I couldn't get the vehicle's registration number. It was obscured by mud.'

'I find that intriguing,' Tweed reflected. 'It suggests Andover is under total surveillance by someone. Did the Land-Rover driver spot you?'

'You think you're dealing with an amateur?' Newman snapped. 'The answer is no. I didn't follow Andover's Rover as soon as it appeared. I tracked it at a distance since he was on the road which could take him to Brockenhurst. The Land-Rover tagged him soon after he'd left *Prevent*. Drove out of an entrance to a field.'

'And yet the whole house is bugged,' Paula remarked.

'Which is why I used the phrase total surveillance,' Tweed told her. 'Now let's list what has happened. Oh, Bob, why did you drive down here to join me? Welcome and all that, but *why*?'

Newman looked uncomfortable. He carefully didn't look at Paula as he replied.

'I found out Harvey Boyd was taking Paula with him on some whim to investigate the disappearance of his pal, George Stapleton, on the Solent. I thought there might be danger so I came down to Lymington. Simple as that.'

Not so simple, Tweed thought, keeping his expression neutral. He was amused: Newman was obviously jealous when Paula found herself a boy friend.

'Now that list of unconnected factors,' Tweed continued. 'One, Boyd also has what Walford called an accident in the fog. A fatal one, unfortunately.'

'No accident,' Paula protested. 'I *did* see something big

52

moving in the fog just before the collision. And I do have exceptional eyesight.'

'Calm down,' Tweed soothed her. 'I said what Walford called an accident. That covers factor one. Two, we find Andover has aged ten years, is a broken man. Before we meet him wandering about outside we discover something macabre in his freezer – the severed arm, presumably of Irene.'

'Presumably?' Paula broke in again. 'We both saw the ring on the finger. And later Andover mentions he gave her an emerald ring on her eighteenth birthday.'

'We only have Andover's word for that,' Tweed pointed out. 'He'd guessed we'd found the severed arm and was desperately upset. You're assuming he was upset about the severed limb – which of course he would be. But I think he was upset with us because we had *discovered* it. A quite different thing.'

'Surely you can't imagine Andover is mixed up in some conspiracy?' Paula protested.

'At this stage, I don't *imagine* anything. I just list facts. Three, his daughter appears to have been kidnapped. We're relying on his strange last-minute remark to me. *No ransom at all has been demanded.* That I find most sinister, if true.'

'Is Andover wealthy?' Newman enquired.

'At a guess he could raise up to half a million, which he inherited from his father.'

'And he lives in that ghastly house with no comfort,' Paula recalled.

'He's an old public schoolboy,' Tweed explained. 'I've noticed many of them are quite indifferent to their surroundings. It starts with their boyhood in stark public schools. Poorly furnished dormitories and schoolrooms. No chance ever to develop any sort of taste.'

'Factor four?' Newman prodded.

'Andover's sudden resignation from public life,

closeting himself away like a hermit. Out of character. He was the top man at INCOMSIN.'

'I'd never heard of the organization before,' Paula remarked.

'Because you weren't supposed to. It operates in great secrecy. A very select – and one of the few which work – think-tank. Based in London, its members try to predict coming global developments. I've attended a few of their secret sessions. So have Burgoyne and Fanshawe.'

'And the significance of Andover becoming a recluse is?' Newman pressed.

'Appears to coincide with the time Irene disappeared.'

'Could be one of those odd coincidences,' Newman commented.

'Don't believe in them. Five, we find three old China hands, as they're called, all living within yards of each other in the depths of the New Forest. I don't swallow that as a coincidence.'

'Burgoyne and Fanshawe did give some sort of explanation as to how that came about,' Paula reminded him.

'Which I didn't believe for one moment. Six – who did we disturb so much that they arranged for that concrete mixer driver to kill us both?'

'Willie did leave us to make a phone call, allegedly to Andover,' Paula suggested. 'But I liked him.'

'And,' Tweed reminded her, 'we were at Willie's place long enough for Brigadier Burgoyne to organize the attack.'

'So it has to be one of them. Horrible thought. Now, if it had been one of their women friends I could believe that,' Paula said.

'Which,' Tweed began, looking wrily at Newman, 'means Paula didn't take to either of them.'

'There was something odd in the relationship of both the women living with those men,' Paula persisted. 'Only another woman would notice. A lack of true affection.'

'You've left out one suspect,' Tweed went on. 'Andover himself. He urged us to visit his neighbours, which would keep us in the area long enough to set something murderous up.'

'You can't possibly suspect him,' she protested again.

'I keep an open mind at the moment. Andover was appalled when he knew we'd been inside his house. He really went berserk. Especially when I suggested calling in the police. It's just possible he felt we had to be stopped at all costs.'

'If you say so. Have you looked at Andover's file?'

'I read through it quickly in bed last night.' Tweed paused. 'I don't know whether it tells me much. It's quite thin. A curious document. I think I'm too short of data to appreciate its significance, if any.'

'I was thinking about Brigadier Burgoyne and Willie Fanshawe,' Paula said with a frown. 'Such different personalities. The Brig. – as Willie kept referring to him – is my idea of a brilliant commander. Decisive, I'd say, sharp as a tack. But something almost sinister in that saturnine smile of his. Willie is such a contrast. Very like a generous uncle I once had and liked. Bumbling – I imagine Helen Claybourne has to look after running the whole place efficiently – and good-humoured.'

'A fair description of both men,' Tweed said, cleaning his glasses on his handkerchief as he watched her.

'And a big contrast in wealth, I'd guess,' she went on. 'The Brig. struck me as rolling in it – whereas Willie has to count the pennies.'

'Anything else?' Tweed coaxed.

'Yes. Burgoyne is living in the past. Look at how he's furnished *Leopard's Leap* – a funny name – with mementoes from his years in the Far East. But Willie hasn't a thing from his past, as though he's put it all behind him.'

'All contrasts so far,' Tweed observed.

'Oh, they do have one thing in common. I got it wrong when I said Willie has left it all behind him. Didn't you notice how both men seemed frozen in a time-warp? I mean the language they used. Burgoyne referred to Irene's French boy friend as a bounder. No one uses that term any more. Except maybe the British expats still living in Hong Kong. The same thing with Willie. He used the phrase stout fellow, talking about Burgoyne. So archaic. They're both mentally tied to China, to their old life in the Far East.'

'If you say so,' Tweed remarked absent-mindedly.

Paula jumped up, annoyed. Without realizing it Tweed had repeated a phrase she'd used earlier. Edgy from her experiences the previous day, she thought he was mimicking her.

'All right,' she snapped, 'I talk too much. But remembering we were nearly murdered last night, don't forget the bricks and the small concrete mixer on Burgoyne's verge. He's in touch with a builder – and that could be where that orange monster came from. I need some fresh air. I'm going for a walk . . .'

She closed the door quietly as she left, fuming. Tweed perched his glasses back on his nose.

'Actually Paula said something very significant. And it could just link up with Andover's report in the file he gave me.'

'And you're not going to tell me what it was?' Newman hazarded.

'Too early. I need to be sure. As I said earlier, I need more data.'

'I remember.' Newman stirred restlessly. 'So when do we start getting that data?'

'Oh, I've already started. I was up earlier than either of you this morning. I collected a load of change from the office here, then drove into Lymington to locate a public phone box.'

'Go on.'

'I called Colonel Stanstead, the Chief Constable. Poor Boyd's remains are now in an ambulance on the way to London. I called Sir Rufus Rabin, the eminent pathologist we sometimes use. Rabin will examine the body and report to me. I called Monica at Park Crescent,' he went on, referring to the HQ of the SIS. 'Harry Butler and Pete Nield are already on their way down to take turns in watching Andover's house, *Prevent.* And you can help, if you will. Go and see that Acting Harbour Master, Walford. Play up to his sense of self-importance. Find out if either – or both – Burgoyne and Fanshawe own a boat berthed round here. If so, what type of craft they have . . .'

'I might have known it.' Newman sighed. 'While we were in the land of Nod you've been purring like a dynamo . . .'

'I have also asked Monica to check with the right contacts to get me all that is known about the history of Fanshawe and Burgoyne all those years they spent in the Far East. Plus a profile on Andover. She'll be up all night, our Monica.'

'The energy of the man,' Newman commented. 'Oh, while I remember it,' he said casually, 'was Paula badly cut up about Boyd's death?'

Tweed kept a straight face. 'Naturally she was shocked. But they weren't very close. They just seemed to get on reasonably well together. Nothing serious.'

'I'm glad it wasn't an earth-shattering blow. But why are you taking all this trouble?'

'Because I've read Andover's file and certain elements came back to me when Paula was talking. My earlier action in rushing into Lymington was prompted by Paula insisting she saw something in the fog last night down at the marina. She *does* have exceptional eyesight. I also don't like one of my men – even a new recruit – killed under suspicious circumstances.'

'You mean Harvey Boyd, ex-SAS, was . . .'

'About to join the SIS after passing our training course with flying colours . . .'

'I didn't know that,' Newman rapped out.

'I'd hardly had time to tell you, had I? Bob, I really am worried. There are several apparently unconnected mysteries here. I'm beginning to feel we've stumbled on to something very sinister indeed.'

'Then I'd better get down to have a little chat with charming Mr Walford. You're going back to London?'

'Not just yet. There may be important clues I can hit on down here. I'm driving round Lymington. Maybe call in at one or two pubs. That's where you find out about the locals . . .'

Tweed was climbing into his Escort in the car park outside Passford House when Paula appeared, back from her walk. She peered in at the window as he fastened his seat belt.

'I'm sorry I was so rude, flouncing out like that. I suppose I couldn't come with you?'

'Hop in . . .'

He drove them out of the hotel entrance and along the winding country road leading to Lymington. A hard frost sparkled on the bare trees and the air was cold and fresh. He was turning on to the main road when Paula made her remark.

'This is Bob Newman's ideal weather. Says he works and thinks better in crisp air.'

'Let's hope he's doing both at the moment.'

'During my walk I was wondering what I could do – the rest of you are so active. I'd like to investigate the backgrounds of those two women – Lee Holmes and Helen Claybourne. I feel there could be more to them than just being so-called housekeepers to those men.'

'Check them out. I don't imagine it will be too easy. And I'd be careful.'

'So *you* think there's something odd about one of them?'

'I just warned you to be careful . . .'

A few minutes later he drove into the public car park behind a Waitrose supermarket. He stopped the car in the Long Stay area where there was nothing to pay. The receptionist at Passford House had told him how to find it.

Walking back to the main street, it was after eleven when they wandered past old Georgian frontages and a mix of shops. Tweed stopped at Pier 68, a bar-restaurant, ushered Paula inside.

'Barmen usually know the locals pretty well,' he whispered. 'I'm after certain information. Those ships that disappeared . . .'

Inside Pier 68 was a long cosy room with a bar counter and stools along one wall. Beyond, through an open doorway, Tweed saw tables laid neatly for lunch. He perched on a bar stool next to a man with a stiff blue cap, a prominent peak, who was smoking a cheroot. He ordered a glass of French dry white wine for himself and Paula. The barman was a jolly type with a fringe beard.

'I hear stories about boats vanishing into thin air after they've sailed from Lymington,' Tweed remarked.

'Sailors' stories.' The barman shook his head. 'I've heard vague rumours.'

'Five boats are supposed to have disappeared for ever this year,' Paula observed.

'All rumours.' The barman shook his head. 'Livens up the place, I suppose . . .'

He moved further away, polishing the counter. The man with the peaked cap put down his glass of beer, leaned close to Tweed.

'You a reporter?'

'No, just intrigued.' Tweed swivelled in his chair to give the man his attention. 'And it might make material for a book I'm writing.'

'Then your best bet is down on the waterfront. Try Ned, barman at the Ship Inn. He's closer to what's going on down there.'

'Thank you. We were strolling in that direction anyway.'

He left his glass half drunk, nodded to the barman as they left. Crossing the High Street, they were soon walking down a steep hill, perched on a high railed pavement. Paula glanced in the shops, at the locals.

'Seems a peaceful enough place.'

'Which could be deceptive.'

At the bottom they crossed a road and continued down a very short and steep cobbled street closed to traffic. Quay Hill. A brief distance later it turned sharply right into another cobbled lane. Quay Street. Mostly tourist shops of high quality but Tweed noticed doors which appeared to lead to private residences. They turned a corner and saw a forest of masts and the Ship Inn.

Paula paused, swallowed, resumed walking.

'Would you sooner wait somewhere while I go there – in view of what happened last night?' Tweed asked her.

'No. It was where I had the last drink with Harvey but I'm not letting that affect me.'

A wave of warmth met them as they stepped in out of the raw cold. Again Tweed made straight for the bar and ordered two glasses of wine. He was paying for them when he asked the barman the same question.

'I bumped into the Harbour Master yesterday. He was telling me about some rather strange accidents round here. I gather no less than five boats which went out at different times this year never came back. Oh, are you Ned?'

'That's me.' There were no other customers and the

barman leaned forward, dropping his voice as he addressed Paula and Tweed. 'They're trying to keep quiet about it. Idiotic. One boat vanishes. OK. Two. Maybe. But not five. Ought to be investigated.'

'They all disappeared just off Lymington, I gather?'

'No, sir. That's not accurate. Three of them, including a Mr Benton – the first casualty – were seen sailing up the Solent during breaks in the fog. I reckon they went down close to the mouth of the Beaulieu River.'

'Correct me if I'm wrong, but doesn't that river run roughly parallel to the Lymington River but further east?'

'You've got it, sir. It's a wild lonely part with few people living in the area. There's another big boating anchorage upriver, Buckler's Hard. Some prefer to berth there rather than here. Funny lot, these boaty types.'

'In what way?'

'Well, I suppose you'd call it snobbery. Because we've got the Royal Lymington Yacht Club here one group thinks this is the top sailing port. A much smaller group has other ideas. Think the real élite base themselves up at Buckler's Hard. There's a Brigadier Burgoyne has his motor yacht there. Wouldn't be seen dead here. Can't see the difference, myself.'

'You said a moment ago it's very lonely on the Beaulieu River. You mean no one lives there below Buckler's Hard?'

'Well, yes and no, sir. There's a funny lot lives at Moor's Landing. The west bank of the Beaulieu belongs to Lord Montagu. But the east bank – or most of it – is owned by Lord Rothschild. Moor's Landing is land he leased out, as far as I know. There was a small village just back from the river – that's Moor's Landing.'

'You said "was". Doesn't it exist any more?'

'Didn't explain myself very well. Some developer bought up all the old cottages, renovated the insides, made them real posh. He then sold the lot in a matter of days.'

'You said they were a funny lot,' Tweed encouraged him. 'That sounds intriguing.'

'Well, they keep very much to themselves. Professional types, I gather. Snooty. Never seen any of them here. They like to keep the place to themselves. Snobbery again, I suppose.'

'Has this Moor's Landing access to the Beaulieu River?'

'It certainly does. A big landing stage which they recently had poshed up. Carefully repaired and freshly painted. Which I thought was odd – so far as I hear not one of the folk who live there has a boat. Status symbol, I suppose. All this is going back a year or more.'

'I'm writing a book on out-of-the-way places,' Tweed remarked, sticking to the same story – it would avoid Ned wondering afterwards about his questions. 'Is there any way I could sail down the Beaulieu River from Buckler's Hard?'

'Last month you could have cruised on the small catamaran which takes tourists downriver. Too late for that now – end of the season come the last day of October. But I'd have thought you might hire a powerboat with crew. Cost you a lot more than the catamaran.'

'I'll think about it.' Tweed finished his drink, looked at Paula. 'Actually now my stomach is thinking about lunch. That restaurant through there looks tempting.'

'They serve a reasonable meal, sir . . .'

After lunch they wandered out on to the front. They were there just in time to see a four-coach red, white, and blue train crossing a bridge on its way to the ferry terminal. At the same time a large car ferry appeared, heading for the terminal on its return journey from the Isle of Wight.

'I wonder who Harvey's friend was going to see when he set out on his last trip to the Isle of Wight,' Tweed said half to himself.

'We'll probably never know,' Paula replied. 'Why are you so interested in Buckler's Hard and this Moor's Landing?'

'I'm looking for anything out of the ordinary. We'd better get back to Passford House.'

Paula realized she wasn't going to be told any more so she said nothing more as they made their way back to the car. She never dreamt of what would be waiting for them.

Pete Nield, summoned by Tweed to watch Sir Gerald Andover's home with Harry Butler, stood by his Ford Sierra outside the hotel. Tall and slim, he was a snappy dresser and had a small dark neat moustache which he was fingering. He rushed forward before Tweed or Paula could leave the Escort.

'Harry's back at *Prevent*. I came to tell you. The house has been broken in to. Andover has disappeared . . .'

6

'Have you by any chance seen a Land-Rover, Pete?' Tweed asked as he drove the Escort close to *Prevent*. 'Really I should have warned you.'

'No need,' replied Nield, sitting in the back of the car. 'Harry spotted it parked back in the undergrowth as we arrived. It left almost as soon as we'd driven past it. Sorry we couldn't get here earlier. Monica had trouble contacting us.'

'When did you get here?' Paula asked as she sat next to Tweed.

'Ten o'clock this morning. We did a recce of the house and immediately discovered the break-in. We didn't go inside,' he continued in his laconic way. 'Waited outside in case the intruders appeared. No such luck. I then drove to tell you at Passford House. Called you from a phone box. You were all out.'

Tweed nodded, slowed down. He turned off the road and parked his car where Newman had waited by the copse the previous evening. Leaving the car, he hurried and the other two had trouble keeping up with him as he went up the drive. Harry Butler stepped out from behind a bank of straggled shrubbery.

'No one around,' he reported.

A man of few words, Butler was more heavily built than Nield. Clean shaven, he was dressed in denims and a windcheater, which contrasted with Nield's business suit.

'How do you know Andover has gone?' Tweed asked, his voice quiet.

'No car in the garage – an outbuilding, but there's oil traces on the concrete floor, shelves of equipment for maintaining a car.'

'He could be still inside, couldn't he?'

'Not unless he'd dead. I stood by the smashed front door and called out for him at the top of my voice. No reply. Let me show you.'

'First I think we should check the grounds at the back of the house. They're pretty extensive – Andover was out there last night, walking like a zombie.'

'Already checked,' Butler replied tersely. 'No one.'

'Have you informed the police, Harry?'

'No. I thought you ought to be told first.'

'You were right, let's explore . . .'

The break-in had been conducted without finesse. Once again the front door was open. Butler pointed out where it had been jemmied open, breaking off a large section of the door-frame.

'That's a taste of what you'll see,' he warned.

With Paula by his side, Tweed followed Butler inside and across the spacious hall. Pete Nield had stayed outside as lookout. Tweed made for the study. The door was open and inside was a scene of carnage. The glass fronts of the bookcases had been smashed, the doors wrenched open. All the books had been hauled out and scattered over the floor.

'It's like this upstairs,' Butler commented. 'In the bedrooms mattresses slashed open, carpets ripped up, eiderdowns torn.'

'Which makes me wonder if they found what they were looking for despite their ravages,' Tweed mused.

He stood in the middle of the room. Drawers had been pulled out of Andover's desk, lay on the floor with their contents tipped out. Even the curtains had been pulled down, lay in heaps on the floor.

'We'll never know what they were searching for,' Paula remarked, picking her way among the wreckage. 'What is it?' she asked.

Tweed stood quite still, hands inside his trench coat, thinking of Andover. His eyes fell on an old bound book lying with its spine broken. He stooped, picked it up. Edgar Allan Poe's *Tales of Mystery and Imagination*. He flipped through the pages, stopped at a page where the corner had been turned down. He showed it to Paula.

'I wonder?'

'Sorry, am I being thick? I've never read him.'

'You should. He was a genius. See the title of the story where the page has been folded in at the top?'

'"The Purloined Letter". It doesn't mean a thing to me.'

'It wouldn't – since you haven't read it. Andover is a clever man. Maybe he's left me a signal.'

'What signal . . .'

But Tweed was walking over to the large old-fashioned

65

mantelpiece above a pile of logs laid in the fireplace. The only items on the ledge were a Victorian clock which had stopped at five to twelve and two candlesticks. Perched alongside the clock against the wall was a brown envelope familiar to all – *On Her Majesty's Service*. A communication from the tax authorities.

He picked up the envelope, and concealed behind it, propped against the peeling plaster, was another envelope. It was made of good-quality paper, was addressed to Sir Gerald Andover, and carried a Belgian stamp.

'Surely they couldn't have wrecked the house looking for that?' Paula protested.

'Depends on what's inside . . .'

Tweed pulled out two folded sheets and again the paper was high quality and thick. He read both pages rapidly. When he turned to Paula his expression was troubled.

'This is a very revealing letter from Gaston Delvauz of Liège.'

'I've heard that name before. Can't quite place it.'

'Delvaux is an armaments manufacturer and one of the world's greatest experts on advanced developments in his field. Not just tanks and guns, but aircraft and ships. Note the last item.'

'You mean he might know something about that ghost ship I swear I saw just before Harvey died?'

'I didn't say that. Delvaux was also a member of INCOMSIN, the International Committee of Strategic Insight I told you about.'

'The think-tank of brain-boxes on likely global developments.'

'And Delvaux, like Andover, is another brain-box. I've met him several times when invited to sit in on one of their secret meetings.'

'What does the letter say?'

66

'We can talk about that later,' Tweed replied, pocketing the letter. 'It probably means a trip to Belgium soon. And I've little doubt this is what the marauders were looking for.'

'But how on earth did you know where to look?'

'Poe's story. It is – briefly – about an important letter which vanishes from a room. They search everywhere and then leave, as I recall – perhaps not too accurately. The main point is the letter was hidden in an *obvious* place – perched on the mantelpiece inside an envelope. It was so clearly on view no one thought to look there. Hence Andover turning down the page of that story. My guess is the book was on his desk for me to see. Now, before we leave, phone the police anonymously from a call box. We have a grisly task, if we can manage it.'

'Brace yourself, Harry,' Tweed warned in the kitchen as he stopped to raise the lid of the chest freezer.

'Enough to put you off your lunch,' the phlegmatic Butler commented.

'I'm just relieved it's still here,' Tweed responded, staring down at the severed arm preserved in its plastic container filled with ice. 'I don't know how we're going to solve this problem. I'd like to have the limb transported to London for examination by my pet pathologist, Dr Rabin. But we can't just take it there by car like that.'

'Yes, we can,' Butler assured him. 'Not knowing how long we'd be out here, I brought a very large cool bag full of food. It's inside my Ford Cortina. Give me five minutes . . .'

It was a long speech for Butler. He disappeared and came back quickly, holding an outsize cool bag.

'Should fit in here. May I?'

Paula had perched herself on a stool as far away from the freezer as possible. She wasn't squeamish, but staring at the severed arm with its bloodstained bandage over the elbow wasn't her idea of duty when it wasn't necessary.

Butler had unzipped the long cool bag. Wearing gloves, he lifted the container out and it fitted easily into the bag. He zipped it up, closed the lid of the freezer, looked at Tweed who was scribbling on the back of one of his cards. He handed it to Butler.

'There's the address. Dr Rabin will be expecting you. I'll call him while you're driving back.'

'I'm on my way . . .'

Paula waited until they were alone. Then she asked the question which had been puzzling her.

'Why a pathologist? And a top one?'

'Because,' Tweed explained, 'although I know very little about medical matters, it seemed to me it would need a very good surgeon to have amputated that arm so neatly. If I can find the bastard who performed that foul act I'll be close to who is behind all this.'

Paula nodded as they prepared to leave. Tweed rarely used strong language: it showed the suppressed rage he was feeling at this brutal act. She didn't look back as they left the ravaged house. Pete Nield appeared out of nowhere, gave a little salute.

'All clear. Not a single car has passed in either direction. Harry is *en route* to London and I buried the food in a gulley. What's the form now?'

'We need to find out what's happened to Andover. First priority. No point in continuing your vigil here. So we get moving. Back to Passford House for starters . . .'

The first thing they saw when they arrived back at the hotel car park was Newman's Mercedes parked in splendid isolation. The next thing they saw was Newman standing up from the far side, holding a polishing cloth.

He strolled over, listened while Tweed gave him a résumé of what had happened.

'Did you find out from Walford if either Burgoyne or Fanshawe own a boat?' he concluded.

'Of course. I was a reporter at one time. I drove friend Walford to a pub, bought him a couple of Scotches. He became quite garrulous. The Brig., as he called him, has a luxury motor yacht based at a place called Buckler's Hard . . .'

'I know that,' Tweed told him.

'Let me go on. Willie Fanshawe has a motor yacht too but his is berthed at Lymington. They all seem to be mad on the sea. Sir Gerald Andover has his own motor yacht, the *Seahorse III*—'

'That's important,' Tweed interjected. 'Based where?'

'Lymington. Do let me finish. Andover has left these shores. Walford saw him aboard the *Seahorse III* sailing downriver and into the Solent early this morning. Just after daybreak.'

'Wish we knew where he'd gone,' Tweed said half to himself.

'I do,' Newman went on. 'He informed Walford he was cruising round the Isle of Wight and down to Devon for a few days. Odd thing, Walford said never before had Andover bothered to let him know where he was going. He described Andover as being very secretive about his sailing trips.'

'Which means,' Tweed said grimly, 'that the one place he isn't going to is Devon. Now, he's being ultra-secretive. We have to track him down later.'

'The coastguard?' Newman suggested.

'No good. Andover is clever. My guess is by now he's well out at sea, whatever his ultimate destination is.'

'So it's checkmate,' Paula commented. 'What do we do now? Go back to London?'

'Not yet. I want to scour this part of the world. I feel

sure there's something strange happening – on top of what we found at Andover's home.'

Tweed stood staring across the frosted lawn which had a *crème-de-menthe* colour. Even at that hour the temperature was close to zero. Knowing him, the others kept quiet. Tweed's mind was racing, examining what they had uncovered, trying to see, dimly, some sort of pattern.

'I've no idea what's going on,' he admitted eventually. 'The alleged kidnapping of Irene is a sinister mystery. And the presence of three old China hands so close together is more than pure chance. Paula said something recently which was significant. The trouble is I can't recall what it was.' He straightened up. 'What we need is even more data—'

'One other thing Walford told me which has just come back,' Newman interjected. 'He wasn't too accurate last night. This morning he told me the three boats which disappeared at the beginning of the year vanished somewhere near the mouth of the Beaulieu River. One of them was Benton. Wasn't that the chap who was a friend of Andover?'

'Yes,' agreed Tweed. 'And what you've just told us links up with the account of the barman at the Ship Inn. We'll take a look at Buckler's Hard and Moor's Landing after an early lunch. Check the map for me, Paula. How close to the Solent is this model village the barman described?'

He paced slowly back and forth while Paula studied the Ordnance Survey map she'd extracted from the Escort. Tweed was disturbed. The whole area seemed so peaceful and yet they'd discovered that severed arm in the house of a broken man.

'Moor's Landing is about a mile from the Solent,' Paula reported.

'So it's close to where those three boats vanished at

70

the mouth of the Beaulieu River. Yes, I think it may well repay a visit . . .'

With Paula navigating, they took the same route to reach Buckler's Hard they had followed the previous evening. Newman was driving them in the Mercedes with Paula beside him and Tweed alone in the back.

Some distance behind them, on Tweed's instructions, Pete Nield followed them as though they were strangers. They were approaching the entrances to *Prevent*, *Leopard's Leap*, and *The Last Haven* when Tweed spoke for the first time.

'Bob, I want you to slow down now. Crawl at twenty miles an hour.'

'If I must,' Newman protested, 'but the Merc. will be rarin' to go.'

'Why, if I may ask?' queried Paula.

'You just did,' Tweed replied, and lapsed into silence.

As they crawled past the entrances Tweed glanced sideways. Just an empty drive at Andover's place. In the morning he'd called the police anonymously about the break-in. The house was as invisible as before. The wrought-iron gates to *Leopard's Leap* were again open. And once more no sign of life.

Paula stiffened as she saw the pile of bricks and the small concrete mixer on the grass verge. It reminded her of their experience the previous evening when they had almost been killed.

Tweed glanced down the open gravel drive to Fanshawe's Swedish-style house. The net curtains across the windows gave it an even more uninhabited look. He waited a minute before he spoke again.

'Could you pull in at the side of the road? I want a word with Pete and there's no one about . . .'

Nield, driving his Ford Sierra, appeared a few minutes

later. Tweed was waiting for him outside the car and gestured for him to stop. Nield jumped out swiftly, leaving his engine running.

'Trouble?'

'Not yet.' Tweed smiled. 'Pete, a mile or two back a lane leads off to the left going back the way we've come. That's where Paula and I had our little encounter with the mobile concrete mixer. It's the only turn-off for miles. I'd like you to go back and drive down that lane to see what – if anything – is happening. I think you studied the map route to Buckler's Hard with Paula. Drive back here as fast as you can later and try to catch us up.'

'All clear. And I'm carrying that route in my head. See you soon . . .'

Before Tweed had closed the door of the Mercedes Nield had turned round over spare ground and was speeding back. Tweed settled himself again.

'Are both of you armed? I should have checked earlier.'

'I'm carrying my .38 Smith & Wesson Special in a hip holster,' Newman replied as he drove on, accelerating.

'And I have my Browning in my shoulder-bag,' Paula reassured Tweed. 'Pete has a Walther. Are you worried this could be a risky trip? This is the New Forest.'

'And we were nearly murdered yesterday evening . . .'

7

They had left the Forest – and after that a flat area of barren heath – behind them when the vintage Bentley overtook Newman, travelling like a demon.

Newman was driving down a curving hill at the approaches to the small town of Beaulieu with the river on their left. He was moving at a safe speed when the ancient open touring car, green in colour with running boards and gleaming old-fashioned headlamps, roared past at insane speed.

Behind the wheel of the four-seater crouched the driver clad in an old crash helmet and huge goggles. Paula had only a glimpse but saw his bright scarf was wrapped round the lower half of his face, presumably to muffle him against the cold.

'Crazy so-and-so,' Newman muttered.

'We turn right in a moment,' Paula warned. 'Don't go on into Beaulieu. Oh, my God! Look at the idiot!'

'I'm looking,' Newman observed nonchalantly.

'And he's going to Bucklers Hard – if he ever makes it alive . . .'

'Actually, he's an expert driver, even if a bit of a show-off,' Newman remarked.

To turn up another steep hill leading to Buckler's Hard the driver of the Bentley had to swing through an angle of about a hundred and fifty degrees. He hardly slowed as he spun off the main road and then accelerated up the hill and out of sight.

In the back of the car Tweed was taking no notice of this demonstration of macho driving. He was twisted round, staring through the rear window, then he switched his gaze to the side window as Newman swung round the same tortuous bend.

'There's a chopper floating round behind us,' he told them. 'A private machine with no markings. Odd, that.'

Newman drove on up the steep and winding hill. At the top he manoeuvred them round a series of bends along a lane with hedges on either side. Then they were on the level. The Bentley had disappeared despite the long straight stretch ahead.

'Lord!' Paula commented. 'He must have moved.'

'Souped-up engine,' Newman told her.

'That chopper is flying on a course parallel to us now,' Tweed reported from the back.

'You seem very intrigued by it,' Paula replied over her shoulder.

'Give me the map,' Tweed said.

A few minutes later, in lonely open country with fields spreading away, Newman reached a private road leading to Buckler's Hard. He was about to turn down it when Tweed called out again.

'That chopper's landing well ahead of us. From the map I'd say it's coming down somewhere on the west bank – on the land owned by Lord Montagu.'

'Just a chopper,' Newman said as he began turning left.

'Should we be going down here?' Paula asked. 'I think this is probably only for use by people who own a boat.'

'Then we own a boat,' Newman rapped back. '*Seahorse IV*, if anyone wants to know. And in my rear-view mirror I see Pete Nield is catching us up. I wonder what glad tidings he brings?'

Half-way down a steep descent the anchorage came into view. The sun was shining and the basin of blue water sparkled like diamonds. It was more like a small lake but towards the Solent the river ran out between tree-shrouded banks. To the north, where it came from Beaulieu, it curved in an S-bend. Newman stopped, turned off the engine. 'I'll wait for Pete . . .'

Tweed, followed by Paula, got out of the car to stretch his legs. On the river deserted yachts and power cruisers, covered with blue plastic sheeting for winter, were moored to buoys. The view was scenic but there was no sign of activity. End of the season. Nield parked his Sierra behind the Mercedes, jumped out.

Paula, who had been wandering about, looking down at the anchorage, began walking back to Tweed.

'Come on, Pete,' she said crisply. 'I'm not a schoolgirl any more. Let me hear the grisly details.'

'They are grisly. The concrete mixer is still there – jammed between two trees. So are the police who told me the road was closed. They'd erected a sheet round the vehicle but a breeze blew it up. The driver who tried to kill you is set solid in concrete. They're having to use pneumatic drills to remove his unwanted overcoat.'

'Better him than you,' Newman commented. 'What next?'

'Paula and I will borrow your Merc. You and Pete take the Sierra down and we'll follow. Try and hire a boat to take us downriver,' Tweed suggested.

'We're on our way . . .'

Tweed parked the Mercedes behind the river front and under the lee of a large yacht propped upright by heavy wooden staves on either side. It shielded the car from easy sighting.

'Why are we hiding?' Paula asked.

'A Mercedes would be noticed. I'm curious about that vintage Bentley which overtook us. And that chopper I saw landing close to the river. I smell danger.'

'From what quarter?'

'I've no idea. But we crawled past Andover's house. The thugs who broke in may have returned and seen us through the shrubbery.'

'Won't the police be there after your phone call?' she queried. 'Although I didn't see a patrol car.'

'They'll have been and gone hours ago. To them it will be just another break-in. Andover probably wasn't there to inform. They'd get their pet builder to board up the front door and leave it at that.'

'Anyone else?'

'We also crawled past both Burgoyne's and Fanshawe's residences. Either could have spotted us, decided to follow to see what we're up to. And someone is going to drastic lengths to stop us, as we know from last night.'

'You're trying to smoke out whoever it is,' Paula stated.

'I would like to know the identity of the enemy. There is one – I know that from reading Andover's file and Gaston Delvaux's letter to him from Liège.'

'And you're not going to tell me anything about either?'

'Not yet.'

They had been walking down a dried mud track scattered with gravel as they talked. When they came round the corner of a clump of trees and undergrowth the track led on to a walk along the river's edge. Newman was hurrying towards them with another man in his mid-thirties.

Tall and slim, the stranger walked with an athletic stride, was well built, clean shaven, and had an aquiline nose. He wore denims and trainers. Paula was relieved by his working clothes, his pea-jacket. She was clad in denims thrust inside knee-length gumboots and a padded windcheater.

'He's good looking,' she whispered to Tweed, 'and he knows it.'

'A piece of luck,' Newman called out as the two men came close. 'This is an old acquaintance of mine. Mordaunt, freelance journalist. He's agreed to take us for a spin on the river.'

Tweed made introductions, using first names only, omitting to mention himself. Mordaunt made a beeline for Paula, holding out a large strong hand. His voice was upper crust.

'I say the day is improving no end. Welcome to

Buckler's Hard, Paula. I've just been putting my boat to bed. A small yacht. Spend as much time down here as I can during the spring–summer. Have a small pad in London. All my money, such as it is, goes on the boat. They're expensive things, boats.'

'Can I have my hand back?' Paula asked with a dry smile.

'Sorry. Didn't mean to offend. It's such a small, shapely hand. Can't really blame me. Now, for the river trip. I've got a large dinghy with an outboard I borrowed. No charge – glad to be of service. This way . . .'

'Isn't there a more stable boat available?' Tweed enquired.

'I'm afraid not. Not to worry. Water is as smooth as silk. Hardly a ripple. You'll enjoy it.'

As he walked off with Newman Paula noticed his thick, dark hair was blow-dried. An odd mix of the matinée-idol type and a practical man of action. She glanced at Tweed, who was following reluctantly.

'You did take your Dramamine back at the hotel,' she reminded him. 'And we're not going out to sea.'

'Heaven forbid. Water always moves and anything on it moves even more. I suppose I shall survive.'

'You can hold my hand,' Paula teased him. 'Lucky this Mordaunt being here.'

'Or department of strange coincidence . . .'

Tweed was following the others across a catwalk leading to the main landing stage. Behind him was a long single-storey building which was a combined shop full of tourist-memento rubbish together with the kiosk where tickets were sold for the catamaran cruise. Everything was shut until the next season in spring.

Paula was suddenly aware Tweed had paused. He was staring to the north where, onshore, was a large collection of vessels of various sizes drawn up on land. He had caught sight of a man's figure disappearing behind the hull of a large yacht.

'Something wrong?' Paula asked.

'I thought I recognized someone up there. Forget it – don't mention it to the others.'

Mordaunt had donned a sailor's peaked cap which he perched on his head at a rakish angle. He stood by a large dinghy inside which Newman and Nield had sat down near the stern. This compelled Tweed and Paula to occupy the seat near the prow, hardly his favourite position for such an enterprise.

'All aboard now?' Mordaunt called out in his confident manner. 'Ready for the Skylark cruise, everyone? But where to? Any preference.'

'What I can do without,' Tweed whispered, 'is the hearty nautical touch.'

'We'd like to visit Moor's Landing,' Newman told their host as Mordaunt released the mooring ropes, jumped aboard, and sat down by the tiller.

'You won't be popular there,' Mordaunt warned. 'They're a very standoffish lot. Don't mix with pleb types like us. Could even be a hostile reception.'

'We'll risk it,' Newman said firmly.

Mordaunt started the engine. Tweed gritted his teeth as the dinghy wobbled and was steered out into the main channel. There was no wind but it was cold as Siberia on the river. Tweed began to study his surroundings as they moved downriver.

'Damn! I hope he didn't see me.'

Brigadier Maurice Burgoyne stood behind the beached hull of the yacht, a pair of glasses looped round his neck. He was positioned in the boatyard and near by was a large lifting machine used to transport beached vessels into the water. The blonde Lee Holmes looked at him with a quirky smile.

'You hope who didn't see you?'

'Tweed, I think. He stared towards me when he was on the catwalk. I'll just check . . .'

Burgoyne was wearing a leather jacket and cavalry twill trousers. The vintage Bentley was concealed inside a shed, his helmet and goggles on the driving seat. He shinned up a ladder perched against the hull, raised his glasses.

The dinghy was moving away from the landing stage. He recognized Tweed crouched at the prow as he turned to say something to the girl next to him. Paula Grey. He climbed rapidly back down the ladder.

'I was right. It is Tweed. And his female sidekick, Paula Grey. This is dangerous. They could ruin everything. We have to find out where they're headed for.'

'How?'

'Do I have to think up all the tactics? Take the small dinghy, follow them.'

'They could recognize me,' she warned him.

'Heavens above!' he snapped. 'Disguise yourself. You have those dark glasses. Put them on.'

'Dark glasses now? In winter? I know the sun is shining. No, it was. They'll just draw attention to me.'

'*Put them on!* Girls wear dark glasses any time. They think it makes them look sexy. Get after those people, Lee. I want to know what they're up to. Quick march.'

Lee moved fast. She twisted her long blonde hair and tied it with a bow at the back. Taking a silk scarf out of her capacious hold-all, she wrapped it round her head so it totally concealed her hair. She put on the dark glasses, ran down to the water's edge, and climbed into the small dinghy. A minute later she was purring across the water in pursuit.

* * *

As soon as their large dinghy had left the landing stage the sun went in and a sold grey mass of low clouds dimmed the light. Despite his dislike of the motion, Tweed was looking all round and not happy about what he saw.

There was not a straight stretch of water resembling a river in sight. From east bank to west the water was cluttered with grassy islands and it was not apparent where the main channel led its devious way south towards the open sea. Paula shivered.

'Creepy atmosphere,' she whispered.

'It could be more stimulating,' Tweed agreed.

Mordaunt seemed to know what he was doing as he guided the dinghy among the islands and out into a clearer channel. But as they moved south down what was obviously the Beaulieu River the brooding sensation increased.

Round a bend, they left Buckler's Hard behind, and when Paula glanced back the anchorage had vanished. They had left all relics of civilization behind. On both sides mushy green flats, an almost sinister acid-green colour, spread out towards the main channel as though trying to strangle it. The flats were interlaced with murky-looking creeks. Even the main river was a sullen green colour.

'This is getting claustrophobic,' Paula said. 'I feel it's all closing in on us.'

There was something in what she'd said, Tweed thought. Beyond the treacherous-looking flats rose the dense jungle of the forest, a tangle of firs and oaks crammed on top of each other. They passed a landing stage and beyond it he caught sight of a Tudor house, buried in the foliage, smoke rising vertically from one chimney. Here and there on the river a lonely yacht was tied up to a buoy. No one aboard. They began to sweep round a wide bend. The sun came out through a hole in the grey overcast, a brief shaft. Tweed looked quickly to his right. The sun had flashed off something in the undergrowth. Were they being watched through field glasses? And this was the point where he'd calculated the chopper had descended. Then the sun went in. Paula glanced back, stiffened.

'There's another dinghy – a smaller one – coming up behind us. I think there's a woman aboard it.'

'Out for a spot of fresh air, I expect. And it's arctic fresh.'

They passed several other landing stages, some of which looked derelict. Then Mordaunt called out: 'There we are. That landing stage ahead of us. That's the one for Moor's Landing. Are you sure you want to go ashore? Private property.'

'A whole village?' Newman snorted. 'Ridiculous.'

'Don't say I didn't warn you . . .'

He steered the dinghy away from the main channel to a very long landing stage. Freshly painted, railed, the planks seemed to have been renewed. A prominent notice carried the message: INTRUDERS TRESPASS HERE AT THEIR PERIL. PRIVATE. Mordaunt steered the dinghy to the steps. Nield was the first to jump out. As he climbed the steps he appeared to slip, grabbed at the notice board, wrenched it savagely. It came loose and Nield shrugged as he watched it floating off and vanishing inside a creek amid the acid-green marsh.

'Accidents will happen,' Nield remarked, brushing off his gloved hands.

Accident my foot, Paula thought. You destroyed the board deliberately. And then made your flip remark for the benefit of Mordaunt. She was about to disembark nimbly when someone gripped her arm to steady her balance.

'Easy does it,' Mordaunt assured her with his broad smile.

81

'Thank you,' Paula said.

Tweed appeared to lose his balance making his way towards the stern from the prow. He grabbed at the end of the landing stage. The board Nield had wrenched free had been held by only two screws. Tweed was holding on to solid timber where a larger ship would disembark passengers. He looked at the smooth area of fresh wood, unpainted. Something very strong and sharp had sliced a piece out of the timber, neater than if a chainsaw had been used. He made the comment as he joined the others without referring to what he'd observed.

'I think we've come to the right place.'

'I'm staying with the dinghy,' Mordaunt called out. 'It needs guarding. Even on the river you get yobbos who make off with any vessel they can lay their hands on. I will wait, of course . . .'

With Newman in the lead they began walking down the long bridge to the distant shore. Paula paced herself alongside Tweed.

'That small dinghy has stopped in midstream. I think the girl aboard is watching us through binoculars.'

'Idle curiosity, I expect.'

'I still think I know her. Something about her movements. And why did you say we've come to the right place? I don't see anything that suggests that.'

'Call it sixth sense,' Tweed replied off-handedly.

'All right, be enigmatic,' she snapped, and quickened her stride towards the invisible village of Moor's Landing.

8

On the surface Moor's Landing appeared to be the kind of village you occasionally see on picture postcards. Stepping off the long railed catwalk they had walked on down a short country lane which ended at the beginning of the main street.

'It's so picturesque,' Paula said.

'It doesn't look real to me,' Tweed said in a neutral tone, registering his first impression. He'd found in the past initial impressions were correct.

They stood close to an old stone well in the middle of a straight cobbled street. On either side were detached cottages with thatched roofs and small walled gardens in front. Tweed counted fourteen cottages, seven on each side. Then the village ended as abruptly as it had started where they stood.

'No sign of shops, not even a general store,' Nield remarked. 'Just an estate agent half-way down on the right. Strange sort of village. And not a soul anywhere.'

He had caught something of the atmosphere which had attracted Tweed's attention. All the windows of the cottages facing each other were curtained. They appeared inhabited except there were no inhabitants.

'Not too keen on this place,' Newman commented. 'It is like a façade carefully presented but hiding something.'

He was right about the presentation, Paula thought. All the cottages had their white walls freshly whitewashed. The thatch was in perfect condition. Each door was painted a different bright colour. And beside each door was a coach-lamp, gleaming even under the grey overcast which made everything seem more unreal.

'I don't believe this place,' Paula said. 'What do we do next?'

'The barman at the Ship Inn did tell us a developer had bought up the place and renovated it,' Tweed reminded her. 'Our next move is to call on the estate agent, pretend we're house-hunting.'

'So you and I are now Mr and Mrs Gulliver,' Paula decided.

She switched the two rings she wore on to the third finger of her left hand. Newman loosened his trench coat to hide the bulge of his Smith & Wesson.

'I'm coming with you. Just in case. I'm your adviser.'

'And I'll keep my eyes open here,' Nield suggested. 'I want to make sure Mordaunt doesn't take off and leave us stranded . . .'

There was still no sign of life as they strolled down to the fourth cottage on the right. Even the cobbles seemed freshly laid to Tweed. They paused outside the cottage. A board attached to the wall, its paint peeling, carried the legend 'A. Barton. Estate Agent'.

Tweed opened the wrought-iron gate, let Paula walk up the path first. She was about to press the bell when the door was opened and a six-foot-tall, heavily built man with remote eyes and no warmth in his manner spoke to her.

'Yes? What is it? What do you want?'

'Are you Mr Barton?' she enquired.

'That's me.'

'You are an estate agent?'

'Says so on the board up there.'

'Mr and Mrs Gulliver. We are looking for somewhere to live. This village seems ideal. This is our adviser. May we come in?'

'Yes, if you want to, but you're wasting your time.'

She entered a front room sparsely furnished with a trestle table, a fold-up chair behind it on bare floorboards, and several photos, curling up at the edges, displayed in a frame on the wall. Pictures of various properties, some of them clearly cottages at Moor's Landing, all with a red *SOLD* sticker on them – except for one. She wandered over to the framed board as Tweed and Newman followed her inside.

A burly man, Barton wore an expensive smart grey suit and a striped shirt with a silk tie, and handmade shoes, which contrasted oddly with his stark surroundings. He stood silently as Paula turned round.

'It's really one of the cottages here we'd like to see. I suppose someone is thinking of moving if the price is right? And may we sit down?'

Barton, hands shoved in his trouser pockets, shook his large head. Without any show of enthusiasm he fetched two fold-up canvas chairs leaning against a wall, opened them on the clients' side of the trestle table. As Tweed sat down with Paula, Barton lowered himself carefully into his own canvas seat. Tweed had the impression he hadn't sat in it much and didn't trust it with his bulk. Newman walked over to study the photos.

'You won't get a cottage here for love or money,' Barton informed Paula in his abrasive manner.

'Why not?' Tweed asked quietly.

'Because none are for sale.' Barton glared at Tweed. 'That clear enough for you?'

'No, it isn't. My wife has decided she wants to live here. Money is no object. Your job is to sell houses to earn your commission. You seem to have a funny way of going about it.'

'I told you,' Barton snapped. 'I know all the owners. Not one will sell. Not for any price.'

'They're all millionaires?' Tweed enquired politely.

'They're just settled. *Settled!* Get it?'

'Then how do you stay in business?' Newman asked as he swung round to stare at the man behind the trestle.

'I do have other properties in other areas. But if it's Moor's Landing you're set on, forget it.'

Paula intervened quickly. She sensed Newman's temper was on a short fuse.

'In that case what about the Brockenhurst property you've got on your board? It looks like a nice house. Belongs to a Mrs Goshawk, I see. Perhaps you could phone her?'

'Not at this time of day. She's always out.'

'Then the best thing is for us to go over there and take a look at it,' Paula persisted. 'I've memorized her address. How do we find Cray's Road?'

'I'll draw you a map. But she'll be out. Is most of the time. Doesn't help to sell a property . . .'

Two minutes later Paula had folded the sheet of paper Barton had used to draw a map on, stood up, smiled, thanked him for his help, and left. Newman was close behind her as she strolled back down the path and looked at the far end of the village.

An old woman dressed in black was scrubbing her doorstep. It was the only cottage with a badly weathered door and no bright colour on it. She whispered to Newman.

'Bob, detain that awful boor for me. I want to go and have a chat with that woman cleaning her doorstep – with Tweed . . .'

Newman reacted instantly. He turned back, let Tweed pass him, and buttonholed Barton, standing in his way so he couldn't reach the street.

'Barton, just how long has Mrs Goshawk's house out at Brockenhurst been on the market? We're going to look at it but from the state of your photo that property has been sticking for months . . .'

Tweed agreed it was a good idea to talk to the old lady

86

since she was the one person who might know something about Moor's Landing. She looked up suspiciously as they walked up her path and used her hand-brush to scrub the stone even more vigorously. Her first words revealed the reason for her suspicion.

'If you've come 'ere to try and get me to sell you can turn round and walk straight back where youse come from. This is my 'ome and they'll carry me out when my time comes.'

'We're nothing to do with that uncouth brute,' Paula reassured her. 'We're trying to find out what's going on here.'

'Dark doin's, no mistake about that. Who are you, then?'

'I'm a Chief Investigator for phoney insurance claims,' Tweed said quickly. 'And this lady is my assistant. I don't quite understand, What dark doin's?'

'I'm Mrs Garnett,' the old lady went on. Her grey hair was tied back in a bun and she continued scrubbing as she talked. 'Know how they got the folk who once owned these cottages out?'

'No, I don't,' said Tweed. 'But I'm interested.'

'That developer offers them all double the price they'd get from an ordinary buyer. Greed took all my friends away.'

'What happened next?' Paula asked.

'Funny business. Every cottage – except mine – done up posh. Spent a fortune they did. Then sold the lot in three days.' She paused in her work to look up with alert eyes. 'I ask you – houses going in three days – all of them. Except mine. I wouldn't sell.'

'What sort of people bought them?' Tweed enquired.

'That's a funny business, too. Professional folk, so I heard. Supposed to work in Southampton. Nearly all men.'

'You mean several men to a cottage?' Tweed coaxed.

87

'That's right. Two or three in a cottage in some. And three of them share the same woman. That's a secret they don't think I knows. Supposed to be married. I never 'eard of one woman being married to three men. They don't fool me with their trick.'

'What trick was that?' Paula asked.

'When she came back with a different so-called husband she dressed differently, wore a wig. But I could tell,' Mrs Garnett went on vehemently, 'from the way she moved. One woman doesn't fool another with fancy dressin' up.'

'You mentioned professional people working in Southampton,' Tweed recalled. 'How do they get there? I don't see any garages – or do they park . . .'

'Garages are round back at end of street. Old barns converted to take their cars. They can drive off in either direction to Southampton.'

'I'm surprised there's no village store,' Paula remarked.

'Was one. Cottage at top end of the street, near the landing stage. When Mrs Rogers sold out they converted it into a cottage to live in, like the rest.'

'Is the landing stage used much?' Tweed asked casually.

'Not in daylight. None of them 'as boats. But I sleep light. In the middle of the night about every three months a couple of new men arrive and move in to two of the cottages. Those there moves out. Lord knows where. But they comes and goes by the river. There,' she stood up with remarkably agility. 'Step's finished so I'm goin' to make myself a nice cup of tea.'

'Thank you for your information,' Paula said. 'Now do take care of yourself.'

'Got my trusty cudgel. Anyone who tries to move me out ends up with a cracked skull. I own this cottage . . .'

As they walked back to where Newman was engaging Barton in conversation it appeared an argument was taking place. Barton was pushing past Newman, red in the face.

'No cars? I should have spotted that earlier. So you came down the river, used the landing stage. That is private. I may sue you for trespass . . .'

'Don't talk such tripe,' retorted Nield, who had joined Newman. 'There's nothing to indicate it's private . . .'

'Bloody blind as a bat, are you? I'll show you,' Barton stormed.

They followed him down the lane. Barton's leather-soled shoes created a drumbeat as he marched down the long catwalk. Newman and Nield were close behind him as Tweed and Paula followed.

'What the devil . . .?'

Barton was standing on the landing, staring at where the warning notice had been. Tweed noticed Mordaunt was carefully not looking in Barton's direction as he stood up in the dinghy. Paula needled Barton.

'You should put up a notice if it's private property.'

'There was a bloody notice . . .'

'Watch your language, old man. Especially when you're talking to a lady,' Newman suggested amiably.

'Vandals!' Barton was beside himself with fury. 'You don't expect them on the river but they come. Wreck things just for the pleasure of it . . .'

As he raved on Mordaunt helped Paula aboard the dinghy to the same seat at the prow. Tweed glanced downriver, joined her as Newman and Nield came aboard. Mordaunt started up the engine after releasing the rope tying the craft to the landing stage. They were moving out into midstream when Paula also glanced downriver and stiffened.

The temperature had nosedived, the sky was almost dark as night. And drifting swiftly up from the Solent was a dense freezing fog.

*　　*　　*

Paula's nerves were on edge but she made a great effort not to show it. The freezing fog – like ice mist – had caught up with them, blotted out both banks. It recalled for her the vigil at Lymington marina when she had waited for Harvey Boyd to return. Something was moving up close behind them.

The fog swirled like dense smoke. She peered back and saw it was only phantom shapes which came and went. At least so they appeared. Tweed sensed her nervousness, squeezed her arm.

'We'll soon be back at Buckler's Hard,' he said quietly.

'But how on earth will Mordaunt find his way up the main channel? We could end up marooned in one of those horrid marshy flats.'

'Seems to know what he's doing . . .'

The fog trailed clammy fingers over Paula's face. Just as it had done at the marina. She was living the nightmare all over again. Gritting her teeth, she continued to look over her shoulder, waiting for something huge to drive them under the water.

They had been talking in whispers. It was an unconscious reaction to the leaden hush which had fallen on the river with the arrival of the fog. Even the sound of their outboard was muffled as Mordaunt followed the familiar course of the channel. Then she heard a slapping noise of water washing against a hull. A second later a distinct shape loomed up to starboard. Paula's gloved hand clenched the plank seat tightly.

'Just a yacht moored to a buoy,' Tweed assured her.

They passed within a foot of the yacht with its mast a dim silhouette spearing up and vanishing inside the fog. Visibility dropped to zero as they rounded a sweeping bend. The freezing cold was penetrating Paula's windcheater. She turned away from Tweed to lick her lips, dry with fear. Then she leaned her head close to his.

'That water slapping against the yacht's hull – something must have disturbed the water. It's like oil. I wonder if that girl in the dinghy we saw coming down is also on her way back?'

'I expect so,' said Tweed in the same calm tone.

'I'd have thought we'd have reached Buckler's Hard by now.'

'We're nearly there. I remember coming round this steep curve. And the fog is thinning. We'll be safe on *terra firma* within minutes.'

'Don't tempt fate . . .'

Lee Holmes steered her small dinghy close to the shore by the boatyard. Brigadier Burgoyne appeared, wearing his driving helmet and goggles, scarf in one hand. As she stepped out he dragged the dinghy ashore up the slope to the hull of the large yacht.

'You took your time,' he snapped. 'I think I can hear them coming back. We've got to be away before they arrive.'

'I haven't a lot to report . . .' she began.

'Then save it until we're well on our way.'

He ran to the shed. So they could leave quickly he had already opened the doors. She ran after him, pulling her sodden scarf off her head, shoving her misted-up glasses into her handbag. He had the engine going as she jumped in beside him. She was shutting the door of the Bentley when he drove off through the dark up the private road, his headlamps undimmed. On the outward journey Lee had remained hidden, huddled on the floor behind the front seats. Burgoyne rapped out his order.

'Now, get on with your report.'

'No need to be so bossy. You're not dressing down one of your subalterns.'

'You cut it too damned fine. Get on with the report.'

'They all – except Mordaunt – got off at Moor's Landing and disappeared for ages. Tweed, Paula Grey, and two men I couldn't recognize – except one looked familiar through my glasses. It will come back to me who he is. When they returned Barton was with them, seemed to be in a rage, waving his hands about.'

'How long do you reckon they were there?'

It was dark now, which didn't stop Burgoyne racing along a straight stretch, headlamps blazing. He was anxious to reach the main road from Beaulieu to Brockenhurst before his targets appeared.

'Exactly thirty minutes. I timed them.'

'As long as that? They must have poked around a lot. I don't like it.'

'Then,' Lee continued, brushing her long mane of blonde hair, 'I saw the fog coming upriver so decided I'd better hare back. Tweed and his friends were leaving, anyway. I nearly lost my way coming back up that bloody river.'

'Did they see you?' Burgoyne snapped, indifferent to her problems.

'I don't think so. I stayed well back from them.'

'Thirty minutes at Moor's Landing,' Burgoyne repeated, jerking to a brief halt, then roaring round on to the main road. 'No, I don't like the sound of that at all. Tweed could ruin everything. He'll just have to be discouraged.'

'How?'

'I'll decide that,' he said grimly.

The fog had dispersed by the time Mordaunt brought the dinghy alongside the landing stage at Buckler's Hard. Paula jumped on to it before Mordaunt could offer his hand. To ease the tension out of her legs she left the others behind, crossed the catwalk, turned left along the river path and past the closed shop.

It was almost dark as she stood at the bottom of a wide gravel path leading uphill. On either side was a row of old terrace houses mounting steeply to the distant brow. They stood well back from a spacious grass verge. Mordaunt appeared beside her.

'I'd regard it as a great pleasure – for me – if you'd have lunch with me in London. Here's my card. Leave a message on the answerphone if I'm out.'

'That's very kind of you. May I think about it?'

'Think on . . .'

Mordaunt refused to accept any payment from Newman, even for the fuel. Thanking him, Newman hurried after the others. Tweed seemed to be in great haste to get away from Buckler's Hard.

'What's the rush?' Newman called over his shoulder as he drove the Mercedes uphill with Paula beside him. 'And Pete will be staying closer to us on the return trip in his Sierra. Doesn't want to lose us in the dark.'

'Stop the car,' Tweed said as they reached the top and turned on to the country road towards Beaulieu. 'I want to listen.'

Newman signalled to Nield, stopped, switched off his engine. He looked at Tweed in his rear-view mirror. Tweed had lowered his window, sat with his head cocked to one side.

'I thought so. I can hear that chopper again. Just taken to the air, I would suggest. After picking up whoever was watching us from the west bank with binoculars.'

'Does it matter?'

'I advise you to drive very carefully from now on.'

9

Newman was heeding Tweed's warning, driving slowly down the steep winding hill close to the approaches to Beaulieu. His headlights showed up a road sign.

'Bunker's Hill,' said Paula, stifling a yawn. 'They got the name right.'

Tweed didn't take in what she'd said. Sitting in the left-hand seat he had his window lowered a few inches as Newman negotiated the dangerous turn, moving up another hill along the B3054 away from Beaulieu. Tweed again had his head cocked sideways, listening.

'Can't we shut that window?' pleaded Paula. 'Even with the heaters on it's freezing.'

'No, we can't. I sense danger. Please keep quiet . . .'

Paula sighed. Zipping her windcheater up to the collar, she closed her eyes, rested her head back, and went to sleep. Sitting next to Newman, the icy breeze played on her neck but she didn't notice it any more.

Ahead, their lights illuminated the lonely, hedge-lined road. They hadn't seen another vehicle since leaving Buckler's Hard. November, Newman was thinking. All the tourists gone. A heavy frost was forming. From the back of the car a hand reached over, shook Paula by the shoulder. She opened her eyes, blinked.

'What the hell is it now?'

'You must stay awake, alert,' Tweed called out.

'Thanks a lot.' Wearily she picked up the map. 'Where are we now?'

'We're approaching Hatchet Gate. It's just a handful of

94

houses. If you remember, on the way out we passed that sheet of water by the roadside on our right – Hatchet Pond. Although it's quite large and more like a small lake.'

'Why did you wake me up?' Paula asked, studying the map.

'Because I can hear that chopper coming closer. It seems to be heading straight for us.'

'Just a chopper,' Paula commented. 'Incidentally, I see from the map we could take the left fork by Hatchet Pond and go back to Passford House via Boldre. It's a more direct route.'

'We'll try it then,' said Newman.

'It takes us across Beaulieu Heath,' Paula went on. 'I do remember that on the outward trip. It's very level and looks like a blasted heath, to quote Shakespeare, I think. Easier driving.'

That was when she heard what Tweed's acute ears had picked up. The steady egg-beater chug-chug of a helicopter. It sounded as though it was behind them and losing altitude rapidly. Worried, she woke up quickly. The chug-chug was a roar and now it sounded to be just above the roof of the car.

'What the devil is he playing at?' Newman snapped.

'I don't think he's playing,' Tweed warned.

Newman rammed his foot down on the accelerator, swerved off the main road on to the left fork. As he did so the undercarriage of the chopper appeared just ahead of them. Paula stiffened. The damned thing was flying barely twenty feet above them.

Newman had just completed his swerve, was straightening up to drive along the road across the desolate moorland which showed up in his headlights. He also saw the so-called pond alongside the road to his right, stretching away for some distance. He was still moving fast, trying to outrace the crazy pilot.

'Brace yourselves . . .'

It was the only warning he had time to shout. Paula pressed her back into the seat, her feet against the front of the car. In the back Tweed took similar precautions, grabbing hold of the overhead handle. Newman braked furiously, bringing the Mercedes to a teeth-rattling emergency stop. He was jerked forward but held on to the wheel.

The chopper had dropped a projectile which hit the road in front of them and burst. By the lakeside another lake had spread – covering a large area of the road surface from verge to verge. In the glow of the headlights a dense dark glutinous liquid gleamed with a sinister reflection.

'Oil,' Newman said, releasing his seat-belt. 'If we'd hit that at the speed I was moving at we'd have ended up in Hatchet Pond. And we had heavy rain a few days back, so it's probably deep . . .'

Behind them Nield, who had been driving at a proper distance from them, slowed, stopped, leapt out of his car. He hoisted the Walther he was gripping with two hands to aim at the helicopter, then lowered it without firing. All the passengers in the Mercedes walked towards him.

'No good,' Nield told them. 'It was out of range. You could have drowned.'

'I'm sure that was the idea,' Tweed agreed mildly.

'I'm going over to that house,' Newman said. 'Someone should inform the police about the mess in the road – or the wrong people could have a fatal accident . . .'

He returned quickly, carrying an illuminated hurricane lamp. By his side walked an old stooped man with a bushy moustache, carrying another lamp.

'We were lucky,' Newman called out. 'And Mr Harmer here is going to call the police when we've got these warning lamps in position.'

'I'll take mine other side of the slick,' Harmer said.

He walked on the grass verge, well clear of the seeping

oil, placed his lamp on the far side of the oil lake. Newman had backed his car and placed his own lamp as the old boy returned.

'Spillage from some oil truck, I suppose,' Newman remarked before the others could speak.

'Come past my 'ouse like express trains,' grumbled Harmer. 'Where are you bound for? You won't get past that.'

'Brockenhurst,' Newman said promptly.

'Then you was goin' the wrong way. Road across moor leads to Boldre and Lymington. Back a bit more and then take this road through Forest. Now, I'd better get home, make that phone call to police. Drive carefully . . .'

Nobody said anything as Newman started up his engine, reversed a few feet, drove back the way they had come along the B3055. Tweed realized they were experiencing delayed shock: reaction had set in. He was the first to break the silence and avoided referring directly to the attack.

'One advantage of this route is we can see who – if anyone – is at home in those houses we visited.'

'I suppose that's the result of your idea that on the way out we crawled past,' Newman told him. 'The chopper.'

'We don't know that,' Tweed replied. 'But the enemy has committed two tactical errors. First, the attempt to kill Paula and me with the concrete mixer. Now this fresh attempt on our lives. I find it rather satisfying.'

'That's one way of looking at it,' Newman responded with heavy irony. 'What enemy?'

'I've no idea. But at least we know there is one.'

There was another spell of silence as they came close to *The Last Haven*, Fanshawe's residence. The Swedish-style house was a blaze of lights. Newman drove on slowly. Passing *Leopard's Leap*, Burgoyne's luxurious home, they saw a faint glimmer of lights beyond the shrubberies. Newman continued driving at low speed.

They reached the entrance to *Prevent*. Tweed was expecting darkness.

Instead he saw two patrol cars parked in the drive and behind the straggle of shrubbery the Victorian house was ablaze with lights.

'Stop!' he called out. 'Something's happened . . .'

A few hours earlier the same day two men in their twenties had anchored their small yacht offshore about midway between the mouths of the rivers Beaulieu and Lymington. It was a clear cold day on the Solent and before any sign of the freezing fog had appeared.

George Day and Charlie Neal worked in a stockbroker's office in London. But both men lived for their fishing trips aboard the yacht. A strong breeze was blowing up as they sat with their fishing rods, saying little, staring across the water.

'Time we started getting back to Lymington,' Charlie said reluctantly after checking his watch. 'And a fog was forecast for this evening.'

'Not yet,' George protested, 'I think I've caught something big . . .'

He began to reel in his line but his catch seemed to be carried towards the hull of the yacht by the current. George stopped reeling in, puzzled by the feel of what his hook was snagged in. He leaned forward. It was coming up from the stern, drifting along the side of their vessel. He waited, leaned further forward to get a closer view.

'Oh, my God!' he gasped. 'Look!'

'What is it?' Charlie chaffed him. 'Bit of driftwood? You and your big catch . . .'

He stopped in mid-sentence as the floating body slid under where they peered over. Charlie was the first to react. He reached down, grabbed, found he was holding a handful of dark hair. George was helping him now.

Leaning over together, they hauled the corpse aboard. White-faced, they stared at their catch as water ran over the deck. Charlie was the first to speak in a hoarse voice.

'Jesus! It's a girl. And she's lost an arm. Dear God! There's a blood-soaked bandage coming loose. It's horrible.'

'We'd better get straight back to the marina,' said Charlie. 'She can't be much over twenty, if that. Let's find something to cover her up. I can't stare at that while we're heading back. And I don't understand that bandage. Come on, let's get moving. This is something for the police. And you won't get me fishing here again.'

10

At the end of the drive leading to *Prevent*, Newman was stopped by a uniformed police sergeant holding up his hand. Tweed jumped out, followed by the others.

'Who are you?' the policeman demanded.

'I might ask you the same question.'

'Might you, sir? I'm Sergeant McCann. You know the owner of this house?'

'Yes. Sir Gerald Andover. My name is Tweed.' He gave the sergeant his card printed with General & Cumbria Assurance. 'I also know the Chief Constable, Mark Stanstead.'

'Colonel Stanstead is inside. These people with you?'

Tweed made introductions, including Nield. McCann was a typical country policeman, in his thirties with a weatherbeaten face and shrewd eyes. He looked at Paula.

'Been trying to trace you, Miss Grey. I'd like you to

give me a statement about your discovery of the man you dragged out of the river last night. Harvey Boyd . . .'

'She can do that inside,' Tweed interrupted. 'It is a trifle chilly out here. And may I ask what is going on?'

'Better ask the Chief Constable that question, sir . . .'

Two other uniformed policemen stood outside the front of the house as McCann led the way past the boarded-up front door. He continued along a path now familiar to Tweed round the side of the house, speaking over his shoulder.

'We entered through the back door by picking the lock. In here, if you would. And, Miss Grey, perhaps we could stay in the kitchen while I take that statement.'

Stanstead was examining the wreckage in Andover's study. Of medium height, well built, clean shaven, he had a thick thatch of brown hair and a ruddy complexion. He was in his forties, dressed in a blue business suit, with intelligent features. He moved quickly. A man, Newman thought as he was introduced, accustomed to swift obedience to his orders and with eyes which didn't miss a thing. After he had greeted Tweed in a warm manner, Tweed said: 'We were driving past, saw the lights, wondered what was up.'

'Grim news, Tweed. Two men fishing in the Solent this afternoon hauled a girl's body out of the sea. Brigadier Burgoyne and Miss Holmes next door have identified it as Irene, Andover's daughter. Minus one arm. An odd business that. The arm had been bandaged – the bit that was left – near the elbow.'

'Where is the body?'

'I had it brought here in an ambulance for Andover to identify – recognized her myself. Trouble is there's no sign of Andover so I was compelled to call on his neighbours.'

'And where is the body now?' Tweed persisted.

'It will have reached the mortuary at Southampton.'

Tweed took Stanstead aside. They held a whispered conversation. The Chief Constable nodded as though in agreement. He was making his way to the phone on Andover's desk when Tweed caught up with him, whispered again.

'Wait till you get back. This whole place has been bugged. Come outside a moment . . .'

It was only when they'd reached the kitchen that Tweed realized he'd overlooked something. Paula had just finished signing a sheet of paper. Sergeant McCann was folding the sheet to tuck it in his pocket with a look of satisfaction.

'There, Miss Grey, that wasn't such an ordeal, was it?'

'Pretty straightforward, thanks to you, Sergeant,' she said.

Tweed gestured for her to follow Stanstead and himself into the garden. The freezing cold hit them and a heavy frost had formed on the spacious lawn.

'Go back quickly,' Tweed urged Paula, 'and take Newman and Nield back to the car. No talking until you're outside. Entirely my fault, I'd forgotten the house was bugged – including the kitchen where you've just made your statement, I imagine.'

'I'm on my way . . .'

'What is this all about?' Stanstead asked as he walked on the lawn with Tweed.

There seemed no point in further secrecy. Tweed explained about their previous visit when they had discovered the break-in and he had noticed the bugs. He left out any mention of the Gaston Delvaux letter he had found on the mantelpiece, the mobile concrete mixer which had almost killed them, and their visit to Buckler's Hard and Moor's Landing.

'I'll get one of my experts in these matters to come and remove those damned bugs,' Stanstead decided.

'I'd much rather you didn't,' Tweed said firmly. 'Leave

101

them in place. We might later be able to turn the bugs back on whoever placed them there.'

'You have your reasons?'

'Yes. We can start now if you'll play along. I suggest we go back into the study and converse in normal tones. You'll get the idea from what I say.'

'You usually know what you're doing . . .'

Stanstead sent Sergeant McCann outside, telling him to fiddle the back-door lock closed after they'd left. In the study Tweed began immediately speaking in his usual tone of voice.

'I doubt if you'll ever solve this case, Chief Constable. I can't spend any more time on it. Too much on the go with other problems. I'll have to leave the whole thing in your lap, ghastly as it is.'

'I'm inclined to agree with you,' Stanstead began, playing along. 'We'll continue our investigations for a few days – but with the body of the girl half-eaten away by some large fish I don't think we're going to get very far. It's quite possible the whole business was an accident. I imagine she went out in a boat – and I don't think she was much good at handling one. Especially if she went out by herself. Andover's gone to Devon so we'll try to contact him there. Not a lot more we can do . . .'

'What's going on?' Newman asked.

They were driving back to Passford House for dinner in his Mercedes. Tweed was sitting next to him and Paula occupied the rear. Nield had been left behind in his Sierra which he'd parked off the road in the Forest.

'First,' Tweed told him, 'I persuaded Stanstead to arrange the immediate transfer of the girl's body, which, I gather, is pretty intact except for the brutal loss of her lower arm, to London. I want our top pathologist, Dr

102

Rabin, to examine the corpse. He already has the missing arm.'

'What about the bugs?'

'As you know, when you organize a set-up like that they need to have, within a reasonable distance near by, equipment to record what is said as soon as a voice-activated bug picks up conversation. Nield is going to conduct a discreet search of the surrounding area. There must be a van or some such vehicle with the recording equipment. Nield has orders to locate it but not to risk being seen. These people, whoever they are, kill.'

'Why are you using Dr Rabin?' Paula called out.

'Didn't you notice? The severed arm you found in that freezer appeared to have been expertly amputated? At least I thought so, with my limited medical knowledge.'

'And where does that lead us to, if anywhere?' she asked.

'If Rabin agrees with my theory, it leads me to tracing some unknown top surgeon who performed the amputation.'

'And I'm going to check out tomorrow Mrs Goshawk who has a house for sale in Brockenhurst. Or so our friendly estate agent in Moor's Landing, Mr A. Barton, told us.'

Having said that, Paula fell fast asleep.

A little earlier, inside *Leopard's Leap*, Brigadier Burgoyne, wearing a smoking jacket and navy blue trousers, was pacing his living-room after his return from identifying the body of Irene Andover. Lee Holmes, who had put on a form-fitting green dress with a gold belt, stood in front of a wall mirror, brushing her blonde hair.

'So Tweed is staying at Passford House,' Burgoyne remarked, his expression bleak.

'That's right,' Lee confirmed again, 'and I had to call

several hotels before I thought of Passford. Maurice, why are we going there to dinner?'

'To check up on him, of course. I wish to God he'd go back to London, leave this area. He's a danger every moment he lingers.'

'You mean he could interfere with your plans,' Lee said in a mocking tone.

'Of course that's what I mean!' Burgoyne exploded. 'If they're there for dinner you latch on to Tweed, get out of him what you can.'

'You want me to seduce him if necessary?'

'I don't like your tone. Just do the job I've given to you. I'll concentrate on Miss Paula Grey.'

'Exerting your irresistible charm on her, I presume?'

'I don't like sarcastic women.'

'You don't seem to mind them after the lights go out,' she retorted as she used her lipstick. 'When do we leave for Passford House? You seem edgy – was it having to identify Irene's body?'

'I've seen enough dead bodies in my time.' Burgoyne's expression was even more saturnine. 'But you were cool enough and I think Stanstead noticed.'

'I'm ready. Are you?'

'I've been ready for ten minutes while you've been tarting yourself up.' His tone became commanding. 'We take the Jag., of course. Mustn't risk them seeing the Bentley. And I've just thought of a good tactic. Pop round to *The Last Haven* and ask Fanshawe to join us. Good camouflage.'

'I don't have to ask that Claybourne bitch as well, do I?'

'Of course you do. Be polite. Make the effort. Just for once . . .'

Pete Nield, clad in a grey boiler suit he'd fetched from his Sierra, crawled slowly through the undergrowth close to

104

Andover's estate. He wore the boiler suit to protect his city clothes – and the grey colour was neutral in the dark.

He had parked his car by the copse Newman had used during the previous day. His hands were protected with gloves and he pressed down the undergrowth ahead of him slowly. The ground was covered with dead leaves, crusted with frost. One false move and the crackle of those leaves would be heard yards away in the uncanny stillness of the bitter night.

His boiler suit was unzipped to his waist: he could grab the Walther out of his hip holster in a millisecond. He pressed down another tangle of undergrowth and froze. A hand had descended on his right shoulder.

'Friend,' a familiar voice whispered. Harry Butler's.

Nield was flaming. He could have shot him by mistake. But his greatest annoyance was that Butler, turning up out of nowhere, had tracked him without making a sound. He'd tell him. Later. There were other matters which had priority. As Butler crouched beside him Nield aimed a finger, pointing.

'Good work,' Butler whispered. 'Think you've found them?'

'Look for yourself. Listen, for Christ's sake . . .'

Twenty feet beyond where Nield had pressed down the undergrowth a large camper was parked. It stood on a narrow track and what Nield regarded as amateurish camouflage had been attempted. Uprooted undergrowth had been piled on the roof, piled against the vehicle's sides.

A large tall aerial speared up towards the branch of the fir tree it was parked under. The noise Nield had heard was the metallic rattle of the aerial being retracted. It telescoped slowly until it was almost level with the roof.

Nield had no doubt they were looking at the vehicle acting as the recording station for all the voice-activated bugs placed inside *Prevent*. The interior would hold all the sophisticated recording equipment registering on tape everything said inside Andover's house.

A burly man, no more than a silhouette in the dark of the Forest, appeared as the rear doors opened. Holding a long pole, he dropped to the ground and used the pole to sweep the roof clear of the undergrowth camouflage hopefully concealing them from aerial observation. He then moved all round the camper, removing the undergrowth piled up against its sides. Walking back to the rear, he disappeared inside, and the doors were closed quietly.

'They're leaving,' Nield whispered. 'We'd better hurry back to my car. Just a minute – how did you get here?'

'In the Cortina after making my delivery to Rabin in London. You tail the camper, I'll guard your rear . . .'

'Just one point, Harry,' Nield said as they reached their cars. 'If you ever creep up on me like that again it will give me great pleasure to break your bloody neck. I had the Walther in my hand when you first spoke.'

'Point taken. Now let's get on with the job. Wonder where that camper will lead us to?'

Tweed was just washing his hands and face in Room 2 at Passford House when he heard a gentle tapping on his door. He opened it cautiously, keeping one foot behind it. Then he stood back as Paula, who had stayed on the ground floor to warn the head waiter they'd be arriving soon for dinner, came in, closing and locking the door behind her.

'We have company,' she said, breathing heavily.

'That's nice. Who is honouring us tonight at this hour?'

'I peered into the bar before coming upstairs. Burgoyne is there with his blonde beauty, Lee Holmes . . .'

'Maybe I can look forward to a lively evening?'

'Stop joking. With them are Willie Fanshawe and Helen Claybourne.'

'Right. You and I will go in for a drink, see just what happens. Could you pop along to Newman's room – warn him. Tell him the situation. I suggest he goes into dinner without us.'

'You find it strange – that quartet turning up?'

'I find it odd that Burgoyne – after identifying Irene's dead body – then trots out for a drink. To say nothing of Lee Holmes. We'll just leave the initiative to them, see what they do . . .'

Ten minutes later they entered the bar at the front of the hotel. A comfortable room, oblong in shape, it had the bar at the far end along one of the shorter sides. Lee Holmes jumped up immediately, swung her long legs as she walked up to Tweed, holding a glass. She ignored Paula.

'Mr Tweed, how marvellous, this gives us a chance to plan our liaison in London.'

She gave the word 'liaison' a certain seductive emphasis. Taking hold of his arm, she led him towards the bar.

'And my glass is empty.'

'So what are you drinking?' Tweed paused as they passed a window table where Burgoyne sat with Fanshawe and Helen Claybourne. 'Do you mind?' he enquired.

'The best man always wins,' Burgoyne said sardonically. He did not look pleased, Paula noted. 'Don't mind me,' the Brigadier added with a final slash. 'I'm just part of the furniture.'

Paula stood still as Fanshawe, beaming, jumped up, came to her rescue. Taking her by the arm, he guided her to the seat Lee had occupied next to Helen Claybourne.

'How nice to see you again, Paula. I may call you Paula? Good. I'm Willie. We're working our way through a bottle of Laurent Perrier, as you'll see. Or would you prefer a different tipple?'

'Champagne is my favourite drink, thank you.'

And there he goes again, she thought. The words had tumbled out of his wide, generous mouth. The use of the old-fashioned word 'tipple'. She glanced towards the bar as Lee laughed, a tinkling laugh full of enjoyment. She was performing a pirouette and her long blonde hair swept in a wave over her bare shoulders. The eyes of every man in the room studied her – furtively when the were with their wives.

'Lots of lovely bubbly champers,' Lee said. 'And the way things are going – with you turning up – I'll end up feeling just like one of those bubbles . . .'

Paula clinked glasses with Willie and watched Helen Claybourne over the rim of her glass as she sipped. Unlike Lee, Helen was wearing the same outfit as when they'd met the previous evening. There was a touch of demure severity about her mandarin collar and pleated skirt. Very businesslike, Paula thought approvingly – compared with Lee, who was the essence of *joie de vivre*.

Helen glanced towards the bar as Lee laughed again. With her refilled glass, she had twined her long bare arm round Tweed, crossing their glasses so each could sip out of the other's. Her greenish eyes glowed as Tweed watched her with a hint of amused tolerance.

'I'm a fun girl,' she confided. 'I think life should be fun. You and I could make that come true. I can tell from looking into your eyes, you secretive man.'

'What do you want to know about me?' he asked amiably.

'You're married, I can tell. But I don't think that you are living with your wife any more.' She squeezed his arm. 'Go on, confess. Am I right?'

'You must be psychic,' Tweed observed. 'It was all a long time ago.'

'The memory lingers on?'

'Not really. It's faded into history. And I live in the present, not the past.'

She had hit an exposed nerve, but he was surprised he was not in the least annoyed with her. Had she done her homework? His wife had run off with a Greek millionaire to South America a hundred years ago. Maybe it was just feminine intuition. Lee nodded solemnly.

'You are an interesting man. Live in the present always. That's my motto.' She drank more champagne. 'Have you a nice pad in London? Somewhere I could come and see you? I'd love that.'

'Maybe we'd better have lunch sometime first,' Tweed said evasively. 'Do you get on well with Burgoyne?'

'Can you imagine any woman doing that . . .'

At the table by the window overlooking the illuminated car park and the lawn Paula decided to drop a bombshell. But Helen was glancing again at the bar and put her spoke in first.

'The trouble with Lee is she has to hypnotize every man in sight. It's a mania with her and she seems to have your friend in the palm of her hand already.'

'It's a nice palm anyway,' Paula said equably. She dropped her bombshell. 'I heard a rumour that you and the Brigadier had to identify a body brought out of the sea. And that it was Irene Andover's corpse.'

'How the hell did you hear that?'

Burgoyne sat stiff-necked, glaring at Paula. His tone was cutting as though dressing down a private soldier. He leaned forward, gazing at Paula as he went on.

'I suppose Tweed is – was –the negotiator for his insurance outfit, trying to act as go-between for Andover with the kidnappers of his daughter.'

'Kidnappers?' Paula sounded stunned.

'Well, it's been obvious,' Burgoyne hammered at her in a bullying manner. 'Andover for the past three months

109

has rapidly deteriorated physically and mentally. A shadow of his former self. And it all coincided with the disappearance of Irene.'

'I thought you said she'd hopped off with a Frenchman,' Paula reminded him.

'Her corpse hadn't materialized then. We were all trying to keep it under wraps.'

'Maurice,' Willie urged, 'you're talking too loud. I don't think anyone has heard you yet in here but go on like that and they will . . .'

'You keep out of this.' But Burgoyne had lowered his voice. 'And you've been as blind as a bat as to what's been going on right on your doorstep.'

'I simply had no idea,' Willie protested. 'What's all this about a body fished out of the sea? I'm completely in the dark.'

'You always are,' Burgoyne said brutally.

Paula was furious. Willie was obviously hurt. He drank a lot of champagne to cover up his discomfiture. Burgoyne was well into his stride. He focused on Paula again.

'Your boss has made a right balls-up of it this time. The poor girl might have been saved if he hadn't been brought in – by Andover, I assume – and stumbled around like the legendary bull in a china shop.'

'He usually knows what he's doing,' Paula said quietly, determined to keep her temper.

'I find all this very perplexing, distressing,' Willie complained in a subdued voice. 'Won't someone please put me in the picture?'

This was the moment when Helen intervened. The only sign that she was irked by Burgoyne was one crossed leg swinging up and down.

'Willie, a lot of this is rumour. Maurice is in one of his moods tonight. There's absolutely nothing for you to feel upset about. We'll hear in good time – and from a more reliable source than the Brig. – what is really going on.

We're supposed to be here this evening to enjoy ourselves.'

She gave him her cool smile. Paula saw Willie relax. He beamed at her and then proceeded to refill her glass.

'Helen's right. We are here to enjoy ourselves. From now on the enjoyment starts.' He looked at her glass. 'Sorry, that's a meagre tot-up. We've run out.'

'Yes,' said Helen. She looked at Burgoyne. 'Maurice – don't you think you ought to order another bottle? I thought you were host and the others may join us soon.'

'Doesn't look much like it to me. Lee's swarming all over Tweed,' Burgoyne growled.

'Maurice,' she repeated, 'please order another bottle.'

To Paula's surprise the Brigadier summoned the barman and placed the order. From that moment the tension drained out of the atmosphere. Willie babbled on cheerfully about his days in the Far East, Burgoyne listened with an expression suggesting he'd heard it all before. Helen relaxed in her chair, produced a large fountain-pen from her evening bag, and began scribbling a list on a notepad.

Tweed eventually brought back Lee to the table. He had a twinkle in his eyes as he drew out a chair for her while addressing the Brigadier.

'You needn't have worried. I've brought her back all in one piece.'

'Why should I worry?' Burgoyne retorted.

Tweed took Paula into dinner and they chose a table well away from Newman's. Paula asked why.

'Best not to let anyone know he's with us,' Tweed replied cryptically. 'Did you learn anything?'

'A lot. You're going to be surprised – maybe even puzzled . . .'

11

Nield and Butler, tailing the camper, had to exercise all their skill in what turned out to be a tricky task. The camper had driven down the track, turned right, and headed through the night along the B3055 to Brocken-hurst. Nield had driven his Sierra out of the copse in time to see it emerging from the track. He was soon glad he'd taken the precaution of keeping well back.

A Land-Rover, occupied only by the driver, appeared from an opening into a field and took up station a short distance behind the camper. It looked as though the tapes the camper was transporting were important – important enough to be guarded.

Arriving at an isolated straight stretch of country road, Butler, protecting Nield's rear, saw the Land-Rover as the moon came out briefly. And beyond it the camper trundling along. He came to the same conclusion as Nield.

'I wonder where the hell you two are going to,' he said out aloud to himself.

He had little inkling of where they would end up as the camper turned right on to the A337 at Brockenhurst and sped on north towards Lyndhurst. A long stretch of rolling straight road extended ahead. On either side they were passing through vast expanses of lonely moorland as the moon broke through again.

At that hour – and at that time of year – there was very little other traffic as they plunged on through belts of the New Forest. The trees were Christmas-like in the moonlight, their branches and foliage covered with a mantle of white frost.

Beyond Cadnam, heading north-east and later bypassing Winchester to turn on to the M3, Butler began to suspect the ultimate objective must be London. On the motorway Butler and Nield began to play the leapfrog game to confuse the targets, to avoid any suspicion they were being followed.

At times Butler overtook all three vehicles, driving on some distance ahead of the camper, watching its lights in his rear-view mirror. Where the devil were they going? Butler wondered again.

At other times Nield overtook all the vehicles, including the Cortina. Butler then slowed, allowed the camper and the Land-Rover to overtake him, dropping well back to the rear. They reversed positions several more times before they reached London.

Only then did both Butler and Nield drop back behind the Land-Rover. As they crossed the Albert Bridge it was very dark and late. Nield was trying to work out where he had seen the driver of the Land-Rover before.

'Because I know I've seen you, mate,' he said to himself. 'Something about the way you hold yourself.'

A little later they were driving along the Fulham Road, quickly turning off to the right and north. Butler slowed down as the Land-Rover pulled up behind the stationary camper. He ground his gears as he crawled past them, working on the psychology that no one following them would make so much noise. Nield pulled in to the kerb. They were in the middle of the curving Boltons, one of the most prestigious addresses in London.

Nield watched as the Land-Rover driver, still wearing his crash helmet, jumped out and walked up to the camper as the rear doors opened. By the illumination from a street lamp Nield saw a burly man hand over to the Land-Rover driver a stack of about half a dozen slim round cartons. Just the sort of containers to hold the tape reels which had recorded all the conversations in Sir Gerald Andover's house.

'So who lives there?' Nield asked himself.

The driver pushed open the wrought-iron gate, hurried along a path and up the stone steps to one of the magnificent mansions set back from the double curve of The Boltons. Dying for a cigarette, Nield waited patiently without reaching for the pack in his pocket.

The driver reappeared quickly. By now the camper had driven off. Climbing back up into the Land-Rover, he also left the area. Nield waited a little longer, then climbed out and strolled along to the mansion where the cartons had been delivered. No. 185. On the second pillar was a gleaming engraved plate. It carried the legend MOONGLOW REFUGEE AID TRUST INTERNATIONAL.

He looked up as Butler appeared. Nield moved away from the entrance before he spoke.

'Moonglow. That's where a pile of cartons were delivered. My guess is they contained tape reels.'

'Then I'd better pay a call on them. Plenty of lights on inside the place. Better go back to your car. I'll let you know what happens . . .'

Butler walked back to where he had parked his Cortina. Opening the rear door, he took out a grubby coat and a cap. Slipping on the coat over his windcheater, he donned the scruffy cap, pulling the peak down over his forehead. He picked up a large yellow canvas hold-all with a stack of newspapers protruding from the top. He slung the hold-all over his shoulder. It was a trick he had used before.

He walked back to No. 185, pushed open the gate, shuffled along the path – in case he was observed from inside. Climbing the steps, he pressed the bell and waited,

114

one hand grasping the top of a newspaper. A porch lamp came on, there was the sound of three locks being unfastened: deadlocks, Butler noted. A chain was removed. When the door opened a tall and large middle-aged woman dressed in black and with a grim expression stared at him. She was holding a Walther aimed at his chest. He stepped back in apparent fear, speaking in a whining voice.

'No cause for alarm, lady. And guns make me nervy. If you shot me it'd be murder. I don't even carry a penknife . . .'

While he was rattling on he was looking at the lighted spacious hall behind her. At the back a curving staircase wound upwards. It was dimly lit. He could see a heavily built man walking slowly down the stairs. With a very deliberate tread. The vague figure reached the bottom and paused. The hall lights reflected off his gold pince-nez. The eyes behind the lenses were invisible, which was disconcerting.

'What do you want?' the woman with the gun demanded.

'Just delivering the local paper. It's free. Tells you what's goin' on round 'ere. New parkin' regulations. And a developer is tryin' to turn one of these 'ouses into a cheap 'otel. Wouldn't want that, would you?'

'What exactly is happening, Mrs Kramer?'

It was the man with the pince-nez who had spoken. His way of talking was strange – he pronounced each word with extreme precision and paused between each word he uttered. His voice was soft-spoken but every word had carried clearly to Butler. He found the voice as disconcerting as the way the man moved.

'Nothing, sir,' Mrs Kramer called back over her shoulder. 'Just a yobbo handing out free newspapers.'

'At this time of night?' the voiced continued. 'I really find that rather odd. Yes, very odd indeed.'

'I'm behind schedule, guv,' Butler whined, raising his voice. 'And in the mornin' I've got a different job.'

'Send – him – packing – Mrs – Kramer.'

The word pauses were even more pronounced. Even more disturbing. And Butler was not a man easily unnerved by any situation.

'Go away!' snapped Mrs Kramer. 'And never call here again. We don't accept rubbish.'

The door was slammed in his face as Butler opened his mouth to say more. He stood there, listened to the three locks being turned, the chain replaced to its secure position. Then he shuffled back down the steps and along the path. A minute later he was relating his experience to Nield and they decided to drive straight to SIS headquarters at Park Crescent.

12

It was after eleven at night when Butler and Nield were let inside the headquarters of SIS in Park Crescent, close to Regent's Park. George, the ex-NCO, who acted as one of the guards, called out to them as they started up the staircase to Tweed's first-floor office.

'You'll find Monica still there, hard at it. She's having meals sent in. Doubt if she'll welcome you two . . .'

They opened the door and walked in. Monica, who was Tweed's faithful assistant, a woman of uncertain age, grey hair tied back in a bun, looked up from her desk. She had a collection of files spread out and her hand was reaching for the phone.

'Hello, Monica,' Nield said cheerfully, 'we've got a

job for you. Stop you from getting bored.'

'Bored!' Monica expressed mock indignation. 'Tweed has given me enough work to last me a week. Building up profiles on Sir Gerald Andover, Brigadier Burgoyne, and Willie Fanshawe. My phone bill for calls to the Far East will be horrendous. I even managed to reach Philip Cardon, our agent in Hong Kong. He's flying home shortly. For your information I can do without your job.'

She liked Pete Nield. He often joked with her and she was secretly rather taken with his dark eyes and easy manner. Nield grinned and went on.

'Better make a note. Tweed will want the data on this. Ready? Moonglow Refugee Aid Trust International. 185 The Boltons. Everything you can dig up about them – and who runs the outfit.'

'Moonglow?' Monica crinkled her forehead, scribbled the full name on her pad. 'I've heard of them somewhere. The Boltons? High living for a charity organization.'

'We've driven a long way,' Butler intervened. 'A mug of tea would go down well for both of us.'

'Then you know where the kettle is. So make it yourself. I haven't got time to fuss over you. And while you are about it, I could do with a drink myself . . .'

When they had left her alone Monica frowned again. She absent-mindedly sucked at the end of her pen.

'Moonglow,' she said to herself. 'I have heard of you – and something odd, but never proved. I'll dissect you down to the bone.'

Monica was not the only one working late. At No. 185 The Boltons Dr Wand sat in a room which served as a cinema. The lighting was very dim and no more could be seen of him than Butler had observed from the front door. Dr Wand preferred the dark.

He was not watching a film tonight. Mrs Kramer was

feeding the tape reels into a machine and he was listening to conversations which had taken place at *Prevent*. His large head was tilted at a slight angle as he memorized what had been said.

At one stage Mrs Kramer glanced in his direction. Wand's gold pince-nez glinted in the low-power illumination provided by a wall light. He was smiling, a smile with pursed lips, a smile which had no human warmth. Even Mrs Kramer, who knew him well, was frightened by the smile.

When the last tape had been played Wand rose slowly to his feet. He gave her the instructions in his slow, soft-spoken voice.

'Contact Vulcan immediately. I think from now on we must keep a very close eye indeed on the man called Tweed. Convey my thought to Vulcan at once. I am going to my study to check further details about Operation Long Reach.'

'I *will* make the call immediately, sir.'

'See that you do, please.'

Mrs Kramer hurried out of the room to the telephone. She had no idea of the identity of Vulcan – only his phone number. She also had no idea what Operation Long Reach meant. And she had learned it was unwise to ask Dr Wand any leading questions. People who made that mistake had disappeared.

At Passford House the following morning Tweed announced he was leaving immediately for London. In Room 2 Newman looked at Paula in surprise. They were so often taken off-guard by Tweed's lightning decisions.

'I shall drive myself back,' Tweed continued, 'in the Ford Escort. Paula wants to check Mrs Goshawk, who apparently has a house for sale in Brockenhurst – according to that estate agent, Barton. I want her protected, Bob.

Could you drive her everywhere in your Mercedes?'

'Will do. But what are you after? Have you any idea what is going on?'

'List the facts.' Tweed counted on his fingers. 'One, Harvey Boyd, who was about to join us as a trained agent, was possibly murdered on the River Lymington.'

'Murdered?' Newman queried. 'What do you base that on?'

'The fact that the right side of his head was sliced off so neatly needs explaining.' He looked at Paula. 'And I trust your exceptional eyesight. I'm convinced you did see something in the fog just before the so-called accident.'

'As a reporter I still regard that as an assumption,' Newman persisted.

'It is not an assumption,' Tweed said sharply, 'that on two occasions someone has tried to exterminate us. The mobile concrete mixer, then the chopper which dropped oil on the road in front of us. Somewhere along the line I said something, asked a question – with Andover, Burgoyne, or Fanshawe – which triggered off those lethal attacks. So we have stumbled on to something. That is fact two.'

'You can't include Andover – after what's happened to his daughter,' Paula protested once again.

'I'm not crossing Andover off my list before I've seen the profile Monica is preparing,' Tweed said firmly. 'At the back of my mind I once heard something odd about the daughter, Irene. Fact three,' he went on briskly, 'I'm sure there is something odd about that isolated village, Moor's Landing.'

'That *is* an assumption,' Newman objected.

'Oh, really?' Tweed's tone was hard now. 'When we have an estate agent who isn't interested in selling us any kind of property? And they're trying to drive out old Mrs Garnett from the last remaining cottage. Strange that Barton didn't say her cottage might become available if we could wait a bit longer.'

119

'It was a weird place,' Newman agreed.

'Finally, fact four – Irene had apparently been kidnapped. Yet Andover whispers to me that no ransom demand had been received. After about three months.'

'You see any pattern forming?' Paula asked.

'I'm completely in the dark,' Tweed admitted. 'I have in my hand a number of pieces of a jigsaw – none of which seem to fit. I need more pieces to build up a picture. And now,' he picked up his packed suitcase, 'I must get off to London. Take great care.'

'We'll see you in London,' Paula assured him.

Tweed turned suddenly. 'I missed out facts five and six. The file Andover handed to me. And the letter from Gaston Delvaux, Belgian armaments genius – and a member of that think-tank, INCOMSIN. I may be in Brussels within the next twenty-four hours . . .'

April Lodge, the home of Mrs Goshawk, was a small detached Victorian house on the outskirts of Brockenhurst. Newman and Paula had agreed it would be better if she visited the house on her own. Having driven past it, Newman parked the Mercedes on a grass verge.

Bearing in mind Tweed's request for him to protect her, Newman followed her at a distance along the country lane and waited by a copse of firs. As Paula disappeared he checked his Smith & Wesson.

Paula walked up the straight drive. On either side was a spacious lawn, neatly trimmed and covered with a heavy coating of frost sparkling in the sun. The house corresponded with the old photograph she'd examined in Barton's office. She entered the porch, pressed a highly polished brass bell.

'Mrs Goshawk?' she asked.

The door, with a stained-glass window in the upper half, had been opened by a well-dressed woman in her fifties.

120

From her coiffeured brown hair Paula guessed she'd just returned from the hairdresser.

'Yes.' Mrs Goshawk smiled. 'I hope you're not selling something?'

'On the contrary, I'm hoping to buy this house.'

'But it's not for sale. What on earth made you think it was?'

'It is shown – with a photo – as being for sale at Barton's, the estate agent at Moor's Landing.'

'This is ridiculous.' Mrs Goshawk flushed. 'I'm sorry, that was rude. I meant ridiculous of that rather rough type, Barton. I decided not to move. He was informed over a year ago and said he'd take it off the market at once . . .'

'Back to Moor's Landing, I suggest,' Newman decided after hearing Paula's story. 'I thought there was something not right about that chap Barton.'

'Something's wrong about the whole place. What it is I just don't know. Maybe another word with Mrs Garnett is a good idea.'

'Let's wait till we get there. See what the situation is.'

Newman was soon driving back along the road to Beaulieu. It was a glorious sunny morning with a clear blue sky and again very cold. The trees were clotted with frost and Newman drove past *Prevent* and the other two houses at top speed along the empty winding road.

Paula was studying the map. To reach Moor's Landing by car they had to drive through Beaulieu, cross the river, then turn south down a country road which eventually led to a village called Exbury. The turn-off to Moor's Landing was several miles earlier. She gave Newman guidance and within three-quarters of an hour they were driving past the lane to the landing stage and into the village. Newman parked as soon as they reached the first cottage.

'That's funny,' Paula said as she stood by the car.

121

'What is?' asked Newman.

'The estate agent's board has disappeared.'

'You're right. Maybe it's taken down for painting. It was peeling badly, I noticed.'

'So did I. Which struck me as peculiar at the time. I would have thought it would have been spick and span to be in keeping with the model-village effect.'

She walked down to the fourth cottage on the right and pushed open the gate. Newman followed closely behind her after glancing down the street. Once more it had a strangely deserted look. Paula tugged at his arm.

'Net curtains at the windows. They weren't there when we called yesterday.'

She raised the brass knocker and hammered several times. A strange man in a smart business suit opened the door and stared at Paula. About twenty-eight, she estimated, clean shaven and with a pleasant smile. A strong waft of perfume met her. Not one of those, I hope, she was thinking. She spoke briskly.

'We've come to see Mr Barton, the estate agent.'

'Mr who?'

'Barton, the estate agent. He had a board up outside.'

'I'm sorry, I don't understand. *I* live here. Martin's the name. You must have come to the wrong village. No estate agent has been at Moor's Landing since the converted cottages were sold, so far as I know.'

'We were here yesterday,' Paula insisted impatiently. 'And we met Mr Barton.'

'Indeed we did,' Newman's voice confirmed over her shoulder.

'He has an office in this front room,' Paula ploughed on. 'Hardly any furniture, blank walls, one with a board of houses for sale. A trestle table and fold-up chairs.'

'This doesn't make any sense,' Martin replied, a trace of impatience in his voice now. 'This is my home.' He looked at Newman. 'The lady is confused.'

'Then would it be too much, Mr Martin,' Paula pressed on, 'to let us just see the front room?'

'If it will convince you.' Martin shrugged. 'Walk right in. I'm sorry about the smell of perfume. My wife spilt a whole bottle on the table this morning . . .'

Paula walked in, followed by Newman, who was holding an unlit cigarette. She stopped, stunned. She was looking at an expensively furnished living-room, mostly in the Scandinavian style. The walls were panelled in oak. She stared around helplessly. Newman wandered past her, dropping his cigarette close to a wall, bent down to retrieve it. Martin waved his hands.

'Satisfied? Try the village of Exbury. The roads round here are confusing.'

'Thank you, Mr Martin,' Paula said coldly.

She waited until they had reached the gate. She heard the cottage door close behind them.

'Am I going dotty?' she asked Newman. 'It's the sort of experience you have in a dream.'

'No dream,' Newman said grimly. 'More like a nightmare. Let's have that word with Mrs Garnett. She knows what's happening round here – up to a point . . .'

'What the devil's going on?' Paula asked. 'Just look at Mrs Garnett's front door. Bright purple. Yesterday the paint was peeling and it was no particular colour.'

'So we'll call on her.'

Paula marched up the path, touched the purple paint and it was bone dry. She pressed the bell and waited, stiffening herself. The door opened and another man dressed in a business suit stood regarding her. Not a day over thirty, she guessed. Dark-haired, he had a more distant manner.

'Yes, what is it?'

'I've called to see Mrs Garnett, please.'

'Well you certainly won't find her here.' A touch of an

American accent. 'She left and went into some nursing home for old people, I understand. No idea where.'

'Left overnight, you mean?' Paula demanded.

'Good Lord, no. I've been here for quite a while.'

'I'm Porter,' Newman interjected. 'Could you tell us your name?'

'Hartford, if it's any of your business. Now, I am very busy, so if you don't mind . . .'

'But I do mind,' Paula snapped. 'Only yesterday . . .'

'We've made a mistake,' Newman said and grasped her arm firmly. 'The roads round here are confusing. Obviously we've taken a wrong turning, got the villages mixed up. We are sorry to bother you, Mr Hartford.'

'Use a map next time.'

Paula was seething as the door was slammed in their faces. Newman, still gripping her arm, guided her down the path and back to the car. She burst out as he was turning the Mercedes, prior to driving back to Passford House.

'You didn't give me much backing. Damn all, in fact!'

'It's a very lonely part of the world here,' Newman reminded her. 'We don't know how many more men they had about the place. And people disappear from Moor's Landing. At times, discretion is the better part of valour and all that jazz.'

'Too bloody right they disappear!' she stormed. 'So what do you suppose has happened to poor Mrs Garnett? She was a gutsy old soul. Something unpleasant?'

Newman checked his rear-view mirror again. No sign of pursuit. He wanted to reach a main road as soon as possible. Paula repeated her question.

'Something unpleasant?'

'I fear it may be something permanent. Time we got away from this area. We'll leave Passford House today, drive back to London.'

'You mean they've killed her, don't you?'

'I fear that is very much on the cards. The question is who? And why?'

Driving up the motorway to London Tweed was well aware he was being followed. He'd been aware of the fact for some time. By a Land-Rover driven by a man wearing a crash helmet.

But there was something familiar about him. Like Nield, he couldn't place where he had seen him. Despite his tail's efforts to avoid being spotted, Tweed had detected him soon after leaving Passford House.

Which was interesting, Tweed reasoned: it strongly suggested that whoever had given the driver his instructions knew his quarry *was* staying at Passford House.

'Which,' Tweed said to himself, 'again brings us back to Willie Fanshawe, Brigadier Burgoyne, and Sir Gerald Andover. Not forgetting Lee Holmes and Helen Claybourne – since either woman could be operating independently under the control of some unknown fourth party.'

Tweed made no attempt to lose the Land-Rover. His tail was still with him when he was deep inside London in the Baker Street area. Driving into the garage where he often bought petrol, Tweed got out, called out to the mechanic.

'Something's not right with the accelerator, I suspect. I may be wrong but perhaps you could check it. I won't need the car for a few hours.'

'I'll give it a thorough check, sir,' the mechanic assured him.

'Looks like rain,' Tweed remarked.

Opening the boot, he took out his rather shabby Burberry and a deerstalker hat. Handing the keys to the mechanic, he put on the raincoat and hat. Leaving the mechanic, he took off his glasses before emerging into the street. He walked towards Regent's Park without glancing back. A few minutes later he paused at a bus stop and pretended to study the timetable, glancing back. No sign of the Land-Rover or its driver.

'You'll have a long wait for nothing, laddie,' he said to himself.

Crossing the road, he walked along Park Crescent and up the steps of the building carrying the doorplate, *General & Cumbria Assurance*. Monica jumped up when he entered his office.

'Have I got news for you – and don't tell me you already know. Because I don't think you do.'

13

At No. 185 The Boltons several hours later Dr Wand sat in his spacious study at the rear of the mansion. In London the sky was overcast and he had the curtains half-closed across the window behind him. A shaded desk lamp provided the only illumination and the rest of the room was in deep shadow. The intercom on his large Regency desk buzzed and he pressed a switch.

'Yes?'

'The messenger you're expecting has arrived, sir.'

'Tell him to wait for a moment or two. I will let you know when I am ready.'

Seated in his swivel chair behind the the desk and facing the door, Wand's large hands began to fold up the maps he had been referring to – maps of Western Europe. He folded them slowly and carefully. Next he covered up a list of names with his leather-bound blotter. He pressed the intercom switch again.

'Send – him – in – please, Mrs Kramer.'

Wand leaned back in his chair out of the glow of the light. He was staring straight at the door when it opened and his visitor came inside, closing the door behind him. Wand steepled his fingers in the shadows.

'Sit down and give me your report. With precision.'

The uncomfortable carver was placed a good six feet beyond the front of the desk. As the man sat down Wand reached out a hand, swivelled the desk lamp so it shone in his visitor's eyes. The man shielded them with a hand briefly, then lowered it.

'I followed Tweed as instructed from Passford House and . . .'

'Was he at any time aware of your presence?'

'I'm sure he wasn't . . .'

'I wouldn't bank on that. Please proceed.'

'I followed Tweed all the way to London without losing him once . . .'

'I don't like the sound of what is coming. Proceed.'

The eyes were blank behind the gold-rimmed glasses and the visitor was not helped in guessing Wand's reactions by the light glinting off the gold. But he could see the mouth which – for a moment – twisted in a most unpleasant smile. The smile always filled him with foreboding.

'He drove into a garage in Baker Street and I waited for him to drive out. He never did. After a while I left my parked Land-Rover and went into the garage. I kidded up the mechanic the driver of the Escort was a friend and got him talking. He didn't even know Tweed's name – he always pays for petrol and any service by cash. I looked all over the garage, pretending I might use it for servicing my car. Tweed had vanished.'

'You – *lost* – him.'

There was an ominous silence while the visitor tried to think what to say next. He hoped Wand would speak again but soon realized he was expected to speak himself. He felt horribly unnerved.

'I plan to go back to the garage and wait until he comes back.'

'He won't. He knew you were following him. Really, you haven't done awfully well, have you?'

'I'm sorry . . .'

'Please don't say that. Apologies for gross incompetence unsettle me. A team is waiting downstairs – I foresaw this might happen. You will take charge and this time it would be safer for your health if you do a proper job. You don't mind my expressing myself like this, I hope?'

Again the twisted smile. And the voice was so softly speaking the atmosphere of menace seemed more terrifying.

'Forget Tweed,' Wand continued. 'Find a Miss Paula Grey. She is Tweed's assistant. At least that is her title . . .' He smiled again. 'It might imply a more intimate relationship. I simply wish to know how much she means to Tweed, where she lives, every little detail about her.'

'I'll get moving on that . . .' His visitor began to stand up.

'Remain seated, please. I will tell you when I have finished. During the break-in at Andover's house are you sure you found no reference to Gaston Delvaux?'

'Nothing, sir. We really turned that place over.'

'Are you absolutely certain you missed nothing? And I do mean certain. As you know, I am a positive person,' Wand concluded.

'I am certain there was nothing connecting him with this Gaston Delvaux,' the visitor replied.

'Then you may go.'

Dr Wand rose, padded round his desk in the shadows. He grasped his visitor by the arm as he led him to the door, his manner amiable.

'Now we're not going to let one silly little mistake – losing Tweed – undermine our self-confidence, are we? I want you to know you have my complete trust. Good day to you . . .'

Alone, he went back behind his desk. Settled in his

chair, he pressed the intercom. Mrs Kramer answered his summons immediately.

'Yes, sir.'

'Our visitor is leaving after taking charge of the waiting team. Have him followed everywhere he goes day and night by Greaves. Have you got that?'

'Understood, sir.'

'Two more things. Phone Bournemouth International Airport, tell the pilot of the executive jet to bring the machine to London Airport. Warn him he will be taking me to Brussels in the near future. And one extra chore, if you would be so good – phone Vulcan and tell him Tweed could be a major menace to our operation, that we may have to take extreme measures, adding him to the target list.'

At Park Crescent Newman and Paula had just walked into Tweed's office. Newman had driven non-stop from Passford House. Tweed welcomed them back with a grave face, asked them to sit down while he listened to Monica.

Newman settled himself into the armchair, stretching the stiffness out of his arms and legs. Paula skipped behind her desk, which faced Monica's, produced a notepad and pen and listened.

'Nield and Butler found a camper close to *Prevent*,' Tweed explained. 'They followed it when it moved to No. 185 The Boltons, with a Land-Rover guarding its rear. They saw the Land-Rover driver carry a pile of cartons – the kind containing tape reels – into this address. Monica has spent half the night checking the organization based there. Moonglow Refugee Aid Trust International. Go ahead, Monica.'

'I managed to contact our agent in Hong Kong, Philip Cardon. Just before he was flying back here. He's good, as you know – speaks Cantonese fluently and, rather like

Lawrence of Arabia, who could pass for an Arab, Cardon can pass for a Chinese.'

'He's top flight,' Newman commented.

'He's heard of Moonglow. A rather mysterious organization. The odd thing is it has an outfit in Hong Kong with a slightly different name. Moonglow Trading and Mercantile International. But no one seems to know what they trade in – and it has limitless funds. Source of those funds unknown.'

'Very odd,' Paula remarked. 'A refugee outfit in London. A trading company in the Far East.'

'Who runs this outfit?' Newman asked.

'A Dr Wand. On the phone Cardon said he's something of a mystery man. No one has ever seen him. He works through his executives. No photos of him. There's a rumour that he once visited the United States for plastic surgery. No one knows why. And Cardon said he heard another rumour – that Wand has a powerful deputy in Britain, an Englishman code-named Vulcan.'

'Vulcan? I find that intriguing,' Tweed commented.

'I also had a Paris call,' Monica went on. 'Lasalle said the situation in France is so bad he can't release his brilliant agent, Isabelle Thomas, to join us. Not yet.'

'Pity,' Paula said without conviction. She hadn't taken to the attractive Isabelle during the previous year's fracas in France. 'And Cardon's call gets us nowhere.'

'Not quite,' Tweed corrected her. 'Remember Nield and Butler tracking that camper? That provides a direct link between the bugging of Sir Gerald Andover's house and the Moonglow outfit. Therefore, also with the shadowy Dr Wand. Track him, Monica. Up to the hilt.'

'I've got a lot more to tell you about my conversations in the bar at Passford House,' Paula reminded him.

'Later.' Tweed checked his watch. 'Monica had surprising news when I got back. I have to drive to London Airport in the next few minutes.'

130

'Someone arriving?' Newman asked.

'The last person I'd expect at this moment. None other than Cord Dillon, Deputy Director of the CIA. And he's bringing a woman with him who has discovered something very strange. If you like, you can come with me – both of you, Newman and Paula.'

'I like,' said Paula.

They stood waiting in the concourse of the terminal at London Airport. Outside the sun was shining and the sky was a clear blue. An atmosphere of peace and well-being, Paula thought. Especially after the horrors of Lymington and the New Forest. Strange that the frenzy of London should seem so comforting – when they had returned from what was normally the restfulness of the countryside.

'When is this damned aircraft due?' Newman asked impatiently.

Tweed had gone to check the arrivals board. He came back in time to hear the question.

'Landing now,' he said. 'It was supposed to arrive this morning early on. Delayed at Dulles Airport in Washington due to a bomb scare. Turned out to be a hoax. Monica was keeping in touch all morning.'

'Let's hope Cord Dillon is in a good humour,' Newman remarked. 'Which he probably won't be after the delay.'

The American had a fearsome reputation for his short fuse. Enormously competent, he expected everyone else to live up to his exacting standards. Fifteen minutes later the passengers started to emerge – far more than Newman had expected. The 747 Jumbo must have been full up.

More passengers appeared and soon the area round the exit was milling with people. Passengers disembarking, drivers of cars holding up names for their customers, friends greeting the new arrivals. Tweed, Newman, and Paula were huddled together in the crowd. You couldn't tell who had just come off the flight and who had arrived to meet them, Paula noted.

'There he is,' said Tweed.

Cord Dillon was a tall, well-built man in his fifties, with a craggy face. He had a shock of thick brown hair, was clean shaven, and above a strong nose his eyes were a startling blue, and ice cold. One hand carried his bag, the other waved a greeting as he pushed his way up to them. He nodded to Newman, shook Paula's hand, gave her a broad smile, then turned to Tweed.

'Could we wait here a minute or two,' he whispered. 'My companion is travelling by herself. Security. She's Hilary Vane. A key element in the catastrophe. Small and slim, she's wearing a light-blue raincoat, dark blue beret. Carrying a small tartan case.'

'Should be easy to spot,' Tweed said to Paula, who had been listening.

The *mêlée* of people became more dense and muddled. Paula saw a tall, elegant, slim woman wearing a wide-brimmed hat with a small veil. Her coat flapped open and revealed a Chanel suit.

Paula saw the small woman he had described. Blue raincoat, blue beret, tartan suitcase. Hilary Vane began to thread her way through the jostling crowd. The woman with the wide-brimmed hat bumped into her, dipped her head in apology. Vane said something, started to push her way forward again. Her face contorted in a grimace of agony. The case fell from her hand. She collapsed.

'Jesus!'

Dillon thrust his way through the crowd, pushing people out of the way. Tweed followed at his heels. The crowd was parting, staring down. Dillon and Tweed reached the inert body. Tweed, moving swiftly, bent down, felt her neck pulse, looked up.

'She's dead.'

'She can't be!' Dillon roared.

132

Even among the babble of voices his own was heard clearly. More people stopped, pushed forward to see. Paula looked round for the woman with the wide-brimmed hat. No sign of her. An airport guard holding his walkie-talkie pushed his way through. Tweed spoke quickly.

'I'm Special Branch.' He showed the card forged inside the Engine Room in the basement of Park Crescent. 'Use that thing. Get Jim Corcoran, Chief of Security. He knows me. Get him damn quick . . .'

They were all inside Corcoran's top-security office. The body of Hilary Vane was stretched out on a table. Bending over her was a doctor. He looked up, shook his head. He pursed his lips, looked puzzled.

'I could have told you she was dead,' Tweed snapped. 'I would now like to know the cause of death.'

'Oh, I couldn't possibly give an opinion on that . . .'

'Well, maybe I can.'

Tweed pointed to a small tear in Vane's raincoat in the upper arm. Gently, he eased up the sleeve of the light material. He pointed to a small puncture on the outer side of the slim arm. Vane's lips were a bluish colour. A tinge of the same colour was spreading over her face. The doctor sucked at the arm of his glasses and Tweed lost all patience.

'Clear enough, isn't it? She was injected with a lethal dose with a needle. The arm is bruised at this point.'

'Only a pathologist . . .' the doctor began.

'I know one of the top ones in the country,' Tweed informed him. 'So, thank you for your attention. But I don't think we need your presence any more.'

'Really! I beg your pardon . . .'

'Time to go, sir.' Corcoran, a tall, burly man, took the doctor by the arm, led him to the door. 'I am the Chief of Security here. It might be better if you did not mention this tragedy to anyone. To anyone at all.'

'I can't promise,' the doctor said peevishly. 'I have a formal report to make and no one is going to stop me.'

'I am. I can.' Tweed showed the same card. 'Now have nothing to worry about. Of course, if you disobeyed you might find yourself in professional trouble. I am invoking the Official Secrets Act.'

'Oh, I see. Why didn't you say so?'

'I just did. So, again, thank you for your time and I hope you haven't missed any important appointments due to the delay. I emphasize that this incident involves a matter of national security.'

'Then there's not a great deal more I can do here.'

'Nothing I can think of,' Tweed said in the same polite tone. 'But thank you for your assistance . . .'

Newman made an observation to Tweed as soon as they were alone. It seemed very quiet inside the confines of Corcoran's office. 'You bluffed him,' Newman pointed out. 'All that stuff about invoking the Official Secrets Act. He hasn't even signed it.'

'I know. But it will help to keep him quiet.' Tweed looked at Dillon who was still staring at the body on the table.

'Was Vane important, Cord?'

'Very. Most of what she knew was inside her head. She had a lot of guts. I blame myself. She insisted that it would be safer if we travelled separately – as though we were strangers. I thought it was a good idea. And it wasn't.'

Tweed was surprised. It was the first time he'd witnessed such a human reaction from the tough American.

'You haven't even a clue as to what she knew?' Tweed insisted.

'Yes. I have one tape of a recorded conversation with her. I'll play it to you in your office. Not here.'

'It could be urgent for me to have a hint.'

'Then this room has to be cleared of everyone except you and me.' Dillon had reverted to his normal abrasive tone.

He looked at Paula and Newman. 'And that includes you two.'

'We can all go into another office next door,' Corcoran volunteered. He grinned to lighten the atmosphere. 'Tap three times on the door when it's safe for us to come back.'

'You mentioned the phrase a key element in catastrophe,' Tweed said when they were alone. 'Go ahead.'

Seated behind his desk Dr Wand picked up the phone, dialled a Brussels number. He waited, leaning back in his chair, adjusting his pince-nez up the bridge of his strong nose.

'Yes?' a throaty upper-crust voice answered.

'Dr Hyde?'

'Yes. What can I do for you?'

'This is the Director speaking. You recognize my voice? Good. Go to a public phone box and call me back. At once, please.'

Wand replaced the phone. While he waited he studied maps of Britain and Western Europe, marked with crosses in pencil. Easy to erase. After ten minutes the phone rang.

'Dr Hyde speaking.'

'I think you should now proceed to the next programmed stage with your patient. A hand will do very nicely.'

'The patient is right-handed,' Hyde informed him.

'Oh, well, let us be merciful. Remove the left hand and dispatch it as planned . . .'

Inside Corcoran's office Dillon was striding backwards and forwards. Tweed had never known him show such agitation. He remained silent, guessing Dillon was deciding how much to tell him.

Eventually the American came very close to Tweed. He began speaking in a whisper.

135

'Catastrophe is not a strong enough word. We are faced with a new ruthless enemy who could overwhelm western Europe – even annihilate the United States.'

'The identity of this enemy?' Tweed enquired.

'Let me tell you this in my own way. Hilary Vane was a brilliant physicist. She worked part of the time on a top-secret project at the Boeing plant in Seattle. Later she moved to Palmdale, California. We now realize that three top scientists – working on the same project – were kidnapped with their families about three years ago.'

'And the project is?'

'One of the largest and most advanced planes in the world. The Stealth B2 bomber. It is practically undetectable by any known radar – including our own. The process may also have been adapted to ships and submarines. The enemy may – probably has – these weapons.'

'So we are faced with?'

'Invisible planes and ships. By Stealth.'

14

'I've remembered now where I think I've seen that woman in the wide-brimmed hat before,' said Paula.

She stroked her raven-black hair with one hand, frowning as she sought to marshal her memories. Sitting behind her desk at Park Crescent, she had as an audience Tweed, Newman, and Monica.

Dillon had decided he ought to pay his respects to the Director, Howard. 'And don't think I'm going to enjoy that,' was his parting shot as he left Tweed's office, 'because I'm not going to. A bag of wind, if you don't mind my saying so.'

'It was some gesture she made just before she bumped into Hilary Vane at the airport . . .' Paula mused.

'And pushed the fatal needle into her victim,' Newman commented. 'Cold-blooded murder in broad daylight amid a crowd of people. That takes nerve.'

'Let Paula concentrate,' Tweed chided him.

'Both women have nerve,' Paula observed.

'Which women, for Heaven's sake?' Newman interjected again. He fell silent as Tweed glared.

'Down in the New Forest. Lee Holmes and Helen Claybourne,' Paula continued. 'One of them. The trouble is I just can't recall the resemblance, the gesture. Either woman is tall enough to have played that fiendish role at Heathrow . . .'

'And both Holmes and Claybourne have acting experience,' Monica added. 'I'm building up a file on both those most unusual ladies . . .'

'One thing I can check,' Paula went on, her mind closed to all interruptions. 'I can phone both places down in the New Forest and see if one of them isn't there.'

'Burgoyne and Fanshawe,' Monica said to herself, checking a local phone directory from her collection. 'Here we are.' She scribbled two numbers on a piece of paper and handed it to Paula.

There was an expectant hush in the office. Paula took a tissue out of a box, crumpled it, put it inside her mouth, then wrapped a silk handkerchief round the mouthpiece of her phone to disguise her voice. First she dialled Brigadier Burgoyne's number. She waited several minutes as the ringing tone went on, put down the phone.

'Interesting. No one there. No Lee, no Brig. Now for Helen Claybourne . . .'

She repeated her performance. Again she waited several minutes. The ringing tone went on and on with irritating persistence. She replaced the receiver.

'No one there either. No Helen. No Willie.'

Newman waited no longer. He spoke with great vigour to Tweed.

'Why the hell, I'd like to know, aren't we doing something about Moor's Landing? Poor Mrs Garnett has vanished, as I told you earlier.'

'What do you propose?'

'Put the police on to it. Contact Mark Stanstead. Since you know him he'll act. The next thing we'll hear is Mrs Garnett's body has been found floating in the Solent – like Irene Andover's. A woman has disappeared, Tweed, and I'd have said that was more than enough to turn over the whole of Moor's Landing.'

'You're a great one for premature action occasionally, Bob,' Tweed replied calmly. 'I am deliberately not stirring up that wasps' nest. Yet. We'll let them think they've got away with it.'

'Why?' Newman shot back.

'Because I'm afraid much greater issues are at stake. Let me read a few extracts from the file Andover handed me.' He took the file from a drawer, opened it, began to read slowly.

'Mrs Kramer, get Vulcan on the phone for me. Rather urgently, if you please.'

Dr Wand spent the time while waiting studying the maps on his desk. They showed the south coast of England from Dover to Lymington. He checked other maps covering the coasts of Western Europe from the Dutch border to Denmark across Germany. All of them carried pencil crosses marking certain locations. The phone rang.

'Vulcan speaking.'

'Go to London Airport with our friends at once. Tickets at Sabena desk. We are leaving for Belgium.'

138

'Understood. There have been intruders at Moor's Landing. Should we evacuate the area?'

'Your opinion, if you would be so kind.'

'Not necessary. I know Tweed. He proceeds step by step until he has all the data before he acts.'

'Then,' Dr Wand replied, 'by going to Belgium we stay a step ahead of him. In any case, arrangements have been made to remove him from this world if necessary . . .'

This terse conversation took place several hours before Paula made her abortive phone calls.

Tweed continued reading from the Andover file:

'"But in the thirteenth century far more momentous events were afoot upon the larger stage of Asia. A Tartar people from the country to the north of China rose suddenly to prominence in the world's affairs, and achieved such a series of conquests as has no parallel in history. These were the Mongols . . .

'"In 1214 Jenghis Khan, the leader of the Mongol confederation, made war on the Kin Empire and captured Pekin (1214 AD). He then turned westward, conquered Western Turkestan, Persia, Armenia, India down to Lahore, and south Russia as far as Hungary and Silesia . . ."'

'I don't see the point of this history lesson,' Newman protested.

'Patience. Let me read a little more . . .

'"His successor, Ogdai Khan . . . continued this astonishing career of conquest . . . He completed the conquest of the Kin Empire and then swept his hosts across Asia to Russia (1235 AD), an altogether amazing march. Kieff was destroyed in 1240 AD, and nearly all Russia became tributary to the Mongols. *Poland was ravaged, and a mixed army of the Poles and Germans was annihilated at the battle of Liegnitz in Lower Silesia in 1241 . . .*"'

'That's getting near to home,' Paula observed as Tweed paused.

'Most intuitive of you. Andover underlined the passage beginning with Poland.'

'You might let me in on what this is all about,' Newman complained.

'Shshh!' said Paula. 'Read on,' she prodded Tweed.

'". . . It should be noticed that the Mongols embarked upon the enterprise with full knowledge of the situation of Hungary and the condition of Poland – *they had taken care to inform themselves by a well-organized system of spies* . . ."'

'Andover has underlined that last passage where I raised my voice,' Tweed commented.

'Still don't get it,' Newman persisted. 'The only Mongols left are a handful of nomadic tribesmen in Central Asia. So what? Andover was a student of history.'

'Andover,' Tweed emphasized, 'is a student of present-day global menaces, trying to foresee the future from past history. Yes, the Mongols are mere nomads of no particular size today. But massive forces exist close to them – forces which Andover believe studied history.'

'Liegnitz is not far from the Atlantic,' Paula said thoughtfully. 'How close, I wonder?'

'You are beginning to detect the shadowy outline of the enormous menace Andover identified,' Tweed told her. 'Andover has written a comment on exactly that point . . .

'"Liegnitz is little more than a hundred and fifty miles from present-day Berlin – and no more than two hundred and fifty miles from Hamburg and its opening to the sea. The Mongols came within a hair's breadth of reaching the Atlantic – *and Britain*."'

'The last two words have been also underlined by Andover,' Tweed explained. 'Apart from his comments, what I have read you are extracts from H. G. Wells' *A Short History of the World*.'

140

'So now we've had our history lesson,' Newman remarked, stretching himself, 'what is the next move?'

'The next move is for us to hurry to Belgium to have a talk with Professor Gaston Delvaux of Liège. A fresh link in the chain, I hope. Monica has tickets for the three of us. But first I must speak to my old friend, Chief Inspector Benoit of the Brussels police. A man who knows everything going on inside his country.'

'Let's hope he doesn't give us a shock,' Paula said.

'Why should he?' Newman demanded.

'I just have a feeling.'

'More intuition?' Newman asked ironically.

Monica phoned the Brussels number and requested the call to be put on a scrambler phone. She was told they would call back. Several minutes later the phone rang.

'Benoit?' Tweed enquired. 'Tweed here.'

'Ah, my old friend has at long last remembered me,' a warm voice greeted him in English. 'How are you? Good. So you must have a problem. Always a problem when you contact me. Shoot, as the vulgar Americans say.'

'I am coming over very shortly . . .'

'Tell Monica to phone me the flight details. I will meet you with a car at Zaventem Airport.'

'A more pleasant welcome to Belgium I can't imagine. Thank you. I need to visit a M. Gaston Delvaux . . .'

'Are you also on scrambler?' Benoit interjected quickly.

'Yes.' Tweed's grip tightened on the phone. 'Why?'

'Delvaux the armaments genius in Herstal outside Liège?'

'That's the man,' Tweed confirmed.

'You may have difficulty seeing him, I fear. There is a mystery there. Very strange.'

'What kind of mystery?'

'I don't know. Yes,' Benoit stated, 'I agree that sounds a

141

peculiar thing to say but it is the truth. We are banned from going anywhere near his château.'

'What on earth is going on?' Tweed pressed.

'I am not making myself clear. Let me try. But it will not be easy to describe the indescribable.'

'The cold facts would help.'

A sigh. 'Gaston Delvaux, so active all his life, and in his fifties still, has withdrawn from all public and commercial activities. He has become a recluse. Possibly a nervous breakdown? Why then has no doctor been to see him as far as I know?'

'How much of a recluse?' Tweed probed. 'And for how long?'

Paula had leaned forward. At the mention of the word 'recluse' her eyes gleamed. She watched Tweed closely. Newman, previously drumming his fingers quietly, had stopped and sat upright, also staring at Tweed's expression, which gave nothing away.

'For three to four months. Apparently his wife has left him, ran off with an American millionaire. I find that a little hard to believe.'

Tweed had a jab of memory. His own wife had left him for a Greek shipping magnate. So far as he knew they were living somewhere in South America. He was surprised how little the reminder affected him. It had happened, after all, quite a few years ago. All this flashed through his mind as he immediately responded to Benoit.

'I also find it hard to believe that about Lucie,' Tweed said grimly. 'Gaston brought her to London once for a meeting of INCOMSIN. I had dinner with them. His wife struck me as a very stable woman, very attached to Gaston.'

'My impression also,' Benoit agreed. 'Of course, you cannot always tell with women. But it still does not sound like Lucie. Not at all. But that's what Delvaux has told people.'

'That's the extent of the mystery then?'

'By no means. There is more. I said he had become a recluse. He suddenly resigned all his posts – Scientific Adviser to NATO, Defence Consultant to the EC, etc. All thrown up overnight.'

'How long ago?'

'Three to four months.'

'Which must have just about coincided with the disappearance of his wife, Lucie?'

'That is so. It was assumed here that caused him to withdraw from public life. Myself, I think the psychology is wrong. To cushion the shock of losing his wife he would have immersed himself in his work. I repeat, a mystery.'

'Monica will let you know when we are coming, Benoit.'

'We? Is the delightful Paula coming with you?'

'She is.' Tweed smiled to himself. Benoit had a soft spot for Paula. 'We'll see you soon . . .'

The phone rang on Dr Wand's desk. He picked it up, glanced at his Rolex watch.

'Yes?'

'I'm phoning from a call box,' a woman's voice informed him. 'I have completed the assignment at London Airport. The job is done.'

'Did anyone see you?'

'Of course not. Conditions were perfect. A large jostling crowd. Ideal atmosphere for the operation.'

'Excellent, my dear,' Wand purred. His pursed mouth smiled with satisfaction. His eyes gleamed behind the pince-nez. 'We shall soon be leaving for Brussels, where I may have another assignment for you. Come here in your usual guise.'

'I'm dressed as a cleaning woman now. I'm on my way . . .'

Dr Wand put down the phone. He rubbed his large

hands together. Everything was proceeding satisfactorily. The next target to check on was in Belgium.

'This is all so weird and disturbing,' Paula said when they had heard Tweed's résumé of his conversation with Benoit. 'It sounds like a repeat performance of the experience with Sir Gerald Andover.'

'It does indeed,' Tweed replied. 'I find it most sinister. Which is an added reason for going to Brussels.'

He handed her Andover's file as Cord Dillon came back into the office with Howard. The Director of the SIS was a tall pink-faced man, clean shaven and immaculately clad in a blue chalk-stripe Chester Barrie suit from Harrods. He also wore the obligatory fashionable striped shirt and his accent was upper crust.

'Most unfortunate – to say the least – this incident at London Airport,' he began.

'To say the least,' Tweed repeated drily, wishing he would go away.

'An appalling welcome for our distinguished visitor,' Howard went on. 'And all the information was inside the dead woman's head . . .'

Tweed glanced at Dillon. His expression was poker-faced – clearly he had not said one word about Stealth to Howard, a man he had never liked.

'. . . so I suppose we'll never know what she was going to tell us,' Howard waffled on. 'I really find this all most regrettable. As you know, Tweed, I'm just back from a visit to Washington.' He looked at Dillon. 'Your Director said there was nothing much going on now. Except the chaos in Russia.' He turned his attention again to Tweed. 'So what about the home front . . .'

Huddled over files on her desk Monica groaned inwardly. *The home front.* Howard would keep using his out-of-date phraseology. His club language.

'Anything startling to report? Any new activity during my absence?' Howard continued.

'This and that,' Tweed replied off-handedly. 'Too early to draw any conclusions. Much too early.'

'Ah!' Howard removed a speck of dust from his lapel, glanced at Dillon, 'Mum's the word?'

Tweed nodded. Howard had assumed that Tweed didn't wish to reveal anything in front of Dillon. A reaction Tweed had stage-managed to avoid telling Howard anything yet.

'I'd better delve into my files,' Howard decided. 'And if you can find the time, Dillon, do come and have dinner at my club one evening. Welcome to the old UK . . .'

Dillon waited until he had gone. He sat in a chair Paula brought for him, started speaking in his usual abrasive manner.

'What the hell I can't understand is how they had someone waiting at London Airport for Vane to arrive. Had to be planned in advance to have an assassin on the spot.'

'Cord, understandably you're probably suffering from jet lag or you'd have seen it yourself,' Tweed said diplomatically. 'This has to be a big, international, organization we're up against. Your flight from Washington was delayed by five or six hours with a bomb scare – which turns out to be a hoax. You must have been seen with Vane at Dulles Airport. The hoax held up your plane's arrival long enough for the assassin to get to London Airport. Diabolically simple.'

'So we listen to a voice from the dead,' Dillon said.

He took out of his pocket a thick velvet sleeve. From it he extracted a slim container and look at Paula. Opening the plastic container he took out a CD disc.

'Paula, that looks like a machine over there that takes CDs. It is? Good. We recorded Vane's edited statement on CD because it's so easy to conceal. Would you mind

145

playing it? I said edited because I want you to hear the guts . . .'

Paula inserted the CD after switching on the machine. She pressed the 'play' button and sat down to listen. It was eerie to hear the soft-spoken voice of the dead Hilary Vane.

'I spent six years working with Boeing in Seattle on the Stealth project. Two of the most brilliant researchers in this field were Professors Bauer and Rockmann. Both were married and had children. Three years ago I was due to be transferred to Palmdale, California. Just before I left, Bauer and Rockmann were about to have their contracts renewed. Their specialty was aircraft – Stealth. A third equally brilliant researcher, Professor Crown, believed the technique could be adapted to ships and submarines. Crown had been working on his own for some time. Just before I left for Palmdale Bauer and Rockmann disappeared. They left notes behind at their homes in Seattle saying they were moving to another company. Agents from Washington couldn't find any trace of the two men – or their families. Professor Crown came with me to Palmdale. He was married but had no children. He also disappeared with his wife, leaving behind in his Seattle home a note saying the pressure was proving too much, that he'd taken a long holiday with his wife . . .'

There was a pause. Everyone waited expectantly and Dillon explained.

'Soon you'll hear me ask her a question. Not much more.'

He stopped speaking as the dead woman's voice continued. Paula thought she now detected a shakiness in her tone.

'Again the agents came from Washington and couldn't find any trace of them – Professor Crown and his wife. All three men with their loved ones had vanished into thin

146

air. I found it most disconcerting, made it difficult to concentrate on my work . . .'

Another pause. Then Cord Dillon's voice asking the question.

'Ms Vane, about three years after Crown vanished, did you suddenly remember something you'd forgotten to mention in statements taken from you at the time?'

'Yes, Mr Dillon. I feel so stupid. It had completely slipped my mind. But Professor Crown went on what I thought was a holiday trip to Belgium before settling down at his new location in Palmdale. When he came back he told me over a drink late at night that he'd found confirmation of his marine Stealth theories from another source. He was very excited . . .'

Dillon stood up, strode briskly to the machine, switched it off. He removed the CD disc and replaced it in its velvet cover.

'That's it, Tweed. It was only one week ago Vane recalled that conversation with Crown over a late-night drink. Only a week ago that Belgium was mentioned. I come here direct from the President. His orders were that I contact you – he knows your track record.'

'And that's it?' Tweed asked.

'Not quite. We guessed no one would try to disappear from the States by plane. We knew the disappearance dates so we checked on shipping which left the ports of Seattle and San Francisco. When Bauer and Rockmann vanished we found a freighter – which has never returned – left San Francisco. Same with Crown. A freighter – which again never returned to the States – left Seattle just about the time he vanished with his wife.'

'You checked the registration of these two ships?'

'Sure. Some obscure outfit we couldn't find anything on. Moonglow Trading and Mercantile International.'

'And the destination of those freighters?' Tweed asked.

'Hong Kong.'

15

It turned out that Cord Dillon was not only suffering from jet lag. He was also recovering from a bout of flu. He had been glad to leave Tweed's office for his room at the Inn on the Park. Shortly after his departure the phone rang. Monica picked it up, listened, put her hand over the mouthpiece and looked at Tweed.

'A Commander Noble is waiting to see you downstairs.'

'Wheel him up,' Tweed ordered.

Newman stood up. He was looking dishevelled and washed out.

'I think I'll get back to my flat and have a bath. That is, unless you think I ought to wait to hear what the Commander has to say?'

'I'd push off.' Tweed smiled. 'I rather think Commander Noble will want to speak to me alone. Naval Intelligence, as you know. I asked him to locate someone . . .'

Newman opened the door as the visitor arrived at the top of the stairs. Nodding to him, Newman disappeared. Commander Noble stood six foot two, had a large frame, was in his late thirties, and had the ruddy complexion of a man who has spent time at sea. He wore a business suit.

Tweed stood up. He held out his hand in greeting.

'Good of you to come. Not something we could discuss on the phone, I gather?'

'Don't trust them. Not even scramblers. No thank you,' he responded when Monica offered him coffee. He looked at Paula and Monica before seating himself in the chair Tweed indicated.

'I don't wish to question the reliability of your staff. But this is a subject strictly between you and me.'

'I was just going to search for a file,' Paula said tactfully and left the room with Monica, who made a similar excuse. Noble sat upright in the armchair, grim-faced.

'Tweed, what's all this about ships vanishing without trace and for no apparent reason?'

'Five in the general area of the Solent this year.'

Tweed pointed to the wall where Monica, on his instruction, had attached three maps. One of the south coast centring on Lymington. Red-topped pins marked the general areas where Walford, Lymington's Acting Harbour Master, had reported they had disappeared.

A second map, large scale, was of the whole of Europe. The third, taking up the most space, was a map of the entire world.

'Know about those,' Noble commented. 'There have been others.' He paused as though wondering how much to reveal. 'Hell, I know you. But this is top secret. I'm in touch with naval intelligence of other nations. Top secret,' he repeated. Another pause.

'Of course,' Tweed encouraged him.

'We've had similar reports of vessels disappearing for no reason off the coasts of Holland, Germany, and Denmark.' He stood up. 'Got more of those pins? Thanks,' he went on as Tweed handed him a glass ash-tray full of red-topped pins.

'How many ships were involved? What types? And what were weather conditions like?' Tweed fired off his questions.

'Two offshore from Holland.' Noble jabbed in pins. 'Six off the German coast. Often near the Frisian Islands, curiously enough. Borkum, Norderney, and Sylt. There's a German naval base on the northern tip of Sylt . . .' He jabbed in more pins. 'And then eight off the western coast of Denmark – south of the port of Esbjerg.' Noble rammed in pin after pin, then turned to face Tweed, his hands on his hips.

'What types, you said. Yachts, coasters, fishing boats, and freighters. In every case no wreckage found. And no survivors. Except in one case. A trifle grisly.'

'Go on, I'm intrigued,' Tweed urged him.

'A German radar expert called Vogel took his small sloop out from Norderney in a dense sea mist. He was number six, had gone out to find out what had happened to a close friend. He never came back. A search the following day by a helicopter located a piece of floating wreckage. A chopper crewman descended with a cradle to bring up the relic. He retched up all his breakfast. Vogel's head was jammed in the remains of the bow. He had been decapitated. Head sliced off below the chin as neat as you like. Same with what was left of the sloop.'

'What did it?' Tweed probed. 'Surely a German pathologist . . .'

'Yes. A German pathologist checked the specimen. He'd no idea what had done it. Said the neck was severed so cleanly he'd have thought a surgeon with a huge knife had done the job. Fantastic idea. He didn't mean it – he was just demonstrating how bizarre it was.'

'And that's the lot? Missing ships?'

'Glory, no.' Noble picked up the ash-tray from a table, moved to the world map. 'Two fishing boats vanished off the west coast of Africa near the Dakar bulge.' Noble stuck in two more pins. 'Then three freighters disappeared well south of the Cape of Good Hope. Blown off course by a gale, then conditions became very foggy. Oh, there was fog off Dakar, too. Now we move much further east. The Timor Sea – midway between northern Australia and the island of Timor. Three large fishing vessels were lost there. Plus a Japanese freighter, the *Subaru*.' He jabbed in the final pin and sat down in the armchair.

'The four vessels which vanished in the Timor Sea did so

150

when a dense fog was present. Seems to be the only common factor. Fog. We're worried and perplexed. Just too many. And no survivors. Except Vogel – if you count his head. Make any sense to you?'

Tweed didn't answer at once. He seemed to have drifted into a daze as he stared at the maps. Noble checked his watch. He spoke as Tweed stirred.

'You're on to something, aren't you?'

'I'm not sure. You used the word bizarre. That describes my theory. I need more data.'

'When you phoned me and mentioned missing ships you asked if I could locate Sir Gerald Andover's motor yacht, *Seahorse III* . . .' Noble broke off, stared at the maps. 'While I remember it, shouldn't I remove those pins before I go?'

'I'd sooner you didn't. And this is probably the most secure room in London. We've tightened up. And each night two armed men guard my office.'

'Leave the pins, then. Now, Andover. I started phoning contacts up at Esjberg in Denmark and worked my way south. I got lucky at Antwerp. This morning. *Seahorse III* is now berthed in that Belgian port.'

'And by train a short ride to Brussels, then another short train trip to Liège,' Tweed said to himself.

'Pardon? Missed that.'

'Nothing. Just talking to myself. I owe you one . . .'

Alone in his office Tweed had swivelled his chair round so he was facing the maps. He studied them through half-closed eyes. Before leaving, Noble had told him that the 'incidents' off Dakar, the Cape of Good Hope, and in the Timor Sea had all taken place well clear of normal shipping lanes.

'Then what were the fated vessels doing there?' Tweed had asked.

'All blown off course by gales and heavy seas we assume,' Noble had replied.

'Significant,' Tweed said.

He roused himself as someone tapped gently on the door. He called out for the visitor to enter. Into his office walked Marler, summoned by Monica at Tweed's request.

Marler, in his early thirties, had been a member of the SIS for several years. He was the deadliest marksman with a rifle in Western Europe. Of medium height, slim, clean-shaven, he was smartly dressed in a check sports jacket, grey trousers with a razor crease, a crisp white shirt and a pale blue tie. Fair-haired, he spoke with an upper-class drawl. On the continent he could pass for the typical Englishman of independent means. He perched on the arm of the large chair as Monica and Paula returned.

'Can we come in, now your naval person has gone?' Paula enquired.

'Make yourselves at home,' Tweed told them. 'You'll be interested in what I tell Marler.'

'Got a job, I do hope,' Marler drawled. 'Hanging around looking in sports-print shops gets a trifle boring.'

Monica watched him. Smart as paint, she thought. And so unlike Howard. Behind the Director's back she referred to him as 'our mobile fashion-plate'.

'Yes,' Tweed confirmed. 'And a very dangerous job I suspect it could be.'

'Better and better. Gets the old adrenalin moving. Any travel involved?'

'That's for you to find out. Monica, before he leaves, give Marler five thousand pounds. Plus two thousand in Belgian currency.'

'Brussels on the agenda?' Marler enquired. 'This sounds up my street. Some good eating-places there.'

'That's a guess,' Tweed warned. 'Belgium, I mean. No more than a hunch. Your job is to track the movements of a Dr Wand . . .'

He explained tersely all he knew about the target, all Monica had been able to dig up so far. He emphasized that no one could be sure what Wand looked like, which made his task difficult.

'Sounds like the blighter Butler saw at The Boltons the night he played paper boy. Not so many men wearing gold pince-nez.'

'If that is Dr Wand,' Tweed warned. 'Apparently he's so far never been photographed.'

'Oh, he will be.' Marler produced a small camera from a pocket. 'If it does turn out to be Brussels, shouldn't I be weaponed up?'

'Essential,' Tweed agreed. 'In Belgium you shouldn't have much difficulty obtaining what you need.'

'Contacts in Antwerp, Brussels, and Liège,' Marler confidently reminded Tweed.

'I repeat, this man could be very dangerous,' Tweed emphasized.

'So a target worth tracking. Is that it? If so I'll get my bag from the Registry – the one I leave there packed for swift departures.'

'One more thing,' Tweed told him. 'I'll be staying soon at the Hilton on the Boulevard de Waterloo with Paula and Newman.'

'Do we really need our world-famous newspaper correspondent tagging along?'

Tweed sighed inwardly. In an emergency the two men could work together, rely completely on each other. But both men had their reservations about the other. Personality clash.

'Newman is coming,' he said firmly. 'I've given you all I can. Sorry it's so little.'

'Makes it all the more interesting. Finding out. So, Dr Wand, here I come. And you'd better mind your p's and q's . . .

*   *   *

Monica picked up the phone, which was ringing. She spoke, listened, briefly. Masking the mouthpiece she called out urgently to Tweed.

'Philip Cardon on the line. Sounds to be short of time.'

'Tweed here. Cardon, where are you? I thought you were flying home.'

'Stopped off at Bangkok . . .'

'Where are you calling from?' Tweed asked anxiously.

'Public phone box, airport. I'll be three days or so late flying back. I'm going up to Chengmai . . .'

'Don't! That's an order . . .'

'Can't hear you. Bad line. Must go . . .'

Tweed realized the connection was broken. He put down the receiver slowly. Paula had been watching him.

'What's wrong?'

'Philip Cardon calling from Bangkok Airport. He's stopped over to visit Chengmai.'

'The huge drugs distribution centre for the so-called Golden Triangle. You ordered him home?'

'Yes. He played the old trick on me. Pretended that the line was crackling, said he couldn't hear me. I'm very afraid.'

'But you do give your top agents a lot of licence to use their initiative,' she reminded him. 'And Cardon is an expert on the Far East. How could drugs come into what we're investigating, if they do?'

'No idea.'

He looked up as Newman came into the office. He was carrying a bag and wore a raincoat over his suit. Dumping the bag, he sank into the armchair.

'Just in case we're on our way. Are we?'

'I want to talk to Dillon if he'll come over now . . .'

Monica was already dialling the Inn on the Park. She had checked, made a note of the number earlier. After several minutes she nodded and Tweed picked up the phone.

154

'Cord, you know who's calling from my voice? Good. Sorry to disturb your beauty sleep, but if you could get back to my office I'd appreciate it. I need more details about the specific subject we were discussing.'

Dillon, sleepy-voiced, immediately caught on to the fact that Tweed was referring to Stealth. To the technique installed in the revolutionary bomber.

'I'd come over, yes.' Like Tweed, Dillon was phrasing his words carefully, knowing the conversation was passing via the hotel switchboard. 'But I don't think I could tell you what you want. That was the point of my thinking in bringing over Vane. She was the only one who carried all the technical details in her head. That is, over here.'

'Then go back to sleep. Sorry to disturb you. I may not be available for a few days. Take a rare rest, get out of London into the country. Call you when I get back . . .'

Tweed jumped up, went over to the cupboard where he kept a packed case ready for instant travel. He spoke to Monica as he hauled out the case.

'You have three tickets, Business Class, booked on the Sabena flight to Brussels today?'

'Yes. I've been moving the reservations from one day to the next. You pick them up from the counter at London Airport.'

'So we are off,' said Paula, collecting her own case from the cupboard Tweed had left open. 'With what aim?'

'To visit Gaston Delvaux in Liège as quickly as I can get to him. I didn't like the sound of what Benoit told me. I just hope to God we're in time.'

Dr Wand stood behind a net-curtained window on the first floor of the mansion in The Boltons. Beside him stood the gaunt, grim-faced Mrs Kramer.

'We are being spied on,' Wand told her. 'That white van parked up the road. Supposedly Straker's the Florist.

A large window in the side. One-way glass, I'm certain. For unseen cameras to photograph who calls or leaves. A job for our Mr Briggs. Rather urgent. The Daimler will be arriving soon to take me to London Airport. Briggs must remove the intruder. Tell him from me, please – any method he chooses.'

Mrs Kramer left the window immediately. She picked up a phone, gave the instruction to Briggs in careful phrases. Describing the van exactly, she put down the phone.

'Briggs says fifteen minutes. He has a vehicle standing by for emergencies.'

Dr Wand turned away from the window, lips pursed, gave his ice-cold smile. Briggs was reliable. He didn't think the van driver – and any other occupants – were due to survive much longer.

Harry Butler sat behind the wheel of the white van parked in The Boltons wearing a white coat – the type worn by florist delivery men sometimes. He was also clad in a peaked cap pulled well down and a dead fag hung from the corner of his lips.

The van was equipped with a large rear-view mirror and several wing mirrors. The rear was always the dangerous area. Despite the raw cold of a sunny November day, he had his window down. On the seat beside him was a large plastic bag containing a dark liquid.

He had seen the net curtain in the first-floor window twitch and guessed he had been observed. Fifteen minutes later by his watch he heard the sound of a large vehicle approaching. Trundling round a distant corner of the curved crescent a huge dustcart was approaching. Butler switched on his engine.

Twenty feet away he saw a man in a dark overcoat with an astrakhan collar, a dark hat, and gold pince-nez

156

walking down the steps of No. 185. He carried a suitcase as a gleaming Daimler overtook Butler, pulled up outside the mansion.

Butler saw all this with a brief glance. His attention was concentrated on the huge dustcart which had paused at the bend. Suddenly the driver accelerated as the Daimler glided away from the curve with its passenger in the rear seat.

The dustcart roared round the curving crescent, moving at such speed that Butler guessed the engine was souped up. He changed gear. The truck was thundering alongside him when the driver swung his wheel right over. Butler reversed at high speed, one hand on the wheel. His other hand threw out the plastic bag, which burst, spilling a lake of oil on the road surface. Tweed had told him of their experience with the helicopter next to Hatchet Pond down in the New Forest. Always learn from the enemy.

Behind the wheel of the dustcart Briggs had expected to smash into the side of the van at speed, crushing it. Instead he saw the massive garden wall of a mansion in front of him. He turned the wheel desperately. His wheels, slithering in the oil, refused to respond. The truck hit the wall with shattering force. Briggs was thrown forward against the wheel, breaking ribs. But it was the least of his worries. The truck, its front crumpled amid the wreckage of the wall, burst into flames.

Butler – who had agreed to help Marler – had already left The Boltons. He was driving at cruising speed towards Cromwell Road with his window now closed.

'Very satisfactory,' Dr Wand thought, relaxed inside the Daimler. 'Perfect timing. I must consider giving Briggs a bonus.'

It never occurred to him to glance back through the rear window. Even had he done so, it is very doubtful whether he would have noticed the Ford Escort tailing him. Behind the wheel, Marler whistled to himself.

Butler, he was thinking, had proved a most successful decoy. While the van was parked in full view of No. 185 Marler, in the Ford Escort, had parked a distance away where he could just see the entrance to Dr Wand's mansion. And he wasn't worried about the explosion which had shaken his car: Butler was very capable of looking after himself.

When he was convinced of the Daimler's destination he picked up the microphone. The car was equipped with a high-powered radio system, tuned to the waveband of the receiving station in the communications centre in another building at Park Crescent.

'Parker Transport calling base. Have collected fare and now on way to London Airport . . .'

Once his message was acknowledged, Marler closed up on the Daimler. He began whistling again. The tune was 'Nothing Can Come Between Us'.

16

Marler parked the Escort in a long-term bay at London Airport. It seemed the logical thing to do: Dr Wand's chauffeur-driven Daimler was parked nine bays away. Marler sat twiddling a king-sized cigarette between his fingers as he watched. The uniformed chauffeur alighted, opened the rear door, and Wand climbed out. Blinking, he adjusted his gold pince-nez.

A perfect opportunity. Marler whipped out a small camera from the glove compartment, raised it to his eyes, pressed the automatic self-focus, and within seconds he'd taken six shots.

The chauffeur, wearing a peaked cap and dark glasses, was opening the boot, taking out two cases. Louis Vuitton. Nothing but the best for Dr Wand. Marler took two shots of the chauffeur. A tall, slim type, well built, aquiline nose, and with an athletic stride. He locked the car and Marler locked his own, following them at a distance.

Looped round Marler's neck was a compact pair of field-glasses as he carried his case. Five minutes later he was watching through the lenses as a motorized passenger trolley carried Wand, chauffeur, and luggage to a waiting Lear executive jet. Marler registered the number, then ran all the way to the office of Jim Corcoran, Chief of Security. He was lucky: Corcoran was sitting at his desk staring glumly at a pile of reports.

'Don't bother about those boring old things, sport,' Marler greeted him. 'I've got something far more interesting for you do do.'

'Oh, yes? And what might that be? Trouble, I'm sure. The last time your boss was here we ended up with a body.'

'And this just might be connected with that,' Marler guessed wildly. 'Lear jet on the tarmac. Registration number—. A Dr Wand has just gone aboard. Apparently Customs and Passport Control go out to OK His Highness.'

'Dr Wand?' Corcoran wrinkled his long nose in disgust. 'He carries clout. All because he's running some refugee aid outfit. What do you want – and I know I'm going to wish I hadn't asked.'

'Nothing much. Just find out where he's going. And delay his departure.'

'Is that all?'

'Tweed would want it,' Marler said, 'and you've got a

superb memory. So you'll recall you owe him. While you're doing that mind if I smoke?'

'With all the "No Smoking" signs glaring at you? Go ahead – you will anyway. I'll check his flight plan. As to delaying his flight, you wouldn't have any ideas how I might go about that?'

'Easy again. You say you've received a bomb threat to an unidentified executive jet. Send men out to the Lear. You can say later it turned out to be a hoax.'

It amused Marler to use the same tactic Tweed had told him on the phone the enemy had used in Washington – to give time for an assassin to be waiting for Hilary Vane.

'This is really important, I suppose?' Corcoran demanded.

'Case of national security,' Marler said jauntily, using the magic phrase.

He wandered round, puffing his cigarette, using a tin lid as an ash-tray, while Corcoran busied himself on the phone. Eventually the tall, red-faced, alert-eyed Corcoran put down the phone, started rattling off information.

'Dr Wand's pilot put in a flight plan for Zaventem Airport, Brussels. A bomb squad has gone out to the jet to do their stuff, God help 'em. Maximum time they can keep the jet on the tarmac three-quarters of an hour. Anything else?'

'Now that you ask, just one more favour. Book me a seat on the first flight to Brussels. Business Class. When is the first flight?'

'They're calling it now, first call, that is.' Corcoran sighed, picked up the phone again. A brief call this time. 'One Business Class ticket waiting for you at the counter. Sabena flight. Now could *I* make a request? Good. Nice to have had you around. And get to hell out of here.'

'One final question,' Marler called out as he reached the door. 'Will my Sabena flight beat that Lear to Brussels?'

'It will do just that. Close the door quietly, won't you?'

Inside the Sabena jet Paula sat in a window seat with Tweed alongside her. Across the corridor Newman occupied the aisle seat. Passengers were still boarding. From the few waiting in the final departure lounge the flight was half empty. Paula nudged Tweed, whispered.

'Look who has arrived.'

Marler, carrying his small case – which meant he wouldn't be delayed waiting at the carousel, could walk straight off the plane – was heading up the aisle. He didn't even glance at the trio.

Reaching the front of the aircraft, he appeared to change his mind, walked back past them. Paula waited a moment, then glanced back. Marler was sitting three rows behind them, occupying a window seat on her side with an empty seat next to him.

'He's taken up a position to watch over us,' Tweed said in a low tone. 'Odd he should be on the same flight.'

Paula glanced back as though to see how many more passengers were coming into Business Class. Marler was staring through the window, his compact pair of binoculars pressed against his eyes. Round the Lear jet in the distance a team of men were swarming. The retractable steps were still down.

As he watched, a heavily built man wearing a dark overcoat with an astrakhan collar padded down the steps. He began to pace slowly up and down. He stopped, stared towards the Sabena aircraft. He had a large head, fair hair, and gold pince-nez were perched on his strong nose.

Marler left his seat, peered back into Economy. More passengers still boarding. He walked up to the front of the

161

aircraft and asked the stewardess a question.

'Can you give me some idea of the flight time to Brussels?'

'Fifty minutes, sir.' She looked at Marler, liked what she saw. The passenger seemed restless. 'There are plenty of other seats if you wish to change,' she suggested.

'I'm the athletic type.' He grinned at her. 'Like to get a bit of exercise – find I get cramped sitting down. And you look very chic in that uniform.'

'Thank you, sir . . .'

Marler was on his way back to his seat, walking slowly. The stewardess watched him with interest. He hadn't made the usual coarse pass she was used to – he'd just paid her a genuine compliment. Marler was timing it carefully, field-glasses clenched in his hand. A woman passenger was coming towards him. They met alongside Tweed.

Marler appeared to stumble as he stood aside to let the new arrival pass. He fell across Tweed, dropped the binoculars in his lap.

'I'm so sorry, sir.' He lowered his voice. 'Lear jet over there. Could be Dr Wand pacing up and down. Destination Brussels.'

Apologizing again, he returned to his seat. Paula picked up her glasses, raised them to her eyes. They were already focused on the Lear. As she studied the large man he stopped and again stared towards the Sabena plane. In the lenses his face came up close. Remote eyes behind the pince-nez. She shivered.

'What's the matter?' Tweed asked in a normal voice.

He'd already checked. No one in the two rows ahead or behind them. Paula swallowed.

'If that is Dr Wand there's a streak of pure cruelty in the man.'

'Well, from what's happened so far the mastermind

162

behind it all is certainly cruel – almost to the point of sadism.'

'You mean the severed arm of Irene, then her body floating in the Solent?'

'That – and many other things. A sadist capable of the most appalling mental cruelty – as well as physical. Unless I'm wrong in the theory taking shape.'

'No point in asking you what theory, I suppose?'

'Not until I'm sure.'

The aircraft was in midair, crossing the North Sea, when Paula decided to go to the toilet. Some instinct made her put on tinted glasses. In the aisle she glanced into Economy section and nearly froze.

Sheer will power – plus SIS training – kept her moving. When she returned she waited until Tweed had settled himself in his seat. Then she leaned close to him.

'I've had a shock. You'll never guess who is travelling with us. In Economy.'

'You know I don't like guessing.'

'Willie Fanshawe, Brigadier Burgoyne, and Helen Claybourne. Helen has the window seat. Willie is next to her. The Brig. is across in the next aisle seat – like Newman with you. Willie was leaning over, chatting to Burgoyne.'

'Did any of them see you?' Tweed enquired.

'No. I'm certain of it.'

'Any sign of Lee Holmes?'

'Absolutely not. And Economy is full up.'

'Maybe she caught an earlier flight to Brussels. I find it significant – the absence of Lee.'

'In what way?'

Tweed ignored her question. Taking off his glasses he began to clean them on his handkerchief, which meant his mind was racing. He asked her the question as he put on his glasses.

'You never got a chance to give me your impressions of the relationships between Burgoyne and Holmes and between Willie and Helen. Now might be a good time.'

'At first I made the obvious assumption – both men had their mistress living with them. Nothing odd about that. Then it did become odd. I decided I was wrong. Perhaps only another woman would sense it. The lack of little things indicating intimacy. Before we left each house I was convinced my first impressions had been wildly off the mark.'

'So what is the relationship?'

'Odd, as I said. Both women obviously manage house and do the normal jobs wives would do – or some mistresses . . .'

'You're becoming as cynical as me.'

'Let me go on. I had the strongest feeling both women are working for the men in some professional capacity. It's a business relationship, if you like.'

'Anything else?'

'Yes. Lee has to handle Burgoyne with kid gloves. Basically he's still the Brigadier, accustomed to giving orders and expecting instant obedience. With Helen I had the opposite impression. Willie is an amiable soul – has all his marbles though. But Helen is calling the shots.'

'I find your conclusions illuminating. Thank you.'

'Good. Glad to be of service,' she said ironically. Her tone changed. 'You look worried.'

'I am wondering how many more have to die before we bring this business to a climax. So far the body count is three, probably four. Harvey Boyd, Irene Andover, Hilary Vane – and I doubt whether we'll ever find Mrs Garnett of Moor's Landing alive.'

'You seem to be in a great rush to reach Brussels. What do you expect us to find there?'

'My worst fears confirmed.'

'I don't understand,' said Paula.

'You think it's a coincidence that Dr Wand is leaving for Brussels aboard that Lear jet? You think it's another coincidence that Burgoyne, Willie, and Helen are on board this plane?'

'Do you? It does seem strange.'

'I never believe in coincidences,' Tweed replied grimly.

'And your remark about your worst fears?'

'I forgot to tell you I called Benoit, stopped him meeting our plane. It could be dangerous to be seen with him. After dumping our bags at the Hilton we're driving straight to Grand' Place – to police headquarters to meet Benoit there. Newman has phoned ahead for a hire car to be waiting for us.'

'You saw Marler go up to the stewardess yet again? My bet is he's had the pilot radio ahead also for a hire car.'

'Probably. He knows what he's doing.'

'And you're not going to tell me about your worst fears?' she persisted.

'I'm certain we're involved in a race against time. The problem is very simple. Who will reach Gaston Delvaux first – while he's still alive?'

17

They were the first off the plane at Zaventem Airport. It was Tweed who led the headlong rush, with Paula and Newman hurrying to keep up with him. Through Passport Control they carried their only bags, the ones they'd taken aboard the aircraft. Newman caught up with Tweed.

'Why the mad scramble?'

'Change of plan. You know where to pick up that car you phoned ahead for in London? Good. Forget the Hilton – drive us straight to police headquarters off Grand' Place. I must check the situation with Benoit, then we race to Liège – to Herstal. To Delvaux's château. Not a minute to lose . . .'

His unusual urgency conveyed itself to the other two. A cool, fast-walking Paula checked her watch. It would be dark when they arrived in Liège. Running outside the airport, Newman swore under his breath. The hire car waiting for them was a *red* Mercedes. Too conspicuous. It couldn't be helped. He hustled through the formalities with the car-hire girl, accepted the keys, told her to wait while he tested the engine.

'Get in,' Tweed said impatiently.

'You might have warned me it was going to be a marathon,' Paula remarked as she dived into the rear.

'I only decided this would save time when the plane was descending. And we lost time droning round in that holding pattern. All right, Bob?'

'Engine seems OK. We're off. Grand' Place and Benoit, here we come . . .'

Paula groaned inwardly as they drove into Brussels, the most muddled and depressing city in Europe. Like Los Angeles, a series of districts in search of a centre. And the fog which had delayed them was drifting in smoke-like trails in the busy streets.

Tall concrete blocks rose everywhere, interspersed with small, shabby, two-storey buildings – centuries old, paint peeling – cafés, bars, and shops illuminated with tasteless neon. Street skiving off in all directions. Drivers of cars jousting for the only available slot left in the middle of a wide boulevard.

The pavements – ankle-breakers – were crowded with Belgian housewives hurrying for metro entrances. The home of the EC commissioners hadn't changed. A worthy home for those fat, well-fed, and over-paid bureaucrats, she thought. The whole place was like a disturbed anthill.

Newman was driving ruthlessly, at high speed, overtaking. Belgian motorists blared their horns as they had to pull up suddenly to let him through. He's exceeding the speed limit, Paula observed to herself. Tweed's burst of nervous energy had transmitted itself to Newman's wild driving.

They pulled up outside a building off Grand' Place, which was barred to traffic with frontier-like poles. One of the truly ancient sections of Brussels, Grand' Place was surrounded with medieval buildings. Newman parked in a no-parking zone, took out a pad of stickers, wrote 'Police HQ' on one, attached it to the windscreen.

Tweed, already outside on the pavement, glanced at the sticker, called out to Newman.

'It's *Politie* here. You should have remembered that.'

Newman scribbled a new sticker. Removing the previous one, he attached the new version, jumped out of the car, locked it, and followed the others. Tweed and Paula were already inside the building.

'Chief Inspector Benoit is expecting us. An emergency. Every second counts . . .'

Tweed had addressed the uniformed desk sergeant in French. He dropped his card in front of the man, a card which gave his name and the fake cover company.

Chief Inspector Benoit appeared almost at once, running agilely down the stairs. He greeted Paula first, hugging her. 'Welcome to Brussels.'

She felt glad she was wearing a smart outfit. Under her open trench coat she was clad in a high-necked white blouse, navy blue jacket, and pleated skirt. Tweed was moving restlessly, a reaction which did not escape the Belgian.

Chief Inspector Benoit, the shrewdest policeman in Belgium, was a jovial portly man in his forties. He had a great, beaked nose, light brown hair, and quick-moving eyes. He ushered them upstairs to his office on the first floor.

'We have to reach Liège very urgently. Precisely, Gaston Delvaux's château at Herstal. We've come straight here from the airport. The Hilton can wait,' Tweed said.

'I'll phone them, book you accommodation. Executive rooms on the twentieth floor, if I remember. Now, Liège. I rather expected this. You must go by train from Midi . . .' He checked his watch. 'You just have time to catch the express from Ostend going through to Cologne. Only one stop. At Louvain.'

'Surely by car—' Tweed began.

Benoit shook his head. 'With the traffic at this time of day? No, the train. I will try and get there by car to meet your train at Liège, but cannot guarantee I will make it, even with sirens and flashing lights.'

'You said Delvaux had banned police coming near him,' Tweed objected.

'True. I have unmarked cars waiting. There will be a silent approach as we come close to the château. We will wait a short distance away.' He raised a hand. 'I insist. My territory. You could be in great danger. Which reminds me. You just have time . . .'

He took them into another room. One glance at the weapons laid out on a table, with ammo, confirmed to Newman what a remarkable memory the police chief had. Paula picked up a .32 Browning automatic, some ammo. She was checking the gun when Benoit spoke.

'Empty. Your favourite gun. Made in Herstal. Although today our armaments industry at Herstal hardly exists any more. The collapse of the Soviet Union and other factors.'

Paula was loading the Browning as Newman picked up a Smith & Wesson .38 Special. Alongside the ammo was a hip holster. Benoit never forgot a thing. Taking off his trench coat and jacket, Newman slipped on the holster, checked the machanism of the gun, loaded it, put extra ammo in his coat packet. That left a 7.65mm. Walther automatic on the table. Benoit looked at Tweed, who shook his head.

'I hardly ever carry a gun.'

'Now for the perishing paperwork,' Benoit continued as he produced two forms which already had details typed in. 'Paula, Newman, sign these. They are permits for you to carry those weapons. Now it is all legal.'

'Benoit,' Tweed said, after checking his watch, 'we will have to buy tickets for Liège before we board that express.'

Benoit produced his wallet, extracted six slips of paper. He handed two to each of them.

'First-class return tickets to Liège. I will drive you to Midi station. Then with a team I will drive on to Liège, hoping to meet you at the station. It is quite a gamble . . .'

'I'm leaving now,' Newman broke in. 'I've got a Merc. outside. I think I can make it by road before Paula and Tweed reach Liège. Along the motorway. See you two . . .'

He was gone before anyone could protest. Benoit threw up his hands in mock horror, then ran to the window. Peering down, he took out a pad, made a note.

'I have his registration number. I'll leave instructions to be radioed along his route. To all patrol cars. That Merc. to be permitted to proceed at all costs. Now, we leave for Midi station . . .'

Tweed and Paula had a first-class compartment to themselves as the express raced eastward well beyond the Brussels suburbs. To Paula's surprise it was still daylight and the fog had gone. They were crossing open country-side and carefully ploughed fields stretched away on both

169

sides. The bread-basket of Belgium. Here and there a dense copse of pine trees reared up. They passed isolated villages with neat rows of old brick-built terrace houses with steep-pitched roofs. In the distance the occasional church spire pointed skywards like a needle. Which prompted Paula's remark.

'I've been thinking about Hilary Vane – how she was murdered at Heathrow. It looked to me as though she was injected with cyanide. Her lips were blue.'

'Undoubtedly,' Tweed agreed. 'Cyanosis was pretty obvious. Her whole face was beginning to turn blue.'

'I was also wondering how the murder was achieved. In a busy airport you can't really produce a hypodermic needle and jab it into somebody. The location was too public.'

'What solution have you arrived at, then?'

'A hypodermic needle disguised as something else. Something very ordinary which no one would think odd a woman holding it in her hand.'

'Sound thinking. The same thought crossed my mind.'

'What about Dr Rabin?' Paula asked. 'Has he told you anything?'

'You know what pathologists are. Won't commit themselves until they've gone through the whole process. He said he would have information for me by the time I got back to London.'

'That place we stopped at was Leuven, I noticed.'

'Which means a Flemish enclave,' Tweed commented. 'Benoit said Louvain, the French – or Walloon-version. It's a real mix-up, is Belgium – which is why the road signs in Brussels are always first in French, then in Flemish. I think we're coming in to Liège.'

'Looks pretty grim,' Paula observed, peering out of the window. 'Can't really see it yet. Just those peculiar hills shaped like mounds. Funny they're all so rounded. They don't look like proper hills.'

'They aren't. Liège was once a great coal-mining centre. They just dumped the coal dust in great slag-heaps on the edge of the city. Not a very tidy lot out here. You'll see the colour of the buildings – coal black from the dust blown down into the city. Prepare not to enjoy yourself.'

The stench of Liège hit Paula as they walked out of the modern station. A revolting smell of greasy food from hot-dog stalls. The street was littered with stained food cartons carelessly thrown down. The brick buildings opposite were soiled with black dirt – the coal dust Tweed had referred to, she assumed.

Waiting cab drivers, wearing shabby clothes, pestered them for a fare. Their complexions were an unpleasant olive colour and several leered at Paula's legs. So this was Liège . . .

Paula stared. On the opposite side of the cobbled street a red Mercedes was parked. Newman stood beside it and beckoned them over. Paula picked her way among the mess of discarded cartons.

'I didn't come over,' Newman explained. 'This is the sort of place where you stay by your car unless you want to lose a wheel, windscreen wipers, the lot. And I have found out the route to Herstal. It's not far. I have marked it on a map, so you can be navigator, Paula.'

'How did you find it?' she asked, studying the map when she'd slipped into the back seat.

'Cost me two thousand francs. These cabbies don't give you the time of day for nothing. This is Money-Grubber Town. Watch your shoulder-bag.'

'Let's get moving,' Tweed urged. 'Any sign of Benoit?'

'He's inside that unmarked car on the corner. Arrived about fifteen minutes after me. Relax . . .'

He was driving down a narrow street walled in by more soot-soiled buildings. It started badly, it became worse.

The gutters were littered with crushed drink cans, with screwed-up paper. The few locals slouching along the dimly lit street were clothed to match their surroundings. The interior of the Mercedes was polluted with the smell of stale food. Newman opened a window wide.

'Don't imagine you appreciate the Liège atmosphere. So a breath of partly fresh air should clear it in a minute. Just relax . . .'

'Relaxing is the last thing I have on my mind,' Tweed snapped. 'I want us to get to Delvaux in time. Assuming we are in time. Benoit isn't going to form up a cavalcade behind us, I trust?'

'He has three cars packed to the gunwales with armed men. And he's promised me not to come within a quarter of a mile of the château. Reluctantly. Ladies and gentlemen,' Newman went on in a lighter vein, 'we have just arrived at the great River Meuse . . .'

It was dark as he drove alongside the major waterway for barges and other traffic, the river from distant Dinant in the south, which progressed via Namur and Liège to become the Maas in Holland before it finally reached the North Sea.

Tweed peered out of the window. Street lamps provided better illumination here. The wide river down below with massive concrete embankments like fortress walls. The water was a muddy colour. Paula touched Tweed's arm.

'Look at those apartment blocks on the opposite bank. They're modern – but even they are hideous.'

Tweed nodded. The apartment blocks were painted in a variety of primary colours, all an offence to the eye. They gave the curious impression they were built of plastic. Newman called out again.

'Now for Herstal. It's roughly north-west of Liège, as you'll see from the map. Not far now.'

Tweed hardly heard him. He was staring out of the

window. There was a large yacht basin, a branch of the river closed in by a low wall. Again the element of water and various craft. As at Lymington and Buckler's Hard.

Headlights undimmed, the woman behind the wheel of the black Mercedes raced through the night, blaring her horn frequently to blast other motorists out of her way. Belgian drivers swore as she overtook them, made rude gestures she never noticed. Her whole mind was concentrated on reaching her destination, and God help anyone who got in her way.

It wasn't easy to identify her as a woman. She was wearing a crash helmet, goggles, her leather jacket turned up at the collar. Her gloved hands rested lightly on the wheel. As always, she was perfectly in control of the situation.

A large truck edged out on to the motorway. She pressed her hand on the horn non-stop, increased speed. The truck driver used foul language as he jammed on his air-brakes. Then the black projectile was past him, its red lights disappearing in the distance.

'Crazy bastard!' the truck driver said to himself.

The black Mercedes, with a taxi sign, raced on and on. Its tyres screeched as she swung round a bend, never slackening for a second. Her hand was on the horn again as she overtook more vehicles, several shaking in the slipstream of her fantastic speed.

She checked a road sign, glanced at the dashboard clock, rammed her foot down another inch. The Mercedes was practically flying, seemed about to take off at any moment. She drove on, ruthlessly forcing other traffic to give way.

Her destination: Herstal.

18

'That must be his armaments factory,' Newman commented. 'I thought Delvaux had gone out of business.'

'So did I,' Tweed replied from the back of the Mercedes.

They had reached Herstal. Tweed peered out of the window at a modern single-storey factory complex of white buildings close to the edge of the Meuse. Across the road from the plant was a large landing stage with two huge barges berthed.

A searchlight perched high on top of the main building was switched on. The spotlight of the beam hit the road ahead of Newman, moved swiftly towards him. Just in time he lowered the visor, half-closed his eyes. The glare of the spotlight focused on the car, paused, followed it for several seconds.

'Bloody traffic hazard,' Newman growled.

'Their security is extraordinary,' Tweed observed.

The factory was surrounded with a high wire fence he suspected was electrified. Behind the fence uniformed guards partrolled, holding Alsatians straining at their leashes. Even above the sound of the engine he could hear their fierce barking. The walls of the buildings had no windows but in the sloping roofs were large fanlights and from these powerful lights glowed in the night. A door opened, a fork-lift truck piled high with crates was driven inside, the door closed. A huge sign proclaimed *Delvaux SA* – with no indication that this was an armaments factory.

'I don't understand it,' Paula said. 'They're working full blast at this time of night.'

'Another mystery,' Tweed remarked.

'You turn off soon now,' Paula called out. 'A curving road to the right, according to the map. Just beyond this bend in the river.'

'Here, I'd say,' Newman replied. 'Yes. See that sign – Château Orange? This is Delvaux's place.'

'Bob!' Tweed spoke quickly. 'Look out for somewhere to park the car out of sight of the entrance to the château. But we're all going in together . . .'

The headlights were sweeping round bends as the Mercedes climbed a hill. On both sides were dense woods and wide grass verges. The headlights shone on open entrance gates. Newman drove slowly, edged the car along a track. It turned almost immediately in a clearing. He swung the car round ready for a swift departure, switched off the engine, opened his trench coat so he could reach his gun swiftly. He locked the car and they hurried back.

The gravel drive beyond the entrance gates bore evidence of neglect. Weeds sprouted through the gravel. Which didn't seem like Delvaux, a tidy man. Tweed paused in the middle of the tarred road. Just above the entrance the road curved again round a sharp bend. The silence created a brooding atmosphere, despite the light of a moon.

'What is it?' Paula whispered.

'Listening for the sound of cars. Looks as though Benoit has kept his word. I couldn't see any trace that we were being followed through the rear window.' He took a deep breath. 'Let's get on with it.'

Tweed walked with Paula alongside him while Newman came up behind them, the Smith & Wesson held by his side. Hemmed in by overgrown shrubberies, the drive had a creepy feel, and Paula's right hand was tucked inside her shoulder-bag, gripping the Browning. Their feet crunched on the gravel, advertising their approach.

The large three-storey château came into view suddenly. It had a mansard roof with circular dormer windows in the roof. A wide flight of steps led up to the main entrance, a pair of double doors. There were lights in the ground-floor windows.

'What a beautiful place,' Paula enthused.

'Must have cost a few million—'

Newman broke off as a small bare-headed man of slight build and small stature appeared round the side of the château. Tweed immediately recognized him as Gaston Delvaux. The night air was cold and there was frost on the shrubs, but the Belgian wore no coat over his dark business suit.

As he came forward Paula was struck by the impression of cleverness – even brilliance – he made on her. Clean shaven, his head was large, his hair grey, and his forehead bulged. He reminded her of a large elf. Newman slipped his gun behind his back, tucked it down inside his trench-coat belt.

Tweed was shocked by Delvaux's slow movements: normally he was so nimble. His face was drawn and he looked hollow eyed. Only his voice seemed normal as he greeted Tweed in English.

'The last person on God's earth I expected to see here. Would you mind if we wandered outside round the back?'

Tweed felt he was witnessing a repeat performance, experiencing the same nightmare of Andover at *Prevent*. His reaction was strengthened as Delvaux lowered his voice.

'There are listening devices all over the château. We shall not be overheard in the garden.'

Paula reacted quickly, after Tweed had made brief introductions.

'Mr Delvaux, could I possibly go inside to your loo?'

'Of course, Miss Grey.' Delvaux paused. 'It is rather a large house. No one else is inside, so do not feel afraid . . .'

Taking a set of keys from his pockets, he climbed slowly up the steps. At one time, Tweed thought, you'd have run up them. Selecting two keys, the Belgian unlocked the right-hand door, opened it, stood aside.

'You go across the hall. On the left you will see a door with *S'il vous plait* on a metal plate. Then perhaps you will join us in the garden.'

'Thank you . . .'

Paula walked slowly across the marble-floored hall. It was illuminated by a huge chandelier suspended way above her head. She paused, looked back, listened. Delvaux would now be well away from her.

Ignoring the door with the plate, she walked on to the rear of the hall where a door was half open, the room beyond lit by fluorescent strips. As she had hoped, it was the kitchen. A beautiful wood-block floor, all the latest equipment, including a de luxe island unit. She was relieved to see the curtains were closed.

Beyond the island unit was another door with a large frosted-glass panel. She opened it quietly. Again she had guessed right. It was the utility room – also equipped with the latest gadgets. Including a huge freezer.

This was what she had been looking for. She sucked in a deep breath as she approached it. Standing gazing down at the closed lid, she gritted her teeth, steeled herself. She was feeling very tired. Already it had been a long day. Get on with it, she told herself.

Stopping, she grasped the lid, lifted it back in one swift motion. Even though she was expecting something like this, the shock was still great. The freezer was packed with food. Motionless she stared at the plastic carton full of ice laid along the top of the food. It was smaller than the carton in Andover's freezer – because what it contained was smaller. The severed hand of a woman, amputated at the wrist, where it was covered with a bandage stained with blood.

She knew it was a woman's hand. The slim fingers suggested a woman. But what confirmed it was a woman's hand – a left hand – were the two rings on the third finger. A ruby engagement ring, a gold wedding ring. The final obscenity was a single wilted rose which had been placed between the fingers.

'*You bastards!*'

Paula's lips formed the words soundlessly. She had not forgotten the listening devices. She closed the lid, walked slowly towards the front entrance.

When Paula had gone inside the château Delvaux had led the way along a footpath beside the building to the grounds at the rear. Newman, following Tweed, almost gasped at what he saw.

Illuminated by lanterns, spaced out at intervals, the estate was laid out like a miniature Versailles. A vast lawn, heavily coated with glistening frost, was criss-crossed with paved walks. Beautiful stone urns were perched on shapely plinths. In the shadows decorative conifers – expensive specimen trees – rose up like small exclamation marks. In the distance a coloured fountain spurted vertically, falling back into a round walled lake.

'I used to love this,' Delvaux commented as he stood on a terrace running the length of the back of the château. 'Why have you come, Tweed?'

Newman, standing with the gun by his side hidden from Delvaux, was staring at the shadow of a man. He stood quite motionless, in the darkness close to the wall of tall evergreens shielding the estate.

'There's someone hiding over there,' he interjected.

'Do not worry,' Delvaux assured him. 'He is a friend.

Why have you come, Tweed?' he repeated.

'Because I've found out what happened to Sir Gerald Andover.'

There was silence for several long minutes. Delvaux's hands began to tremble. He hastily shoved them inside his jacket pockets. Before he could answer Paula walked on to the terrace. She looked at Tweed, jerked her head towards the château.

'The same situation as at *Prevent*,' she whispered as she stood closer to him. She extended her left hand, made a chopping motion with her right on her other wrist. 'The freezer again.'

'What have you been doing inside my house?' Delvaux demanded in a high-pitched voice. He had moved near enough to catch her last three words. 'What have you found?' he screeched, his facial muscles working.

Over Paula's arm were folded some clothes she had found inside a cupboard in the hall. She turned to face the Belgian. Just before she turned round Tweed nodded to her and she knew he wanted her to talk.

'Your coat and a scarf, Mr Delvaux,' she replied. She helped him on with the coat, wrapped his scarf round his neck. 'You'll catch your death out here in this temperature.'

'Thank you, my dear. Most considerate. It is chilly.'

'It is even more chilly inside the freezer,' she told him. Only shock tactics would make this man talk. 'And I found a woman's severed left hand. Lucie is supposed to have run off with a millionaire. Would he send that to you?'

Delvaux crumbled. He shook like a leaf in a breeze. He was shuddering all over. He came to Paula and she put her arms round him as he hugged her close for comfort. Then he stiffened, let go of her, stood back, stood upright.

'I'm sorry. I'm making a fool of myself. Yes, that is

Lucie's hand. She's been kidnapped. Over three months ago.' He had spoken calmly. Now he became agitated, speaking in an anguished manner to Tweed. 'You must *not* tell the police. Please! *Not* the police! They will kill her.'

'Which is why I came alone,' Tweed said in a matter-of-fact tone. 'What are their demands? How much?'

'No ransom has been demanded. I was given precise instructions. I must go into retirement, resign from all public bodies – including INCOMSIN. They emphasized INCOMSIN. Otherwise Lucie's body would be delivered to me in a casket. I did everything they told me. I fended off Chief Inspector Benoit, who was suspicious.'

'And the listening devices all over the château?' Tweed probed.

'One day when I was at the factory they broke in and placed the listening devices. As soon as I returned I had a phone call from a woman. She told me what they had done. She warned me they would know if I interfered with – removed – any of the devices. She said I knew what the ultimate consequences would be. Ultimate. That is why we are talking out here . . .'

He stopped talking. Newman had raised his gun, holding it with both hands. The man in the shadows was walking towards them. Newman's voice rang out clear in the crisp silent night.

'Raise both hands above your head or get a bullet in the guts.'

'Put the gun away,' Tweed ordered. He had recognized the way the approaching man walked. 'It's all right,' he called out.

Sir Gerald Andover, clad in a heavy overcoat, lowered his hands. He walked towards them as though his shoes were made of lead. God! Tweed thought. Shall I tell him now about Irene – that she is dead, dragged out of the Solent?

'I recognized you, Tweed,' Andover began. 'And Paula.' He turned to her, gave a formal bow. She realized he was making a tremendous effort to appear to be in control of himself. Delvaux spoke.

'Gerald sailed to Antwerp in his motor yacht to come and see how I was getting on, to ask my advice about a certain matter.'

'Instead,' Andover said with a note of irony, 'I found myself advising Gaston. You might say we're in the same boat. You've told him, Gaston?'

'Some of it,' Delvaux replied cautiously.

'I don't understand the severed hand, Gaston,' Tweed remarked in as casual a tone as he could muster. He looked at Andover. 'Just as I didn't understand the severed arm of Irene.'

'We think – we know,' Delvaux intervened, 'that these barbaric acts were to encourage us not to inform anyone in the outside world of what was happening. Including the police. The woman phoned me again, said so after I found that horrible carton in the freezer. It happened last night after I'd returned from a discreet visit to the factory. She told me to look in the freezer, was still on the phone when I got back. I swore at her, called her a sadistic fiend. She said it was a reminder – not to go to the police – and rang off.'

'Tweed,' Andover said grimly, 'that's what we are up against – sadistic fiends. And we don't know why.'

'What I would like to know,' Tweed remarked, turning to Delvaux, 'is why your plant is working full blast – also why you are making discreet visits, as you phrased it.'

'I have nothing more to say,' the Belgian said. 'But I ask you as a friend – do not inform the police. For the sake of Lucie. Now, you had better go.' He turned to Paula. 'Please do not think me discourteous, but I find myself in an impossible position.'

'Then we will leave,' Tweed decided.

'May I come with you?' Andover asked. 'I came by taxi – and left it outside the factory, then walked the rest of the way.'

'By all means, Gerald. We have a car – concealed, by the way, Gaston. *We* have been very discreet . . .'

Delvaux had started to walk away. He nodded to show he had heard, and shuffled out of sight. Tweed shook his head, looked at Andover, and then all four of them walked towards the drive. Tweed was silent: he had still not been able to bring himself to tell Andover about Irene. Best to wait until they were in some comfortable hotel suite.

Newman had slipped his Smith & Wesson back into its holster. Paula felt tense, full of foreboding. Again the claustrophobic drive felt creepy. Lifting the flap of her shoulder-bag, she gripped the butt of her Browning.

Near the entrance gates Paula quickened her pace. Ahead of the others, she reached the road, glanced to right and left, ran across it, and waited on the track in the shadows.

Andover was walking on Tweed's right. He began talking as they approached the deserted road. He still moved with a dragging step, but his voice was brisk and vigorous.

'Gaston is a broken man. Can you wonder at it? It's a bloody waste – a genius like that subjected to such a frightful ordeal.'

'You've had a pretty bad time of it yourself,' Tweed remarked. 'You sound better now. Ready to face anything, however grim.'

'Oh, I have braced myself for whatever the future may hold. I've still got a lot of fight left in me . . .'

Newman was walking a few yards behind them. Like Paula, he was tense. And very alert. The two men ahead of him reached the road. They began to cross it. Newman heard the sudden thunderous roar of the car coming as it accelerated round the bend higher up the hill to his right. Both men in front of him were crossing the road when the black Mercedes descended on them like a tornado. Andover threw up a hand to shield his eyes from the ferocious glare of the headlights.

Newman knew he could only try to save one man. Rushing forward he charged into Tweed's back, hurtling him forward to sprawl on the grass verge by the track. Newman's impetus was so great he was carried across by his own momentum, falling beside Tweed.

Paula alone saw what happened in fractions of a second. The black Mercedes smashed into Andover, lifted him high into the air, sped on as Andover crashed with a terrible thud on to the tarred surface of the road. Paula had whipped up her Browning. She fired off one shot which penetrated the rear window. Then the car was gone, skidding madly round a lower bend.

Winded, Tweed took a deep breath, clambered to his feet with surprising agility, ran to the crumpled form lying in the road. He bent down, felt Andover's neck pulse, and straightened up slowly as Newman reached him.

'Christ!' Tweed hardly ever swore. 'He's dead. At least the poor devil never knew about his daughter.'

'I'm sure the driver was a woman.' It was Paula, holding her Browning. 'The murdering bitch. I put a bullet into her rear window but I'm sure it did no damage.'

'What makes you think it was a woman?' Tweed asked quietly.

'She wore a crash helmet, goggles. It was the way she turned her head. I swear it was a woman,' she repeated.

'Help me carry the body back to the château, Bob,' Tweed suggested. 'I want Gaston to see it. He's got to start talking now.'

19

Inside the château kitchen there was furious, urgent activity. Paula was perched on a pair of steps taken from a cupboard. In her hand she carried a new instrument like a small torch with a grille over the front – what was known in the surveillance trade as a 'flasher'.

It detected the presence of listening devices and she had been taught how to use it by Butler on a refresher training course at a large isolated house in Sussex surrounded with extensive grounds. She had also learned certain physical skills which had tested her powers of endurance.

Newman stood on a working surface close to her, removing the bugs as she detected them. One was hidden in a corner on top of a tall cupboard; another behind the tall refrigerator. She even detected one concealed on top of a fluorescent tube.

Earlier they had witnessed a tragic scene on the terrace outside the front entrance when Delvaux had opened the door in response to Tweed's insistent ringing. The Belgian stared at Andover's body which Newman was holding. He came forward, his face tortured with anguish.

'They have killed my old friend, Gerald . . .'

Tweed had briefly told him what had happened beyond the entrance gates. Anguish was replaced by fury as Delvaux had stroked the back of his neck, a mannerism Tweed recalled when the Belgian was worked up.

'Now you have to tell me everything,' Tweed had lashed out in a cold voice. 'But first we must find a room inside where we can talk – after the listening devices have been removed.'

'I agree,' Delvaux had responded. 'They will know the devices have been tampered with – but I am now resigned to the fact that my wife Lucie is dead. I am going to hit back . . .'

They had laid Andover's body on a couch in the hall – after Paula had insisted on fetching a cushion for the head. The back of the skull was crushed in and bloody. She didn't want a blood-stained couch left to remind Delvaux of the murder on his doorstep every time he was crossing the hall.

Thirty minutes later Paula was satisfied they had traced every bug. Tweed said something about making assurance doubly sure. He switched on a radio which was playing a programme of classical music, then he turned on a tap.

'Even if you've missed one,' he told Paula, 'they will never be able to filter our conversation out of both the music and running water . . .'

Paula found that no one had eaten for hours. While Tweed talked with Delvaux and Newman perched on stools round the island unit she prepared food and drink. In a larder she found crusty rolls in a crock. Butter and ham were in the fridge. The larder had also contained coffee.

She made coffee in a cafetiere while slicing ham, cutting the rolls, buttering them, slapping ham inside. She passed round a large plate of the rolls, poured coffee into large mugs. Her customers began devouring the rolls and drinking large quantities of coffee. Tweed noticed the nourishment was stimulating Delvaux. He began probing.

'Gaston, your wife had been kidnapped. No ransom was demanded. You were forced to go into retirement. The same thing happened with Andover – but it was his

185

daughter who was kidnapped.' He paused. It might help prepare Delvaux for the worst. 'They sent him her severed arm . . .'

'I know,' Delvaux nodded. 'Andover told me.'

'What he couldn't tell you – and thankfully I delayed telling him – is that his daughter's body was later dragged out of the sea. Who are these murdering swine?'

'I don't know . . .'

'But you must know what it is about.'

'I think it's about Stealth . . .'.

Dr Wand sat in his luxury suite on the third floor of the Bellevue Palace Hotel on the equivalent of Park Lane in Brussels – the Avenue Louise. The only other occupant in the spacious room was his dark-haired, uniformed chauffeur, who still work dark glasses and sat behind a desk. He had just poured his employer a good measure of Napoleon brandy. Wand was swirling the liquid in the glass when the phone rang.

'Be so good as to answer that,' Wand requested.

The chauffeur picked up the gold receiver. He asked the caller to identify herself and she gave him a code-name.

'It's her,' the chauffeur reported.

'Then perhaps' – Wand checked the time on his Rolex – 'you would pass the phone to me, please.

'Yes,' he said into the mouthpiece, 'you have progress to report?'

'The first consignment has been dispatched to its ultimate destination,' the woman's voice told him. 'I emphasize ultimate.'

'And there were no problems, I trust?'

'Nothing I couldn't handle,' the woman assured him.

'Splendid. I congratulate you. What a pleasure to know someone who is always reliable. I will see you then. At the agreed time, at the agreed place. So, thank you for calling.'

The chauffeur was on hand to take away the phone. Wand swirled the liquid in the glass he had continued to hold in his large, right hand. Cognac needed warming and Wand was a very particular man. He glanced up at the chauffeur through his gold pince-nez, pursed his lips, twisted them into his cold smile.

'Very satisfactory,' he remarked. 'Most satisfactory indeed.' He swallowed some of the brandy. He had been referring to the execution of Sir Gerald Andover.

Not a dozen yards from the entrance to the Bellevue Palace Marler sat parked in his hired Mercedes. He was eating the last of three ham rolls purchased from a nearby café. Perched on the small platform beside him behind the gear lever was a cylindrical carton of coffee.

Marler felt pretty sure that would be the extent of his dinner for the night. Earlier he had used the car phone to call a Brussels number. A rough voice had answered in French. Speaking the same language, Marler had indicated in a roundabout way that he required one Armalite rifle and plenty of ammo.

There had been the usual haggle over price after Marler had identified himself as Charlie – the name known from previous transactions to the illegal supplier of guns. Marler had explained where he would wait for five minutes at an agreed time. No point in letting such a character know he expected to be staying there for hours.

He had the engine running when a shabbily dressed hulk of a Belgian appeared carrying a large, equally shabby, briefcase. Marler lowered the window but kept the door – which was locked – closed. The Belgian giant looked round the deserted street, leaned down, and his breath smelt of garlic as he spoke in French.

'The money first, my friend.'

'Not until I've checked the merchandise.'

Marler had shown the Belgian a handful of notes rolled up in his left hand.

'Then switch off your engine.'

'I'm in a hurry,' Marler snapped.

But he switched off the motor, held up the key, and dropped it on the seat beside him. The briefcase was passed in through the window. Inside was a dismantled Armalite rifle. With expert and swift movements Marler assembled the weapon. Keeping it below the level of the window he pulled the trigger. It was in excellent shape and there was a generous supply of ammo in the case. He counted out a large number of thousand-franc notes, rolled them into a wad, passed them to the Belgian. The roll disappeared inside a pocket as the giant slouched off, vanishing down an alleyway.

Marler had then started up the engine, had driven to the end of the Avenue Louise where it met the Place Louise. He performed a complicated manoeuvre and drove back the way he had come, glancing down the alley, which was deserted. It was just a precaution in case the giant had taken it into his head to spy on him.

He had then parked in the same place. It took him no time to dismantle the rifle, to put it back inside the briefcase. He was glad he'd taken care to buy a carton of coffee with a tight lid. It was rolling on the floor.

That had taken place some time before. And earlier still he had followed Dr Wand's limousine from Zaventem Airport to this extremely expensive hotel. What had puzzled him then – and still did – was that the chauffeur had handed over the car to a porter to drive it into the underground garage.

The chauffeur had accompanied Dr Wand into the hotel and had not reappeared since. Which made Marler wonder whether the chauffeur was far more important than he had thought him to be.

'Can you explain in layman's language how this Stealth technique works?' Tweed asked in the kitchen of the Château Orange. 'An American scientist was going to tell us but she became unavailable.'

'I had one of the top American scientists working on the project here to visit me about three years ago,' Delvaux recalled. 'A brilliant man – Professor Crown from the Northrop plant at Palmdale, California. He was not only applying the technique to aircraft but also to ships. I found we were working on exactly the same lines.'

'How did you know about each other's work?' asked Paula.

'Oh, there's a confidential international grapevine. We co-operate with each other. But I'll come back to that later.'

'How does Stealth *work*?' Tweed prodded.

Absorbed in his own subject, Delvaux became positively voluble. Words tumbled out and his eyes were glazed in concentration.

'Have you got some English coins? I need one to demonstrate my point.' Paula opened a section of her purse, handed him a collection. 'That's the one I was after,' Delvaux continued. He held up a gleaming fivepenny coin. 'I hear it's not liked – so easy to lose. Now take the American B2 Stealth bomber. It's quite enormous – a wingspan of one hundred and eighty-nine feet, seventeen feet high. Normally a plane with such a huge wingspan would show up on radar about the size of this fivepenny piece. Which is a *very* big image. Flying towards hostile territory it would be picked up immediately. Now guess the size of the radar image of the Stealth bomber. I'll tell you. About the size of a pin-head, if that.

The B2 could slip through any radar defence, under any satellite system on earth. We are talking about a bomber which is totally *invisible*.'

'Sounds deadly,' Newman commented.

'It is. No defence against it. No antidote. Imagine the payload of bombs a machine that size can carry.'

'But why can't it be spotted?' Tweed insisted.

'Partly a question of shape. It looks like a gigantic manta ray – so thin. But that is backed up by applying special coatings to the machine of a certain material. The coatings create fake reflections back to any rader, breaking up those reflections into tiny waves which are meaningless to the radar. Its own radar uses a laser device to make it undetectable by other planes. On top of that the jet engines are concealed inside the slim structure. And on top of that a diffuser mingles cool air with the exhaust gases – so the plane can't even be detected by satellite heat sensors. There's just nothing in the design any defence system can lock on to. I repeat, this enormous machine is invisible.'

'Sounds frightening to me,' Paula commented. 'But why does Stealth affect what happened to Andover, what is happening to you?'

'Let us take Andover first,' Delvaux went on precisely. He seemed to have forgotten temporarily the terror of his own situation. 'We must be logical, take the factors in their correct sequence. Andover is the great world authority on geopolitics – a global outlook on politics and warfare. His mentor was Professor Haushofer . . .'

'Who?' Paula queried.

'Professor Haushofer was the expert on geopolitics in his time. The close confidant of Adolf Hitler. And Hitler absorbed his views. By mentor, I mean Andover studied the views of Haushofer, long since dead. He then developed his own theory adapted to present world conditions today. He predicted the new great menace to the

190

West would come from the East – and not Russia.'

'But how does this link up with Stealth?' Tweed asked.

'The new enemy – potentially the most powerful Europe and America have faced yet – has, Andover suspected, acquired through devious means the know-how to build a fleet of Stealth bombers . . .'

'Three American scientists working on the project – including Professor Crown – have been kidnapped,' Tweed told him. 'About three years ago. It is believed they were taken to Hong Kong.'

'Which confirms Andover's theory . . .' Delvaux was in full flood. 'I have little doubt that those three American scientists, forced to direct a team of reasonably competent technicians, could supervise the building of a Stealth bomber fleet. Three years ago, you said? They probably have Stealth bombers now . . .'

'You mentioned Professor Crown was adapting the Stealth technique to ships,' Tweed intervened.

He was anxious to obtain every item of information as swiftly as possible. It was only a matter of time before Delvaux's sudden burst of energy ran out of steam.

'Yes,' the Belgian agreed, 'Crown was a marine specialist. Oddly enough he was working on the same research aspect as me. How to adapt Stealth to ships.'

'And how is that done?' asked Newman.

Perched on a stool, he had a notebook in his lap below the level of the counter. He was surreptitiously recording what Delvaux was saying.

'Again there are basically two problems to overcome. The *shape* of the average ship – easily registered by radar. And the exhaust from the vessel's engines – exhaust easily detected by satellite heat sensors. So we have designed a ship with a very low profile – almost like that of a semi-submerged submarine, but without the prominent conning tower. You want the details – in simplified language?'

'Yes, we do,' urged Tweed.

'The propellers at the stern have an exceptionally low noise level. The funnel is constructed so it hardly projects above the low deck level. In addition, it is equipped with a cooled exhaust system – like the bomber. It has a retractable mast – like the automatic radio aerial on a car which retracts completely inside the chassis of the vehicle. Its radar system is also constructed so it hardly projects above the surface of the deck. The hull has a rounded profile to reduce to nothing the normal radar and infra-red signatures it would emit. And missile launchers can be built inside the bow.'

'An ordinary ship needs a bridge,' Tweed pointed out.

'That also has been dealt with. A Stealth ship has both command and weapons control centres below decks. So, we have an invisible ship. A fleet of invisible ships – if the enemy establishes a conveyor-belt system of production like that American shipbuilder did on the West Coast of the States during the Second World War. What was his name? I have it. Kaiser. The Liberty ships.'

'You're scaring the daylights out of me,' Tweed commented. 'And I think you said there was no antidote earlier. No way of detecting Stealth bombers and ships. While I remember it, why is your plant working non-stop, apparently at all hours?'

'You are quick, Tweed. Very quick. I said there *was* no antidote. Past tense. So why do you think I take the risk of working my factories on three shifts twenty-four hours a day?'

The phone was ringing again in Dr Wand's suite at the Bellevue Palace. The chauffeur answered it, handed the phone to his boss.

'It's the lady again, sir. Anne-Marie . . .'

'It always gives me pleasure to hear from you,' Wand began. 'Such an enchanting voice. You have a problem?'

'I am sorry to disturb you. Could you take down this phone number?'

'Of course. One moment.'

Wand extracted a thin morocco-bound notebook from his pocket. He held a slim gold pencil poised.

'I am ready.'

'The number is—. A public phone box, Place Louise. May I call you there in fifteen minutes?'

'I will most certainly be there waiting . . .'

Wand understood exactly what that meant. Some information his caller did not wish to pass through a hotel switchboard. Night operators were notorious for passing the boring hours by listening in.

Five minutes later he emerged from the Bellevue Palace, making a remark to the doorman that he needed a breath of night air. Proceeding on foot down the Avenue Louise in his dark overcoat he walked with the chauffeur on his right towards the Place Louise.

Inside his parked Mercedes Marler reacted swiftly. He rammed on his fair hair a beret he'd purchased from a shop next door to the bar after buying sandwiches and coffee. He was now wearing a shabby windcheater earlier taken from his travelling case. Stubbing out his half-smoked king-size, he tucked the remaining half at the corner of his mouth. He hadn't shaved for hours and his chin was covered with a prominent stubble. It was a very disreputable-looking Marler who followed the two men, slouching along on the opposite pavement.

Reaching the Place Louise, very quiet at that hour, Dr Wand checked the time by his Rolex, an action noted by Marler. He also noticed that the chauffeur had tucked his right hand inside his uniformed jacket. Marler had little doubt he was clutching a gun.

The two men walked across the Place Louise to the Boulevard de Waterloo. Arriving at the entrance to the metro, they disappeared down inside it. Marler followed, stepped on the moving escalator. At the bottom he was just in time to see the two men moving down a second escalator.

He waited a few seconds before he stepped on it himself. As he was carried down deeper he passed a series of crude and bizarre wall murals. He wrinkled his nose. Belgian art! At the bottom of the second escalator he entered the main Metro complex. Against a wall a slovenly man was seated on the floor, his back to the wall, his legs sprawled out.

Close by was a row of phone booths. Dr Wand entered one, paused a moment, came out, entered the next one. Marler realized he was checking the numbers. Wand stayed inside the third one, made no attempt to use the phone. The chauffeur stood outside, staring in the opposite direction.

Marler sagged against the wall, spread out his own legs, the fag protruding from his mouth, still unlit. The slovenly man called out to him in French in a stage whisper.

'Got a joint, mate?'

'Shut up or I'll stick a knife in your gullet,' Marler hissed back.

The phone rang inside the booth. Dr Wand picked up the instrument. He spoke immediately in his slow, deliberate manner.

'Who is this speaking, may I ask?'

'Anne-Marie,' a woman's voice answered, using the code-name. 'I am sorry to trouble you in this way. Later I remembered something I thought you'd wish to know. In the headlights of my car I saw a competitor.'

'Then you were most wise to call me, most wise. Price is a major consideration with the contract we are bidding for. So it is important we know who are our competitors.'

'Tweed is the competitor.'

Dr Wand was silent. He had received a shock, a

194

surprise. One thing Wand did not like were surprises. They were dangerous.

'Are you still there?' the woman's voice asked.

'I really am very sorry. I was thinking how we should go about countering this competition. We may have to employ robust measures. Yes . . . robust. Let me think on it. And I look forward to seeing you soon. Thank you so much for calling . . .'

Through half-closed eyes Marler watched Wand walk towards him with the chauffeur. They glanced at the sprawled junkie to Marler's left but never spared even a glance in his direction. Marler had the impression Dr Wand was disturbed: his thin lips were pressed tightly together.

Waiting until they had disappeared up the lower escalator, Marler scrambled to his feet, followed them at a distance. They had crossed the place and had just reached the Avenue Louise when Wand reached under his coat into his back pocket, and taking out a silk handkerchief mopped his forehead.

At that moment a macho motorcyclist raced down the boulevard with a deafening burst of speed. In taking out the handkerchief Wand had dropped his wallet. They walked on and Marler realized that the motorcyclist had muffled the sound of the wallet hitting the pavement. He picked it up.

Leaning against a wall, he waited until he had seen the two men go back inside the Bellevue Palace. He then slipped inside a doorway alcove, put on surgical gloves, checked the contents of the wallet.

It contained a fat wad of 10,000-franc notes. And one note was worth over £150. What interested him most were the business cards. All embossed with *Dr Wand, Director, Moonglow Refugee Aid Trust International*. No address.

Marler was careful to replace everything as he had found it. Taking off the gloves, he shoved them into his

195

pocket, bent down to the grubby floor, rubbed one hand in the dirt and smeared it all over his stubble. He had changed its colour and made himself look even more like a no-good.

Five minutes later he walked inside the Bellevue Palace, followed by a protesting doorman. He went straight up to the reception counter and addressed the night clerk in French.

'One of your guests just dropped this wallet. I want the Assistant Manager.'

'I can take charge of that . . .'

'You deaf or something? Get me the bloody Assistant Manager . . .'

A small portly man in a formal black suit came over to the counter. His fat face expressed extreme distaste.

'What is going on, Jacques?'

'This is the Assistant Manager,' Jacques informed Marler. He turned to his superior. 'This man has . . .'

'All right! All right! I'll tell him,' Marler snapped. 'Sir, one of your guests dropped this wallet in the street. He's just come in with a chauffeur.'

The manager examined the wallet. His eyebrows rose when he saw the wad of money. He looked at Marler.

'There could be a reward . . .'

'No reward. Don't want no reward.' Marler was backing to the door. 'I'm just out on probation. I'm not taking a franc . . .'

He was gone before the manager could recover from his surprise. He walked past his parked car and then looked back. No one in sight: not even the doorman. He unlocked his car, slipped behind the wheel, closed and locked the door.

He spent the next few minutes using wet-wipes from a container in the glove compartment to clean his face. Then he finished the job, using a handkerchief to brush away any remnant of wet-wipe that might be clinging to his stubble.

Marler felt it had been a very successful outing. He now

196

knew positively he was tracking Dr Wand. And he had the photos of him taken at the long-term garage back at London Airport. What Marler didn't realize was he possessed the only photographs of Dr Wand ever taken.

20

Beyond the entrance to the Hilton on the Boulevard de Waterloo the reception counter stretches away to the right. It faces a huge sitting area furnished with comfortable chairs and small tables.

After dinner Brigadier Burgoyne was sitting upright in an armchair. Opposite him sat Willie Fanshawe and Helen Claybourne. Lee Holmes was stroking her long blonde hair as she settled herself in her own chair.

'You've been away a damned long time,' Burgoyne observed.

'Just to the powder room,' Lee replied. She smiled wickedly at the Brigadier. 'Women to tend to linger in a powder room. They're making themselves presentable for their men.'

Burgoyne grunted. He looked very smart in a blue pin-striped suit. Willie, as always, looked crumpled although also wearing a suit: his plump bulk made it impossible for him to keep any suit decent for more than a few days.

Both men had a glass of Grand Marnier which Burgoyne had paid for. Willie's income was a fraction of the Brigadier's. Helen, wearing a pleated white blouse with a mandarin collar and a navy blue skirt, studied Lee. The blonde was clad in an off-the-shoulder purple dress slit to her thigh. You do like to display your assets, she thought. Instead she said: 'Is your business trip proving successful, Brigadier?'

'Of course it is,' Willie broke in cheerfully, leaning forward. 'He's arming the world . . .'

'Do keep your voice down,' Burgoyne snapped. 'You came at your own urging.'

'We did? My recollection is you suggested we join the party. And don't think we're not having the time of our lives, because we are. That's so, isn't it, Helen?'

'The time of our lives,' Helen repeated in a neutral tone.

'I think,' Lee intervened, 'we ought to amuse ourselves. What about a game of poker?' She looked at Burgoyne. 'I'm going to take the pants off you.'

'I wouldn't mind taking the pants off you,' Willie told her and chuckled.

'Don't be coarse,' Helen scolded him. Willie had had a lot to drink. Lee was producing a pack of cards out of her large Gucci handbag. 'I think we ought to set a limit if we're playing for money,' Helen went on firmly.

'Of course we're playing for money,' Willie chattered on. 'What else is there to play for? I remember in Hong Kong we often stayed up all hours and . . .'

'Willie,' Helen interrupted, 'Lee has dealt the cards.'

'Of course. Sorry, my dear . . .'

Four heads bent over, studying their hands. Lee glanced up. Silence had descended. She had achieved her objective. Unusually for her, Lee didn't feel like talking.

'I have been working on an antidote to Stealth for months,' Delvaux explained in the kitchen of the Château Orange. 'The work was speeded up since my wife was kidnapped. It kept me from going crazy with anxiety.'

'I admire your concentration,' Tweed remarked. 'How far have you got?'

198

'I have solved the problem. The whole history of warfare is based on the invention of counter-measures. The tank was followed by the creation of the anti-tank gun. The fighter plane compelled us to invent the ground-to-air missile . . .' Paula watched, fascinated, as Delvaux spilt out the words non-stop. 'So Stealth has driven me to invent a radar system – the most advanced in the world – which can actually *see*, register on the screen, the presence of a Stealth bomber or ship. And that is why my plant is working night and day. Come, let me show you something.'

Delvaux trotted over to the large fridge, the first time Tweed had seen him move normally. Opening it, he pointed to a modest-sized tin.

'What is that?'

'A tin of biscuits,' Paula answered, mystified.

'That is what it is *intended* to look like. In fact, it is a specially designed container impervious to extremes of heat or cold and which can be dropped without damaging at all the delicate instrument inside.'

Taking out the tin, he placed it on a table, prised off the lid, stood back and gestured. Tweed, Newman, and Paula peered inside. The walls were lined with some kind of protective material. Delvaux reached into the tin, carefully lifted out an intricate mechanism. The only part Paula recognized was what appeared to be a large circular TV-like screen. Delvaux then extracted a thick bound file.

'None of you will understand the file,' Delvaux warned. 'But hand it to one of your radar boffins and he will at once understand how the system works. Tweed, please take this with you back to London. Arrange for a fleet of trucks with armed men to travel to my works. We will load them with a large number of these devices. Have you a card?'

Tweed produced one of his cards printed with only his

name and General & Cumbria Assurance. Delvaux took it, extracted a pen from his pocket, underlined the 'T' of Tweed, showed it to him, then slipped it into his own wallet.

'All the drivers of those trucks must carry such a card. It will identify them to my General Manager, Alain Flamand. I will write that down for you. Another card. So the drivers deal only with Alain Flamand. He practically lives at the plant. Now, I have designed an executive-style case which just takes the biscuit tin.'

Packing the mechanism inside the biscuit tin, he opened a drawer under the table, laid an executive case on top, slipped the tin inside the case, closed it, handed it to Tweed.

Tweed had secreted the card with Alain Flamand's name written in Delvaux's neat hand inside his wallet. He lifted the executive case and was surprised at its lightness. His expression was grim as he put it on the table.

'Thank you, Gaston. A feeble way of congratulating you on what you have achieved – and under the nerve-breaking conditions you are suffering. But we now have to think of Andover's body. The police – Benoit – must be told.'

'I suppose they must,' Delvaux said slowly.

Paula watched him crumble. The brisk vigour with which he had been speaking dissolved. The terror had returned. He held out his hands in a helpless gesture.

'Then the kidnappers will know . . .'

'Listen to me!' Tweed gripped his arm. '*Think!* The men – or man – masterminding this hideous business know Andover has been murdered. Because they planned it. So they will expect a police ambulance to arrive to take away poor Andover's body. Benoit will be discreet, I promise you.'

'But the listening devices you have removed from here?'

'Can you put them back exactly where you found them?' Tweed asked Paula.

'Yes, we can. Come on, Bob. Back to work . . .'

She took a dishcloth, damped it slightly under the running tap. Each bug had a rubber sucker used to attach it to wherever it was placed. For the next half-hour she worked with Newman's help, damping a sucker, pressing it against the surface precisely where she had found it. Delvaux had collapsed into a chair long before she had finished the job. Climbing down from the ladder, she put it back where she had found it.

'Everyone keeps quiet from now on,' Tweed whispered. He tapped Delvaux on the shoulder. 'Time to phone Benoit. We are going to turn off the tap and the radio. Tell Benoit an English friend, Sir Gerald Andover, called on you – a professional colleague and an old friend. He came to warn you his daughter had been killed. Did he know about your wife?'

'Yes, I told him after he arrived here . . .'

'And he phoned you from England earlier after Irene, his daughter, had been kidnapped.'

'But he didn't . . .'

'Say he did. It establishes an iron-clad reason for him to come and see you. There must be *no* mention of the real subject – Stealth. Have you got it?'

'Yes. It's simple – close to the truth. Only the timing was different,' Delvaux continued, whispering.

'And you tell him about me. About Paula and Newman. We suspected the same hideous technique was being employed on you. Luckily I was the one who found your letter to Andover – on his mantelpiece at *Prevent*. The letter in which you said you had solved the technical problem. By the way, how did you solve it?'

'Oh, from my researches, we built a Stealth light aircraft inside the works. I used the most advanced – at that time – radar and none of the available equipment detected it. So I analysed why – that involved complicated mathematical equations and the development of a theory. Laser is one element in the new apparatus you have in that case, but only one . . .'

'Now!' Tweed pounced. 'Repeat what you are going to tell Benoit. And not as though you've learned it by heart . . .'

While explaining about the Stealth light aircraft Delvaux had spoken briskly. Paula found it pathetic to hear him relapse into his broken state as he repeated the story he had to tell. Tweed had the same reaction, but was also relieved – his story would be that much more convincing.

'Everybody else keeps quiet until we're out of the château,' Tweed warned again.

He switched off the radio, turned off the running water.

Paula had already cleaned and put away the crockery they had used, leaving out only Delvaux's. Otherwise Benoit might wonder why they had spent so much time there.

Delvaux phoned Benoit's headquarters in Brussels. He was told that as it was an urgent matter his call would be passed on to Chief Inspector Benoit immediately. It was possible he might arrive at the château very quickly.

Tweed patted the Belgian on the shoulder to indicate he had done well. To his surprise, as they walked across the hall Delvaux, snatching a coat from a cupboard, followed them outside.

'I can't wait in there alone.'

'You must get back inside soon. Benoit might fly here by helicopter.'

Tweed was worried, knowing that Benoit was in the vicinity. It was a fact he thought it best Delvaux did not know. They walked down the drive and Newman, remembering what had happened to Andover, put out an arm to make them stay still.

'I'll just check,' he said.

Holding his Smith & Wesson in both hands, he darted across the road, paused on the grass verge, listening, looking both ways. Then he approached the Mercedes cautiously. Only when he had checked the underside of the chassis with a pencil flashlight and looked at the engine was he satisfied. He went back and beckoned for them to cross.

He started the engines and switched on the heaters – the interior of the car was like an icebox. Delvaux sat in the back with Tweed while Paula occupied the front passenger seat next to Newman.

'Something very important I forgot to tell you,' Delvaux said suddenly. 'Hugo Westendorf in Germany was a member of INCOMSIN. Somehow the refugee problem is mixed up in all this.'

Two uniformed policemen were patrolling the dubious Marolles district of Brussels. Marolles lies behind the immense bulk of the Palace of Justice and is only a five-minute walk from the Hilton.

Both men were alert: it was not an area to go to sleep in. They peered into a bar. Marc, the younger, swivelled his eyes swiftly over the customers. No one 'known' to the police. They walked on, came to the entrance to a narrow cobbled street.

Armand, the older, paused, frowned. A few paces into the street a black Mercedes taxi was parked. He unfastened the flap of the holster on his right hip, making it easy to grab the butt of his pistol.

'Marc, might as well take a look. I think that cab is empty. Taxis don't park round here.'

His colleague had a pair of handcuffs and a truncheon slung from his belt on his left hip. His right hand was holding a walkie-talkie. They approached the car in the usual tactical manner – one man taking the right-hand side, the other the left. It was Armand who approached the driver's seat.

Marc noticed the sticker advertising a restaurant plastered across the rear window. Armand aimed his flashlight at the dashboard, saw the key in the ignition. He called out quietly to his colleague.

'Very odd. An empty cab and the key in the ignition.'

'Except it isn't empty.'

Marc had opened the rear door. The cab driver was bent over in a huddled position so he couldn't easily be seen by a casual passer-by. Armand opened the other rear door, aimed his flashlight. The driver's head rested on the floor, sightless eyes staring up in the beam of the flash.

'Call headquarters,' Armand ordered. 'We have something here which is going to raise all hell ... And that sticker is covering a bullet-hole in the rear window ...'

Inside the parked Mercedes across the road from the Château Orange Delvaux was shivering despite the fact that the heaters were quickly warming up the interior. Tweed knew he was on the verge of another collapse.

'What is this about the refugee problem being mixed up with this whole strange affair? Andover used the word 'catastrophe' to me. And how does Hugo Westendorf fit in?'

Tweed was hugely intrigued, although his manner was casual. Hugo Westendorf was – had been – a major player in the world of Western politics. He had been known as the Iron Man of Germany and – until recently – had held the post of Minister of the Interior. Suddenly, to everyone's surprise, he had resigned, pleading reasons of ill-health.

'Andover,' Delvaux continued, 'told us that a major part of the menace facing Western Europe was the tidal wave of refugees waiting on Poland's border to flood across the Oder–Neisse river line into Western Europe. He said they were being organized by the enemy.'

'You just said "us",' Tweed reminded him. 'Who does that mean?'

'Oh, Westendorf was here several times when he was Minister. He travelled to Herstal secretly – incognito – to attend meetings with Andover and myself. Westendorf was very strong on stopping those refugees, employing drastic methods.'

'You will have to leave soon and get back to the château before Benoit arrives,' Tweed warned.

Delvaux wasn't listening. 'And the terrible mistake the Americans have made is not to protect themselves against the Stealth threat. A move to save money – to help their economy. They are wide open to a horrendous attack.'

'I have heard that,' Tweed assured him. 'Now, you must go. At once, please. And remember, Benoit will be discreet.'

Delvaux opened the door slowly, as though reluctant to leave. He stood outside with the door still open while he pulled up his coat collar. Tweed leaned over to speak to him.

'Gaston, one important thing you haven't told me. That is, if you know the answer. Who is the new enemy?'

'Didn't I tell you? I thought I had. Andover – with his expertise on global power – had worked it out. And Westendorf agreed with him, completely.'

'Who?' Tweed pressed urgently.

'The most menacing force we have ever faced. Forget Hitler, forget Stalin. They were small beer, as you say in England. The new enemy is the People's Republic of China. Over a billion people, one-quarter of the world's population. Andover called them Fortress China – Communism which is economically successful. They read history.'

As he walked away, shoulders bowed, feet dragging,

across the road back to the château, Tweed looked at Paula. She had twisted round to stare at him.

'Yes, I had wondered,' Tweed said grimly. 'And Dr Wand is Director of Moonglow Refugee Aid Trust International. It is all coming together, the vague pattern which has been building in my mind. You remember the extracts from Andover's file I read out to you?'

'Which bit?'

Tweed quoted from memory. ' "In 1214 Jenghis Khan, the leader of the Mongol confederation . . . turned westward, conquered Western Turkestan, Persia, Armenia . . . and south Russia as far as Hungary and Silesia . . . His successor, Ogdai Khan, continued this astonishing career of conquest . . . a mixed army of the Poles and Germans was annihilated at the battle of Liegnitz . . ." And I pointed out Liegnitz is no more than two hundred and fifty miles from Hamburg.'

'So the Mongols are coming?'

'The People's Republic of China this time . . .'

21

'There's been a murder of a cab driver in Brussels.'

Chief Inspector Benoit made the statement as he was driving Tweed and Paula from the château to Liège railway station at breakneck speed. Paula sat beside him while Tweed was occupying the rear with the unmarked police car's driver.

'We can just catch the express,' Benoit had decided after spending half an hour with Gaston Delvaux on his own. He had earlier been intercepted by Tweed when he arrived and before he could enter the Château Orange.

Tersely, Tweed had explained the situation. He had told Benoit about the kidnapping of Lucie, Delvaux's wife – but had omitted all reference to Stealth and Hugo Westendorf.

'I'll be discreet,' Benoit had promised before following the ambulance up the drive. 'And hand-picked men will watch the château from a distance . . .'

This outcome had been inevitable: Andover's murder on Belgian soil dictated that the police must take over the case. Benoit had checked train times, had shown relief when he realized they could return by fast train.

'I've had enough of travelling in a car for one day,' he explained.

'So why are you behind the wheel now?' Paula chivvied him mischievously. 'When you have a perfectly good driver behind us?'

'Oh, Jean is cautious. I drive like a madman – I used to do a bit of race-driving.'

'I can see that,' she commented as he swung round one of the bends practically on two wheels.

'What about this murdered cab driver they informed you about over your car phone?' Tweed called out.

'Well, you said this car which mowed down Andover was a black Mercedes taxi. Two uniformed men found his body inside the same type of vehicle abandoned in Marolles – behind the Palais de Justice. Paula told me she fired one shot through the rear window. The cab they found has one bullet-hole in the rear window. Draw your own conclusions.'

'Would it be possible for me to have a word with the policemen who found it? And even see the body?' Tweed suggested.

'You and I can go to the morgue where they've taken the body. The policemen have been told to wait there for me.'

207

'I'd like to come too,' said Paula.

Benoit grinned at her. 'A moment ago you suppressed a yawn. Now the lady wants to see a corpse.'

'I've been with Tweed since this business started. I'm not going to miss anything now.'

'The lady has stamina,' Benoit said, and grinned again.

'Flattery will get you nowhere,' Paula shot back.

'Have you any idea how this cab driver was murdered?' enquired Tweed.

'It was only a brief message. Maybe we'll know when we get there . . .' Benoit shrugged.

'If we do reach Liège station alive,' Paula needled him.

Which was not entirely fair. It was only on traffic-free stretches that Benoit rammed his foot to the floor. Now they were threading their way through the dank gloomy streets of Liège Benoit was driving slowly, despite his frequent glances at the dashboard clock. The cobbled streets had a greasy, sweaty look, and as Benoit pulled up in front of the station and Paula stepped out the same appetizing smells of cheap fast-food stalls assailed her nostrils.

Benoit collected their bags from the boot, his portly figure moving at great speed as they rushed for the train. The express was standing by the platform and moved off the moment they had jumped aboard into an empty first-class coach.

Benoit sat opposite Paula while Tweed sat alone, also in a corner seat, staring out into the night as the express raced west. Glancing across at him, Paula guessed his mind was racing as fast as the express. Benoit leant forward.

'I have arranged for a car to meet us at Midi station. First stop, the morgue. Are you sure you want to come with us?'

'Quite sure. But thanks for asking again. Later we can go back to the Hilton.'

'Which is not so far from where the cab driver's body was found,' Benoit said thoughtfully.

'I presume,' Tweed called across, 'that Andover's remains will eventually be sent home to the address I gave you?'

'But certainly,' the Belgian agreed. 'That is, after the pathologist has examined the body. It is the law.'

'Was that all the ambulance contained?'

'No.' Benoit paused. 'Delvaux showed me his wife's hand in the chest freezer. I persuaded him it must be sent to the pathologist in the same ambulance. What sort of people are we dealing with? Psychopaths?'

'We are dealing with a man of exceptional intelligence and not even an atom of humanity – a man working to a plan, if my theory is right.'

'What plan is that?'

'The élite of Western Europe are being targeted. The plan is to break their spirit, to remove them from any position of influence – to use fiendish psychological methods to turn brilliant men into useless wrecks – both mentally and physically. Especially mentally. How long ago is it since Hugo Westendorf resigned as German Minister of the Interior?'

'About three months or so,' Benoit replied. 'Surely you don't suspect . . .'

'I don't suspect anything. Like you, I deal only in facts. But the timing is right.'

'I could get in touch with Chief Inspector Kuhlmann of the Criminal Police in Wiesbaden.'

'I would greatly appreciate it if you didn't do that under any circumstances,' Tweed said.

'Then I will not do it . . .'

'But what I would like you to do is to ask your pathologist to concentrate first on examining Lucie's severed hand. As a matter of top priority.'

'I can – will – do that. May I ask why?'

'You just did.' Tweed smiled. 'I want to know whether your pathologist considers only a top-flight surgeon could have carried out that amputation.'

'You're going to track them through him,' Paula said.

'I am going to work night and day on every possible lead. There is something enormously menacing behind all this. It could well be a race against time.'

'What about Newman?' Benoit asked. 'He said he would see you in Brussels.'

'He has the car. At this moment he will be driving at top speed through the night. He drives like you, Benoit. So, he might just be waiting for us at Midi.'

'I doubt that,' Benoit said.

They fell silent and Paula closed her eyes as the train stopped at Leuven, then thundered on west again. Tweed had his eyes wide open. He seems tireless, thought Benoit. The pace of his investigation is accelerating.

The morgue was noticeably colder than even the outside world. A white-coated man with greying hair and an authoritative manner, introduced as Dr Leclerc, glanced at Paula and then at Benoit.

'It's all right,' Benoit reassured him in French, 'Miss Grey has seen dead bodies before. You might say it is part of her job.'

Behind Benoit and Paula stood Tweed and Newman, who had been waiting for them in his hired Mercedes when they'd arrived at Midi. Leclerc, a small, well-built man wearing rimless glasses, pulled out one of the rows of large metal drawers. A sheet covered what lay inside. Tweed and Newman stood on one side while Paula joined Benoit on the other. Leclerc drew back the sheet. Paula stifled a gasp. She looked across at Tweed, spoke in French.

'Cyanosis.'

210

'The lady has had some experience,' Leclerc remarked. 'I have not started work yet but the cause of death does appear rather obvious, subject to my examination.'

The cab driver's lips were blue. His whole bony face had a bluish tinge. Paula bent forward, peering at the side of the neck.

'Come round here, Tweed. I think you can see where the fatal needle was inserted.'

'Again the lady is correct,' Leclerc agreed.

Tweed bent down alongside Paula. A small reddish bruise disfigured the side of the neck. Paula was frowning. Tweed caught her expression.

'Yes?'

'That's an odd place to reach easily. I suppose from the back seat his passenger could have inserted her instrument, but it seems unlikely. The driver would see it coming. On the other hand, suppose she pretended to take a liking to him, put her arms round his neck, one hand concealing the needle – in whatever form it is disguised. During the embrace the driver would be off his guard. Then would be the moment she could press in the needle.'

'You think the murderer was a woman?' Leclerc sounded surprised.

'Just an idea,' Paula replied evasively.

'But possibly the right one,' Benoit intervened. 'Tweed, you wanted to interview the two policemen who found the cab driver. They are in the next room.' He noticed Leclerc had raised his eyebrows at the suggestion. 'Tweed,' he explained, 'was once the youngest Superintendent of Homicide at Scotland Yard.'

'That was a little while ago,' Tweed said wryly. 'Now, I would like to see those two men . . .'

Benoit took them all, leaving behind Leclerc, into a small office further along the corridor leading to the morgue. Two uniformed men stood up. Benoit made introductions, using the men's first names, Armand and Marc, and told them to answer Tweed's questions.

'Have you had time,' Tweed asked, addressing Armand, who seemed to be the senior, 'to contact the cab company, to check the mileage on the clock?'

'Yes, sir. It was my first thought. Most cabbies spend their time doing local jobs – to one of the stations, to a restaurant or hotel. Short distances. This cab had been driven a long distance.'

'Could it have travelled to the Liège area and back?'

Armand thought for a moment. 'Yes, sir, it could. The gas tank was almost empty – but I'm going by the company records and the clock mileage.'

Tweed looked at Benoit. 'To me it seems conclusive. It was this cab which the murderer used to kill Andover. And there was a bullet-hole, you said, in the rear window which Paula fired through.'

'We found that bullet, sir,' Armand informed him. 'It was embedded in the rear of the front passenger seat. And it was within millimetres of penetrating the seat. If only it had struck the back of the driver's seat it might have got him . . .'

'Her,' the younger man, Marc, corrected.

'Why do you think it was a woman?' Tweed enquired.

'All the vehicle's windows were closed when we found it. And, incidentally, there are traces in the boot suggesting the body spent some time in there.'

'So why would it be moved?' Tweed pressed.

'We think we know,' Armand intervened. 'While it was being driven – to Liège, you suggested – the body would have to be concealed. But when the killer left the Mercedes in the Marolles some yobbo could quite easily have jemmied the boot open, hoping to find something worth taking. The body was jammed down inside the rear of the car. It was dark. So unless the door was opened it would appear empty.'

'And why do you think it was a woman?' Tweed persisted, turning to Marc.

'As I told Chief Inspector Benoit when he came to see us just before you visited the morgue, I am a non-smoker. I have an acute sense of smell. When I opened the rear door of the cab I immediately caught the aroma of a perfume – Guerlain Samsara.'

'And just how were you able to identify that particular perfume?' Tweed asked sceptically.

He was standing very erect, both hands shoved inside his coat pockets, staring straight at Marc. He suddenly realized his stance was exactly the same he'd adopted when interrogating a suspect at the Yard. Old habits died hard.

'Because,' Marc explained, 'I'd had a win at the casino in Ostend. I used some of my money to buy my girl friend a bottle of Guerlain Samsara. I should know that perfume now.'

'The cab driver could have picked up a previous passenger, a woman, before he encountered the murderer,' Tweed probed.

'I think not, sir. Samsara is a subtle perfume – expensive. Any woman passenger earlier would have opened the door to get out. She swings her legs out first – I have often observed this – and then she climbs out of the cab. With the door open even that amount of time the aroma would have gone.'

'I'm convinced. Thank you, Marc. In due course you will undoubtedly be promoted. You use your eyes as well as your nose.' He turned to Benoit. 'I think that is all. Except for that matter about the priority for Dr Leclerc.'

'Which I will tell him as soon as I have seen you off the premises. You would like an unmarked police car to take you to the Hilton?'

'I can drive them there,' Newman said.

Tweed shook hands with Benoit. It was the custom in

213

Belgium: when you met, when you departed, and on any other occasion when the opportunity presented itself.

'Now all we need,' Newman said when the bags had been transferred to his boot, 'is a woman who uses Guerlain Samsara.'

The first people Tweed noticed on entering the Hilton were Burgoyne, Lee Holmes, Fanshawe, and Helen Claybourne playing a game of cards. He wondered how Lee had travelled to Brussels.

'We want three executive rooms for two days,' he told the girl receptionist behind the counter. 'I believe there is a special reservation room for those on the twentieth floor.'

'No longer, sir. We do have the rooms but you register here. Chief Inspector Benoit phoned us.'

She asked for a credit card but Tweed paid in cash for the three rooms in advance: you can track a man's movements by tracing credit-card transactions, if you know how. Tweed, still clutching the executive case containing Delvaux's new radar system, then asked for a safety-deposit box.

The girl guided him round a corner at the end of the reception counter, pressed a button inside, let him into a glass cubicle. He closed the outer door, she opened the inner door and led him to the deposit room.

'For that case you will need our largest box . . .'

Attaching the key to his ring, Tweed thanked her, went outside where Paula and Newman were waiting. Paula came close, whispered.

'You've seen who is in the lounge area?'

'Yes. I think we should make their acquaintance later. What about dinner?'

'I'm beyond it. Ham sandwiches and coffee is all I can cope with.'

'Me too,' said Newman.

'Agreed. We're all on the twentieth floor. We'll meet by the lift up there. When, Paula?'

'I'm going to treat myself to a five-minute shower. A bath is too much effort . . .' They walked inside one of the elevators, the doors closed, the ascent began. 'I will be ready in ten minutes,' Paula decided. 'Time me . . .'

Tweed found he had Room 2009, a spacious room the size of a suite. After a swift wash and change of under-clothes, he switched off the lights, peered out behind the closed curtains. The view was panoramic – the enormous green dome surmounting the Palace of Justice seemed near enough to reach out and touch. A building larger than St Peter's in Rome. And Marolles is down there, he was thinking – where the murdered cab driver had been found. So close to the Hilton.

In his suite at the Bellevue Palace Dr Wand was working late. When the phone rang the chauffeur answered, handed him the instrument.

'Someone called Vulcan wishes to speak to you.'

'Yes,' Wand opened the conversation. 'You recognize my voice. What is it, please?'

Wand always kept his communications with Vulcan short. It was so important to keep his caller's identity secret.

'I thought you should know,' the voice said in English, 'that the Hilton has three new visitors. Your good friend, Tweed, Paula Grey, and Robert Newman, the foreign correspondent. Just in case you wished to have cocktails with them sometime.'

'Thank you so much for your call. I will think about it.'

Wand put down the phone. Vulcan had phrased the information carefully. Any switchboard operator listening in would not understand the implications.

Wand pursed his lips and did not smile. Watching him furtively, the chauffeur knew he was disturbed. And he was right.

Wand sat thinking, tapping a slow tattoo with his gold pencil. Tweed first in Liège and now in Brussels. He is coming too close, he thought. He picked up the phone and dialled a number from memory, a Brussels number. A woman with a working-class voice answered and Wand asked to speak to Dr Hyde.

'Hyde speaking. Who is this?' The voice was hoarse, and spoke in English. 'I said who is this?' Hyde repeated.

'You know who I am, my friend,' Wand replied. 'I think it might be wise if you moved to a hotel in Liège. It is possible you could have a patient requiring treatment. Either in Belgium or Germany. In the near future. Good-night . . .'

Handing the receiver to the chauffeur, Wand took out his slim notebook. He turned to the last page where he had noted down in pencil – easy to erase – twenty-five names. They comprised the élite of Western Europe – and there were few politicians. These were the men – and women – Wand feared might detect the plan. Operation Long Reach.

The first three names were Andover, Delvaux, Westendorf. He drew a line through Andover. Dealt with. He paused, his pencil poised. Then he inserted a fresh name after Westendorf. Tweed. Alongside the name he put a question mark. It was a little early to be sure whether Tweed should be subjected to treatment.

Brussels has three main stations, running roughly from east to west – towards the sea. Midi, Centrale and Nord. The undistinguished Hotel Hermitage was situated in a small side-street near Centrale station – not the most upper-crust section of Brussels.

Dr Carberry-Hyde – to give him his full name – was packing his case after receiving the phone call. A tall, heavily built man in his fifties, he had a permanent stoop from bending over patients' beds. He had a large head, a hooked nose, thinning grey hair above a tall forehead. Clean shaven, he possessed a perfect set of teeth which he often showed when he smiled at nervous patients. It was not a sincere smile and never reached the eyes behind rimless glasses: he assumed it for his bedside manner.

Dr Hyde wondered whether Liège would offer him the same facilities for relaxation as Brussels: he doubted it. He had recently returned from a certain street where the company of an attractive girl could be obtained for money – rather a lot of money.

He opened a smaller case. Neatly arranged inside were his surgical instruments. He picked up a scalpel and lovingly polished it. Dr Hyde was a man who enjoyed his work.

22

Tweed, Paula, and Newman walked out of the elevator on the ground floor and headed straight for the poker-playing quartet. Burgoyne was just sitting down again in his chair. Tweed, threading his way between tables, caught his words.

'Sorry about the interruption. Could do without business calls at this hour. In any case, the game is over. Lee has cleaned us out.'

In front of Lee was the hand she'd displayed. A Royal

Flush. Fanshawe jumped up, insisted that Paula took his chair. He began talking non-stop.

'What a coincidence. And what a pleasant one. Delighted to have your company. No, I'll get more chairs for our welcome guests. Yes, amazing coincidence. Last time it was the New Forest. Who'd have thought we'd have the pleasure of your company here in Brussels? Tweed, you sit here next to Lee. Rich woman. So just your cup of tea. You two will get on famously . . .'

Newman was helping Willie to bring more chairs. Tweed noticed Burgoyne hadn't stirred a muscle to give a hand. He introduced Newman to the party. Burgoyne then reacted with a barbed comment.

'The notorious foreign correspondent. Everyone will have to watch their words. We'll find ourselves reported in the national press.'

'I'm taking that as a joke.' Newman leaned forward towards the Brigadier. 'In case you hadn't heard, I retired.'

'So would I,' the Brigadier retorted, 'if I'd made the fortune you did out of that sensational bestseller you wrote. What was it now? *Kruger: The Computer That Failed.* Read it. Not bad. Must have made you a millionaire.'

'It depends on which currency you're talking about,' Newman countered.

'Why don't you two stop fencing and enjoy yourselves?' Lee remonstrated. 'This is supposed to be a fun party.'

'Then let's have some more to drink,' Burgoyne decided. 'More champagne?'

'Perfect,' Lee agreed. 'I have something to celebrate.'

'Then you ought to pay,' Burgoyne growled. He summoned a waiter with a beckoning gesture of his index finger. Just like summoning some poor squaddie in the officers' mess, Tweed thought. 'Two more bottles of Krug – same as last time,' Burgoyne specified.

Tweed took the opportunity to order ham sandwiches for three. And a glass of white wine for himself. He wanted a clear head for this gathering.

Paula was watching Lee. She had a pile of Belgian-franc notes in front of her. Methodically, she was sorting them into a neat pile. That girl likes money, Paula was thinking: there was an aura of pure delight in the way Lee handled the money, a considerable amount. She moved her chair closer to Tweed's, rested her bare arm against his sleeve. She turned to face him with a glowing smile.

'I'm paying for your order. Now, no argument. And when you've eaten please join me in a cognac.'

'Let's see how I feel later. It's a bit stuffy in here.'

'Then if you feel like a breath of fresh air later I'll be glad to join you for a walk. To the Copenhagen Tavern.'

'We might do that,' Tweed agreed amiably.

She was pressing her arm against his and he could feel the warmth of her body through his suit. Helen Claybourne had stood up, was collecting the cards, shuffling them into a pack. She paused next to Lee, bent down and picked something off her right shoe.

'A few bits of undergrowth and pine needles,' Lee remarked. 'Which I must have collected when I had a stroll in the Parc d'Egmont behind the hotel.' She looked at Tweed. 'That before dinner with Willie at the Café d'Egmont. It's high-class coffee house, but the food is good.'

'It's better at the Baron de Boeuf on the first floor,' said Burgoyne. 'That's where you get a first-class meal.'

'At first-class prices,' Willie commented. Newman was reminded of a doleful St Bernard. 'Still,' Willie brightened up, 'we're all having one helluva time. I like nothing better than good company, good food. What else is there in the world?'

'Hard work.' The Brigadier grunted, tasted the Krug the waiter had poured. 'That'll do.'

219

Paula had her first chance to look at the shoes Lee was wearing. Sensible walking shoes. Which didn't go at all with the glamorous purple off-the-shoulder outfit.

Newman had moved his chair so he sat close to Helen Claybourne. Lee had blood-red nail-varnished finger-nails, a colour he disliked intensely. Looked as though she'd dipped her fingers in blood. As a contrast, Helen's slim strong-looking fingers were varnished a pale pink. She turned to him and her grey eyes held his unblinking.

Out of the corner of his eye he saw Lee stroking back her blonde mane so she could see Tweed clearly. Again a contrast: Helen sat quite still, her hands clasped in her lap, still staring at him with the hint of a smile.

'Are you enjoying all this?' he asked her quietly.

'I am now. I've read quite a bit about you in magazine profiles. I'd imagine you're a very resourceful man – someone a woman could depend on in an emergency. Which is more than you can say for most men nowadays.'

With any other woman it would have sounded like flattery. But Helen made it sound like a simple statement she believed. They clinked glasses and she gave him her half-smile again.

I'm not doing very well tonight, Paula thought. Lee appears to have Tweed in the palm of her hand. Newman can't take his eyes off Helen. I must be losing my touch. Willie seemed to sense her feeling of isolation. Turning to her, he clinked his glass with hers, beaming at her.

'You must have had the appetite of a lady who hasn't eaten for weeks. The way you devoured those sand-wiches. I know a rather nice little restaurant just up the boulevard. The Copenhagen Tavern. It has a bar. Why don't we go up there, get away from this lot?'

'I'd love to – and thank you, Willie. But it's been a long day. Maybe tomorrow . . .'

She was watching Lee who had twisted round in her chair. She was straightening Tweed's tie. Willie glanced in

220

the same direction, then went on chatting.

'Tell you what. There are some pretty good exhibitions on at the moment. Helen,' he called out, 'hope I'm not interrupting. I wonder if you could find out all the exhibitions on in town early tomorrow, give me a list?'

Helen produced a notebook from her handbag. Newman kept quiet as she produced her expensive fountain-pen, took off the top, make a note.

'Consider it done,' she assured Willie.

'That's a nice pen,' Newman remarked. 'Fountain-pens are coming back into fashion. And it suits your neat handwriting.'

Pile it on, Bob, Paula thought. Helen was playing with the fat pen, made a movement as though to show it to Newman, then dropped it back inside her bag.

'It was a present from my favourite uncle. I guard it with my life . . .'

Tweed seemed totally absorbed by Lee. She took out her jewelled cigarette holder, inserted a cigarette, and put the holder between her lips. She made no attempt to light it and Tweed, a non-smoker, produced the lighter he always carried. Igniting it, he leant forward. Lee snatched the holder out of her mouth away from him.

'Sorry. I'm giving up smoking. I do this as a test of will power. So far I haven't lit a cigarette for over four weeks.'

'Damn silly idea,' Burgoyne commented. 'Just don't buy any cigarettes. These pseudo-psychological methods never work. I suppose that crank doctor you consulted suggested it.'

'Maurice,' Lee said sweetly, 'why don't you mind your own damned business?'

'And are you here on business, Brigadier?' Tweed asked, seizing on the opening.

'Yes. What about you?' Burgoyne barked.

'The answer is yes,' Tweed said slowly. 'In my capacity as Chief Claims Investigator for my insurance company. I

221

am actually investigating a particularly grim kidnapping.'

Was it his imagination or had a sudden hush descended on the party? Paula, who had pushed her chair back, was in a better position to see everyone. She could have sworn someone froze for a second. The trouble was she couldn't identify who it was.

'Anyone we know?' Burgoyne asked eventually.

'I would assume probably not,' Tweed replied in the same slow tone. 'And I am close to my target.'

'I'm going to bed,' the Brigadier announced abruptly, and stood up. 'The rest of you can chatter the night hours away.'

On this polite note he left them. Lee insisted that she and Tweed walked up the boulevard to the Copenhagen Tavern. Willie turned to Paula as Lee went to fetch a coat.

'Now you *are* going to join me for a nightcap. We can get one just up the street at Les Arcades. You'll like it. Quite atmospheric. Be a devil, say yes.'

'I'll get my own coat,' Paula agreed immediately. At least someone was showing interest in her. 'Won't be a tick . . .'

Helen waited until she was alone with Newman before she made the suggestion. Facing him, she fiddled with a brooch under her mandarin collar, her grey eyes staring straight into his.

'If you feel like it, we could slip into the bar over there and have a quiet drink and a chat. Get to know each other better.'

'Then why are we still sitting here?' Newman asked, and gave her a warm smile.

Tweed didn't let on to Lee that he was familiar with the Copenhagen Tavern. At that time of night there were only a few customers – some finishing a meal, others sitting over drinks.

A spacious establishment, it had an intimate atmosphere

– largely created by the fact that the walls were lined with brown cloth, combined with subdued lighting from brass wall sconces supporting brown shades.

Tweed guided Lee to the back of the split-level room, avoiding the steps leading up to a large alcove on the right. He chose one of three empty tables at the back of the room with brown banquettes against the wall. Lee slipped round the table on to the banquette, tapped the space beside her. Tweed took off his coat, walked round the other end, perched the coat on the banquette between Lee and where he sat. She stripped off her coat, folded it carefully, placed it on top of his and pushed the pile towards him. Then she eased herself closer.

To his surprise she ordered a glass of dry French white wine when the waitress came and he followed suit.

'I'm floating in champagne,' she confessed in a husky voice. 'God! The Brigadier is a pain in the proverbial.'

'Why work for him then?'

'For a secretary-housekeeper the pay is very good. And I still haven't a clue about his business. He seems to dictate letters in some sort of code.'

'You mean a code like the Secret Service are supposed to use?'

'No. But his phraseology is strange. I always have the feeling there is a double meaning to the words. Still,' she smiled and for a moment left her full red lips half open, 'don't let's talk about him. Let's talk about us.'

She sipped at her glass of wine, watching him over the rim of the glass. Her greenish eyes glowed with excitement.

'Isn't that Guerlain Samsara? The subtle perfume I caught a whiff of?' Tweed enquired.

'Yes. You seem to know a lot about women. Helen Claybourne has a bottle, let me try it.'

'Maybe the Brigadier would buy you a bottle,' Tweed suggested.

'Not Maurice.' She smiled warmly again. 'He reckons he pays me too much. He'd say I could afford to buy it myself. Which I suppose I could.' She sipped more wine. 'Your Paula is a striking-looking girl,' she said suddenly. 'And sharp as a tack.' She smiled again, wickedly this time. 'I bet she's a marvellous asset – in every sort of way.'

Tweed evaded the probe. 'She is extremely efficient. Incidentally, whose idea was it for the four of you to come on this trip together?'

'Are you interrogating me?' she needled him good-humouredly. 'It was Maurice's. I'm afraid he treats Willie as a pet lap-dog. I hope that doesn't sound cruel. I gather the friendship started ages ago out in the Far East.'

'Any idea what Willie did in those days? To earn his living, I mean.'

'More interrogation,' she chaffed him. 'You're not a top claims investigator for nothing. According to Maurice he – Willie – was known as Mr Fix-It. Let's suppose two trading companies were trying to take over each other. And things were getting nasty. They'd call in Willie – as a kind of mediator. You know how he rambles on. And apparently his amiable personality helped. Plus his stamina. You might not believe it, but he can stay up all night and be as fresh as a daisy in the morning. I imagine he used a mix of diplomacy and wearing everyone else down until he got them to agree to a compromise. There's more to Willie than meets the eye.'

And there's more to you than I'd thought, Tweed said to himself. The fun-loving blonde was turning out to have a good head on her beautiful bare shoulders. Which must have fooled a lot of men.

'Thank you for the drink – and especially your company,' Lee said and kissed him on the cheek. 'Let's do this again. And now I think I'd better get my beauty sleep. Poor Paula – God knows whether she will get to bed tonight. Willie really does have the stamina of the devil.'

She put away the jewelled cigarette holder she had been twirling between her fingers after removing the unlit cigarette.

Earlier, as Willie had walked up the boulevard with Paula, they had passed the Copenhagen Tavern. Its wooden frontage was painted an over-bright blue. Paula had glanced through the closed door, wondering how Tweed was getting on with the glamorous Lee.

'We're nearly there, my dear,' Willie had said, rubbing his hands. 'Just a few more steps. It's bit brisk out tonight. You are warm enough, I trust?'

'Very comfortable, thank you,' Paula replied, grateful for his consideration.

Willie wore a heavy check overcoat and no gloves on his large hands. When they arrived at Les Arcades he took her arm to escort her into the warmth. A small but gallant gesture. Sometimes I prefer older men, Paula said to herself.

'Ladies first,' Willie said as he had opened the door.

Typical of Brussels, Les Arcades was a long narrow, deep room stretching away with a bar midway along on the right. Framed oil paintings and sketches of horses decorated the walls, the ceiling was oak-beamed and the banquettes were a pale green colour. Discreetly lit by wall sconces, it had a cosy atmosphere. A well-built Belgian came from behind the bar to greet them.

'Hallo there again,' Willie said cheerfully. 'You'll see I have a different lady with me tonight. I'm going up in the world. A bottle of Sancerre would go down very nicely. That should get us in the mood, Paula. Let's see the night out . . .'

There were only two other couples in the room and the barman ushered them to a banquette by the wall on their

225

own. Willie tasted the wine after their coats had been taken, pronounced it good, very good indeed.

'I like this place,' said Paula. 'You come here often?'

'Only every time I'm in Brussels! Drink up!'

'And the Brigadier suggested you should join him?'

'Not on your life! My suggestion. Not going to let him traipse off from the New Forest and leave me behind. He isn't in a very good mood, I'm afraid. But I'm used to it. He was so often down in the mouth out in jolly old Hong Kong. I do my best to cheer him up. These old ex-officers think they're still on parade.'

'What did he do out there – in Hong Kong?'

'After the Army chucked him out, you mean?' Willie put a hand over his mouth in mock horror. 'There I go – always blowing the gaff. Forget what I said.'

'Well, what did he do? Afterwards?' Paula persisted.

'Spent half his time in the bars. Set up a few tinpot companies. Never could understand how he afforded the high life. Nothing but the best for the Brig. Always the top restaurants, the five-star hotels. Don't misunderstand me – Maurice is a good chap. Always gets his wallet out first when there's a big bill to pay – and always pays in cash. Won't touch credit cards with a barge-pole. Bit of a mystery man, Maurice.'

'And Lee? Is he going to marry her?'

Paula was asking direct questions she would normally never have dreamt of putting so pointedly. But with Willie she felt she could ask anything. She suspected he thrived on indiscretion.

'Shouldn't think so for a moment. Not Maurice. He likes to keep people dangling – off balance so they're never sure where they are with him. Probably learnt that when he was in the Army. A lot of politics when you get up to the higher ranks.'

Paula was sipping her wine slowly. Willie kept topping up her glass, then refilling his own empty glass. He must have a head like a rock, she thought.

'And how did you spend your time in Hong Kong all those years?' she asked.

He beamed. 'And how do you know it was all those years?'

'Someone told me. Can't think who.'

'Doesn't matter. Me? I did a bit of this and a bit of that.' He moved closer, lowered his voice to a confidential tone. 'You could say I was some kind of diplomat – not in the FO I hasten to say. A and B were at each other's throats. I'd be asked in to cool the fires. Get them to come to some agreement. I'd get a commission on the deal. Sounds like a Somerset Maugham character – a commission man. Not very nice. But when I'd saved them millions I reckoned I was worth a crust of bread. Knew a lot of the top people – went to their parties. Oil on the troubled waters and all that.'

'And now you are happy with Helen?'

For a moment Willie looked like a sphinx. He swallowed more wine, refilled his glass. He drank some more, then twiddled the stem.

'Helen is Helen. She likes managing things – including me, as I believe I once told you. Would you believe it – she never makes a mistake. I fumble about like a whale wallowing in a pond.' He chuckled. 'I'm lucky – Helen likes the country, you see. The New Forest enchants her.'

'If you don't mind, I'd better get to bed. Thank you for a lovely outing.'

'Do it again . . .'

When they had entered the bar at the Hilton Helen had led the way, clasping Newman's hand. Illumination was almost non-existent. They settled in a corner close together. The few other guests drinking were out of sight. Helen ordered a glass of Laurent Perrier and Newman asked for the same.

'Tell me about yourself, Mr Newman,' she invited, still clasping his hand.

'I'm Bob, and I'm going to call you Helen. Ladies first. I want to hear about you.'

'That makes a change. Most men gabble on about themselves. And I've noticed you listen to every word I say. A most attentive companion.'

'Now, about yourself.'

'Oh, I'm that dreary old thing, a career woman . . .'

'Nonsense. You're not dreary. Old? That's a laugh. And these days it's the custom – a lot of women manage two jobs very well.'

The champagne arrived, Newman paid for it in cash, they clinked glasses. Helen sipped a little, put down her glass, sighed.

'You asked for it. Willie found me through an agency that specializes in secretary-housekeepers. He's easy to work for. Unlike Maurice, who must be pure hell. Before that I worked for a banker in Singapore. My little fling to see the world. Once was enough. It was so humid. All right inside cars, shops, hotels – air-conditioned. Hit the streets and they hit you. So I came back.'

'Parents?'

'Not any more. They died in a car crash. I wasn't close to them. Too independent-minded.'

She leaned close to him to slip off her shoes. He kissed her lightly on the cheek. Her grey eyes held his and she sipped more champagne.

'That perfume,' Newman said. 'I like it. Guerlain Samsara.'

'How clever of you to identify it. I wasn't too sure it suited me. Lee has a bottle, urged me to try it.'

'It suits your personality perfectly. By the way, what made the four of you come away together?'

'Willie's idea. He heard that the Brig. and Lee were coming here and said why don't we make it a foursome.'

'And how did the Brig. react to that?'

'I'm not sure. You never can be sure what he's really thinking. Willie didn't give him much option – except for an outright refusal. Since we're next-door neighbours I imagine even Maurice thought an objection would not go down well. On the other hand, I had a feeling that maybe he welcomed the idea. I think he's in the armaments business.'

'Think? You're not sure?'

'I'm never sure about anything with Maurice.'

She had released his hand a while ago. Now she wriggled herself more comfortably against the banquette. At the same time she crossed her legs and eased her pleated skirt up above her knees. Newman had the feeling that she wanted him to lay a hand on her knee. He kept it firmly holding his glass. She had very good legs.

'Maybe we could meet in London?' she suggested.

'I haven't any cards left,' he lied. 'I can give you my phone number.'

In no time she had produced her notebook from her handbag. She held her fat fountain-pen poised. He gave her the number, but not his Beresforde Road address in South Ken.

'There's an answerphone if I'm out. Leave a message for me,' he suggested. 'And now I suppose we'd better hit the hay. Might see you in the morning.'

She stood up, eased her way out, paused for him to catch her up. Suddenly she turned round, clasped both hands round his neck, stroking it as she kissed him full on the mouth. As he followed her out he saw Paula standing in the entrance, her expression neutral.

'Damn!' he said under his breath.

Paula said good-night with undue pleasantness to Helen who disappeared inside an elevator. She looked at Newman.

'You're wearing the wrong shade of lipstick.'

229

23

Marler had decided to take a risk. It was very late, and sitting in his parked car, he'd seen no sign of life from the Bellevue Palace. He needed to clean up ready for the morning.

He took off his shabby windcheater, his beret, revealing his smart sports outfit underneath. Getting out of the car he opened the boot, shoved beret and windcheater inside, collected what he needed from his case, locked up the car.

He left two windows an inch or so down. The atmosphere inside was pretty fetid with the smoke from his king-sized cigarettes. An icy breeze was blowing in the right direction. Clad in his Aquascutum trench coat and clutching his shaving-kit case, he walked down the Avenue Louise, crossed to the Boulevard de Waterloo, entered the Hilton.

He mingled with a party of late-nighters just returning, smelt whiffs of alcohol, heard their none too sober conversation. He walked straight up to the reception and spoke to the man behind the counter.

'I've been driving non-stop for hours. I want to get a shower and clean up before I drive on to Ostend. I need a single room – which I'll pay for – for the night. Even though I'll only be there an hour . . .'

Paying in cash, he went to the elevator, stepped out at the right floor, used the blasted computer card – which he loathed – to open the door. Then he moved swiftly, stripping down, stepping into the shower, and towelling himself five minutes later.

He used his electric razor to remove the stubble from his face, put on the rest of his clothes. He checked his appearance in a long mirror. Now he looked quite different – even respectable.

Returning to the lobby, he ordered sandwiches and coffee. Eating everything, he drank the last drop of coffee, paying for the meal before he walked out again and returned to his parked car.

When he got behind the wheel the first thing he did was to feel under his seat. The Armalite rifle was still there. Using a copy of the *Herald Tribune* he had picked up in the Hilton, he spread sheets out over the weapon, further concealing it.

He then settled down to rest, but not to fall asleep: Marler could survive for forty-eight hours without one wink of real sleep. When morning came he was glad he'd taken the precautions of making himself look like a respectable tourist. Very glad indeed.

It was the middle of the night and Dr Wand was fast asleep when the phone rang. He woke instantly, switched on the bedside lamp, put on his pince-nez, glanced at his clock, and guessed who was calling. He picked up the receiver.

As he had expected it was long distance – from Hong Kong. The operator informed him Moonglow Trading & Mercantile were on the line. So it would be in the morning in Hong Kong, and urgent for them to call him at this hour. He identified himself and listened to the caller who spoke in English.

'Philip Cardon, did you say? Could you please repeat?' he asked after a short conversation which appeared to concern a business transaction.

'I see,' he continued after listening to a few more words. 'Here are my instructions. Kindly terminate Mr

Cardon's contract. Yes, terminate. He is totally redundant . . .'

Having ordered the murder of another human being, Wand took off his pince-nez, placed them carefully on the table, switched off the light, and fell fast asleep.

Tweed paced slowly round his room as he spoke. Newman and Paula had both come to see him early in the morning after Helen Claybourne had disappeared inside an elevator. They had given Tweed a résumé of their conversations with Helen and Willie. In return, Tweed had tersely reported his experience with Lee Holmes.

'It appears we still don't know the truth,' Tweed began, 'but we do know one of those women is a liar.'

'You mean about the Guerlain Samsara,' Newman suggested.

'Exactly. Lee told me Helen had a bottle and had let Lee try some of the perfume. Helen said the exact opposite. That is sinister.'

'It means then,' Paula said grimly, 'that one of the two of them could be a murderess twice in one evening?'

'Exactly,' Tweed repeated. 'The victims being Andover and the cab driver found in Marolles. Presumably – if it was one of them – she injected the cabbie with cyanide to use his cab to drive to Liège, then brought it back here. It could be significant that it was abandoned a few minutes' walk from this hotel. Not conclusive – but why should one of them lie about the perfume?'

'And Willie and Burgoyne?' Newman asked.

'They could be liars too. Willie tells Paula it was his idea that the four of them came together to Brussels. Helen confirms this arrangement with Bob while talking in the bar. On the other hand Lee told me quite clearly it was Burgoyne's idea. So we don't know about that either.'

232

'Helen hinted to me,' Newman recalled, 'that Burgoyne is mixed up in arms deals. Sounds plausible – with his military background. And he seems to be loaded with money. It must come from somewhere.'

'I think the important thing is to concentrate on the two women,' Paula emphasized. 'You two had them on your own, so what impression did they make?' She looked at Tweed. 'I suppose Lee played the coquette with you madly?'

'As a matter of fact, she didn't. I was surprised – she isn't the dizzy blonde I'd imagined. She talked a lot of horse sense and has a native shrewdness. Lee can look after herself.'

'And Helen?' Paula asked Newman.

'She was like I expected her to be. A mature woman with her feet planted firmly on the ground.'

'You know,' Paula said, 'when we were all gathered round the poker game in the lounge I had the same impression I had when we visited them in the New Forest. That we were witnessing an elaborate charade put on for our benefit.'

'You mean that the four of them are in it together?' Tweed queried.

'Maybe. I'm not sure yet,' she said, frowning with concentration. 'But at least one of them isn't what he or she seems. I'm damned sure of that. And it's creepy – this idea that either Helen or Lee could be a three-time murderess. Hilary Vane, the cab driver in Marolles, and Andover.'

'You caught a glimpse of the driver who mowed down poor Andover,' Tweed reminded her. 'You seemed sure it was a woman wearing a crash helmet and goggles. Surely that cancels out Lee – with her long mane of blonde hair.'

'Which just shows how little men know about women. She could have worn her hair piled up on top of her head

233

under the helmet. That doesn't cancel out Lee.'

'We've talked enough for one night,' Tweed decided. 'I suggest you all get off to bed now . . .'

It was the middle of the night when the phone woke Tweed. Earlier, on arrival in his room at the Hilton, he had made a brief call to Monica in London, giving her his hotel and room number. He switched on the light, picked up the phone, and it was Monica. She phrased her message carefully.

'Sorry to disturb you, but I've had a call from Cardon, our Far Eastern representative. From Bangkok. He's had a three-day holiday in Chengmai. He's flying home later today via the Persian Gulf. He'll be calling me before he boards his flight to give me his ETA.'

Tweed's blood ran cold. *Chengmai*. The Thai centre of drug distribution from the notorious Golden Triangle area. What on earth had drugs to do with this crisis? Nothing at all, he'd have thought.

Tweed's sixth sense was working overtime. He had the most awful foreboding. All this flashed through his mind in seconds while Monica waited for him to reply. He took an instant decision.

'He's travelling under his own credentials?' he asked.

'I gather so.'

'Monica, when he calls you again give him this order. Stress in the strongest terms it *is* an order. He is to fly straight back to Hong Kong – using his other credentials. He is then to take the Pacific route, repeat, the Pacific route, to San Francisco, cross the States, catch Concorde to London.'

'I'll tell him. Rely on me. Good-night – or rather, good morning . . .'

If Tweed had been asked, he couldn't have explained why he had taken this decision. But he had learnt over the

234

years his sixth sense never let him down – that it could be fatal to ignore it.

Sitting up in bed against a propped pillow, he reached for his copy of Anthony Trollope's *Barchester Towers*. He didn't go to sleep again. The shadowy pattern formed in his mind of what was going on had been shattered. Drugs? On a huge scale? That meant vast sums of money. A glimmer of an idea twitched at the back of his mind, then faded.

It was still dark when he got up, had a leisurely bath, dried himself, got dressed slowly. Then he watched dawn break over the muddled mess of a city which was Brussels.

Marler made his move some time after dawn broke but before the city had woken up. If Dr Wand was going anywhere he wasn't likely to start out as early as this.

It was cold and the streets were pretty much deserted as he hurried along the Avenue Louise between tall, boring-looking buildings. After a night inside the confines of the car he welcomed walking into the spaciousness of the Place Louise with its two main one-way highways – the first one he crossed to the wide pavement island in the centre dividing it off from the Boulevard de Waterloo.

He walked briskly up to the Hilton. He still had the room he'd paid for and the computer-card key was in his wallet. The uniformed doorman saluted him, suppressing a smile. He thinks I've had a night out on the tiles with some girl, Marler thought.

He continued his brisk pace past the empty lounge on his left, heading for the bank of elevators. Then he slowed down. A familiar figure, hands clasped behind its back, was pacing slowly up and down near the entrance to the Café d'Egmont. Tweed.

Marler was stunned. He paused as Tweed saw him,

walked swiftly towards him, took his arm, guided him to the bank of elevators, pressed a button. No. 20.

'You're on top of the world,' Marler remarked to say something.

'Twentieth floor,' Tweed replied once they were inside the elevator and the doors had closed.

There was no more conversation until Tweed had ushered Marler into Room 2009. Marler spread his hands in amazement and smiled ironically.

'You won't believe this but I came here to phone Monica to find out where you were . . .'

He explained tersely how he had tailed Dr Wand from the airport, the incidents at the Bellevue Palace, how he had taken a room at the Hilton. Tweed listened, then spoke.

'I woke very early. I was downstairs waiting for the coffee shop to open. You have done very well – very well indeed. So Dr Wand is a mere ten-minute walk or less from here. I find that interesting – in view of what has happened.'

'If you can tell me later, I think I'd better hoof it back to the Bellevue Palace. If Wand goes somewhere I want to know where to.'

'Agreed. But you need some back-up. No, don't argue . . .'

Tweed phoned Newman's room. The phone was answered but Newman's tone was disgruntled.

'What is it, Tweed? At this hour?'

'Come and see me immediately.'

'I was in the shower. I'm in my birthday suit. Be with you in ten minutes . . .'

Tweed had just put down the phone, was going to explain the situation to Marler, when someone tapped three times on the outside door lightly. Tweed looked through the spyhole, opened it. Paula, dressed in a navy blue suit, carrying a trench coat, her shoulder-bag over her arm, walked in.

'Couldn't sleep,' she said. 'I wondered whether you'd be up. Marler, you look dressed for action.'

'He is . . .'

Tweed swiftly explained the problem. Marler was spreading prints of Dr Wand taken at London Airport on a table. The special small camera designed in the Engine Room in the Park Crescent basement automatically developed and produced high-definition prints.

'Here is the devious bastard,' he said cheerfully. 'I will keep one, leave the rest to you.'

'We can't wait for Newman,' Tweed said impatiently. 'So Paula is coming with you instead.'

'Then let's get out of here fast before Newman comes rushing in,' Marler snapped.

Paula settled herself in the passenger seat beside Marler and handed him one of the two covered plastic cups containing coffee. She had slipped into a nearby bar while Marler moved the car a few yards.

'They had ham rolls,' she said. 'I could go back . . .'

'Don't. Thanks, but I'm up to here with ham. I've eaten nothing else for the past twelve hours or more.'

'Me too.'

Paula liked Marler. On the continent, with his upper-crust drawl and London clothes, he was often taken for the typical Englishman, an impression he cultivated. Paula was also amused at the speed with which he'd hustled her out of the Hilton. Newman and Marler were old sparring partners, neither really liking the other – but in an emergency they knew they could rely on their colleague to the limit.

They chatted animatedly and Paula gave Marler a brief outline of their grim experience in Liège and, later, their encounter with Burgoyne, Willie, and their two women. Marler watched her as she eyed him through her long lashes while she talked.

'Something's happening,' he said suddenly.

237

It was almost two hours since they had reached the car. Marler was glad he'd slipped into the toilet while Tweed was phoning Newman. In those two hours Brussels had come alive. Street cleaners wearing yellow jackets and trousers, pushing rubber-wheeled trolleys carrying tall rubbish bins had appeared. Small ochre-coloured trams were trundling towards Place Louise.

'What is it?' Paula asked.

'That big Mercedes 600 coming up out of the garage. It brought Dr Wand here from Zaventem Airport.'

Paula watched as the huge black limo paused half-way out of the exit. A car was blocking the way. The uniformed chauffeur with a peaked cap and dark glasses opened his door, got out to call to the doorman. Marler stared as the doorman, a guest's keys in his hand, rushed to move the vehicle.

'There's no one else in the car,' Paula objected. 'Do we want to know where a chauffeur is going?'

'No. Except I don't think that is the chauffeur. His build is too bulky, he moves more ponderously. Someone is playing Clever Dick.'

'I don't get it . . .'

'I'll bet a month's salary that's Dr Wand inside that uniform. So where is he off to that he doesn't want anyone to know about? Here we go. Hold on to your hat.'

The Merc. 600 reached the Place Louise, turned right up the Avenue de la Toison d'Or, running parallel to the Boulevard de Waterloo where traffic moved in the opposite direction. And there was traffic now. Marler was in his element, weaving in and out among private cars and rumbling juggernauts. Belgian drivers are aggressive but Marler beat them to it every time, leaving behind tooting horns as he skilfully kept one vehicle between himself and the Merc. 600.

Dr Wand – Marler was convinced it was him – was a mean driver himself, using the size of his car to make smaller cars give way. Sooner than Paula expected they were outside Brussels. She saw a signpost. *Gent* (French version), then *Gand* (Flemish version) underneath.

'Lord, he's moving,' Paula commented.

'So are we!' Marler said breezily.

They passed through turn-offs to numerous villages, and the Merc. 600 kept going. Marler had a juggernaut in front of him and ahead of that was the limo. They passed through flat open countryside – ploughed fields and colonies of greenhouses, their slanting roofs reflecting a glare from the sun. Above them was a clear blue sky and the air was cold and fresh.

Beyond Ghent the limo turned off the main highway down a tarred country road. Marler dropped back: concealment was now more tricky. The frequent bends in the road helped – he could just keep in sight the roof of the outsize limo. He came round a corner and stopped.

When he switched off the engine a heavy silence descended. Paula sat erect in her seat, staring, as though hypnotized.

'What's the matter?' Marler asked.

A hundred yards or so ahead was a new village. On either side of a freshly tarred road stood a row of small two-storey houses. They were built of red brick with steep-pitched roofs of grey slate.

The limo had been driven round the back of the first house on the left. The 'chauffeur' reappeared, walking slowly. Marler guessed he had the key in his hand because he opened the door quickly, disappeared inside, shut it.

Paula counted the houses which faced each other along the sides of the ruler-straight road. Eight dwellings on either side. And not a sign of life anywhere. Not even a single shop. She blinked, shook her head.

'I don't believe it,' she said.

'Don't believe what?'

'They're new, not old, of course. But they remind me –

239

the atmosphere – of Moor's Landing on the Beaulieu River in Hampshire.'

'Tweed told me about that place.' Marler lit a king-size. 'Incidentally, there's a canal just over there.'

Paula looked in the direction he'd indicated. A barge was waiting to pass through a lock. The uncanny silence persisted. Marler switched on the engine, backed his car almost out of sight of the village at a point where he could turn round.

'That was Dr Wand,' he told her, 'inside the chauffeur's uniform. I could tell from the way he moved. I watched him pacing up and down outside the Lear jet at London Airport.'

'And that place is a Flemish version of Moor's Landing,' Paula said. 'All the houses are curtained and I'm sure people live there. But no sign of any of them. Creepy – like Moor's Landing.'

'Let's go back into Ghent. I'll show you the Old Town. And if we find a restaurant or bar we'll ask a few questions about this place.'

'Wait a sec. I'm going to mark its position.' Paula picked up her map, made a cross at the approximate location of the village. 'It's not even marked on the map . . .'

Marler turned the car round and soon they were back on the highway, driving towards Ghent. He glanced several times in his rear-view mirror.

'You saw that blue Audi parked on the verge at the entrance to the side road?'

'Yes. Why?'

'We have company. It's following us . . .'

24

'I'm leaving for London today,' Tweed announced. 'I am booked on an afternoon flight. It's urgent that I take Delvaux's new radar device and hand it over to Naval Intelligence. And it was a false alarm, Bob.'

In response to his phone call Newman had just hurried to Room 2009 from his own bedroom. Newman had a double surprise – Tweed's sudden decision and the presence of Harry Butler and Peter Nield sitting on a couch. Tweed saw his glance in their direction. He smiled drily.

'Not like me to have such protection. I phoned Monica yesterday and asked her to contact Butler and Nield, to get them to fly over here immediately.'

'It's that Delvaux device,' Newman hazarded.

'You're right. It could be so important I decided I must travel with guards. I've also contacted Benoit. He'll be at the airport and we'll bypass Customs and Passport Control. Tell Paula and Marler when you see them. With a bit of luck I'll be back tomorrow. I have to see an officer at the MOD.'

'Ministry of Defence?' Newman sat down and raised an eyebrow. 'May we know what's going on there?'

'You may. I want to find out everything they can tell me about Brigadier Burgoyne – his military career and the years afterwards he spent in the Far East. And Monica has dug up more on Willie Fanshawe – and Dr Wand . . .'

He broke off as the phone rang. He listened to the operator, put his hand over the mouthpiece for a second.

'Talk of the devil – Dr Wand is calling me.'

'Yes, this is Tweed speaking. Did you say Dr Wand? What can I do for you?'

'I – think – it – is – time – we – met – Mr Tweed . . .'

The voice was a sibilant hiss and counting each word as if it was worth a great deal of money. Tweed checked his watch. He played for time while he thought.

'Can you give me some idea of the reason for this meeting? And the subject for discussion? I have an urgent appointment later.'

'Mr Tweed, I am given to understand you are a man of great discretion. The telephone is hardly the medium for a frank talk.'

'As I said, the timing could make a meeting impossible.'

'So, Mr Tweed, I am at your disposal. Could you come this morning? I have a modest villa at Waterloo, the headquarters of my refugee aid organization in Europe. I can, of course, send a car to collect you from the Hilton.'

'I can spare thirty minutes,' Tweed said abruptly. 'And I have my own transport.'

'My dear Mr Tweed, in thirty minutes – with your quick brain – we can cover the affairs of the world. And perhaps you would like to bring Miss Grey with you. It would be my pleasure.'

'I will be coming with someone, but it will be a man.'

'Excellent! Excellent! Now, if you would be so kind as to note down this address . . .'

Tweed scribbled it on a pad. He was annoyed to see that he was pressing hard with the pencil. His voice, however, remained cool and calm.

'I've got that. We will be there shortly. For thirty minutes.'

'I look forward to our meeting with the greatest of pleasure. Take good care of yourself in the mean time. Until we meet . . .'

Tweed put down the phone carefully. His expression was grim. He paced slowly round the room as he repeated the gist of the conversation. Newman reacted immediately.

'I am coming with you. The bastard! That reference to Paula. And how did he know you were at the Hilton? For my money he knows a little too much. And I am coming with you,' he repeated.

'I'm quite happy for you to join me,' Tweed agreed. 'Dr Wand is a very dangerous man. He was needling me, but I didn't react. As to how he knows so much, the answer must be Lee, Helen, Willie or Burgoyne. The question is, which of those four?'

'And also why has he suggested this meeting?' Nield asked. 'Maybe Harry and I should also accompany you?'

'It is a small victory on our part that he wants to see me. One of the four people I mentioned has passed on to him my remark in the lounge last night that I was getting close to my target. So my ploy worked. But I don't want four of us turning up – it makes us look nervous. But thank you for the suggestion, Pete.'

'To get to Waterloo we should leave in half an hour if we're to arrive soon,' Newman said firmly. 'And I'll check that address you have on my street map . . .'

Tweed handed him the sheet of paper with the address and stood by the window, his hands clasped behind his back. Waterloo lay to the south of Brussels, was one of the most expensive residential areas in the whole city. He was rather looking forward to crossing swords with the mysterious Dr Wand.

'Mr Audi is still following us,' Marler remarked as he drove into the Old City of Ghent.

It was obvious when they had left modern Ghent behind and reached the Old City centre. The tarred roads had become cobbled streets which the Mercedes bumped over. Ahead of them a heavy truck shuddered and shook drunkenly with the vibrations.

Paula liked the look of the Flemish town. There was an atmosphere of relaxation about the way the people strolled slowly but purposefully. The frenzied rush of Brussels seemed far away – another country. The buildings were ancient, built of mellow stone. Paula felt she had been transported back into the Middle Ages.

'This is about the centre – the Koornmarkt,' said Marler. 'And there's a parking lot free near the Post Office.'

'Isn't that a restaurant?' asked Paula. 'I don't understand the Flemish at the top but it says brasserie underneath. I'm so hungry I could eat a horse.'

'You won't here. Flemish food is very good.'

He had stopped the car. Across the cobbled street was the place Paula had spotted. The first legend read DENTER-GEMS WIT. Underneath in French was the second legend, BRASSERIE DE POST. Paula pointed to an ancient grey building with a spire at one corner and a clocktower at the other end. The façade was festooned with stone decoration.

'What on earth is that place?'

'Post Office. And Mr Audi is going to park one vehicle behind us. Yes, we'll eat at the brasserie. For one thing I'm famished too. For another I can keep an eye on my car. And Mr Audi . . .'

He locked the car and crossed the open square with Paula by his side. Marler was careful not to glance in the direction of the Audi and the fat man behind the wheel who sat smoking a cigar.

'Oh, Lord,' said Paula, standing at the entrance. 'My Flemish is non-existent and that's the language on the menu.'

'Nothing wrong with your French, is there? Wait till we get inside.'

The restaurant had panelled walls, a tiled floor, wooden chairs and tables covered with paper cloths patterned to look like linen. Already the place was a hive of activity as waitresses bustled to serve, their heels click-clacking on the tiled floor. Marler pulled out a chair for Paula at a window table. As he sat down she was studying the menu. Marler glanced outside. Across the street Fatman was still seated behind the wheel, puffing his cigar, and gazing straight ahead rather too fixedly.

'This is great,' said Paula. 'The menu is in French as well as Flemish. I'm fillets of sole and loads of chips.'

'Sounds good, me too.'

The waitress was already standing over them. Marler gave her the order in French and asked for a carafe of Macon and some mineral water. The waitress stared at him.

'*Pas de potage?*'

Marler looked at Paula who shook her head. He looked up at the waitress, smiled, said, '*Non.*' She looked amazed and hurried off to place their order.

'I'm ravenous,' Paula remarked, 'as I told you. But I've seen the soup at the next table. It's a plateful of solid liquid. A meal in itself.'

'I agree. Takes the edge off your appetite. But the Flemish work hard, eat well to stoke up. Macon is all right, I hope? The waitress was dizzy with impatience to push off and get on with it.'

'You know it's one of my favourite wines. And thanks for remembering the mineral water . . .'

Paula thought how strange the situation was. In Marler's company she was feeling as relaxed as she did when out with Newman. But across the street was that sinister fat man waiting for them to leave.

'Mr Audi could be a problem,' she mused after the waitress had served the wine and the mineral water. She also brought a basket of sliced pieces of a baguette. Paula took a slice and devoured the crusty bread. 'This is good too,' she commented.

'Forget Mr Audi,' Marler suggested. 'I've been in this town before and know the geography. I may deal with our friend before we leave. Now, concentrate on the meal . . .'

Drinking her wine, Paula looked outside, fascinated by the Dutch-style architecture. Slim old buildings sheered up to the typical Dutch rounded triangular façade at the top. Five or six storeys high, some buildings had heavy wooden doors on the fifth floor – doors which had once opened to take deliveries hauled up from wagons in the street.

'Looks good to me,' she said as the food arrived. 'And no bones to fiddle with. Glory, look at the amount of beautiful chips.'

'Bet we get through the lot,' said Marler.

They said nothing more as they attacked the meal. More customers flooded in. Obviously locals, Marler thought from their appearance. And regulars, from the way they were greeted by the waitresses. The restaurant was a babble of conversation mingling with the rattle of cutlery and the clink of glasses.

A man in a white coat appeared from the back. He had a characteristic strong Flemish face. He spoke to Marler in French.

'Is everything to your satisfaction, sir?'

'Quite splendid,' Marler enthused. 'A meal fit for a king. By the way, we were touring round at random outside Ghent and arrived at what appeared to be a new model village . . .'

Paula produced her map quickly. She pointed to the cross she had marked for its location. The white-coated man bent over, noded his head, continued in French.

'We won't get any business from that place. They are very standoffish. All young executives, apparently. They work in Brussels, I gather. Very little is known about them, but they keep themselves to themselves. Enjoy your meal . . .'

'There *is* something funny about that village,' Paula

insisted after the white-coated man had gone. 'The more I think about it, the more I'm reminded of Moor's Landing – even though that place is renovated thatched cottages.'

Another tram screeched as it passed slowly across Koornmarkt. It was a loud penetrating noise, Marler noted. Trams had rumbled past at frequent intervals while they ate.

'Well,' Marler pointed out, 'Dr Wand is linked with the village outside Ghent. I'm certain the chauffeur was Wand in disguise. So there's one connection. But what connection have we between Dr Wand and the New Forest?'

'A solid one,' Paula reminded him. 'As solid as lead. Butler and Nield followed the camper which had been recording the conversations inside Andover's house. Where does it lead them to? The Boltons. No. 185. The home of Dr Wand in London.'

'You're right. Now what about dessert?'

'Couldn't.' Paula patted her stomach. 'It's full to the brim. And we did finish off all those chips. I don't think I even want coffee.'

Marler glanced out of the window. Fatman was still inside the Audi. He was lighting a fresh cigar. Some lunch, Marler thought. He leaned forward.

'Paula, I'm going to get the bill. I'll leave you the money to pay. Then I'm going outside. As I told you, I know this area. Here are the keys of the car. When you see Fatman disappear go straight to the car and sit in the passenger seat. Put the key into the ignition. Then wait for me to reappear.'

'What makes you think Fatman will vanish?'

'Trust me.'

He waved to the waitress. She hustled up to the table. Marler asked for the bill. She looked stunned.

'*Pas de dessert?*'

'*Non.*'

She wrote out the bill. Her expression again was one of

247

disbelief. These English, they do not eat! Marler thanked her, passed several banknotes across to Paula when the waitress was summoned to another table. Then he stood up and walked slowly out of the restaurant and across the square.

Paula handed the money to the waitress, and watched with trepidation as Marler reached the far side and drifted to the left past the Post Office. Fatman leaned forward. Even at that distance Paula could sense his indecision as Marler walked past his parked Mercedes.

Reaching the corner of the building, Marler turned right and disappeared. Fatman moved. Clambering out of the Audi, he locked the car, then followed the way Marler had gone, his short fat legs moving clumsily. Paula guessed he was not accustomed to using his feet: the car was his mode of travel.

She watched him arrive at the same corner, disappear out of sight. Marler's prediction had come true. But what could Marler do to lose him – put him out of action – in the centre of a crowded town? She left the restaurant, paused as another tram screeched slowly past, before running to the Mercedes. Unlocking the car, she ran round the front, slipped into the front passenger seat, slid the ignition key into place, waited.

Meanwhile Marler had strolled along the side of the Post Office. He turned right again at the back of the building into Graslei, a cobbled road running alongside a canal. In the near distance a bridge crossed it. Here he realized luck was on his side.

About half-way along the third side of the building was a group of American tourists clustered together for protection in a foreign land. Well dressed, they were the wealthier Americans who came abroad out of season. A girl courier was lecturing them on the history of Ghent as they huddled close to the wall.

Marler edged his way round the back of them as though

part of the group. He smiled at a blue-rinse matron. 'Isn't this just all too wonderful?' she drawled as Marler sidled further into the group. He nodded and glanced back. Fatman had appeared, had stopped, unable to see his quarry.

Marler was now standing at the entrance to a narrow alley – Hazewindstraatje. Flemish names could be jaw-breakers. He knew the paved alley led straight back to Koornmarkt. Walking swiftly down it he came out close to where the Audi was parked.

The pavement was crowded with people away from the kerb. Marler had one hand in his trouser pocket as he approached the Audi. Taking his hand out of his pocket, he let a handful of small change fall.

Crouching down, he began to pick up the coins. No one was taking any notice of him as he unscrewed the dustcap from the front wheel. He had noticed three trams were trundling towards Koornmarkt. Perfect! Taking a biro from his pocket, he jammed the pointed end hard down on the spring-loaded valve. The hiss of the air escaping from the tyre was muffled by the screech of the trams. Inside two minutes the tyre was flat as a pancake.

He stood up, walked swiftly to his Mercedes, throwing the dustcap into the gutter. Paula leaned over, opened the door for him. He slid behind the wheel, slammed the door shut, switched on the engine.

'That was a damn near-run thing, as Wellington said about Waterloo,' he remarked. 'Appropriate, as Waterloo is not so far away.'

In his rear-view mirror he saw Fatman appear at the end of the alley. He looked towards the Mercedes, fumbled with his key, dived inside, switched on his own engine.

'Now for some fun,' Marler said.

He drove out of Koornmarkt, heading for the highway to Brussels. Fatman was in such a panic that he was going to lose them that he threw caution to the winds. Ramming his foot down, he pursued the Mercedes.

'What fun?' Paula asked.

'Fatman has a flat front tyre. Watch in your wing mirror. These cobbles will play havoc with him. Any second and one wheel will be riding on the metal rim.'

He increased speed. A cab driver coming in the opposite direction had to be moving at 100 k.p.h. – a little over 60 m.p.h. Marler increased speed. Behind him Fatman was desperately trying to keep his target in view. Then it happened. Marler checked his rear-view mirror as Paula watched in the wing mirror.

At far too great a speed the Audi was racing with a wheel grinding over the cobbles on its metal rim. For a second the vehicle rocked madly, then Fatman lost all control. The Audi skidded, swerved into the back of a stationary garbage-collection truck, ramming into it like a sledgehammer. The front telescoped. An avalanche of garbage flooded down over the bonnet, piled up over the windscreen. Fatman had not taken the precaution of fastening his seat belt. He was hurled forward, his head shooting through the glass like a shell from a gun.

Marler turned a corner and the grisly sight vanished from view. Paula let out her breath, thought of something inconsequential to say.

'You mentioned Waterloo. I've never been there. Maybe I can see it sometime.'

'Don't bother,' Marler replied. 'Nothing to see. And nothing ever happens at Waterloo these days.'

25

'He referred to "my modest villa" – it's a palace,' Tweed commented.

Newman had driven Tweed in the Mercedes and they had arrived at Waterloo. He had been driving slowly and now he stopped close to a pair of tall ornamental gates between two large stone pillars. Beyond the pillars stretched an endless ten-foot-high wall. On top of the wall extended a wire which, Tweed felt sure, was electrified. And the gates were closed. On one pillar a large metal plate carried the legend, in English: MOONGLOW REFUGEE AID TRUST INTERNATIONAL.

'He seems to feel himself in need of a lot of security,' Tweed observed.

Newman got out of the car, went to the speakphone below the name-plate, pressed the bell, spoke into the grille when a voice asked in French who was calling.

'Mr Tweed. By appointment. To see Dr Wand . . .'

He didn't wait for a reply. As he sat behind the wheel and closed his door the electronically controlled gates began to move slowly inward. Fifty yards or so beyond the gates, perched on top of a terrace, was a wide three-storey mansion with a mansard roof and the walls painted dove grey. On either side of the straight drive the gardens were laid out with a series of sunken paved areas surrounding a fountain. On a larger scale, it reminded Tweed of Delvaux's estate, but without the taste.

Newman drove inside, stopped just beyond the gates and jumped out. Grabbing one of the white-painted stones lining the drive, he carried it behind the car and laid it against one of the open gates, returned to the car.

'What are you up to?' Tweed enquired.

'When the gates close automatically – which they are beginning to do now – the right-hand gate will be stopped by that small boulder and won't close. Just in case we find we have to make rather a swift departure . . .'

Arriving at the foot of the terrace, Newman turned his car so it pointed back down the straight drive. Side by side they mounted ten steps to the terrace, walked up to two large wooden double doors. Before Tweed could press the bell the door opened. A heavily built man with dark hair slicked back and dressed like a butler stood to one side.

'Dr Wand is waiting to see you now, gentlemen.'

Tweed walked in first, followed by Newman. There was a loud pinging noise. Which was when Newman realized the door was framed with a metal detector. The butler closed the door. He addressed Newman.

'One moment, sir. Are you carrying any weapons?'

'Yes,' Newman said promptly. 'A Smith & Wesson.'

'If you don't mind,' the butler went on in French, 'I'll take care of that while you see Dr Wand.'

'No you won't.'

'It is the custom of the villa. No one carrying a gun is permitted into Dr Wand's presence.'

'Then open the bloody door again, flunkey, and we'll go back to Brussels.'

Newman saw his right hand twitch in an upward movement, then relax. During this verbal duel Tweed had remained silent. This could be a dangerous outing and he felt quite prepared to let Newman handle it in his own way. The butler gave Tweed a little bow.

'If you don't mind waiting a few moments, I have to consult my employer.'

'Go ahead,' Tweed urged him.

252

While waiting in the enormous entrance hall with a polished wood-block floor decorated with Persian rugs casually laid here and there, Tweed, hands clasped behind his back, strolled over to examine a small framed painting of a woman wearing medieval clothes.

'That's a Holbein,' he remarked to Newman. 'An original if I'm not mistaken. It must have cost a mint.'

'Dr Wand doesn't seem to be short of a bob or two,' Newman commented. 'Aiding refugees.'

The butler had walked to the rear of the hall where a large Regency desk stood. Presumably his station to which he summoned servants to give them orders. He was speaking into an old-fashioned phone with a gold handle. Replacing it on the cradle, he walked back.

'Dr Wand is prepared to make an exception in your case. Please follow me. I will be waiting outside his study door.'

'Eavesdropping?' Newman enquired genially.

Marching ahead of them, the butler missed a step, then resumed his military-style walk. Pausing before a heavy door inlaid with panels, he knocked twice, opened the door and stood aside, closing it as soon as they had entered.

Tweed blinked. The study was a very large room but all the heavy velvet curtains were drawn over the windows. The only illumination came from a shaded desk lamp, tilted so it shone on two low arm chairs in front of the Louis Quinze desk. Behind the desk, seated high up in a tall-backed chair, was a shadowy figure. Still in the shadows, the figure stood up slowly, remaining behind his desk.

'Mr Tweed, it is my great pleasure to be honoured with your company. So please come forward both of you and sit down. I am sure that with men of your intelligence we shall find much of interest to discuss.'

Conscious of the deep pile carpet under his feet, Tweed

walked forward more slowly than usual, glancing round as his eyes became accustomed to the dim light. Then he moved sideways, lifted a carver chair, pushed the low armchair out of the way, sat down.

'I prefer this type of chair,' he remarked.

'So do I,' said Newman, bringing forward another carver, seating himself with his legs crossed.

'Mr Newman, I believe?' said Dr Wand, who had settled himself back in his own chair. 'The famous international foreign correspondent. I trust our conversation is – as they say – off the record? I would find it disconcerting to read an account of our meeting later in *Der Spiegel*.'

'I retired a few years ago,' Newman told him.

'Of course. I recall you wrote an international best-selling book which brought you in a fortune. I read it with fascination. Such a villain.'

'Oh, there's a lot of it about.'

Tweed saw Dr Wand's large head dip forward. For a brief second he saw the eyes behind the gold pince-nez, a flash of pure malevolence. Newman's retort had hit home. Then the head withdrew into the shadows. Wand spoke again in his soft careful voice.

'I must apologize for the paucity of illumination, but strong light affects my eyes. Now, in what way can I be of assistance to you, Mr Tweed?'

'I thought the reverse was the case,' Tweed reminded him. 'We are here at your invitation.'

'Of course. Of course.' Wand paused. 'I find myself intrigued by the fact that you have found it worthwhile spending your valuable time investigating me.'

Now we come to the crunch, Newman thought. He wondered how Tweed would handle the situation. Tweed responded instantly.

'What leads you to think I have the slightest interest in your activities?'

'Come, come, my dear sir. A man in my position – with

254

world-wide interest in the plight of refugees – has of necessity an acute ear to the underground grapevine.'

'Mind if I smoke a cigarette?' Newman asked to throw their host off balance.

'If you must. And you should understand that it is a major concession on my part to allow you in, armed as you are, with a gun.'

His tone of voice had changed. There was an abrasive note. Tweed sensed a dynamic energy in the man he still hadn't seen clearly. Newman responded immediately, removing the cigarette from his mouth.

'Then I would advise you to have a word with your butler. The gun *he* is carrying in a shoulder holster bulges out for all the world to see.'

'Thank you, Mr Newman. Most kind of you.' An edge of sarcasm now. 'I will most certainly have a word with Jules about his armament. But we live in violent times.'

'Talking about armaments, you are quite right,' Tweed shot back quickly. 'Sir Gerald Andover was murdered outside the estate of Gaston Delvaux in Liège last night. You've heard of Andover, of course – on your underground grapevine.'

Newman smiled to himself. The pace was hotting up. Tweed was seizing on every opening. He had the impression Dr Wand was furious he had opened a chink in his armour.

'Yes,' Wand said reflectively, 'somewhere I have indeed heard of Andover. I believe he is – was – a crackpot who propounded bizarre theories.'

'Or a genius who saw what was coming next to menace the Western world,' Tweed snapped with a bite.

'And what is coming next, if I may be so bold as to enquire?'

'The refugee problem, for one thing, is a horrendous menace. Thousands – maybe millions – on the move from the East. Europe would be swamped if they were allowed through. And yet, apparently, your organization is dedicated to infiltrating these people into our midst.'

'Infiltrating!' Wand sounded horrified. He shifted in his chair and his head appeared briefly in the light. Cruel eyes regarded Tweed from behind the flashing of the pince-nez. 'Would you kindly be more explicit? What precisely are you suggesting about my organization, when its only purpose is to help poor and helpless people?'

'It was a figure of speech,' Tweed said smoothly. 'Why is the subject of refugees such a sensitive point?'

'We have to be so selective – distinguishing between political and economic refugees. Surely you have heard the topic argued about?'

'Is there any connection between your trading company operating out of Hong Kong and your refugee organization?'

'None whatsoever.' Wand's tone was very abrasive. 'My understanding is your own company is concerned with the negotiation of wealthy men who have been kidnapped. You are supposed to be an expert negotiator in such cases – so how does that link up with what you have been talking about?'

'Because a prominent man has been kidnapped. And I am negotiating his release,' Tweed lied.

There was a long silence. Dr Wand shifted restlessly in his chair. He adjusted his pince-nez. Suddenly his manner changed, became amiable.

'And you are near success in your difficult undertaking, I trust?'

'Oh yes. Vital information has come to light. At the moment you might say we are closing in on our target. There are certain people in Brussels and I wonder why they are here. I think I may have found out why.'

Another pause. Newman, the unlit cigarette still clamped between his lips, was fiddling with his throwaway lighter under cover of the desk. He was using his tough thumb-nail to revolve the wheel controlling the power of the gas, converting it into a miniature flamethrower.

'Then may I wish you good health, Mr Tweed. And also success in your – I am sure – most difficult task. One wrong move and, I suppose, the whole thing could blow up in your face.' The voice became so soft Tweed only just caught the words. 'That would be a tragedy for you – and for all those involved.'

Newman chose that moment to lean forward, to flick the wheel of his lighter. A large flame speared up, he held it steady while he touched the tip of his cigarette, then he released the wheel and the scorching flame died. In those few seconds both men had a photo-flash image of Dr Wand. He threw up a hand to shield his face, but not before they had seen him.

Tweed caught an expression of satanic fury. The eyes glared savagely. Wand had prominent cheekbones, a nose like the prow of a ship, and swiftly he smiled, which was not a pleasant sight, his thin lips twisted in a smile like Siberia. He rose behind his desk, now back in the shadows.

'Mr Tweed, I wish to express to you my deep gratitude for spending a little of your undoubtedly precious time in travelling all the way from Brussels to see me. As I expected, I have found our conversation stimulating and illuminating. You appear to be engaged in a most danger-ous occupation. Let us hope you survive for many more years.'

'I expect to do just that,' Tweed replied tersely.

Dr Wand must have pressed a button. The door opened and the butler appeared, holding the handle and standing erect as he gazed straight ahead. Wand ignored Newman, made no further reference to him, and again he made no attempt to shake hands in the Belgian fashion.

Escorting them across the hall, the butler opened a small metal casing attached to the wall. He frowned.

257

'The gates do not appear to have closed properly.'

'Well, just make sure you open them properly,' Newman suggested jovially.

When they drove away down the drive the gates were wide open. Newman stopped in the road, ran back, replaced the stone by the garden border, returned to the car, and headed back for Brussels.

Inside his study Dr Wand sat in the gloom, his hands clasped in his lap. He sat quite motionless, thinking at top speed. When the phone rang he reached for the receiver automatically, half his mind thousands of miles away.

'Yes?'

'This is Anne-Marie,' a woman's voice said, as always using her code-name. 'I am speaking from a call box.'

'A most wise precaution, I am sure. You have some news for me?'

'Yes. From a fairly brief observation of Miss Grey and her employer I would say they are very close to each other.'

'You believe that she is his mistress?'

'No. I don't think it's that kind of a relationship. I do think he is very fond of her, that he regards her as invaluable as well as a friend.'

'I find that interesting, most interesting indeed. A man may discard a mistress without a qualm, but pure friendship goes deeper. Continue, if you would be so kind, to communicate with me regularly. Goodbye . . . .'

The phone call decided Wand to take certain action he had only been contemplating. Earlier Dr Hyde had called him from Liège, giving him the name of his hotel, its phone number and his room number. Wand dialled the number of the Liège hotel, asked to be put through to Dr Hyde.

'Who is this calling?' the soothing voice of Dr Hyde enquired cautiously.

'Your patron is calling you . . .' The use of this word amused Wand: Dr Hyde was a loyal servant only because he was paid so well. 'You recognize my voice?'

'Indeed I do. How may I be of service?'

'There may well be another patient requiring treatment at your hands. A woman. There may be a delay. It is a question of securing her availability. I will call you when the time is right. In the mean time I suggest you remain where you are. You can always sample the delights of Liège . . .'

'Dr Wand is an even more evil character than he appears in the photos Marler took of him,' Newman remarked as he parked in front of the Hilton.

'That trick of yours with the lighter was clever,' Tweed replied. 'And I agree with you. Some villains are difficult to detect – they have the charm of the devil. But in that brief moment when your lighter flared I had the impression we were in the presence of the Devil himself. A man capable of ordering the bizarre and horrific treatment of Irene Andover. To say nothing of arranging for the Liège assassin to drive down poor Andover.'

'Whom he referred to as a crackpot,' Newman recalled.

'And that was a tactical error. An unusual mistake for Dr Wand to make, I'd guess. His object was to discredit Andover's global theories. Why? Because they are true, I suspect,' he remarked as they stepped into the elevator.

'You went overboard yourself a bit when you talked of us closing in on our target.'

'Deliberately. I wanted to disturb him. I think that I succeeded. A disturbed man can make a fatal blunder.'

'You talked a moment ago about the horrific treatment of Irene Andover,' Newman reminded him. 'You really think a top-flight doctor is involved – the amputations I'm thinking of. Irene's severed arm. Lucie Delvaux's severed hand. Sheer cold-blooded butchery.'

'I'll know whether it took a skilled surgeon after I've seen Dr Rabin in London.' He checked his watch. 'I'll just have time to pick up my packed bag and the radar device from the deposit box.' They entered Room 2009.

'And both Butler and Nield are going back with you?'

'No. A change of plan. You are in charge while I'm away. Harry Butler will accompany me back to London. But Pete Nield will stay in Brussels. He has a special job to do. Give him this instruction from me. He is to guard Paula night and day – and I do mean guard. He must never let her out of his sight. Warn Marler, too . . .'

He had just spoken when there was a tap on the door. Newman opened it and Marler walked in with Paula.

'I've got five minutes,' Tweed told them.

Marler gave him a terse report of their locating the colony of new houses outside Ghent. Tweed looked grim as he picked up his case.

'The Mongols infiltrated spies ahead of their armies. It looks as though Wand's apparatus is already widespread. We may well move fast when I get back from London.'

26

Landing at London Airport, Tweed made a brief call to Dr Rabin after passing through Passport Control and Customs. No one asked to see inside the large executive case he was carrying.

Butler waited close to the phone Tweed made his call

from. He thought Tweed looked relieved when he joined him after completing the call. Taciturn by nature, Butler made no enquiry as they hurried out to locate the car Tweed had phoned for from the Hilton.

'A good trip, sir?'

It was George, one of the ex-Army men who acted as guards at Park Crescent. Tweed nodded and George led them to the car parked in the short-term garage. Climbing into the back, Tweed gave George an address in Harley Street. Dr Rabin, a widower, had kept on the rooms he had used as a general consultant before specializing in pathology.

After the bustle and shabbiness of Brussels Tweed found it a relief to get out into the peace and quiet of Harley Street with its solid buildings. Butler sat in the waiting room, hugging the executive case with the rest of their luggage by his side.

'I have the results of my examination,' Rabin informed Tweed briskly. 'Something very strange here.'

They were sitting in a cheerfully furnished living-room, facing each other in armchairs across a low table. On the table was a silver tray with a Spode tea-set which had been laid by a neatly dressed housekeeper.

Rabin was a short, stocky man in his late fifties. He had a large round head, white hair, a trim white moustache, and wore a blue business suit. His crisp manner always reminded Tweed of that out-moded phrase, an officer and a gentleman – without a trace of snobbery.

'Strange?' Tweed queried, revelling in the tea he was sipping. 'In what way?'

'Let's take the girl first. The severed arm was amputated by an exceptionally skilled professional surgeon. No doubt about it. This was further confirmed when I examined the body. She was killed, by the way, with an injection of potassium cyanide. The hypodermic

261

was thrust into the upper arm through her clothing. Nothing professional about that.'

'That is why you used the word strange?'

'Partly. So two different people were involved. A surgeon who carried out the amputation – and someone else who killed her.'

'Do you mind if I phone Brussels? We may have a similar case there.'

'By all means . . .'

Tweed checked his notebook, dialled police headquarters, asked to talk to Chief Inspector Benoit, speaking in French. Benoit came on the line very quickly.

'Lucie Delvaux,' Tweed said. 'Have you any opinion on how her hand was taken off?'

'Pathologist's report just came through to me over the phone. They have a nice way of putting things, these chaps. He said the amputation of the hand was a really beautiful job. Must have been executed by a top surgeon. Plus a lot of technical data you won't want.'

'Thank you, Benoit. How is everything in Brussels?'

'A close but very discreet watch being kept on Delvaux. Even he isn't aware of it. No developments so far. I will keep in touch . . .'

Tweed put down the phone, offered to pay for the call, but Rabin waved the idea aside. He listened as Tweed repeated the gist of his conversation with Benoit.

'I see,' he said slowly. 'This is all rather disturbing.'

'The point is,' Tweed said quietly, 'do you know of a surgeon who could have done this? Someone brilliant but possibly struck off the Register for conduct unbecoming, etc.?'

Rabin's ruddy complexion seemed to grow a little redder. Tweed saw him glance at a framed photograph on the wall. The photograph showed a group of men gathered together in apparently exotic surroundings. Rabin's tone became a little sharper.

262

'Then you had the body of Harvey Boyd sent to me. I've also completed that examination. Quite a different kettle of fish from Irene Andover – but again strange.'

'Strange in what way?' Tweed queried for the second time.

Rabin's mind seemed now to be only half on what he was saying.

'Well, first there can be no question at all that this was a professional amputation. Nothing of the sort. But I am puzzled. The side of the head, as you know, was fairly cleanly sliced away. Note I used the word fairly.'

'Sliced away by what?' Tweed pressed.

'Ah! that is the point. According to what you told me on the phone Boyd was in a small powerboat when he died. A boat in motion on the River Lymington when there was a dense fog. So the obvious assumption is another far larger and more powerful vessel sank him. But the portion of the head removed was taken off so cleanly. I am further puzzled when I tell you I found in the skull minute fragments of what I imagine was the wreckage of his powerboat at the time of the collision.'

'So why are you puzzled?'

'Because the normal hull of a larger vessel would have smashed up his skull far more brutally. That's all I can say.'

'You could tell me about the surgeon capable of amputating Irene Andover's arm with such skill.'

Rabin cleared his throat. 'Now we are in the realm of professional ethics. My lips are sealed.'

Tweed put down his cup carefully. He stood up, reached for his Burberry placed over the arm of a chair, put it on slowly, then stood erect, hands shoved inside his coat pockets. Rabin, thinking he was leaving, looking uncomfortable, also stood up. Tweed braced himself, stared hard at his host.

'Then you'll have to unseal your lips, won't you? Throw

so-called medical ethics to the winds.' His voice was cold and grim. 'Now you listen to me. There have been two cases so far of eminent men having close relatives kidnapped. No ransom demanded. Just an order that they must retire prematurely from all professional activity. And, to encourage them, at a certain stage one receives the severed arm of his daughter. The other, the severed hand of his wife. Later, the father of the first victim, Andover, has to be told his daughter's dead body has been washed up in the Solent. You've just examined her body. Murdered by the cold-blooded injection of cyanide. Rabin, this is a matter of national security. I know now I have stumbled on a conspiracy of global proportions. My only lead is the fiend who carried out the amputations. I need a name.'

'You make out a very strong case,' Rabin commented.

'And, if necessary, I can make out a much stronger one,' Tweed continued in the same controlled voice. 'I think you know who the surgeon might be. Who?'

'This conversation has to remain strictly between the two of us . . .'

'Did you have to say that, knowing me?' Tweed demanded.

Rabin gave him a quick glance, walked over to the wall. He took down the framed photograph he had looked at earlier, laid it on the top of a sideboard.

'This was taken at an international medical convention in Mexico City just a few years ago. Look at this man.'

He pointed to a figure seated next to Rabin. Tweed examined it. The print was very clear. A large, heavily built man with a paunch. Clean shaven, he wore rimless glasses, had a high forehead and thinning hair. He was smiling, exposing a perfect set of large teeth. Tweed had the impression of a clever man with a high opinion of his own cleverness.

'Dr Carberry-Hyde,' Rabin said. 'Knew him for years –

we trained at medical school together. He always made a point of keeping in touch even when he'd become one of the country's top surgeons.'

'So why might it be him?' Tweed probed.

'He has an insatiable appetite for women. There was a case when he tampered with a woman who was drowsy during a preliminary examination. A nurse he'd sent into the next room witnessed the incident through a half-open door. The woman's husband complained. The nurse kept quiet. Then, blow me, he does the same thing with his next woman patient. This time two nurses – including the one who witnessed the previous incident – watched him. When there was an inquiry both nurses gave evidence. Flagrant cases. He was struck off. The case never made the press – too full of a political scandal.'

'That cut him off from a lucrative income,' Tweed pointed out. 'So what happened to Dr Carberry-Hyde?'

'He went to live in the New Forest. Dropped me a line just once. I think I've got the letter still. And now I come to think of it, there was a brief mention in the press.'

Rabin opened a lower drawer in the sideboard, sorted quickly through a pile of papers. He stood up with an envelope in his hand.

'Got it. Says he's managing to earn a pittance as a salesman for a pharmaceutical company.'

'And this Carberry-Hyde could have carried out these amputations?'

'Standing on his head. A great loss. Brilliant chap.'

'Any address on that letter?'

'Yes. April Lodge, Brockenhurst.'

Nothing of Tweed's reaction showed in his expression. His encyclopaedic memory was flashing back to the house supposed to be for sale in Brockenhurst, the house Paula had visited with Newman. What was the woman's name? Yes, he recalled it. Mrs Goshawk. Of April Lodge, Brockenhurst.

'You can rest assured,' he told Rabin, 'that no one will know – outside my organization – how I obtained this information. And may I borrow this framed photo? Thank you. I'll let you have it back, of course . . .'

Tweed had no regret that he had fooled Rabin in saying he had had to tell Andover about his daughter's death. Any pressure was justified to trace the hideous doctor who had carried out the amputations.

On their way back to Park Crescent – with George driving and Butler hugging the executive case – Tweed had the car stopped near a public phone box. He called Commander Noble of Naval Intelligence.

'I have something technically unique to hand over to you,' he told the Commander. 'The sooner you reach my office the better . . .'

Tweed was surprised by the speed with which Noble reacted. He had hardly taken off his Burberry and settled himself behind his desk when Monica answered the phone.

'It's Commander Noble again. Waiting downstairs.'

'Wheel him up . . .'

Noble sat down in the armchair, gratefully accepted a cup of coffee from Monica, and listened without interruption. Tweed told him quite frankly about the dramatic interview with Gaston Delvaux, about the small Stealth plane he had constructed inside his plant. Then Butler handed over the executive case.

'I wonder?' said Noble.

He opened the case, examined the new device, handling it with great sensitivity. Then he replaced it inside the case.

'I wonder,' he said again, 'whether this device really does work in the way Delvaux claims?'

'You'd better test it.' Tweed leaned forward. 'And may I suggest your boffins get their skates on? Delvaux has always known what he's doing before. He turned down that super-gun idea with the incredibly long barrel the Iraquis pinned their faith on. Delvaux did some mathematical calculations, said the theory was unsound.'

'Oh, we'll test it,' Noble assured him. 'Both Naval and Air Intelligence. And as a top priority. Did you notice my car parked outside with three men inside?'

'Yes, I did,' Tweed replied. 'A big job. Heavy looking.'

'Should be. It's armour-plated. And my escort is armed. Thank you, Tweed. If you don't mind, I'll get the show on the road . . .'

When Noble had gone Tweed swung round in his swivel chair. He faced Butler as he gave him the instruction.

'A job right up your street. Drive down to April Lodge, Brockenhurst. It's somewhere on the outskirts. Owned by a Mrs Goshawk. I think she had a lodger, a Dr Carberry-Hyde. Try and find out if she knows where he is now. If necessary, put on the pressure.'

'I'm on my way . . .'

'A man of few words but plenty of action,' Tweed commented to Monica when they were alone. 'And I have a job for you. Come over and look at this photo taken in Mexico City.' As she leant over his shoulder he pointed to the figure Rabin had identified.

'Dr Carberry-Hyde. I want the Engine Room wizards to blow up his picture to a size about five inches wide by five deep. Glossy prints. One hundred copies. If they kick up tell them I'm expecting another miracle . . .'

Monica paused at the door, the framed photo under her arm. Tweed looked up and waited.

'I was just wondering whether they really do exist – invisible ships. We know Stealth planes do – the Americans built the Stealth B2 bombers. But ships? I ask you.'

'I'm relying on Paula's eyesight that night when Boyd died in Lymington.' Tweed paused. 'But you're right – it does stretch the imagination.'

PART TWO

Fog of Death

27

Latitude 39.55S. Longitude 18.22E. Several hundred miles south of the Cape of Good Hope, the ferocious gale had died as swiftly as it had blown up. The sea was now an oily calm and a dense fog was forming.

It was the strangest vessel ever built. The *Mao III* was proceeding on a north-westerly course, well clear of all traditional shipping lanes. A 20,000-ton ship, it resembled a huge submarine travelling on the surface – but minus the give-away conning tower.

It moved with a sinister silence, the low-noise-level propellers at the stern emitting little more than a whisper. The entire hull had a rounded profile which reduced its radar and infra-red signature almost to zero. No satellite would detect its steady forward movement.

The *Mao*'s cooled exhaust funnel was nearly level with the rounded superstructure. The command and weapons control quarters were not lcoated inside a normal bridge – which would have destroyed its non-image. Instead, they were buried below decks.

Captain Welensky stood in front of a battery of highly sophisticated Stealth laser-radar screens. A six-foot-two giant, the ex-hardline East European Communist dwarfed the neatly uniformed slim man beside him. Welensky, unable to pronounce his Oriental name, called him Kim. The common language they conversed in was English.

The neat little man of forty had a European-type face. The high cheekbones and narrow eyes of his original face had been 'attended to' by one of America's foremost plastic surgeons in Shanghai. The same surgeon had 'attended to' a large number of Oriental patients.

When he had completed his work the American had suffered a fatal 'accident'. After drinking a cup of poisoned tea his body had been buried in an unmarked grave. The large fortune in dollars paid to him had been 'confiscated' and transferred to the Treasury of the People's Republic of China.

'There is a vessel sailing straight towards us in the fog,' Welensky reported. 'If I alter course I should be able to avoid it. But I need a decision now.'

'Sink it. Put it below the waves,' Kim ordered in his smooth voice.

'I promise you I could evade it,' Welensky persisted.

'Is there something wrong with your hearing?' Kim asked. 'We have a smaller vessel travelling in convoy with us at our stern. Sink the intruder. Put it below the waves.'

Welensky shivered inwardly. He had made a bad mistake questioning Kim's first order. He knew it was a mistake he must not repeat.

The Stealth vessel, *Mao III*, its missile launchers housed for'ard, aft of the knife-like prow, maintained its course. The fog was growing denser.

'Do not forget to use the laser gun to wipe out their radio room,' Kim reminded the captain.

The Dutch freighter, *Texel*, 8,000 tons, had been forced badly off course rounding the southern tip of Africa by a ferocious gale. She was now well south of the course planned by her skipper, Captain Schenk. He was worried.

First, bound for Indonesia with his cargo, he was well behind schedule. Second, there was something wrong with his engines and he could only move at half normal speed. Third, when the storm had abated, it had been replaced by freezing fog. Ice was forming on the super-structure.

'Jan,' he ordered the first mate, 'keep your eyes glued to the radar screen.'

'I'm watching it non-stop,' Jan protested. 'Nothing to report. And there won't be any other ships as far south as this.'

'So why,' Schenk rejoined, staring through the window as he held the wheel, 'why am I certain I saw something in the fog – sailing towards us?'

Jan, as short and stocky as the ship's master, began to worry. Schenk's eyesight was legendary back in Amsterdam. Throughout Dutch shipping circles he was nick-named Mr Radar. Jan stared fixedly at his radar screen and blinked to clear his vision.

Technically there couldn't be another ship within miles. The empty radar screen told him that. The trouble was Jan couldn't forget one famous occasion when Schenk had saved another ship from collision with an iceberg – despite the fact that the radar hadn't even shown a blip.

'I am sure there's something close to us,' Schenk repeated.

'Nothing on the—'

Jan never completed his sentence.

A huge shape loomed through the freezing fog on the port side. The *Texel* shuddered horribly under the impact of a frightful collision. The murderous tragedy happened in seconds.

The sharp, immensely powerful bow of the *Mao* sliced the *Texel* amidships. It cut clean through like a monster shark's teeth severing the body of a man at the waist. In his wireless room the Dutch radio op. sat in front of his high-powered transmitter. His fingers started to repeat *Mayday . . .!* At the same moment the beam from the

273

Mao's laser gun – adjusted to target radio equipment – struck.

The radio op. reacted like a man in the electric chair when the switch is pulled. His body jerked rigid, his hair stood on end. A stench of burnt hair filled the cabin, his transmitter burst into flames, the radio op. sagged to the floor. Dead.

The freighter split in two, was sinking rapidly. Jan was outside on deck. He stared in stunned horror for a second as the stern floated away, amazed at the clean-cut break. He saw crewmen, wearing lifebelts, jumping overboard. Poor bloody fools – the sea was ice cold. They wouldn't last five minutes.

Captain Schenk was shouting: 'Lower lifeboats . . .'

Jan knew there was no time for that. He manoeuvred a large inflated dinghy with an outboard motor over the side, looped a rope over the handrail, shinned down it into the dinghy. He might be able to pick up some of his comrades. He started the engine, steered the dinghy away from the bow section, now submerging rapidly.

Jan lit the signal light so any survivors could find him. The hull of something enormous loomed over him. A rope ladder was thrown over the side of the mysterious vessel. Jan attached the end to his large dinghy, began to climb the ladder to safety, his body and hands frozen by the pentrating fog.

He reached the top, grabbed the rail with one hand. Above him a heavily swathed figure held in his gloved hands a large block of ice brought from the freezer. The fatal act was timed well. As Jan's head appeared over the rail the huge figure brought down the block of ice, cracking Jan's skull open. He let the block leave his hands, following Jan's corpse into the icy sea.

As Kim, clad in a sheepskin, watched, the large seaman descended the ladder, holding a boathook. Three swift thrusts with the business end of the boathook punctured the dinghy. A slash with a knife cut the rope, releasing the dinghy as it swiftly filled with water. The sea closed over it.

As the *Mao* prepared to get under way a desperate cry was heard. Kim peered over the rail as the large seaman dropped back on the deck. A life raft was floating close to the hull with three survivors from the *Texel*, wearing lifebelts, aboard. One called out, a pathetic cry in English.

'Save us! Save us . . .'

'I'll fetch a rifle,' the seaman said.

'No!' Kim grabbed his arm. 'Stay where you are.' Kim spoke to Captain Welensky on the bridge through the walkie-talkie he always carried. 'Life raft close to port side. Turn your wheel a few degrees to port. Sink it. Now!'

He watched as the *Mao* turned slowly. Its hull smashed into the side of the raft, overturning it, breaking up the raft into separate pieces. Kim continued to watch as the three men in the sea drifted away, two waving their hands futilely. He turned away.

'A few minutes more in that ice-cold water and they'll be meat for the fishes.'

Kim knew it was a million-to-one chance that the corpses would be picked up in these latitudes. But he never took even such chances: corpses found with bullets embedded in them could cause serious questions to be asked.

Both sections of the *Texel* had now sunk countless fathoms deep. Thirty seamen and ten passengers – four of them women – died when the *Texel* sank to its watery grave. Kim then went below to a section furnished as spacious and comfortable living quarters.

Twenty Scandinavians, all between the ages of twenty-five and thirty, smartly dressed and looking like executives, had been playing cards or reading books. They had

275

spent time at the special training camp in the interior of China. There they had been mentally and physically instructed intensively. All had been selected for their Communist leanings – and more especially for their liking for large sums of money. They looked up as Kim entered.

'Nothing to worry about, gentlemen,' Kim assured them. 'A minor collision with floating wreckage. The *Mao* is in perfect shape . . .'

Purring no louder than a cat, the *Mao*'s engines carried the Stealth vessel on its north-westerly course, which would take it well clear of the west coast of Africa. It was now heading for its rendezvous at sea with a refuelling tanker.

A short distance behind its stern the smaller Stealth ship maintained the same course. Even in the fog its skipper had no trouble following the *Mao* – which at frequent intervals emitted a brief signal only capable of being registered by the sonar equipment aboard the second ship.

From the refuelling rendezvous the *Mao* would continue on its northward course to its ultimate destination.

Denmark.

28

In London Tweed was hyperactive, dealing with half a dozen different problems before flying back to Brussels. Arriving at the Ministry of Defence, he showed his SIS card and was immediately ushered by a guard up a flight of stairs and down endless corridors. Colonel Fieldway, his contact and confidant at the MOD, rose behind his desk to greet him as the guard closed the door.

'I have checked the data we have on Brigadier Burgoyne, as he likes to call himself. Do sit down. That cup of tea has just been poured. Can't recommend it but if you want to wet your whistle . . .'

Fieldway was a man in his mid-forties, tall and thin and sporting a trim brown moustache the same colour as his carefully brushed thatch of hair. He had a long face, alert blue eyes, and, Tweed thought, looked in the pink of physical condition.

'As he likes to call himself,' Tweed repeated. 'What does that mean?'

Fieldway settled himself in his chair behind his desk. Before replying he shuffled papers on top of a file. Tweed recognized the trait: John Fieldway did that when he was unsure of what line to take. He spoke briskly.

'He was *Acting* Brigadier, but his substantive rank is Colonel. Likes to overawe people by pulling rank – one he's not entitled to.'

'His history?' Tweed asked.

'Burgoyne was a brilliant young officer in the Korean War back in 1950. He gained rapid promotion – the sort that only happens in wartime. He was the only commander who out-manoeuvred the Chinese army when it crossed the Yalu river to support the North Korean lot. He got an MC. Brave as a lion. And a shrewd strategist. The two don't often go together.'

'So far so good,' Tweed commented, sensing a reservation.

'That's about it. In a nutshell.'

'What went wrong?' Tweed probed.

'Oh, you know about that? Very few do. It was kept a bit hush-hush. For the sake of the Army's name and all that.'

'Refresh my memory,' Tweed urged him.

He hadn't a clue what Fieldway was referring to. There

277

was a pause before Fieldway resumed his crisp summary.

'Let's go back to that war. At one stage Burgoyne vanished off the face of the earth. He appeared four months later at his HQ. He'd been trapped behind enemy lines as the UN forces under General MacArthur retreated. He lay low, lived off the country, avoided being spotted. One of your natural guerrillas. Promoted again, he took over command of another unit and the situation stabilized.'

'John, I don't think that was what you had in mind when I asked you to refresh my memory. And, talking about nutshells, that's a pretty big one you've got in front of you. His file, I mean.'

'This is all rather delicate. Must you hear me go over it again?'

'Commander Noble of Naval Intelligence is interested in every aspect of the investigation I'm carrying out. And several people have already been murdered.'

'Good Lord! You do live an exciting life.' He paused again. 'All right, here goes. But this is confidential. Burgoyne resigned from the Army when the Korean business was over. I say "resigned" advisedly.'

'Go on. No point in leaving it there now you've started,' Tweed pressed.

'For one thing there were rumours – no more – that he'd embezzled Army funds on a large scale.'

'And for another?'

Fieldway, now looking unhappy, shuffled some more papers.

'Well, there were stories that he had contacts with the Chinese High Command after he'd left the Army.' Fieldway was consulting his file for the first time. 'No proof. Just more rumours.'

'What would be his purpose in doing that – if the rumours were true?'

'He had formed several trading companies in Hong

Kong and quickly became a well-known businessman. Mixed at the highest level with the so-called taipans in the colony.'

'So, how does that link up with the Chinese High Command?'

Fieldway looked up. 'I did say all this was highly confidential?'

'You did.'

Tweed was the soul of relaxation. Settled in his chair he sipped a little more of his tea. It tasted awful.

'The official version,' Fieldway explained, 'is that he was buying timber from Peking – Beijing – I do wish that these new countries, regimes, would stop mucking about with familiar names.'

'You were saying,' Tweed reminded him.

'Buying timber from the Chinese at prices way below the world market price. That put him in a position to make huge profits when he sold the timber to other countries.'

'And the *unofficial* version?'

'That the timber deals were a cover for smuggling banned high-tech equipment to Peking. And that,' Fieldway emphasized, 'was a very vague rumour.'

'So what eventually brought Burgoyne home from the Far East?'

'He sold out his companies to locals at a high price before leaving Hong Kong at short notice. He was on a plane flying home before the buyers of his companies found out the catch.'

'Which was?'

'The Chinese overnight raised the price of the timber they were selling to world market prices. No more easy profits for the new owners of Burgoyne's companies.'

'So Burgoyne out-manoeuvred some of the shrewdest businessmen in the world.'

'Looks like that.' Fieldway closed his file with a snap. 'That's all I have.'

'I'm very grateful.' Tweed rose, shook hands with Fieldway, who leaned across his desk, stood up. 'No, don't bother to show me the way out. I know the drill.'

Tweed turned round suddenly as he was opening the door. Fieldway was still standing up and looked uncomfortable, even embarrassed. Why?

As Tweed travelled back from Whitehall to Park Crescent in a taxi he totted up in his mind the data assembled so far. In a taxi no one could get at him.

On the flight to Brussels Burgoyne, Willie, and Helen Claybourne had been aboard the same plane. A coincidence? Tweed didn't believe in them. He remembered Paula and Marler telling him about the trip to the new village outside Ghent.

From their description it sounded like a Belgian replica of Moor's Landing on the Beaulieu River. Tweed's mind recalled a certain passage in Andover's file about the Mongol invasion of the West.

Then there was the macabre murder of Hilary Vane when she arrived at London Airport with Cord Dillon. The murder carried out by another woman, with a wide-brimmed hat. He played back in his mind Vane's report he had heard on the tape. Three top Stealth scientists vanishing to the Far East, according to Dillon. Always the road led to the Far East.

Dr Wand owned Moonglow Trading & Mercantile International – based in Hong Hong. No one knew what he traded in. Mercantile? That suggested shipping to Tweed. Then there was his verbal duel with Wand at the luxurious Waterloo villa. A more sinister man Tweed had never met.

First he had been glimpsed by Butler in London inside his mansion in The Boltons. Then he turned up in Brussels at a deluxe hotel, followed from the airport to the

Bellevue Palace by Marler. A very mobile man, the mysterious Dr Wand.

And also the director of Moonglow Refugee Aid Trust International. Refugees? Hugo Westendorf, the Iron Man of German politics – before his sudden retirement – had had a tough programme worked out to stop Europe being swamped by refugees. According to Gaston Delvaux.

Andover. Delvaux. Westendorf. All outstanding among the brains of Western Europe. All now men broken by a hideous conspiracy of kidnapping – involving the maximum of psychological pressure to break them. A pattern was forming in Tweed's mind. But he still needed more data.

Prior to his visit to the MOD, Tweed had met Cord Dillon, American Deputy Director of the CIA – more important, he had been sent over as special emissary of the American President. During his brief meeting with Dillon he had reassured the American.

'I've been sitting on my ass waiting for you, Tweed,' Dillon had begun in typically abrasive fashion.

'So you had a chance to get over jet lag and the after-effects of your flu bout,' Tweed had responded genially. 'No, wait until I've finished. I am tracking this vital Stealth problem . . .'

He had told Dillon frankly about the visit to Belgium, the bizarre murder of Andover in Liège, his conversation with Gaston Delvaux. Mollified, Dillon had nodded and stood up, grabbing hold of his suitcase.

'Then I can catch my flight back to Washington. I now have enough to tell the President you're on the job . . .'

What a responsibility, Tweed thought. He shrugged. It was part of his vocation. His mind flashed back to the interview with Fieldway. When he got the chance he must take Willie Fanshawe aside, question him about Burgoyne's view of life.

FAR EAST AIR CRASH. ALL DEAD.

He saw the poster next to an *Evening Standard* newspaper seller. Why did he immediately think of Paula and wonder how she was getting on?

Paula came out of the Brussels shop, the carrier containing her purchase looped over her left arm. She had just bought an expensive pair of knee-length leather boots. The weather had turned even colder.

Walking along near the kerb, she glanced into other shop windows. The green Lincoln Continental cruised slowly behind her. She saw its reflection in a shop window. Why did the Americans have to go in for cars as big as battleships? Gas-guzzlers, they called them – and they were.

The car parked a few feet in front of her. The rear door was thrown wide open. Pursing her lips, she moved to her right to avoid it. As she drew level two powerful hands grasped her by the shoulder. A rough voice growled in heavily accented English.

'Get into the car, lady. Take you back to the Hilton . . .'

Paula resisted the impulse to struggle. She remembered Harry Butler's instruction during the tough training course. 'The moment to stop being kidnapped is when an attempt is first made. Later is too late . . .' Relaxing her body briefly, she allowed herself to be thrust towards the interior. The driver, cap pulled well down over his head, was watching in the wing mirror, keeping his engine running.

Paula rammed her left hand on the roof of the car to gain leverage. Her relaxed body suddenly stiffened. With all her strength she rammed her backside away from her. It hit a flabby paunch. She heard her attacker let out a grunt. What happened next was so swift she didn't see it.

A scooter whizzed up out of nowhere. The rider jumped off and let it fall over. Nield, a knuckle-duster on his right hand, slammed his fist into the side of the rough-neck's jaw. Blood smeared the assailant's face. A second later Newman came up behind him, slammed into his side with a vicious kidney punch.

The large fat man gave a horrible groan, started to sag to the pavement as Paula slipped out of the way on to the sidewalk. Newman grasped the thug by his greasy hair and the back of his pants. He threw him bodily into the back of the car, where he collapsed.

Nield had already darted round to the open window, where the driver had a dazed look. Nield hit him with less force, then hissed at him in French.

'Bugger off or I'll break your neck . . .'

Newman had slammed shut the rear door with the groaning body inside. The driver fumbled for the brake. His trembling hands grasped the wheel. The huge car moved away from the kerb as Newman noted down its registration number.

'No need,' Nield called out.

The Lincoln was zigzagging into the main stream of traffic. A juggernaut coming up behind applied its brakes. Not enough time. It hammered into the back of the car. Another car with 'Politie' in large letters along its side pulled up. Two uniformed policemen dived out and opened the doors of the Lincoln.

'Just stroll,' Newman said, taking Paula by the arm. 'We're not interested in getting involved . . .'

Paula glanced back as she forced herself to walk nor-mally. Pete Nield was astride his scooter, crawling along behind them. She hugged Newman's arm.

'Thank you, Bob,' she said. 'But I left you in the shop.'

'And I followed you out at a discreet distance.'

'So I've become a target.'

'Tweed has become the ultimate target. Through you.

283

And you did well. But from now on you'd better be more on the alert than you've ever been in your life."

'Understood.'

'And now, if Messrs Fanshawe and Burgoyne are still sitting in the Hilton with their aperitifs, let's see how they react. When they spot you.'

The four of them were still sitting in the lounge area with full glasses in front of them: Burgoyne, who sat next to Lee, Willie, who sat next to Helen. Newman reckoned they must be on their third aperitif. Paula watched them closely as they approached their table.

It was Willie, of course, who jumped up with a beaming smile and started fetching chairs. As he arranged them he chatted away.

'Looking in the pink. Both of you. Can't beat a walk in the sun. Used to stroll about a lot myself back in Hong Kong. Get brown as a berry in no time at all out there. In the season. Ah, for the old days of sunlight and swarming humanity. Really felt alive. Paula, you come and sit between me and Helen. This do you, Newman? There's a good chap.'

'I suppose you'd like a drink,' Burgoyne said in his usual offhand manner.

'If there's one on offer,' Newman replied, staring directly at him. 'What about you, Paula?'

'Mineral water, no ice, no lemon, please.'

'I'll have a double Scotch. Neat,' Newman decided.

Burgoyne summoned a waiter in his usual lordly manner – beckoning with an index finger. Undoubtedly, Newman was thinking, servants had come rushing forward in Hong Kong when signalled with the same gesture. Burgoyne ordered the drinks.

'Don't go away,' he snapped. 'I'm not finished. I'd like a cigar.'

The humidor was brought instantly. Burgoyne, taking his time, performed the ritual. After examining the array on offer, he lifted out a cigar, put it close to his ear, rolled it round in his fingers, sniffed it briefly.

'That'll do.'

'A cigar cutter, sir?'

'Got my own. And hurry up those drinks. My guests will die of thirst.'

'Maurice,' Willie protested mildly, 'you do rather trample on these waiters.'

Burgoyne glared at him. 'They deserve it. If they had any guts they wouldn't be waiters – spending their lives fawning on people.'

'I've met some very good waiters,' Paula contradicted him. 'Trained at the best hotels.'

'You wouldn't damn well think it – the time they take to bring a couple of drinks.'

'They haven't been long,' Paula responded, refusing to back down.

Burgoyne stared at her, his ice-cold eyes seeming to gaze right through her, to read her mind. She stared back. How many poor subalterns had dropped their eyes before that stare, she wondered. The man had the soul of an iceberg. Helen intervened to lower the tension.

'I see you've been shopping. Something nice?'

Her cool grey eyes watched as Paula pulled out from the carrier the pair of boots. Leaning forward, Helen ran her strong slim fingers over the leather. She looked at Paula as she commented.

'They're so supple. Even so, I couldn't wear them – boots always chafe my legs.'

'And a very choice pair of legs to chafe,' Burgoyne remarked, his expression more saturnine than ever.

'We're talking about the boots,' Lee snapped. She reached over, took one, smoothed her hand down its surface. To do so she had placed her fat jewelled cigarette holder on the table. Paula's hand stretched out to examine it. Lee snatched it up with her other hand. 'Don't think me rude, but the jewels drop out easily. It was a present from a rich boy friend. When I didn't come across with what he'd expected he turned ugly. So I dropped him – but I kept the present.' She handed back the boot, inserted a cigarette in the holder without lighting it, and turned to Burgoyne.

'Maurice,' she said, throwing back a wave of blonde hair, 'you could buy me a pair like those.'

'I could,' he agreed cynically.

Quite clearly he had no intention of granting her suggestion. At that moment a waiter came up and spoke to Willie.

'A phone call for you, sir.'

'What a bore.' Willie stood up immediately, moved far more quickly than was his custom, beaming round the table. 'Please excuse me, I'd better take the call in my room. So much noise down here . . .'

Willie had scarcely left them when the waiter returned and spoke to Burgoyne.

'There's a phone call too for you, sir.'

'Must be Liège,' Burgoyne said to himself. He raised his voice. 'Transfer it to my room – my files are up there. You do know my room number by now, I hope. And I'll sign that bill for the drinks which were eventually served . . .'

A few minutes earlier, inside his study at the Waterloo villa, Dr Wand glanced up as the uniformed chauffeur he'd summoned entered the room. He was still wearing his dark glasses.

'Joseph, get me Vulcan on the phone, if you would be so kind. You know his hotel and room number . . .'

He had to wait a short while as the chauffeur talked to

286

the switchboard operator at the Hilton. Wand's lips were pursed as he took the phone.

'I am here,' a man's voice said. 'Who is this?'

'I am speaking and I have to tell you I am most displeased. A young woman was to be our guest, collected by car. I have just heard that instead of having the pleasure of her company the invitation was mishandled. Very badly mishandled, if I may say.'

'My apologies . . .'

'I am, as you know, extremely uninterested in apologies. I am only interested in results.'

'It was a rush arrangement. I warned you when we last spoke that such hurried arrangements are dangerous.'

'Now, how right you are,' Wand said in a deceptively soft tone. 'I distinctly recall some such comment. I also recall that you assured me my instruction would be dealt with nevertheless. I would even go so far as to say you have created a complete fiasco. To such an extent, the next invitation will be that much more difficult.'

'I assure you . . .'

'I am also extremely uninterested in assurances. Your new instruction is to co-operate with Joseph. I feel that he may well succeed where you have failed. Would you feel offended if I asked whether you have grasped my instruction? I repeat, you will be so good as to co-operate with Joseph. He will be in touch with you in due course. In fact, my dear sir, very shortly.'

Wand put down the phone before the man at the other end had a chance to reply. He sat back in his chair and the chauffeur remained very still and silent. The eyes behind the gold pince-nez were blank as he studied Joseph.

His manner changed suddenly, became amiable. He waved a hand and the desk light flashed off a ruby ring.

'Paula Grey is the lady whose company we wish to enjoy. I have the utmost confidence in your ability to accomplish this small task. Study the lie of the land – as a successful commander always relies on first carrying out a thorough reconnaissance.'

'I will make my move at the earliest opportunity,' the chauffeur replied.

29

'Did you notice any reaction – surprise, chagrin – among those four when we walked in?' Newman asked.

He was alone with her in the lounge of the Hilton. Lee and Helen had gone to their rooms to freshen up and both Willie and Burgoyne had not returned from taking their phone calls. Newman sipped his whisky as Paula frowned.

'It was disappointing,' she decided. 'I was watching all of them like a hawk. Willie seemed pleased to see me. The Brig. was his usual distant self. I particularly kept an eye on Lee and Helen. Nothing registered.'

'Someone is a good actress – and maybe a good actor . . .'

'Bob!' Paula grasped his arm. 'I've just remembered – checking on their backgrounds it came up back in London that both Lee and Helen were once actresses. Your remark triggered off that recollection. And you studied their men?'

'Like the proverbial hawk you just mentioned. So we've drawn a blank. But from now on you've got to take even more care. That was an attempt to kidnap you in broad daylight.'

'I know.' She shivered, the delayed reaction hitting her. 'Thanks to you and Pete I survived. I'm not sure I would have on my own.'

'You do realize why they picked on you? Remember that I said Tweed was the real target. It was intended to be a repeat performance of Andover and Delvaux. One had the severed arm of his daughter sent to him, the other the severed hand of his wife.'

'Are you trying to frighten me?' she asked quietly.

'I'm trying to scare you witless. Then you'll do as I tell you.'

'Which is what?'

'Until Tweed gets back you eat all your meals here in the hotel . . .'

'That's going to get claustrophobic . . .'

'For Heaven's sake, wait till I've finished. There are three restaurants – including the one on the roof. So that gives some variety. Then there are two outside up the street – Lee Arcades and the Copenhagen Tavern. But you only go up to one of those if you're with either Pete or me.'

'I suppose you're right.' She brightened up. 'And I can concentrate on getting to know both Lee and Helen better.'

'Which is a positive aim.' Newman paused, drank more of his whisky. 'Bearing in mind that one of them is likely to be a cold-blooded murderess.'

FAR EAST AIR CRASH. ALL DEAD.

As usual, Tweed had directed the taxi to Regent's Park Underground station. From there it was only a ninety-second walk round Park Crescent to his building. He had bought a copy of the *Evening Standard* but hadn't looked at it. He walked into his office with the paper tucked under his arm and stopped.

Monica rose slowly from behind her desk with a frozen expression. Spread out in front of her was a copy of the *Standard*. She waited while Tweed put his Burberry on the coat stand, went behind his desk, sat down.

'Tell me. Now.'

'Philip Cardon is dead. Not only our top agent in the Far East but such a nice man.'

'How do you know for certain?' Tweed asked in a neutral tone.

'The newspaper. It was a flight from Bangkok for London. Soon after take-off it blew up in midair, crashing into the jungle. No survivors. A bomb suspected.'

'But how,' Tweed insisted, with a touch of impatience, 'can you know at this stage that Cardon was aboard?'

'The list of passengers on the manifest has come through with exceptional speed. You can see for yourself,' she said with unusual vehemence, bringing over her paper.

Tweed looked at where her finger pointed. *Philip Cardon, Business Consultant.* He pushed the paper aside.

'Monica, I told you when I phoned from Brussels to tell Philip to fly back to Hong Kong, to return via the Pacific route. Didn't he call you back as arranged?'

'Yes he did. And I gave him your instruction. As you told me I insisted it was an instruction, an order.'

Tweed stood up. 'I always, as you know, give my people in the field maximum flexibility. I'm not out there – they are. Who can tell what influenced Philip to take that flight? Maybe someone was closing in on him – so he decided to adhere to his original plan.'

Monica was on the verge of tears. Tweed put his arm round her firmly. He gave her an affectionate squeeze, and when he spoke his voice was deliberately matter of fact.

'I could do with a cup of coffee. Probably you could.'

After she had hurried out Tweed walked over to the window, hands clasped behind his back. He didn't see the grey November day, the steady drizzle, the people hurrying in the cold, shoulders stooped, hands inside their pockets.

Philip Cardon had been his best man in the Far East. A wizard at disguise with his prominent cheekbones, he had in the past dressed himself as a peasant, had travelled deep into the interior of the People's Republic of China without being detected. His fluent command of Cantonese had helped. And he *was* a nice man.

As at other times of setbacks, Tweed turned his mind to different pieces of the mosaic he was building in his mind. Dr Carberry-Hyde. Beyond the window the number of people was increasing. It was late afternoon: rush hour was starting. Carberry-Hyde fitted the bill as the man he was so anxious to track down in several respects.

The timing was right. The surgeon had the skills needed to carry out the hideous amputations. He'd been thrown on the scrapheap – with justification. He had an appetite for consorting with different women – an appetite likely to grow after his experiences, if Tweed's knowledge of that type of man was anything like accurate. He glanced over his shoulder as two people entered the office.

Harry Butler was holding the door open for Monica. Under his arm he carried several plastic wallets containing glossy prints. Monica held a tray with three cups and saucers, a coffee pot, milk, and sugar – for Harry.

'You've already visited Mrs Goshawk at Brockenhurst?' Tweed asked.

'I have. I drove like the wind, but always within the speed limit.' Butler gave a rare grin. 'Just.'

'And,' Monica said as she poured coffee, 'I've discovered something strange about Burgoyne. He's the nephew of the old brigadier you met at Aldeburgh last year. The one who, it turned out, you suspected was still helping Military Intelligence.'

'That is a weird coincidence,' Tweed replied. 'And

these are the enlargements of Dr Hyde, I presume.'

Tweed picked up a wallet, extracted one print to examine it closely. A first-rate print. Enlarged, he disliked the look of the doctor even more. Something crafty about the smirking smile for the photographer. But this was a welcome diversion from the topic of Philip Cardon.

'Harry, how did you get on with Mrs Goshawk?'

'Bull's-eye. She didn't want to talk to me to start with. Showed her my Special Branch card. Told her she was in dead trouble. She couldn't spill the beans fast enough then. Dr Carberry-Hyde – she knows him as Dr Hyde – had stayed with her as a paying guest. I imagine it was for a substantial sum – she was shy about the amount.'

'The timing?' Tweed queried.

'Hyde had been with her about two months. He left April Lodge two months ago.'

'That would fit in with the operation which severed Irene Andover's forearm. No idea where he went, I suppose?'

Not normally given to making theatrical gestures, Butler grinned. Tweed waited patiently.

'Belgium. Mrs Goshawk had a postcard perched on her mantelpiece. Oostende. I walked over, read the brief message on the back. "I miss your simply splendid cooking. I may be back for more soon. Hyde." Postmarked two months ago.'

'So Hyde was in Belgium at the time when Lucie Delvaux's hand was amputated. I suspect that second sentence is intended to mislead.'

Tweed felt a tingle of excitement, although his manner remained calm outwardly. This had happened so often before: the long period of gathering data which seemed to lead nowhere. Then the breakthrough! And so often from an unremarkable incident. In this case, Rabin revealing April Lodge as Hyde's address.

'Hyde had stayed with her before,' Butler added.

'About three years ago the Goshawk woman said.'

And that, Tweed thought, adds fuel to the flames of this fire. It was three years ago when Hyde had been struck off, losing his lucrative livelihood. Why had he buried himself near the New Forest? Had he been contacted after a news item in the papers, however brief? If so, who had contacted him? Fanshawe? Burgoyne? Tweed became very active.

'Monica, get me Benoit on the line. While I'm talking to him phone London Airport, book me a seat through to Brussels for late tomorrow. Get a ticket which will then take me on to Hamburg. When you've done that pack up a batch of thirty of these Dr Hyde prints. Then arrange for a courier to rush them urgently to Benoit. He's to hand them to Benoit personally.'

'And should I also stand on my head while I'm doing these things?' Monica enquired wryly.

Tweed nodded. Her deep regret at the death of Philip Cardon would return. But for the moment the activity had put it out of her mind. Monica nodded back, indicating the Belgian police chief was on the line.

'I'm on scrambler, are you?' were Tweed's opening words.

'As it happens, I am. Can you tell me why I always make the mistake of being in the office when you call? And no more developments on the Delvaux front. Our friend is spending nearly all hours at his plant. So? What can I do for you?'

'I may have traced the fiend of a doctor who cut off Lucie Delvaux's hand. A Dr Carberry-Hyde. I'll spell that . . . May simply be going under the name of Hyde. But I think he's in Belgium. Thirty good prints of this character are coming to you by courier. Can you try and locate him?'

'Your timing is good, my friend. Crime seems to be taking a holiday. That won't last long. But I can put a large team of men checking the hotels . . .'

'Concentrate on the smaller places. This fox will be trying to stay under cover. The courier should reach you this evening.'

'My pleasure. We'll turn Brussels over . . .'

Tweed put the phone down. Butler was drinking his large cup of coffee. Monica had placed thirty Hyde prints inside a plastic wallet, the wallet inside a shabby briefcase which didn't look worth stealing. She handed it to George, the doorman and guard, who had just entered, gave him instructions. Waiting until he'd left, she turned to Tweed.

'You're booked on a flight to Brussels late tomorrow afternoon. Here are the details. Apparently the only way you can fly from Brussels to Hamburg is via an outfit called Hamburg Airlines. I think it's a private set-up. Why Hamburg, if I may be so bold as to ask?'

'I want to interview Hugo Westendorf, Germany's one-time Iron Man. And I'm not looking forward to it. I expect to find another broken man – with a close relative who has been kidnapped.'

Dr Wand looked up from a map of Denmark in his study at the Waterloo villa. He folded it up as Jules, the butler, approached his desk.

'Please excuse my interrrrupting you, sir. Vulcan is on the phone. He says he hasn't much time. You always told me that when he called . . .'

'Thank you, Jules. That will be all."

As soon as the door closed Wand picked up his phone.

'Yes. I am here. Now, what is the difficulty?'

'I am calling from the Post Office but there is a queue for the phones. Tweed has disappeared.'

'Are you really quite sure? And, if so, where has our acquaintance gone?'

'I am sure,' the man's voice continued in a hurried tone. 'And I have no idea where he has gone.'

'To London, perhaps?'

'It seems unlikely since he has left Miss Grey behind. My impression is they usually travel together.'

'Could it be Hamburg?'

There was a menacing note in Wand's voice which had been absent up to this point.

'I suppose it is just possible. Yes, it might be. It has just occurred to me that Delvaux might have mentioned Westendorf to Tweed at the Château Orange.'

'Which had already occurred to me. Kindly continue to proceed with the system which has proved so successful . . .'

Ending the call, Wand pressed the button under his desk to summon Jules. He began talking before the butler closed the door after entering the study.

'I would be obliged if you would treat this as a matter of top priority. The Lear jet must be ready to take off from Zaventem Airport at any moment tomorrow. The pilot will prepare a flight plan for Hamburg.'

'I will phone immediately . . .'

'I think possibly I did not express myself with sufficient clarity. I thought I had used the phrase top priority. Jules, may I suggest that instead of using the phone you would be so good as to use one of the cars to drive now to Zaventem. In other words,' Wand emphasized softly, 'you are to pass on my instructions to the pilot personally.'

Inside her executive bedroom at the Hilton Paula was reading a book while Newman stared out of the window at the heavy evening mist moving in on Brussels from all directions. Marler sat smoking a king-size, watching Newman. He stubbed his cigarette.

'So it is decided that we shall be having dinner at the Baron de Boeuf here on the first floor?'

'Not much point in going out,' Paula replied, closing her book. 'I think a fog is closing in.'

'In that case,' Marler decided, standing up, 'I think I'll drive out for a quick spin to the airport.'

'What for?' Newman asked.

'Just to see whether Dr Wand's Lear jet is still here.'

30

As Tweed walked into the Albemarle Street entrance of Brown's Hotel Commander Noble jumped up from a chair in the lobby. To Tweed's surprise Noble had phoned him earlier, inviting him to dinner.

'I won't say any more – even on scrambler – would six thirty p.m. suit you?' he had suggested.

Tweed, intrigued, had agreed. They walked straight into the luxurious panelled dining-room to a quiet table in a corner. Tweed said he would just have mineral water, ordered for himself a steak and boiled potatoes. When the waiter had gone he turned to his host.

'Why here?'

'Because the tables are set well apart. No one can hear us. That is important.'

'You've taken some decision?' Tweed suggested.

'I have had a private conference with the First Sea Lord. Just the two of us.'

'With the Admiral himself. You are treating this seriously.'

'We are. Do you think that light Stealth aircraft which

Delvaux had constructed inside his plant at Herstal still exists?'

'I'm sure it does. Why?'

Tweed waited while the waiter opened Noble's half-bottle of red wine. He glanced round the comfortable restaurant. Very few other guests so far: Noble had timed the dinner well.

'Because,' Noble continued, 'our boffins need that plane. They think the device could work – could detect Stealth vessels. The Admiral's opposite number on the Air Staff is of the same opinion – it may well locate Stealth aircraft.'

'In that case, as it's a plane, won't the Air Staff people want to grab it?'

'They would have done.' The ruddy-faced Noble grinned and raised his glass to Tweed. 'But fortunately you came to me. I get first bite of the cherry.'

'You can't phone Delvaux,' Tweed warned. 'As I told you his château is bugged.'

'So we go straight to the plant. I'm taking experts with me. They'll dismantle the light aircraft and bring it back here.'

'You'll need a fleet of trucks. That was the arrangement with Delvaux.'

'Which is another reason why I wanted to see you. Trucks will take too long. Loading them aboard a ferry at this end, disembarking at Zeebrugge, then the whole process repeated in reverse.'

'You have a better idea?'

'Yes. And much quicker. A small fleet of large heli-copters is being assembled at this moment. Liège has an airport, Delvaux's company will have its own transport. We use his trucks to carry the dismantled aircraft and the consignment of his new radar devices he offered to Liège airport, then the choppers fly them here.'

'It is a better idea,' Tweed agreed. 'Much faster. But

there is one problem – Liège airport. How are you going to explain to the airport traffic controllers why a fleet of choppers is descending on them?'

'I hoped you could help there.' Noble grinned again. 'Which is why I asked you to dinner.'

'Benoit,' Tweed said suddenly. 'Of course. Chief Inspector Benoit, a man I would trust with my life. And he doesn't ask a lot of questions. I'll call him, arrange for a team of plain-clothes men to close down Liège Airport while your choppers are there. And it's a good idea to use Delvaux trucks. The airport people will think it is some confidential export order. The Belgians take the view they can sell armaments to anyone with the money to pay for them. Unofficially. Even more so now – when the armaments industry is depressed. Apart from Delvaux, the once huge armaments complexes in Liège are closed down.'

'The paperwork at Liège worries me,' Noble remarked.

'There won't be any. Benoit will see to that. When do the choppers fly there?'

'Tomorrow evening.'

Tweed was stunned. Admiralty was taking Stealth very seriously indeed. They were moving like lightning.

'I am relying on a woman with a lot of brains plus her exceptional eyesight,' Tweed insisted.

'Paula Grey?'

'Yes.'

'Years ago it was a girl who detected the flying bomb on its launch pad in the Baltic,' Noble reminded him. 'I'm willing to put my money on Paula Grey. Come to think of it, I may be staking my whole career on her.'

Later that night Tweed went home alone to his new pad in Walpole Street, Chelsea. He was renting it from Howard, his chief, who had once used it as a rendezvous for his secret liaisons with a variety of feminine friends.

Nowadays Howard dutifully went home each night to his estate in Berkshire to spend his evenings with his wife. Monica's theory was he 'had run out of steam'. Tweed doubted that, had a different explanation.

Cynthia, Howard's wife, he knew, had had a long fling with an eminent banker. It was when that affair had broken up he had overheard a snatch of conversation. The door to Howard's office had been half open as he walked past, his mind miles away. Then he had heard Cynthia's shrill voice.

'Ten women I don't mind. Most of you men can't resist a fresh pair of legs. But if there's a number eleven that will be one too many. So, I want to see you at home in the evenings from now on. Or not at all . . .'

Before taking the long walk to Walpole Street, Tweed had taken a taxi from Brown's back to Park Crescent. Monica had phoned Brussels for him.

'Again,' Benoit had mocked Tweed, 'I find myself in the office at the wrong moment. Well, you had better get on with it. What is it at this hour?'

Tweed had outlined tersely Noble's plan. Benoit had listened without comment as Tweed avoided all reference to Stealth.

'. . . it's the paperwork at Liège we are worried about,' Tweed had concluded.

'What paperwork?' Benoit had replied. 'I will be at the Liège Airport myself. Closing it down to other flights will be no problem. The old chestnut – a bomb alert. I will be there until this consignment is airborne . . .'

'Did you remember the plant manager at Herstal will want proof of identity?' Monica asked as Tweed finished the call.

'Yes. I gave Noble my card with the "T" in my name underlined. The plant manager will co-operate.' He walked over to the largest of the three wall maps – the map he had marked with pins showing where ships had disappeared without trace all over the world. He stuck in a fresh pin.

'What is that for?' Monica asked.

'Commander Noble told me another vessel has vanished off the Cape of Good Hope. The *Texel*, an 8,000-ton Dutch freighter. Blown a long way south off course and then it disappears like a puff of smoke.'

'By a gale? I suppose it could happen.'

'Then the gale died out as suddenly as it had blown up.' Tweed paused. 'And was succeeded by a dense fog. And again no Mayday signal reported by other shipping further north.'

'It does sound strange.'

'Even stranger when you know the *Texel* was due to call at Port Elizabeth, three hundred miles or so from its last reported position on its way to Indonesia. When it didn't arrive planes were sent out immediately to search. Not one piece of wreckage was found. No survivors . . .'

After his long walk home to Walpole Street Tweed should have slept like a log. Instead he tossed and turned the whole night long: at the best he slipped into a brief doze. He came wide awake, a vision of Dr Wand in his mind at the moment when Newman's lighter had flared at the Waterloo villa. The satanic expression behind those glinting gold pince-nez.

Over a thousand miles off the African coast of Angola – and midway between two shipping lanes – the refuelling operation with the Chinese tanker had been completed.

The *Mao III* was still proceeding on a north-westerly course to sail well clear of the huge bulge of Africa at Dakar. Inside the low-level bridge Captain Welensky checked his chart, then ordered the engine room: 'Full speed ahead!'

300

'You should have checked with me before giving that order,' reprimanded Kim.

Welensky turned his large bulk to stare down at the small Chinese. He was beginning to lose patience with what he privately referred to as 'the Chinks'. His tone of voice was gravelly.

'I was under the impression that I am skipper of the ship. You want me to slow down? It's still night but soon it will be dawn. We want to be a long way from that tanker when day breaks.'

'I do not wish you to slow down,' Kim replied smoothly. 'Neither do I wish you to try and read my mind.'

Welensky shrugged, turned away. He pressed the button which would emit the signal indicating to the smaller Stealth vessel following in their wake his position. In Welensky's opinion he had done well. He was still on schedule for the ultimate rendezvous, which had to be reached during the hours of darkness.

He had now completed roughly two thirds of their long voyage from Cam Ranh Bay, the great anchorage in Vietnam. And without incident – except for that crazy and totally unnecessary encounter with another vessel south of the Cape of Good Hope.

Behind the *Mao III* the smaller Stealth vessel, *Yenan*, continued to keep pace with the larger ship. Aboard, in the spacious living quarters, fifteen more Danish-speaking passengers, all between the ages of twenty-five and thirty, passed the time watching videos, playing games, or reading. Every man had undergone the very special training carried out at secret camps on the mainland of the People's Republic of China.

Some had become highly skilled saboteurs, others spies. But every man had a second skill – in advertising, accountancy, radio, or the television industry. Every man could merge into the European way of life as a normal member of the community. His reward? Money.

They were the vanguard of the revolution planned to sweep the world.

At Park Crescent the call from Benoit came through in the middle of the night. Monica was still at her desk – trying to disentangle the finances of Moonglow Refugee Aid Trust International.

They were complex. A certain amount of funds came in from subscriptions to the cause, but nothing like the money needed to keep up a house in The Boltons, let alone a millionaire's villa at Waterloo. Through certain mainland contacts Monica had obtained confidential information. Which all led back to Liechtenstein, the toy state on the eastern borders of Switzerland. Liechtenstein – which prided itself on its secrecy where bank accounts were concerned. The phone rang.

'Benoit here . . .' Sounded in a hurry. 'Is Tweed available?'

'He's fast asleep at his Chelsea pad.'

'Monica, I must try that some time. Sleep. And you can tell him I said so. Our friend Dr Hyde has been staying in Brussels.'

'That's quick work, Chief Inspector.'

'Oh, we got lucky. One of my men called at the Hermitage Hotel. Sounds very grand. Over there you'd call it a run-down boarding-house. He stayed there for the past two months. Under the name Dr Hyde.'

'Past tense, Chief Inspector?'

'I am afraid so. He left a few days ago. No forwarding address. But it was him. The slattern who runs the place identified his photograph after a little gentle persuasion from my man.'

'Tweed will be interested. Very.'

'Monica, I'm now spreading the net – concentrating on

302

Liège. Since that is where Sir Gerald Andover was murdered. Will report any further developments. Tell Tweed I hope he slept well . . .'

Tweed was up late in the morning. As the light of a grey dawn filtered through the curtains he had thought about getting up, making a mug of tea. While he was thinking about it he fell into a deep sleep.

Cursing, after he'd put on his glasses and checked the time, he forced himself to get out of bed. Feeling like nothing on earth he went into the kitchen, put on water to boil for the coffee. Returning to his bedroom he dressed slowly.

It was eleven o'clock when he mounted the staircase to his office, step by step. Like climbing Everest. He opened the door. The first thing he noticed was Monica, almost beside herself with joy. He opened the door further and stood still, stunned. A small man wearing a crumpled suit of American clothes jumped up.

Philip Cardon.

31

'We thought you were dead,' Tweed said as he shook Cardon's bony hand. 'The plane crash. The bomb . . .'

'I didn't travel aboard that flight. As you suggested, I took a flight to Hong Kong which was leaving almost immediately. Thailand can be hopelessly inefficient. Clearly they must have left my name on the passenger manifest.'

'I didn't think you'd obeyed Monica,' Tweed said. 'I thought you'd decided to board that plane.'

He sat behind his desk as Cardon sagged into the armchair again. Philip Cardon had a bony face, narrow alert eyes, was of slim build, and with a nervous energy which made his movements swift and agile. He reminded Monica of a squirrel.

'I heard her all right,' Cardon explained. 'What worried me was that someone else might be listening in – even when I was in a public call box at the airport.'

'Sounds unlikely, I'd have thought.'

'Not in Thailand. Corruption is universal. Information is bought everywhere. From Hong Kong I caught another plane to San Francisco, then straight across the States to New York. That was the only delay – they wouldn't let Concorde take off for several hours. Ten-tenths fog. Which is why I scared Monica out of her wits when I rolled in here a few hours ago . . .'

'I tried to phone you,' Monica told Tweed.

'Thor couldn't have woken me. Philip, don't you need some rest? You must be jet-lagged out of your mind.'

Cardon had dark circles under his eyes. His face had a drawn look. He swallowed black coffee from the mug Monica had provided, shook his head.

'I can keep going a while longer. I must. Things you've got to hear. The adrenalin is roaring. Start at the beginning, shall I?'

'Go ahead then. But only until the fatigue catches up with you. Then I'm packing you off to your flat.'

Tweed, suddenly thoroughly awake, relaxed in his chair. He perched one elbow on his desk, his knuckled hand supporting his chin as he studied the man back from the dead.

'I managed to reach Lop Nor,' Cardon began in a casual way.

'Lop Nor!' Tweed was astounded. He jumped up,

walked to the wall map of the world, pointed to a certain position. 'You can't mean Lop Nor in Sinkiang where the Chinese have their atom-bomb plant? That's a vast distance.'

'Yes, that Lop Nor,' Cardon agreed as Tweed returned to his chair. 'I was disguised as a peasant. I hopped on board a plane in Chungking bound for Lop Nor. I'd made friends with a dubious individual who wanted me to carry a package for a small sum. He sat in the opposite seat as though we were strangers. A rocky old crate it was. Lord knows how it crossed the mountains, and breathing was difficult for a while. Just before we landed I got up to go to the loo and slipped the package back into my so-called friend's coat. On landing we were searched. He was arrested by the security service for carrying drugs.'

He paused to drink more coffee. Monica stared at him in amazement.

'You make it sound so easy,' she commented.

'Oh, it's like anywhere else in the world. Security is lousy. You need cheek, bags of self-confidence – plus the ability to look like a Chinese and a knowledge of the lingua franca. Mind you, the Chinese can travel for hours without saying a word, which helps. They just sit there liked stuffed dummies.'

'What happened after you got off the plane?' Tweed asked, fascinated. 'You said the security service was present.'

'Easy again. They were so taken up with grabbing the drugs smuggler they didn't look at anyone else. He was shot, of course. But there were other peasants on the plane. Coolie labour for building more underground hangars for Stealth bombers. They enlarge caves in the mountains, then erect huge doors the same colour as the rock. I mingled with the crowd, listened to them chattering once they were back on Mother Earth.'

'And Security didn't check them?' Tweed queried.

'Lord, no. It's chaos up there. So many coolies earning a pittance. Rather like they built the pyramids. Men with muscle – thousands of them. Amazing what they can achieve with an endless supply of cheap labour.'

He drank more coffee from the mug Monica had refilled, thanked her, resumed his report. He spoke in a sing-song English and Tweed realized his way of talking was still reflecting his use of Cantonese.

'You mentioned Security,' Cardon went on. 'Seeing them was a lucky break. I recognized the uniform. I went into a drinking shop. A lot of the customers were gambling. Never cure the Chinese of that pastime.'

'I thought it was forbidden,' Monica observed.

Cardon grinned. 'It is. But Lop Nor is a long way from Beijing. And out there all they care about is keeping the work force happy. I saw a uniformed man sitting at a little table by himself. Security. Had a special badge attached to his breast pocket and some insignia of rank. He's as drunk as a lord. I buy some more of the local liquor – pure poison – keep filling up his glass. When I first went in I'd heard him shouting for more – in Cantonese.'

'You took a big chance,' Tweed remarked.

'Not really. Not yet. This prat starts boasting about what a big man he is. Head of Security to General Li Yun. The name struck a chord. He tells me he's in charge of security at the War Room. To cut a long story short, we end up outside and I have to hold up my new friend. We walk arm in arm.'

'Wasn't it cold up there?' Monica asked, to make Cardon pause.

'Cold enough to freeze a brass monkey's whatnots. But I'd piled on the clothing at Chungking. That helped. You know me – all bone and muscle. The clothes made me look like a typical stocky Chinese. Where was I?'

'Arm in arm with—' Tweed began.

'I'm there. We walk past the entrance to a military HQ

built of rock to conceal it from the air. Drunky says that's where he works, that he'd better get back on duty. I say you'd better sober up a bit first. He agrees and we leave the town and walk into the wilderness. Huge bare mountains, no one about, have to watch your footing. Big deep fissures and ravines in the ground. Drunky does the job for me. Sits down on a rock and falls asleep. I pick up a small rock, tap him on the skull to keep him that way. He's about my height and build – with all the clothes I'm swaddled in. Guess what comes next.'

'We'd sooner hear it from you,' said Tweed, who didn't want to miss a word.

'I change into his uniform and peaked cap. He has Security passes and identification in his pocket. I lower him into a shallow fissure. At least I thought that it was shallow. He disappears and I never hear him hit bottom. Can't be helped. I hurry back to the HQ. His shoes hurt, but you can't have everything. Then I walk inside past all the checkpoints.'

'You did what?' Tweed enquired. 'Just how did you manage that one?'

'Like I said. The place is swarming with Security personnel. More cheek. I realize I outrank everyone in sight. Probably plus that funny badge. Only one man asks me in Cantonese if he can help. I stare him down. Say "the General" and walk on. Later a guard opens a door for me. I walk inside. A long polished wood table with lots of chairs. No one in sight. At the far end a lot of maps on the wall. Above them the legend – in Cantonese – War Room West: Operation Long Reach. I know I'm in business.'

Cardon drank more coffee from the mug refilled by Monica. Verbally he was on a big high, the words tumbling out.

'There's a door open an inch or so to another room. I

307

can hear a Chinese – presumably General Li Yun – addressing what was probably a meeting of operational officers. The General is from Canton so I catch a phrase or two – but I'm busy with my little camera provided by the Engine Room downstairs here. Taking pictures of those maps on the wall. I do catch something the General is saying. It prickles the hairs at the back of my neck. I quote. "Operation Long Reach – to take over Europe – is well advanced in its first phase, the planting of saboteurs and spies in their midst – Europeans. But the supreme and first objective is Britain." I beat a hasty retreat out of the War Room.'

'Can I quote you something from a file Sir Gerald Andover handed me?' Tweed interjected. He looked at Monica. 'And you haven't heard this.'

He unlocked the deep drawer in his desk, opened the file, turned the pages rapidly. He read from the file.

'Operation Torch: the World War Two Allied invasion of North Africa. The final plan for the initial assault was that *24,500 American troops embarked in the United States* should land north and south of Casablanca . . . They had to convoy, in the face of submarine and air attack, more than 600 vessels, carrying an assault force of *90,000 men, and 200,000 more to follow*, with all their supplies and weapons, across 1,500 miles of sea from Britain and *3,000 miles from America* . . .' Tweed paused. 'That is the end of Andover's quote from *The Turn of the Tide* by Arthur Bryant – from Field Marshal Viscount Alanbrooke's diaries, published after the war.'

'I saw that very volume on General Li Yun's bookshelf,' Cardon remarked.

'What on earth are you two suggesting?' asked Monica in a horrified tone.

'I raised my voice where Andover underlined certain passages,' Tweed added.

'But what are you suggesting?' Monica persisted.

'Oh, it's quite simple,' Cardon went on, 'the Chinese are great students of history. They've spotted that what defeated Hitler was his failure to invade Britain. He left it as a gigantic floating base off the continent – a base the Americans could use to pour in their might ready for the invasion of Europe. Without Britain they'd have had nowhere to build up their forces.'

'Hence,' Tweed intervened, 'their first objective when the time comes is to seize Britain. That isolates the Americans completely.'

'It sounds horrifying, fantastic,' Monica protested.

'As would Hitler's ultimate conquest of Europe back in 1933,' Cardon retorted. 'Tweed is right. China is the successful Communist state. It has been clever enough to adopt private enterprise and has a sound economy – and a satisfied and obedient population. And what a population! Over a billion people – nearly a quarter of the earth's population.'

'So?' Monica said less confidently.

'The Chinese do not have a reverence for human life. With a population like that they could afford to lose fifty million to establish control of Europe. They'd overwhelm us.'

'They have to get here first,' Monica objected.

'If the Americans could transport such huge numbers in 1942 by sea,' Cardon reminded her, 'how many do you think the Chinese could move by sea and air in giant ships and planes?'

'You two are frightening me,' Monica told them.

'That's nothing,' Cardon said. 'Now I'm going to scare the living daylights out of you. China, as I said, is the one successful Communist state. With the collapse of the Soviet Union it regards itself as the keeper of the Holy Grail. And it feels itself to be one gigantic fortress under siege from a capitalist world. So what is the answer? Stalin's. Unlike him they have this colossal population, this vast land mass. The answer? To strike first before liberal

309

ideas take hold inside China. To occupy Europe. Then they are safe. More than safe – they'll be in a position to dictate to the rest of the world with that much power. And generals like military action – that's what they live for.'

'China is a long way from London,' Monica said, without much conviction.

'Liegnitz in Silesia – about two hundred and fifty miles from Hamburg – was a long way from East Asia,' Tweed reminded her. 'And yet the Mongols reached it – and they travelled on horseback. Think of the speed at which a Stealth plane could move. We're talking hours instead of years.'

'You have scared the daylights out of me,' Monica admitted.

'And now just to reassure you,' Cardon said ironically, 'I'll show you those photographs I took inside General Li Yun's War Room West. Developed and printed in the Engine Room before you arrived, Tweed.'

He took out a plastic wallet from his pocket, extracted some prints, spread them out on the desk. Tweed stared at them with rising apprehension.

They were photos of British Ordnance Survey maps – and the first one showed a section of the south coast from Bournemouth to Beaulieu River with Lymington in the centre. A cross marked a location he was certain was Moor's Landing.

Five more photos – also of Ordnance Survey maps – linked up with the Lymington map and were marked with the most rapid routes to London.

He examined the next prints, which were of Belgium. A second cross just west of Ghent marked another location. He must show this one to Benoit when he returned to the Belgian capital.

310

Tweed used a magnifying glass to study another print. He read the words *Ost Friesische Inseln*. The Frisian Islands looping in a semicircle off the west coast of Germany – including Borkum and Norderney. Tweed recalled his first conversation with Commander Noble. Vessels had disappeared in this area – the area where a crewman lowered from a helicopter had been sick when he found Vogel's decapitated head jammed in the floating bow of his craft.

And this was also the area written about before the First World War by Erskine Childers in his classic novel, *The Riddle of the Sands*. A wonderful story about how the Kaiser's Germans planned to assemble a fleet of barges to invade Britain. Had the diabolical General Li Yun also got a copy of this volume on his bookshelf?

No longer dealing with Ordnance Survey maps, he peered through his glass at the final print, of the coast extending north off Germany and including the west coast of Denmark.

The map included the northern tip of the German island of Sylt – also marked with a cross. But Tweed's attention was drawn to the stretch of Danish coast south of the port of Esbjerg – a bleak and lonely area out of season as he knew from a visit. It was off this coast that most vessels had disappeared. And there was another cross midway between Esbjerg and the German frontier – close to the sea.

He double-checked the print of the Frisian Islands. It extended inland up the River Elbe to include the great port of Hamburg. Another cross, downriver and outside the city. He looked at Cardon.

'I suspect this is the most ingenious and brilliant military planning I've ever encountered.'

'Takes the biscuit,' Cardon agreed. He was still bursting with energy as he stirred restlessly in his chair. 'Now, anyone like to know about Dr Wand?'

* * *

In the lounge area of the Brussels Hilton Paula idly turned over the pages of a fashion magazine. She was feeling rather like a prisoner – not able to go out unless she had escorts guarding her. You just want some action, she said to herself.

'Miss Paula Grey, I believe?'

She looked up. A tall, handsome man with jet-black hair and an engaging smile was looking down at her. Where had she seen him before? In his early thirties, she guessed, he was smartly dressed in a blue pinstripe suit, a snow-white shirt, and a blue polka-dot tie. The shirt was a change from the striped effort most Englishmen were affecting at the moment. She put down her magazine, saw the brief glance of admiration at her crossed legs. Not a trace of lechery in that glance.

'You've got to remember where you last saw me,' he teased her as he sat down.

'I'm sorry. I do know I know you . . .'

How feeble can you get, she thought as she heard herself utter the words. And really she was ready for a change of company: just for a few hours. He suggested a drink and she said she wouldn't mind a glass of champagne.

'Or is it a bit early?' she wondered, checking her watch.

'Some people have started lunch already,' he assured her. He ordered two glasses from a waiter, then again gave her his full attention. 'I was dressed differently – in rather casual clothes . . .'

'Buckler's Hard! You took us by boat to Moor's Landing. Mr Mordaunt!'

'Mr Mordaunt it is,' he agreed. 'I knew you had a good memory. Not that I'm the sort of person people do remember.'

She liked that. It suggested a degree of modesty many men she'd met seemed totally devoid of.

'You're a friend of Bob Newman's . . .'

312

'Who is using my name in vain?'

It was Newman who had materialized from nowhere. She wondered why she felt slightly annoyed. Newman sat down and stared at Mordaunt.

'Where did you spring from? Last time you were ambling round Hampshire. What brings you to Brussels?'

'A hot tip. Could be a right royal scandal brewing up. Involving one of those fat-cat EC Commissioners. Could also be the big one I've been hoping for.' He looked at Paula. 'If it's not too brash an approach, would you join me for lunch at the Tête d'Or? It's a very good restaurant off Grand' Place.'

'That's very nice of you.'

She thought it over quickly. Tweed had once taken her to the Tête d'Or. It was a very plush restaurant and the food was excellent. Also police HQ and Benoit were just off Grand' Place.

'I'd like that very much,' she decided.

Mordaunt stood up. 'We're having a glass of champers, Newman. You'll join us, of course?'

'No, thank you.'

'When the waiter comes I'm picking up the tab. Please excuse me for a moment while I visit the bathroom . . .'

'Did you have to be so rude to him?' Paula snapped. 'I need a bit of variety.'

'Some variety,' Newman commented. 'Mordaunt is a snout, a so-called freelance journalist scrabbling in the gutter for snippets of information he can fob off on professional journalists. For money, of course. A hand-to-mouth character.'

'Have you finished?' Paula enquired in a dangerously soft tone. 'A snout? I think that's a disgusting term. And have you, by any chance, used his services yourself in the past?'

'I have,' Newman told her cheerfully. 'I've asked him for info I didn't want – to send the opposition off in the wrong direction. Knowing he'd go and sell what I'd said to him to a rival.'

'I've heard quite enough,' Paula snapped again. 'More, in fact, than I want to hear. And I am lunching with him at the Tête d'Or.'

'Suit yourself.' Newman took the bill off the waiter as the drinks arrived. He signed it with his own room number. Paula was biting after the waiter had left.

'Mordaunt wanted to pay that bill. Do you have to interfere?'

'You don't have to say thank you,' Newman informed her with the same infuriating smile. He had seen Mordaunt coming back, stood up quickly. 'Excuse me.'

Newman had also noticed Marler emerging from the elevator, then standing some distance away while pretending to study an advertisement for an exhibition. Newman spoke quietly, pausing close to Marler as he lit a cigarette.

'See that dark-haired berk sitting down with Paula? She's soon waltzing off with him to have lunch at the Tête d'Or off Grand' Place. Mordaunt by name. Fringe journalist. Looks as though he's prospering by the cut of his suit. Mordaunt doesn't know you. Follow them. I'm just going to alert Nield to do the same on his scooter. I'll follow at a distance in a taxi. And Paula is in an uptight mood. I think it's a reaction to the kidnap attempt.'

'Three of us,' Marler commented. 'You're using the heavy brigade.'

'I don't trust Mordaunt.'

'I'll collect my hired Merc. from the garage. Oh, by the way, Dr Wand's Lear jet is being prepared for a flight to Hamburg.'

'How did you find that out?'

'You know me. Bribery. I got talking to a mechanic in the airport bar when he'd finished servicing the Lear. He heard the pilot talking about his flight plan . . .'

314

32

Lee Holmes came up to Newman at the moment Paula left the Hilton with Mordaunt. She wore a green dress, form-fitting and with a plunging neckline which didn't quite reveal the tops of her well-moulded breasts. Over one arm was folded a camelhair coat. She smiled with her full red lips.

'I'm free – for anything,' she said mischievously. 'Are you?'

'For lunch possibly.' Newman thought quickly. 'I know a nice restaurant in Grand' Place.'

'Sounds divine. I've had Maurice up to here.'

She raised her hand and rested it across her throat. Her greenish eyes stared at him invitingly. What the hell, he thought: maybe I could find out something about this woman and be in the right place at the same time. Don't kid yourself, he told himself: Paula has irked you.

He helped her on with her coat. She used both hands to lift her golden mane over the collar, took him by the arm. Outside the doorman summoned a taxi, Newman told the driver to take them to Grand' Place.

Lee crossed her legs, her coat fell open, exposing her elegant legs. She sat closer to Newman as the taxi moved off, looped her arm again inside his, squeezed it.

'I'm really so glad you're available, Mr Newman.'

'Call me Bob.'

'Then I'm Lee . . .'

How did she manage it? Without appearing to be in any way a tart she used words like 'available' in a way as though they'd known each other a long time. The taxi dropped them outside a street leading into Grand' Place: the barriers prevented him taking them inside the old cobbled square. Newman escorted Lee into a restaurant facing across the square, chose a window table.

From his seat he could see Marler leaning up against a wall, reading a newspaper. He was perched at the corner where the rue Tête d'Or led off Grand' Place. He'd have parked his car near by, Newman guessed. Doubtless at the other end of the short narrow street Nield was close by with his scooter. They had Paula and Mordaunt in a pincer movement.

'Do you like Chablis?' Newman asked, naming his favourite wine.

'I adore Chablis,' Lee assured him.

When they had ordered she leant forward, inserted a cigarette in her fat jewelled holder. Her tone was mocking in a warm way.

'I saw some other man walking off with your girl friend, Paula. I hope she hasn't deserted you.'

'She isn't what is normally known by the term girl friend.'

'So what is the relationship? I'm jealous, Bob. She is a very attractive girl. With brains too.'

She described Paula without a trace of bitchiness. Her eyes never left his.

'She's in the insurance business. Rather high-powered stuff.' He watched Lee closely. 'It can involve negotiations with kidnappers.'

'Sounds dangerous.' Lee bit gently on the tip of her holder. 'Do you mean her outfit insures important men in case they're kidnapped for a ransom?'

'Something like that.' He hadn't seen any flicker of an unusual reaction. But she had been an actress. 'Don't let's talk about her,' he suggested. 'Let's talk about someone who is beginning to intrigue me. You.'

'Thank you,' she said, accepting the compliment gracefully. 'Let me think a moment where to start.'

Newman found himself falling under her spell. It wasn't just her physical beauty. Her voice was soothing and he felt he could listen to her for hours. She sipped her wine, still staring at him, but her mind seemed to be far away. He prodded her.

'Why are you fed up with Maurice?'

'The Brig. can be such a pain. He's so goddam stiff – unyielding in the smallest thing. Everything has to be just so. It's his military background, I suppose. He still thinks he's in charge of the brigade – that I'm his aide-de-camp, or whatever . . .' Newman realized he'd pressed the right button: the words came out in a torrent.

'I trained as an accountant,' she went on, 'so that made me pretty meticulous in everything I do. I gave it up. Figures are boring. They never talked to me – the way they seem to do with some accountants. I drifted from one job to another, then I saw this advertisement. For a housekeeper-cum-personal assistant. "Meticulous attention to detail required", was one phrase used. So I thought: that's me. I keep his papers in order – those he'll let me handle . . .'

'There are some he keeps to himself?'

'Oh, yes!' Her eyes opened wide. 'The Brig. keeps a lot of them locked in a safe like a bank vault. I'm never allowed access to those. Maurice can be very secretive. And he's not relaxing company – like you are, Bob. You're memorizing every word I say, aren't you?'

'I wouldn't go so far as that,' Newman lied. 'Do you travel a lot with him?'

'Indeed we do. Traipse all over Europe. He's meeting what he calls business associates – some of them very peculiar characters . . .'

'In what way are they peculiar?' Newman asked casually.

317

'Pretty rough diamonds. I wouldn't like to meet them in a dark alley. God knows what these business deals are. If he wasn't the Brig. I'd say they were villains. He once told me to go to a certain bar in the Reeperbahn in Hamburg late at night to collect an envelope. I had to dress in a certain way so whoever had the envelope would recognize me. Talk about rough types – it's a wonder I got out of there with any of my clothes still on.'

'So how did you handle that?'

'I grabbed a bottle by the neck, smashed it on the bar, and shouted in German that anyone who came near me would carry the scars for life.'

Newman looked at her. With her soothing voice and perfect complexion he found it difficult to picture her as a raging tigress. But he had no doubt the incident had taken place.

'Get the envelope?' he asked.

'Of course.' She looked surprised. 'A big fat sealed envelope. I felt it afterwards in the taxi back to the hotel. I was pretty sure it was crammed with 500-Deutschmark notes.' She smiled again. 'You're listening to every word I say with hardly an interruption. The Brig. wouldn't let me talk for sixty seconds without interrupting. We really ought to get to know each other better.'

'Great idea.' Newman stood up. 'The food will be here soon. Mind if I pop out for a paper? Back in a minute . . .'

He strolled across the cobbled square in the cold sunlight before the shadows of the ancient buildings blotted it out. Marler, who had seen him coming, had melted out of sight. Newman found him just round the corner.

'What's happening?' he asked Marler. 'I'm bothered about Paula.'

'She's inside the Tête whatnot with her sleek friend. So not to worry. How are you getting on with your blonde lovely?'

'Hearing some strange things about Brigadier Maurice

318

Burgoyne. Keep an eye on Paula and that jerk she's taken a crazy fancy to. Anywhere I can get a paper?'

He arrived back with a copy of *La Libre Belgique* under his arm and stood stock-still. The wine, the glasses, the crockery and cutlery, and one crumpled napkin were still on the table. But Lee Holmes had gone.

Inside the Tête d'Or Paula had enjoyed the excellent food. At the same time she had been wary of the pleasant compliments Mordaunt paid her. Was he leading up to something more intimate? She asked the question over the coffee.

'It's a small world – excuse the cliché – but it really is rather amazing that we should first meet at Buckler's Hard, then you pop up in Brussels at the Hilton.'

'I always stay at the Hilton,' he replied in his debonair manner. 'And this is where journalists congregate these days. The headquarters of the EC fat-cats and all that. Put it down to a lovely coincidence – from my point of view.'

'So what were you doing at Buckler's Hard? Not a lot of material for a journalist there, I'd have thought.'

'On holiday. Drifting.' He sounded vague. 'I do like messing about in boats.' Paula felt sure he was lying: for the first time he seemed uncomfortable. 'You have the most beautiful hands,' he said suddenly.

She prepared to remove her hand off the table, expecting him to reach out for it. But instead he sat back in his chair. She had the impression he couldn't take his eyes off her. If I allowed my vanity full rein, she thought, I'd think he was falling for me. So get that silly idea out of your head.

'Thank you,' she said quickly. 'And I ought to get back to the hotel soon. I'm expecting a phone call.'

Mordaunt summoned the head waiter immediately,

asked for the bill. Paula was puzzled by his attitude. He seemed almost genuine, which she hadn't anticipated.

'I would like to meet you again,' he said, leaning his arms on the table. 'I've never met a girl quite like you.' He looked uncomfortable again, a complete contrast to his normal assured manner. 'Sorry, I heard myself say that. God, it sounded like the usual cheap come-on. I hope you'll excuse me?'

'You're excused,' she replied, smiling, more confused than ever.

'Then could we make a date for dinner? I don't want to put any pressure on you. It's entirely for you to decide.'

'Maybe.' She pondered. 'It would have to be at the Hilton. I get important phone calls at all hours.'

'The Hilton would suit me fine. The Baron de Boeuf or the Sky Room? It's up to you.'

'My, we are pushing the boat out.' She smiled again. 'The Tête d'Or first, now the Baron de Boeuf. This is costing you a mint.'

'I have a job with a big salary at the moment,' he replied curtly. Then he moderated his tone. 'So it is a date – when you can manage it?'

'If I can manage it,' she corrected him.

He paid the large bill – in cash, she noted. On their way to find a taxi he didn't again take hold of her arm as he had done when they'd left the Hilton. She sensed he was being careful not to push her, an action she appreciated.

'When we get back,' he said, 'I'll see you safely inside and then I've got to go across the road to the money exchange. And, if you don't mind my saying so, don't go out alone at night. Brussels isn't the safest city any more . . .'

'I can't go on calling you Mr Mordaunt,' she said in the cab. 'What is your first name?'

'Joseph.'

* * *

320

Dr Wand sat behind his desk in the Waterloo villa studying a map of Africa. He checked the date on his calendar and then measured a distance from the Cape of Good Hope with a plastic ruler. On the floor by his side a copy of *La Libre Belgique* was spread out. A short story carried the headline in French:

DUTCH VESSEL DISAPPEARS
OFF CAPE OF GOOD HOPE

He pursed his lips in annoyance at the distraction when Jules entered the darkened room. His instinct was to throw down the ruler but instead he carefully placed it parallel to the top of the map. A very precise, controlled man, Dr Wand.

'Yes , Jules.'

'Joseph is on the phone. Speaking from a public call box. He sounds agitated.'

'Wait. Sit down.'

Only the unusual terse instruction told Jules his chief was annoyed. Wand spoke in his usual mellow tone as he answered the phone.

'It is, as always, a pleasure to hear from you, Joseph. Is there some unforeseen problem I may be able to help with?'

'There is.' He heard Joseph swallow as though gearing himself up to continue. 'I'm asking to be relieved of the assignment you asked me to carry out.'

'Really, Joseph. Now that I find a most intriguing request. Would it be possible for you to give me your reason for this unique attitude?'

'Certainly. It is quite simple. I doubt whether I am capable of carrying out the assignment. I wouldn't like to let you down.'

'Quite simple?' Wand repeated softly. 'I think that I understand. And, as always, Joseph, you are right. I would not wish you to let me down as you put it. May I express my appreciation for your being so honest with me. Under the circumstances, our mutual trust remains unbroken. Now, I have a quite different instruction for you. Behind the Hilton is a large garden area, the Parc d'Egmont. You know it? Good. This is what I wish you to do . . .'

When he had ended the call Wand leaned forward to replace the receiver. For a moment his face was reflected in the desk lamp. To Jules it seemed the Devil incarnate. Wand leaned back out of the light, steepled his large hand under his chin.

Jules Starmberg was from Luxemburg. He had undergone intensive training at a camp in the countryside outside Hankow, deep in the interior of China. Stocky, powerfully built, he possessed great physical strength and part of his training – to test his nerve – had been for him to break a man's neck, a man like a bull. Starmberg had passed that test with flying colours.

Officially the butler, Starmberg was really Wand's right-hand man. Reflecting his profession, Wand sometimes called the Luxemburger his Chief of Staff. There were two men in the West completely trusted by Wand – Jules Starmberg and Vulcan.

'Jules, we are faced with one of those little problems, I fear.'

'Of course there will be a solution, sir,' Starmberg responded.

'The problem is Joseph.' Wand sighed regretfully. 'Oh dear, human nature can be a problem. Who would have foreseen Joseph would fall madly for the charms of Miss Grey?'

'He refuses to carry out your order?'

'Not expressed in the most subtle way – but in your blunt manner I am afraid you have summed up the problem. Could you be so good as to phone Vulcan? Please tell him to go to a public phone and call me. I have to give him some instructions to pass on to Anne-Marie. The

322

groundwork is already laid. Joseph will be waiting in the Parc d'Egmont at an agreed hour. And, Jules, this solution has also the advantage of rattling Miss Grey and Newman. Tweed, too, if he returns to Brussels.'

'We have to crush the weak sisters as we would a cockroach,' Jules agreed.

'Not quite how I would have phrased it,' Wand commented. 'I have just been studying the map. I calculate the *Mao III* and the *Yenan* – bearing in mind the considerable speed at which they move – should by now be well north off the west coast of Africa. The news in the paper rather confirms this since it gives the date when the Dutch vessel *Texel* left behind the woes of this world.'

'And that is the really important team those ships are carrying to Denmark,' Jules remarked, standing by Wand's side to look at the map.

'We are still at an early stage of Operation Long Reach,' Wand pointed out. 'At least I think so. And you are quite correct – the trained men aboard those ships are the élite leaders trained to take command. On the other hand, events may be moving faster than was anticipated. Europe is throwing away its defences. I have had a signal warning me that the operation may be launched much earlier than originally planned.'

'You said you wished me to contact Vulcan,' Jules reminded his chief.

'I was just about to ask you to call him. The Parc d'Egmont will be famous by nightfall.'

The sky was a sea of grey storm clouds as Mordaunt walked up to the narrow entrance to the Parc d'Egmont. He checked his watch by the illuminated hands – it was so damned dark it might have been night. He wore a trench coat, collar turned up against the cold, and a trilby hat. No one else about and he was on time.

He felt relieved about the outcome of his phone call to Dr Wand. Before lifting the receiver and dialling the number he'd had to assert all his will power. He had never disobeyed an order before. Looking back, he wondered how he'd had the nerve to do it. His mind had been half on Paula. She had given him the impetus to refuse the order.

Mordaunt's brain was still reeling with the impact the girl had made on him. For the first time he had become infatuated with a woman whose personality had – over one lunch – captured him body and soul. He smiled at himself for thinking in such terms.

He was walking now quietly along the the soggy path into the area of grass and trees. As he'd expected, no one else was in the park. It had rained heavily for a short time in the afternoon. He stopped and listened. The only sound was the steady dripping of water off the trees, a noise which for some reason got on his nerves. Like the Chinese water torture.

Get a hold on yourself. You're only a few yards from the back of the Hilton. At times he could see the lights inside the Café d'Egmont, the matrons of Brussels in their expensive clothes taking tea. He was in the middle of civilization.

He wandered deeper into the park – away from the Hilton and towards the distant walls of villas at the bottom of the sloping grass. Who was he supposed to meet? And where the devil were they?

He stopped again in the small neglected wilderness. The drip-drip-drip of water dropping off the trees *was* getting on his nerves. Apart from that unsettling sound it was so silent. He could be miles from any city . . .

'Joseph! Over here . . .'

A woman's muffled voice. A vague shadow slipped out from behind the trunk of a tree, waited for him to approach. She was muffled too – in a long raincoat, the

324

hood pulled well down over her head. He walked towards her. She held something in her hand.

'Joseph, put on these dark glasses. You must not risk being recognized when we meet someone to give them the package.'

He guessed now what his role was: to act as bodyguard during some transaction. He reached out his right hand, took the dark glasses, raised his arm to put them on. The woman's right arm jerked up, plunged down. He felt something sharp rip the cloth of his raincoat, penetrate his suit and shirt, stab painfully into his upraised arm.

There was a brief flash of pain, then a ferocious attack of white-hot burning inside his body. He gurgled horribly, waved his hands futilely for a millisecond, sagged to the soaked grass, lay very still.

33

In London it was afternoon as Tweed slowly paced round his office while Monica watched him. Philip Cardon had completed his report, then had been overwhelmed by fatigue.

He had phoned his girl friend's flat to tell her he was coming home. She'd told him her flat was no longer home for him: in his long absence she had acquired a substitute boy friend. Tweed had immediately called in Butler, who had agreed to take Cardon by car to his own pad. When he came back he said Cardon was sleeping like a babe . . .

Tweed had told him to stay in the office he shared with Pete Nield.

'I may need you at a moment's notice. Be ready to

travel abroad. Monica will supply you with Belgian and German currency . . .'

'You're getting geared up for a big push,' Monica had suggested late in the morning.

'We may have to move very fast. I'm trying to out-think Dr Wand – as I'm sure he's trying to out-think me. It all depends on which of us successfully deceives his opponent . . .'

There had then been a flurry of phone calls – some of which had surprised Monica. First, Tweed had phoned the PM, asking permission to take a certain course of action. He had then waited to give the PM time to make his own phone call. Later Tweed had called SAS HQ at Hereford, speaking to the officer in charge of the stand-by team.

'I may need you to fly your men urgently to somewhere in Europe.'

'North or south?' the officer had queried. 'It makes a difference.'

'Definitely northern Europe. I may phone you from quite a distance to give you the objective. I'll use the code-word Hurricane.'

'I favour transporting my men by a fleet of choppers,' the officer had suggested.

'So do I. It may be a small airfield where you land. And it could be vital to be equipped with powerful limpet mines. To sink ships.'

'No problem there.'

'I'll be in touch, Conway . . .'

Tweed doubted whether that was his real name. When he called Noble the Commander of Naval Intelligence insisted on dashing over to see him – as opposed to talking even on a scrambler phone.

When the ruddy-faced Noble arrived he seemed very cheerful. He accepted coffee from Monica and then began talking at top speed.

'I speeded up the operation to bring back the consignment from Liège. We flew there last night. Benoit was very co-operative, had the airport closed down by the time we arrived. Plus unmarked cars to transport us to Delvaux's plant. Delvaux was there himself. Looked strained, but he's got all his marbles.'

'You can't mean you've brought everything back here already?' Tweed asked, not bothering to conceal his surprise.

'It's all at the Admiralty Research Establishment now. Has been for many hours. That Stealth light aircraft we dismantled is amazing. We assembled it – worked all night non-stop – and none of our most advanced radar could detect it. But Delvaux's device does – from the first reports our boffins phoned me just before I came over here.'

'How long before you're sure?' Tweed asked anxiously. 'Time may not be on our side.'

'A matter of hours. That light aircraft Delvaux had constructed actually flies. A pilot is taking it up – then we'll be certain. And we brought back fifty of Delvaux's unique radar systems. I'll stick my neck out – I think you've brought us the answer to Stealth ships. Between you and me, we've been worried sick about the prospect that a hostile power might build them.'

'Could you tell me whether you have a naval vessel operating in the North Sea? Specifically, within reach of the coasts of Germany and Denmark?'

'Strictly between us – but I owe you a lot – the missile-armed frigate *Minotaur* is cruising in that area. Will be for some time. Why?'

'If,' Tweed emphasized, 'you find Delvaux's device is fool-proof, could you fly one out to the *Minotaur*?'

'Very quickly in an emergency. The *Minotaur*'s captain is a young chap, Tug Wilson. Hates the nickname Tug, but he's resigned to it now. He's one of the old school.

His motto? "If necessary, ram the bastards."' He turned to Monica. 'I hope you'll excuse my language.'

'I've heard worse round here,' she assured him.

'So could I contact this Tug Wilson by getting in touch with you by phone?' Tweed enquired.

'Easily. And I'm sleeping aboard while this action is on.' Tweed realized that by 'aboard' he was referring to sleeping on a camp bed in his Admiralty office. 'You are taking all this very seriously,' Noble observed as he stood up. 'Is this an emergency? If I can tell my people it is, then I'm going to get full co-operation from the Admiral which would put everyone on their toes.'

'I don't want to be melodramatic, but it could involve the survival of the West,' Tweed said slowly. 'And if I call you from abroad I'll use the codeword Hurricane so you're sure it's me speaking.'

'Hurricane,' Noble repeated as he prepared to leave. 'It sounds as though you're expecting one. We'll expect one, too. I think I'll contact Tug Wilson as soon as I get back. Good hunting . . .'

After he had gone Tweed had asked Monica to arrange for a meal of sandwiches to be brought in. He was eating the last one when he began pacing round his office.

'What do you think about what Cardon told us about the mysterious Dr Wand?' Monica asked.

Tweed didn't reply for a while. He was playing back in his mind what Cardon had told them.

'I stress these are only rumours,' Cardon had begun, 'but they come from three very different contacts – and all three said the same thing. Wand is thought to be General Chang, a top member of the Chinese High Command. He appeared out of nowhere in Hong Kong after spending months in the United States. There he is believed to have been treated by an American plastic surgeon – who died in a car accident soon afterwards. He established his trading company . . . seemed to have unlimited funds. His company prospered in two years, then he expressed an interest in the world-wide refugee problem. So, he came to Europe and organized his Trust for aiding refugees—'

'Just a moment,' Tweed had interrupted. 'Any idea where these huge funds came from?'

'Let me tell it in sequence. He cultivated men of influence in all the key European countries – men also concerned with the refugee problem. He's on dining-out terms with several EC Commissioners – they like his lavish hospitality. Most of them think he was born in Hong Kong – a Chinese mother and an English father. When I said he was suspected of being General Chang I referred to underground contacts. None of the taipans he mixed with in Hong Kong have even heard the rumour . . .'

Cardon had stopped speaking to swallow a whole tumbler of water. Tweed watched him carefully, seeing signs that he was running out of steam.

'Now we come to the money,' Cardon had continued. 'Which is why I spent three days in Chengmai in North Thailand, close to the so-called Golden Triangle – the great centre for illegal drug distribution on a colossal scale.' He had paused to make his next point.

'The Chinese Government is controlling the vast drug industry spreading havoc in the West . . .'

'But they shoot drug traffickers inside China,' Monica had objected.

'Of course they do,' Cardon had told her. 'They don't want their own people weakened by the scourge. Just the West. It is a classic case of the Chinese liking for the double-edged sword – they sell the drugs to the West via second parties. The drugs break down the moral and physical fibre of the West – and provide Beijing with vast sums of hard currency. So, without knowing it, drug users over here, in Europe, and the States, are financing Operation Long Reach, and ultimately their own destruction . . .'

329

Later Tweed had put to him the question which was intriguing him.

'Philip, how on earth did you get out of Lop Nor alive?'

'Oh, it was quite easy. I'd realized by then I was wearing the uniform of a high-ranking Security Service officer. I went back to the airfield, found another of their old crates was just leaving for Chungking. The steward made one of the passengers get out of his seat and crouch down in the aisle at the rear. Didn't ask him – he just did it. It was almost night when we landed at Chungking. I beat a hasty from the airport, walked out into the countryside, took off the uniform and burnt it. Which left me in my original rags. I then smuggled myself aboard a hovercraft going down the Yangtze River as a crewman—'

'Hovercraft!' Monica had interjected. 'You're joking.'

'No, I'm not. A bit of a rocky ride but the engines were almost silent. Make a dangerous war vessel. I got off at Hankow and took the long train ride to Canton. From there it's no distance at all to slip across the frontier into Hong Kong. A piece of cake . . .'

At that point Cardon had closed his eyes and fallen fast asleep until Butler had escorted him to his car.

Tweed answered the question Monica had asked earlier, pacing back to his desk and sitting in his chair.

'I think Cardon could be right about Dr Wand. During the brief moment when I saw Wand clearly by the flare of Bob's lighter it struck me there was something Oriental about his features. I suspect I wouldn't have noticed it in broad daylight.'

'What I couldn't get over was the way Philip kept saying it was easy, a piece of cake, phrases like that.'

'I don't think for a moment it was easy. That is just Philip's throwaway confidence. And remember, the British have been good in the past at disguising themselves as another race, infiltrating all sorts of dangerous

330

places. Lawrence of Arabia – passing himself off as an Arab. In India, during the Raj, a clever soldier would dress himself up as a native and move around in hostile territory on the north-west frontier to spy on some rebellious khan. Cardon belongs to that age.'

'What did Philip mean when he said the great anchorage at Cam Ranh Bay in Vietnam has been closed to all shipping?'

'Look at the map.' Tweed jumped up, walked over to the wall map of the world. 'I think that's where Stealth vessels are sailing to Europe from. The logical secret route, avoiding the major shipping lanes, is via the Timor Sea – where ships have disappeared. Then via the Cape – where more ships disappear. And Vietnam is the other major power where the Communists are firmly in the saddle. They've secretly linked up with China, I suspect.'

'It really is frightening. And just when we thought we could relax . . .'

'Which is just what we're not going to do,' Tweed said grimly, returning to his desk. 'I need the strongest team I can muster when I reach Brussels tonight. Book a seat on my plane – and through to Hamburg later – for Butler.'

The phone rang. Monica answered it, placed a hand over the mouthpiece.

'Guess who. It's Philip Cardon . . .'

'You are supposed to be sleeping,' Tweed snapped. 'Why are you calling? Before you answer tell me just where you are calling from.'

'To talk to you briefly, from a public phone box,' Cardon said laconically.

'You didn't go to bed?' Tweed demanded.

'Yes. Couldn't sleep. I'm wearing a heavy overcoat and a pair of trousers over pyjamas. Look, I got the feeling something big is breaking. After a bit of kip I want to be included in on it.'

'You need a holiday . . .'

'I said I wanted to be included in it. Are you deaf?'

'All right,' Tweed said in a resigned tone. 'Phone Monica but only after a long sleep.'

'Agreed. And don't forget what I said about Chengmai . . .'

Tweed told Monica the gist of the conversation after he put down the phone. He drummed his fingers on the desk.

'We could use every man. Book Philip an open ticket to Brussels and on to Hamburg. Then another one on a direct flight to Hamburg.'

'You really are mustering the troops,' she commented.

'I'm sure Dr Wand will be doing the same thing.'

'Do you think he's right about this character, Vulcan? A top mole who is one of Wand's chief associates. And English, too.'

'Not a mole,' Tweed corrected her. 'Philip emphasized his contacts in Hong Kong said he existed. That he'd spent time in the colony. Yes, I think he does exist. Interesting that he's an Englishman . . .'

Benoit, accompanied by plain-clothes officers, followed Newman into the dank wilderness of the Parc d'Egmont. Behind him walked Paula and Nield.

On Benoit's order to the General Manager of the Hilton the windows of the Café d'Egmont overlooking the park had been masked. It was night and the only illumination came from torches held by the police and Newman.

It was Newman who had phoned Benoit. He had received a strange call in his room. The muffled voice sounded like a man's, and the message had been delivered in English.

'You will find something interesting if you go now to the Parc d'Egmont. Better go back home. Don't trip over anything . . .'

'I can take you straight to it,' Newman said as he led the way.

332

'I don't for a moment think you imagined what you saw, my friend,' Benoit replied.

Newman trod carefully down the wet grassy slope. Close to a tree, he stopped. Silently he aimed the beam of his torch. The body lay on its back, legs tangled, the eyes staring sightlessly upwards. Benoit and another officer stooped to examine it.

'Cyanosis,' Benoit commented. 'Lips blue, whole face has a bluish tinge.'

'My verdict,' Newman agreed. 'This is Joseph Mordaunt. Freelance journalist I know slightly. Last saw him in the New Forest area in England.' He paused. 'And then in the lounge area of the Hilton about noon.'

Paula stepped forward, shocked. Only a few hours ago she'd had a long and very pleasant lunch with the heap lying on the ground which had been a live human being.

'I can tell you something about him,' she said.

'Back in the hotel,' Benoit said tersely. He looked at Newman. 'This is the second case of murder by cyanide within walking distance of the Hilton. The driver of the cab which was stolen and driven to Liège was found in Marolles. And whoever drove that cab murdered Sir Gerald Andover. Three murders close together. For me that is three too many.'

'I think you can see how it was done.' Newman crouched down. He aimed his torch at the sleeve of the right upper arm. A rip in the coat's cloth showed clearly. 'My guess would be the hypodermic was rammed straight through his clothes into the flesh.'

'Same technique as was used on the cab driver,' Benoit remarked, crouching beside Newman. 'Which suggests it could be the same person.'

'I think it was a woman,' Paula said suddenly.

'Why do you say that?' Benoit asked sharply, looking up at Paula.

'Because Mordaunt was a man who liked women. But

333

he wasn't stupid. This is a lonely place. Only a woman, I'd have thought, could have got close enough . . .'

She broke off as a fresh group of men appeared with torches. A short, plump, bald-headed man, carrying a bag, put on his glasses, peered at Benoit after a glance at the body.

'You do choose the most original locations to find your corpses,' he observed.

'Pathologist,' Benoit whispered to Newman as they straightened up. 'And the forensic boys. Let's get back to the hotel and leave them to their work. I'll come back with you by myself. The hotel manager is nearly doing his nut about a murder just outside his café.'

Despite the macabre atmosphere Paula smiled to herself. *Doing his nut*. Benoit prided himself on his command of English slang.

'I do have grim news for you,' Benoit whispered again to Newman as they made their way out of the park.

Entering the hotel Paula noticed Helen Claybourne curled up like a cat on a couch, reading a book. She looked up, raised a hand in a small salute, returned to reading her novel.

Benoit shook his head, frowned as the hotel manager began to approach them. Standing in front of the closed elevator doors, no one said anything. The doors opened and Lee Holmes stepped out. Paula caught an aroma of fresh talc. Lee had just had a bath. She grabbed Newman by the arm.

'Bob! Give me just a second. Please! I do want to explain,' she pleaded.

'I'll be up in a minute,' Newman said. 'Here's the key to my room,' he went on quickly, handing it to Benoit. 'Paula knows the number. I'll join you very shortly . . .'

*　　*　　*

334

Newman suggested to Lee they could talk in the bar. She nodded and he was glad she didn't take hold of his arm. He was still slightly irked by her disappearance from the restaurant in Grand' Place without a word, although his mind was mostly filled with the murder of Joseph Mordaunt.

She led him to a secluded corner banquette. He sat beside her, leaving a gap between them. She ordered a brandy and Newman asked for a glass of Chablis.

'I really am sorry to treat you in the way I did,' she began. 'The waiter gave you my message?'

'No. But the place was busy and I paid a different waiter for the drinks. What message?'

The drinks arrived and she grasped her glass immediately, sipping a little of the brandy. Then she turned to face him.

He caught a whiff of her perfume. Guerlain Samsara, Tweed had said. There was still that mystery as to who had the bottle: Lee or Helen.

'I suddenly felt sick – very sick. The smell of food in the place made me feel worse. I drank a whole glass of mineral water at one go, asked the waiter to tell you that I was feeling off colour and was going straight back to the hotel.'

He wasn't sure whether he believed her or not. He couldn't read her eyes, let alone her mind.

'I'm sorry you felt unwell,' he said. 'Feeling any better now?'

'I lay down for most of the afternoon, then had a bath. I think I'll soon feel half-civilized. The brandy is helping.'

'Good. Sip it slowly.'

She laid a hand on his arm. 'Am I forgiven, Bob?'

'Nothing to forgive. You can't help feeling unwell. I'd recommend a quiet evening.'

'I suspect I dragged you away from a business meeting. So, if you want to go please do.'

335

'If you don't mind . . .'

He paid for the drinks, left the bar, and saw Helen Claybourne standing in front of an exhibition poster. She swung round, walked towards him with her slow, elegant step. As always, she looked neat as a new pin, clad in a pale blue blouse, a dove-grey pleated skirt, and low-heeled shoes. Her cool eyes had a mischievous look which Newman found rather fetching.

'I'm an abandoned woman,' she told him. 'No sign of my Willie. The Brigadier has gone missing. Would you think it very forward of me if I asked if you were free for dinner later?'

'I might be. I'll know later. Sorry to be so vague but I'm going to a business meeting. Never know how long they're going to last. I'll try and cut it short,' he said and smiled.

She showed him the little folder the hotel provided with the room number. Leaning forward, she spoke in her soft voice.

'If you could let me know by eight o'clock. Meantime I'll live in hope . . .'

Going up in the elevator Newman was a disturbed man. *I think it was a woman*, Paula had said while they stood close to the dead body of Mordaunt.

Had he – within the past ten minutes – been talking to the murderess?

34

In Liège Dr Hyde returned to the obscure 'hotel' where he was staying. He had just sampled the local offerings of feminine companionship. The quality was way below that available in Brussels. The nosy woman, who ran what was no more than a lodging house, met him as he entered.

'You have had a phone call,' she said in French. 'They wouldn't leave a name or a number,' she went on regretfully, 'but they said it was urgent.'

'It will have to wait,' Hyde said quickly. 'I have just remembered something I forgot to buy. Be back soon.'

He hurried to the nearest public phone box. The only person who knew where he was staying was Dr Wand.

He dialled the number and, to his surprise, it was Dr Wand who took the call. Normally he spoke first to the man called Jules.

'Are you packed and ready to leave, my dear sir?' Dr Wand asked after checking where he was calling from.

'I'm always ready to move on at a moment's notice,' Hyde assured him.

'Then that is what I would much appreciate your doing. If you would be so good, leave Liège at once. Catch the first express to Cologne. From there you fly to Hamburg. As soon as you have found a suitable resting place, be so good as to leave an anonymous note for me at the Four Seasons Hotel. A note which simply gives me your phone number. Dr Hyde, I would earnestly advise you to go now without losing a minute. I am most concerned for your safety. And be ready to treat a new patient. A German who is seventeen years old . . .'

When Newman arrived in his room he found Pete Nield seated on a couch, staring out of the window at the lights of Brussels, a blaze of cheap neon on the far side of the Boulevard de Waterloo. Benoit was sitting at a desk, a large sheet of paper in front of him covered in his neat handwriting. Paula sat beside him.

'We have been working,' Benoit said with an impish grin, 'while you go off with the first curvy blonde who catches your eye. Why, I can't imagine, when you have the delightful Paula in your room.'

'I thought I'd leave you to enjoy her company for a while,' Newman retorted. 'What work?'

'She has been making a statement about what she saw in the Parc d'Egmont, about her earlier lunch with the victim. Now I want one from you . . .'

Ten minutes later Newman signed his own statement. Benoit countersigned it, as he had done after Paula's signature.

'Strictly speaking,' he explained, 'I should have asked one of my men to witness these statements. But I am, after all, the chief of police. Anyone who questions the procedure will get my boot up a tender part of his anatomy.'

'You had news for me,' Newman reminded him. 'Grim, you said.'

'Would you like the good or the bad to start with?'

'The bad.'

'Then I think I'll give you the good first. I phoned Tweed recently, told him we'd traced this Dr Hyde to a boarding house here in Brussels. But the bird had flown. So now we are concentrating on Liège. A team is checking every low-down dump in that beautiful city.' He looked at his watch. 'They will be starting about now.'

'I can't make out why Mordaunt was murdered,' Newman ruminated. 'And just after lunching with Paula – so if by chance he was leading up to luring her away to be kidnapped . . . Although that's a pretty wild theory.'

'Maybe not so wild,' Paula said quietly. She sat down next to Nield, looking depressed. 'He was playing up to me to start with, turning on the charm. Then, during lunch, his attitude changed. He' – she searched for a wording which would not sound conceited – 'seemed to genuinely like me. Was going a bit overboard, I thought. Supposing he decided not to go through with it?'

'Then, remembering our interview with Dr Wand, I'm sure he became expendable. If that is what happened it really is alarming – the speed with which Wand moved.'

'No proof.' Benoit threw up both hands. 'And Dr Wand is a man of great influence in high places. I would need a cast-iron case before I dared approach him.'

'So what is the bad news?' Newman asked.

'They dragged the dead body of Lucie Delvaux out of the Meuse. Killed by a cyanide injection. Gaston Delvaux has gone to pieces.'

Tweed travelled to catch his flight at London Airport by taxi. At his suggestion, Butler had taken a different taxi and would not sit anywhere near Tweed on the plane. It did no harm to conceal from the opposition the team he was building up against them.

He was walking towards Passport Control when he saw Jim Corcoran, Chief Security Officer and his old friend. To his surprise Corcoran looked away, started walking in a different direction. Tweed caught up with him.

'Something on your mind, Jim? You looked right through me.'

'Sorry. I was miles away. You're off somewhere again?'

'Brussels.'

'Have a good flight . . .'

'Thank you.'

Tweed moved on, holding his boarding pass. Corcoran had seemed distinctly uncomfortable. Three-quarters of an hour later he was in his seat aboard the aircraft. Butler sat two rows behind him.

As the plane took off and climbed, Tweed settled back to think. He preferred travelling on his own: no phone calls to interrupt his flow of thought. Refusing all refreshment, he concentrated on the pattern of events now taking definite shape in his mind.

His last act before leaving Park Crescent had been to get in touch with a powerful contact at Special Branch. He'd given them specific instructions – to be put on hold – about Moor's Landing. He'd emphasized they mustn't go near the place. Not until they received his signal.

Vulcan. His brain had switched to another tack. Philip Cardon had been very confident that the unknown Vulcan existed, that he was an Englishman, that he had long ago left Hong Kong for Britain. Vulcan – a key figure in the elaborate preparations for Operation Long Reach. Who was most likely to be Vulcan? Because Tweed was convinced he had already met him.

The executioner. The killer of Hilary Vane, the American woman who had been murdered at London Airport when Cord Dillon had arrived. It had been a woman who'd done the job. Cyanide poisoning. Paula had seen her bump into Vane just before the victim died so unpleasantly. A woman in a wide-brimmed hat which hid her face.

Then there was the cab driver found dead inside his own vehicle in Marolles. After it had been driven to Liège where the woman using the cab had driven down – killed – Sir Gerald Andover. Paula had sworn that had been a woman. It was a new and deadly idea – a woman who was a professional assassin.

Stealth. Tweed began to think about all that involved, and fell fast asleep.

Latitude 37.50N. Longitude 21.50W. The *Mao III*, with its sister ship, *Yenan*, was sailing at thirty knots – over nine hundred miles west of the Straits of Gibraltar.

The sea was an oily calm and another heavy mist was forming. Captain Welensky was relieved to be alone on the bridge. Kim had gone below decks to check something. As he stared at the radar screen, about to issue an

order, Kim suddenly appeared, padding silently in his
cloth shoes. He took Welensky by the arm with an iron
grip and shook him.

'There is a small fishing vessel . . .'

'I know. Dead ahead . . .'

'Dead. Ram it! Now!'

'I was about to alter course to avoid—'

'I said ram it! I have just returned from the radio room.
That vessel is beginning to send out a Mayday . . .'

'It's cold-blooded murder.'

Welensky regretted the outburst the moment after he
had uttered the words. Kim's grip tightened.

'I am beginning to think your efficiency is impaired,
Captain. Do I have to give the order myself?' he purred.

Welensky was frightened. Kim's voice had shown no
sign of emotion. But he was quite capable of thrusting his
knife into Welensky, weighting the body, and throwing it
overboard. Welensky gave the order.

It was a small vessel. Proceeding on the same course,
Welensky watched the radar. He hardly felt the tremble
as the *Mao* sliced clean through the fishing vessel amidships. Kim, his night glasses raised to his eyes, went first
to port.

He saw two men flailing in the water. One raised his
arms as though in a desperate plea for mercy, then the
arms vanished under the waves with the head. The other
fisherman had already disappeared. Kim walked swiftly to
starboard, raised his glasses again. The bow of the fishing
vessel had already sunk. He watched the stern slide below
the waves. No heads floated on the surface of the ice-cold
sea. No survivors. He went back to stand alongside
Welensky.

'I think you require a lesson in seamanship, Captain. If
a vessel sends out a repeated Mayday signal the chances
are other vessels will detect it, will change course to hurry
to the scene. The object of this voyage is to avoid any risk

whatsoever that our presence will be discovered. Do you grasp the meaning of my little lecture, Captain?'

'It is quite clear,' Welensky replied, staring ahead.

'Good. We are on course. We are on schedule. Now we shall proceed west of the British Isles and Ireland. We shall then turn south between the Shetland Islands and Norway and descend on the west coast of Denmark. To be precise, on Jutland.'

'I studied geography at school,' Welensky remarked.

Kim made no reply, but by now Welensky had realized he had no sense of humour.

Tweed had asked Monica to leave a message at Benoit's HQ giving him his flight number and ETA. He didn't expect the police chief to be waiting for him but, as he walked out of Zaventem Airport, Benoit appeared, smiling with pleasure as they shook hands.

'I have an unmarked car waiting. Where to? The Hilton?'

'As usual.'

Butler had stayed in the background. He took a taxi to the hotel. As Benoit sat in a traffic jam he turned to Tweed, who sat beside him.

'It gets grimmer, this business, I fear. While you were away there have been two more murders.'

'Who?' Tweed asked in a normal voice, masking his anxiety.

'A man called Joseph Mordaunt, an acquaintance of Newman's, I understand.'

'I met him briefly near Lymington on the south coast. I wouldn't have thought he was important.'

'Important enough to someone to have him killed,' Benoit commented. 'By cyanide injection.'

'The same technique as used on the cab driver in Marolles,' Tweed recalled. 'Someone has an instrument disguised as an everyday item. I have the feeling I have seen it. I've no idea when. And the second murder?'

'Lucie Delvaux's body was dragged out of the River Meuse. Again, first killed by a cyanide injection. Delvaux is a broken man – mentally and physically.'

'As you say, it is getting grimmer. Poor Gaston.' Tweed was frowning. 'Water,' he said. 'Always an element near by is water.'

'Please explain,' Benoit suggested as the car began moving again.

'Irene, the daughter of Sir Gerald Andover – her body was taken out of the sea near Lymington. Also killed by an injection of cyanide.' And Moor's Landing was located on the banks of the River Beaulieu, he was thinking, but kept the thought to himself. 'Water,' he repeated, 'Lucie's body is found in the River Meuse.'

'You think water is significant?'

'Probably just a coincidence.'

Tweed no longer believed what he'd just said. A Stealth ship would operate on water. Something else he had no intention of broadcasting.

'We have been busy in another direction also,' Benoit informed him. 'Dr Hyde. I phoned the news we'd found he stayed at a dump called the Hermitage here in Brussels. Since then I sent teams to Liège. One of my men showed this Dr Hyde's photograph to a boarding-house landlady in that city. We missed him by one hour. He told her he was leaving for Brussels.'

'Which means Brussels is the last place he's heading for next. But the information is valuable. Thank you for your efforts.'

'I could now blanket Antwerp,' Benoit suggested.

'Don't bother. I think Hyde has left Belgium. Perhaps for Holland, maybe Germany.'

They were now driving down the side road parallel to the Boulevard de Waterloo which led to the Hilton.

Tweed was encouraged by the news about Hyde. He felt they were catching up with him.

Tactfully, Benoit did not accompany Tweed into the Hilton. Earlier he had examined the guest list in search of a suspect. It had proved hopeless: too many people and no familiar name. Also he was not exactly popular with the manager.

Tweed found the executive room he'd paid for in advance for several days was still available. He paid out more money to keep them happy. As he stepped out of the elevator on the twentieth floor he saw Marler leaving Newman's room.

'You've come back to Murder City,' Marler greeted him with black humour.

'I know. Where is everyone?'

'In Newman's room. You want to see someone?'

'All of you. Urgently . . .'

Two minutes later Paula was unpacking his case while Newman sat on a couch next to Pete Nield. Marler took up his usual stance, leaning against a wall while he lit a king-size. Tweed was pacing the room, hands behind his back, his manner brisk as he spoke.

'We're leaving tomorrow as early as possible. Butler has come with me. At reception I was able to scribble a note with my room number and a request for him to join us.' He had hardly finished speaking when someone tapped on the door. Newman slid his hand inside his jacket, gripped the butt of his Smith & Wesson, unlocked the door, and Butler walked in.

'Mobilizing a heavy team,' Newman observed, relocking the door.

'Yes,' Tweed confirmed. 'And Philip Cardon may be joining us later.'

'Why are you assembling all this manpower?' Paula

344

asked as she put a pile of Tweed's shirts into the drawer. 'Normally you work with the minimum of personnel – so they won't be noticed.'

'True. But this situation is really menacing. We have no idea how many thugs – killers – Wand has at his disposal. I suspect far more than would give us a good night's rest. I've little doubt it's going to take all the resources we can muster to cope with the devious Dr Wand.'

'Your trip to London was successful?' Paula enquired.

'I think so . . .'

Tweed proceeded to give them all a concise account of who he had met, what they had told him, and the plans he had made for co-operation from certain key people.

'I'd say you've been on the trot,' Marler concluded.

'You could say that. One important point we must deal with at once. The weapons Benoit loaned us. Marler, I need that hold-all you carry about – with the Armalite inside it . . .' He continued as Marler left the room. 'All those weapons must be dumped into the hold-all and I'll give them back to Benoit. Airport security . . .' Marler returned, and when the weapons were inside Tweed zipped it up.

'Back in a minute. Benoit, who met me at the airport, said he'd wait in the car half an hour in case I wanted to consult him.'

Newman looked round the room when Tweed had gone. Paula had finished her unpacking and was staring out of the window where a grey drizzle was gradually blotting out the city.

'We'd better brace ourselves,' Newman said. 'He's in his dynamo of action stage . . .'

Walking outside into the wet, Tweed saw a new doorman by the side of Benoit's car, obviously enquiring who he was. Benoit, without looking at him, held up his identity folder, staring ahead. The doorman retreated rapidly. Benoit leaned over, opened the front passenger-seat door, and Tweed sat beside him.

Handing back the hold-all containing the weapons, Tweed thanked him. He then showed him a photo.

'Does the place marked with a cross on the map mean anything to you?'

'Odd you should bring that up. I was talking to one of the officials at Ghent's Town Hall recently. It's a new housing development. Only recently occupied – six months or so ago. Vieux-Fontaine. Not even signposted.'

'Who lives there?'

'No one seems to know. The rumour is they're calling themselves executives – but really they're top security personnel who guard our high-life EC Commissioners. I happen to know that's rubbish. Since they haven't committed any known criminal offence no one is bothered.'

'They may well be saboteurs and spies smuggled into the country. Please leave them in peace – until I contact you. Then raid the place at a mutually agreed time.'

'You usually know what you're doing.' Benoit paused. 'I'm going back to headquarters now. I'll organize a strike force to be ready for when you warn me.'

'I'm leaving Brussels tomorrow. Thank you for all your co-operation – especially with that helicopter armada which descended on Liège Airport.'

'It was nothing.' Benoit gripped Tweed's arm. 'Now I urge you to take care of yourself. I sense you could be walking into a zone of maximum danger.'

'Hamburg.'

'I couldn't interview Dr Wand, but I did send men to watch his Lear jet on standby at Zaventem. The security officer told them the pilot had filed a flight plan. For Hamburg. Late this afternoon Dr Wand left aboard that jet with a Luxemburger called Starmberg. A zone of maximum danger,' Benoit repeated.

35

The flight for Hamburg aboard Hamburg Airlines was due to take off at 11.15 a.m. As Paula walked alongside Tweed towards the waiting aircraft she asked the question which had been intriguing her.

'Why Hamburg?'

'To see Hugo Westendorf, the one-time Iron Man of Germany who retired three months or so ago without warning. He was Minister of the Interior.'

'Retired? Suddenly? You don't think . . .'

'That it's another case like Andover and Delvaux? Yes, I think exactly that,' Tweed said grimly. 'We're going to meet another broken man. I suspect the charming Dr Wand has a long list.'

Newman, followed by Nield and Butler, caught up with them as they approached the aircraft. A staircase led up to the entrance. Newman stared in disbelief.

'What are those things sticking out at the front?'

'Propellers, as you well know,' Tweed replied.

'A prop aircraft? I'm not mad keen on them. I prefer a jet.'

'Aircraft with only one propeller won us the Battle of Britain,' Tweed reminded him, suppressing a smile. 'It will get us there.'

'When does this thing reach Hamburg?' Newman asked in a disgruntled tone.

'Thirteen hundred hours. I'm sure it will be prompt.'

'Sounds as though it goes via Paris . . .'

Paula was settled next to Tweed, who had a window

seat, when she nudged him. She could hardly believe her eyes.

'Look who else is coming on board. I don't understand what is happening. Are we being followed? How did they find out we'd been on this flight?'

'Too many questions,' Tweed replied, gazing out of the window.

Brigadier Burgoyne, carrying an expensive case, was walking down the aisle. He looked neither to right nor to left as he followed the steward and barked out the order.

'We want four seats at the back of the plane . . .'

Lee Holmes followed him at a more leisurely pace. Stopping by Paula, she leaned across her to speak to Tweed.

'What a super coincidence. I did enjoy our frolic at the Copenhagen Tavern.'

'My pleasure.' Tweed was still staring out of the window.

'Where are you staying in Hamburg?' Lee persisted, throwing a wave of blonde hair over her coat collar.

'Four Seasons Hotel,' he said brusquely.

'May see you . . .'

She had to move on as Helen Claybourne nudged her back with her own case. Helen walked straight past without saying one word, hurrying to catch up. Willie brought up the rear, halted with a beaming smile as he addressed Paula.

'I really had a fabulous time with you. Best company I had by far in Brussels. Everybody else seemed utterly second-rate. Love to repeat the experience at the earliest opportunity. Oh, dear, I'm holding up the troops. Until next time . . .'

The aircraft was equipped with thirty-six passenger seats. It was half empty when they closed the door and Paula glanced back. The Burgoyne quartet was seated at the rear, well out of earshot. Newman had his face buried in a newspaper: she suspected he hadn't looked up as the new arrivals passed him. Butler and Nield sat away from each other in separate seats. The propellers began to spin, jerkily at first, then racing into a circular blur. Slowly the machine moved forward, accelerated, and then they were airborne.

Paula waited until the pilot announced, first in German, then in English, that they would be flying at a maximum altitude of 21,000 feet and at a speed of 500 k.p.h. Paula looked back at Newman who made a gesture of disgust. The vibration was greater than on a jet.

'You didn't seem pleased to see them come aboard,' she said to Tweed.

'That was the impression I wished to create,' he replied cryptically.

'The Burgoyne quartet.' Paula rather liked the phrase. 'It sounds like a jazz combo.' She chuckled.

Tweed's expression was blank. He felt sure Vulcan was on board. But who was he? To say nothing of a woman who was a professional assassin. And who was she?

He went on gazing out of the window. For the first part of the flight they might have been passing over the Arctic. Tumbled masses of white clouds gleamed in the sunlight. Here and there a towering cloud summit looked like some massive iceberg. As they came closer to Hamburg the weather cleared. Tweed looked down with interest on a mosaic of neat green and brown cultivated farmland. They passed over a blue lake, dense islands of green forest. From this lower altitude he had a much better view. The plane had begun its descent . . .

'Why did you tell her where we're staying?' Paula asked. 'Are you looking forward to another frolic – I think that was the word she used – with her?' she teased.

349

'They could have followed us in another taxi.'

'I think you want to keep an eye on them,' she probed.

'I want us to be first off this plane,' he told her.

Tweed was always pleased to arrive in Hamburg. It had the reputation of being the most 'English' of all German cities. Not that it was a bit like London: the description referred to the friendly attitude of the inhabitants.

'That plane flew like a rusty sewing machine,' Newman remarked. 'And vibrated like one.'

Tweed and Paula were travelling with him in a taxi from the airport. The vehicle had been crawling in a traffic jam down a tree-lined boulevard. The air was fresh, the atmosphere rural.

'It got us here,' Tweed reminded him. 'And in interesting company.'

'Lee nearly had a row with the steward after we'd at long last taken off. She put a cigarette into that fat holder of hers. The steward told her it was a non-smoking plane. She eventually got it across to him she had no intention of lighting the cigarette. And how the blazes did they come to be aboard?'

'I think I've worked it out,' Tweed said. 'Don't ask me yet. I want to be sure.'

'It doesn't seem possible,' Paula insisted. 'You brought us the tickets. As soon as we arrived we boarded that funny little bus which dropped us close to the plane. So where did they get the time to work it out? Maybe it is a coincidence.'

'Don't believe in them,' Tweed advised.

Newman looked back through the rear window. Butler and Nield had taken separate taxis. Marler had told him before they left the Hilton that he'd be hiring a car. A man who always liked independent transport.

They arrived at the palatial entrance to the Hotel Vier

350

Jahreszeiten – the Four Seasons – and uniformed porters appeared immediately to take their luggage. Tweed hurried up the wide steps into the luxurious interior. Monica had booked rooms for them and the receptionist informed Tweed their accommodation was ready. After registering he showed Paula his room number, entered the lift by himself, then walked straight out again as he spotted the concierge who had been so helpful on his last visit.

'I want to visit a friend of mine who lives near Blankenese. Hugo Westendorf. Can you give me the exact address and his phone number?'

'The Schloss Tannenberg,' the concierge replied promptly. 'But not quite as far as Blankenese. The schloss is in the district of Nienstedten. You reach it before you arrive at Blankenese. Now, the phone number – and I will draw you a little map to locate the schloss. It is difficult on a printed map . . .'

Tweed had his old room, number 311, which was more like a suite. There was a lounge area near the windows overlooking the lake – the Binnen Alster. Tipping the porter, Tweed sat down to phone the number as soon as he was alone. The odd atmosphere began with his phone call. He tried speaking in English first.

'My name is Tweed. I know Mr Westendorf. I have just arrived from England and would like to speak to him.'

'I understand,' the man's voice at the other end replied. 'It would be helpful if you would stay on the line for a moment or two . . .'

Tweed waited. The butler? The voice had sounded very official but hardly that of a servant. Tweed realized the line was probably tapped – as had been Andover's and, later, Delvaux's. He had reached the stage where he wanted to stir up the opposition. The voice came back.

'Mr Westendorf will be happy to see you this evening. If you could arrive at 6 p.m. May I ask where you are staying?'

'The Four Seasons Hotel, room number 311.'

'Thank you, sir. We will be expecting you. At 6 p.m.'

Tweed was disturbed as he put down the phone. Nothing had been as he'd expected. He had anticipated Westendorf answering the phone – if anyone at all had responded to his call. He had pictured the German existing on his own inside the schloss – his wife had died several years ago.

Westendorf had one seventeen-year-old son. Tweed had assumed he might well have been kidnapped. Something strange had compelled the German to throw up his career without warning. What was going on in Germany? Tweed sensed the pattern he had uncovered with Andover and Delvaux was now being repeated in Hamburg. Someone tapped on the door. It was Paula.

'What a lovely room,' she enthused. 'And a super view from the window.'

'I think they've installed that lovely fountain gushing in the middle of the lake since I was last here. Maybe I've forgotten it.'

'And if I know you, you've forgotten it's time we went down and had some lunch.'

'Something quick. I don't feel like a full-dress effort. I know. The bar . . .'

Newman was about to knock on the door when they went into the corridor. Paula was revelling in the peace of the hotel. A chambermaid wished them 'Guten Tag' as they entered the lift. The bar opened off the spacious lobby which had a large sitting area. Small and comfortably furnished with leather banquettes, the bar was empty except for the barman who came forward.

'I can make do with ham sandwiches – if that's all right with both of you,' Tweed suggested.

'And to drink, sir?' the barman enquired.

'A bottle of champagne,' Newman decided.

'Mineral water for me,' Tweed ordered.

Once the barman had gone Tweed told them about his call to the Schloss Tannenberg. He had just finished when Marler peered in. He gave a discreet thumbs-up sign and disappeared.

'That means he's got a car,' Newman said.

'It will be after dark when we get there,' Tweed ruminated aloud. 'Odd the emphasis that man put on six p.m.'

'We'll find out when we get there,' Newman assured him.

At 5.15 p.m. Tweed, muffled against the cold in an overcoat, collar turned up, was walking up and down outside the hotel with Paula. She also wore her coat buttoned to her neck. The night was clear, star-studded, and the temperature had dropped below zero. It was the first day of December.

Newman stood smoking a cigarette as a very large black Mercedes 600 pulled in to the kerb. Paula stared at its size as, behind the wheel, Marler called out through his open window.

'Don't just stand there freezing. Hop in.'

They had left the outskirts of Hamburg behind when Tweed asked the question. They were moving through a district of impressive two-storey villas in spacious grounds behind high railings. Hardly any other traffic.

'How on earth did you get hold of this mobile palace?' he asked.

'Oh,' Marler drawled, 'I said I was driving a top official to visit a Minister. After all, he was one – once.' He eyed Tweed in the rear-view mirror. 'This chariot is costing you a bomb. And from the map you gave me we're nearly there.'

Paula, revelling in the space, the warmth from the heaters, caught glimpses of the solid villas as the

353

headlights swung round bends. A very expensive area.

Marler suddenly stopped, stiffened like a fox scenting danger. He had been driving slowly for the past five minutes, peering at elaborate name plates by the side of high gates and illuminated with lanterns. All the gates had been shut but this pair was open. *Schloss Tannenberg.* Tweed sensed his alertness.

'Something wrong?'

'I think you ought to go in equipped.' He opened a hold-all on the seat beside him, produced a .32 Browning automatic which he handed Paula with spare ammo. For Newman he had a hip holster, a Smith & Wesson .38 Special with ammo. Before replying to Tweed he waited while Newman strapped on the hip holster, checked the gun, loaded it, slipped it inside the holster, put his jacket and coat on again. Paula had slipped her Browning into her shoulder-bag after checking and loading it.

'Something is wrong,' Marler reported. 'Look out of the window. Gates wide open – and one of those dragon's teeth chains laid across the drive a few yards beyond the entrance.'

'But where did you get the weapons?' Tweed demanded.

He was annoyed: they had no permits to carry weapons inside Germany. On the other hand Benoit had warned about 'a zone of maximum danger'.

'This afternoon – while you were all having a kip – I was busy,' Marler said in an ironic tone. 'I visited a chum, a German arms dealer on a barge along the waterfront. He told me business had tailed off something shocking since the Berlin Wall went down. I got this lot for a song – plus Walthers for Butler and Nield. And an Armalite for myself. All a question of knowing the right people.'

'Or the wrong ones,' Tweed rebuked him. 'Now I'm going to walk up that drive. Bob, Paula, you can follow at a distance. I don't want to startle Westendorf.'

354

'I'll find somewhere to park the car,' Marler decided.

Tweed walked slowly up the tarred drive, his footsteps making no sound. He stepped over the dragon's teeth chain – which would rip a vehicle's tyres to pieces and stop it in seconds. It was too quiet.

He could see the old two-storey stone villa in the distance. Lights on in the ground-floor windows behind closed curtains. On either side of the drive high, dense banks of rhododendron bushes concealed the grounds. He reasoned that the oppressive silence was due to the German occupying the villa by himself. Like Andover. Like Delvaux . . .

The muzzle of a gun was rammed into the back of his neck. At the same moment a hand descended on his shoulder, a voice growled the command in English.

'Make one wrong move and I'll blow your head off.'

Inside the Four Seasons, Pete Nield, smartly dressed as always in a business suit, wandered into the spacious lounge area adjoining reception. A very attractive woman with a blonde mane, wearing a form-fitting black dress, sat on a couch. The dress was slit up one side and she had her elegant legs crossed. Lee Holmes.

Nield paused by a table of German newspapers and magazines. He pretended to be looking for something to read. Lee called out to him in her husky voice.

'Don't I know you? Surely you were at the Hilton back in Brussels? You were.' She patted the seat beside her. 'Do please come and sit with me. I'm bored to distraction. I desperately need some entertaining man. You fit the bill.'

'I would have thought there'd be a queue of men – waiting to distract you.' Nield fingered his trim moustache as he sat close to her. 'And of course I do remember seeing you, but you were always chaperoned by some

355

man. Severe-looking type. My bad luck, I thought.'

'A gallant man.' She sighed, her bosom rising. 'How rare these days.' Her bare arm touched his sleeve as she took out her jewelled cigarette holder, inserted a cigarette. Nield flicked his lighter into flame. She shook her head and smiled warmly. 'I'm giving it up – this is testing my will-power. Absolutely silly, really.'

Nield smiled. He had known about her technique, but wanted her to feel he knew nothing about her.

'Why are you so bored?' he asked. 'I saw you with a military type who seemed very distinguished.'

'Brigadier Burgoyne. Distinguished for wanting his own way. Now he's trotted off on some official business, indulging in one of his investigations. He regards me as a piece of the furniture.' She smiled again. 'The only compensation is the pay is good.'

'Thank Heaven for small mercies. What would you like to drink?'

'Champers! To celebrate the beginning of our friendship.'

Tweed froze, remained quite still. The gun muzzle against his neck felt cold as ice. The hand on his shoulder was large and had a strong grip. Then he heard a new voice.

'This gun is pressed into your spine. Drop your own or you'll be a cripple for life. At the best,' Newman concluded.

Tweed heard a tiny click: the safety catch being put on. Then a much louder sound as the weapon hit the tar. He turned round slowly. The first voice had sounded familiar, so he was not too surprised to face Chief Inspector Otto Kuhlmann of the Criminal Police from Wiesbaden.

'A nice warm friendly welcome to Germany, Otto,' he said genially. 'But what the hell are you doing here?'

Newman had holstered his weapon. Kuhlmann bent

356

down, retrieved his own gun, straightened up, and glared at Newman. The German police chief was short in stature but had very wide shoulders. He always reminded Newman of old films he'd seen starring Edward G. Robinson. The same wide mouth, tough face, thick dark hair and eyebrows. The same alert eyes and dynamic energy. A powerhouse of a police chief – and one of Tweed's old friends.

'My apologies,' Kuhlmann began, 'but we get a call from a man who says he is Tweed. That is, one of my officers took that call. Can we be sure of your identity? And in the dark you were just a shadow. We are taking no chances.'

'Neither am I,' Newman told him. 'Like you, I just saw a shadow with a gun. I'm not apologizing.'

'You have a permit for that weapon?' Kuhlmann asked in a gentle voice.

'He hasn't,' Tweed said quickly. 'But if I am right about what has been experienced by Hugo Westendorf protection was in order.'

'I may forgive you, Newman.' Kuhlmann turned to Tweed. 'Shall we see what is going on inside *Schloss Tannenberg* – before we freeze to death out here . . .?'

Tweed braced himself for his first sight of Westendorf. He remembered him well from the time the German Minister, as he then was, had visited Britain incognito to attend a meeting of INCOMSIN – the International Committee of Strategic Insight.

The German had been six foot two inches tall, of slim build, and with a strong-boned face and a high forehead. His mind had been like quicksilver, his manner courteous, and his energy phenomenal. Tweed dreaded what he was about to witness.

Kuhlmann pressed the bell beside the heavy closed door four times in quick succession, then once again after a pause. As it was, when the door was opened a few inches the first thing Tweed saw was the muzzle of a Heckler and Koch 9mm sub-machine-gun. The man holding it came into view, a plain-clothes detective without a smile. Was this the voice which had answered him on the phone, Tweed wondered.

They were admitted with Kuhlmann ushering in Paula, whom he hugged, and then the other two. Tweed then had the shock of his life.

'We shouldn't talk,' Tweed warned quickly. 'This place is probably bugged.'

'It was,' Kuhlmann replied. 'I ripped out every listening device myself.'

But it was Hugo Westendorf Tweed was staring at. The German had crossed the large hall with a brisk step, holding out his hand. He carried himself erect, his grip was strong. There were no signs of strain on his face and he greeted his visitor with a warm smile.

'Welcome to *Schloss Tannenberg*, my friend. It is so very good to see you.'

'And I thought someone – maybe your son, Franz – had been kidnapped.'

'But he has been. Three months ago. Which is why I resigned. It was a demand of the kidnappers – which I at once acceded to.'

36

They were sitting in a comfortable library Westendorf had suggested as a good place to talk. Their German host stood in front of a blazing log fire inside a huge stone alcove. The walls were lined with bookcases from floor to ceiling and Tweed had the impression the books were read. He was mystified by the situation and phrased his question with care.

'As far as you know, is Franz in good health?'

'You mean,' Kuhlmann intervened, 'has Westendorf received a severed arm or hand – like Andover and Delvaux. The answer is no. Westendorf communicated with me as soon as Franz had been kidnapped. I have worked in great secrecy. The press have no idea of what happened.'

'What action did you take?' Tweed asked.

'I launched the greatest dragnet ever mounted in the Federal Republic. I turned over Germany. Always in secrecy. I contacted informants in the underground criminal world and they started looking. Like so many respectable citizens, they hate the alien refugees – many of whom compete in the rackets.'

'The object was to locate Franz if you could?'

'Only partly.' It was Westendorf who explained. 'I had heard from Andover and Delvaux the dreadful experience they had suffered – I travelled to meet them in Liège. Kuhlmann's main purpose was to keep the kidnappers and my kidnapped son on the move. The doctor who carried out amputations on Andover's daughter, on Delvaux's wife, would need peace and quiet – above all, security – to perform his fiendish work. Kuhlmann made sure they never had the time. He missed trapping them three times by hours – but they kept running like scared rabbits.'

'But what is the present situation?' Tweed enquired.

Kuhlmann had lit one of his cigars. He waved it in the air like a baton as he replied.

'Franz Westendorf was freed from an isolated farm-house outside Bremen a few hours ago. His three captors were shot dead. I obtained permission from the new Minister of the Interior – a friend of Westendorf's – to use our élite anti-terrorist team.'

'That ends the chance of identifying the mastermind behind all this,' Tweed observed.

'No chance!' Kuhlmann snapped. 'The kidnappers were gypsy rubbish from the East. They'd had no idea who was controlling them. I emphasize I only took this line of action with the full consent of Westendorf.'

'It was blackmail.' The German ex-Minister stiffened as he spoke. 'I will never give in to blackmail. And Franz, who is eighteen in three days' time, holds the same view.'

'You showed a lot of courage,' Tweed remarked. 'But you did resign as Minister, as well as your membership of INCOMSIN and other organizations.'

'On Kuhlmann's advice,' Westendorf told him. 'The aim was to confuse the man behind the kidnapping. At first, he thinks I'm reacting like Andover and Delvaux. Meantime Kuhlmann is harassing the kidnappers, keeping them on the move, always looking over their shoulders.'

'How did you eventually trace Franz?' Tweed asked.

'As I'm sure you know,' Kuhlmann replied, 'from your one-time experience as Scotland Yard's youngest superintendent in Homicide, you need a little luck. But you must have the wit to know it when you are given the luck. A schoolboy identified the original vehicle used in the kidnap as a grey Audi. One of his friends found the empty Audi parked near this villa, little knowing the kidnap was in progress. The schoolboy – for a bit of fun – burst the yellow balloon his friend had attached to the rear of the Audi. I found this fact in a routine report. So I knew the Audi might still have a limp balloon dangling from it – something the kidnappers might not have noticed. I circulated the report.'

'And then?' Tweed enquired as Kuhlmann took a puff at his cigar.

'Having switched cars many times, I'm sure, the damned fools hung on to the Audi. Earlier today a motorcycle

360

patrolman in Bremen saw an Audi stopped in the traffic – and noticed a limp yellow balloon hanging from its rear. It was foggy and he followed it into the country to this farmhouse. He used his radio to Bremen police HQ and I heard the news inside thirty minutes in the Action Centre I'd established here at Berliner Tor. A unit of the anti-terrorist team was flown to Bremen . . .'

'On rather a long shot,' Tweed commented.

'Not too long. I'd first phoned Bremen and the locals said the farmhouse had been rented three months ago with a bank draft from Luxemburg City. That was enough for me. I ordered the raid to go ahead. You know the result.'

'I congratulate you,' said Tweed.

Westendorf had earlier poured glasses of hock for his guests. He walked over to Paula, sitting next to Newman, placed a gentle hand on her shoulder.

'All this must have been very tiring for you. I have heard you go almost everywhere with Tweed. How is the hock?'

'Very refreshing,' she replied gratefully.

'Then, gentlemen, I have a suggestion.' Westendorf's blue eyes were alert, his manner decisive. 'I wish to discuss certain very important matters with Tweed. The next step we take. But I find the villa has become claustrophobic, so let us drive to my motor yacht, the *Holsten V*, moored at Blankenese harbour on the Elbe. And I would be glad of your company,' he said to Paula. 'Intelligent women often think of angles men overlook.'

'Good idea,' agreed Tweed. 'But I'm curious about one thing, Kuhlmann. Why did you destroy all the bugs?'

Kuhlmann removed the cigar from his mouth. 'I toyed with the idea of using them – arranging rehearsed conversations. Westendorf vetoed the idea.'

'Why?' Tweed asked his host.

Westendorf made a chopping motion with his hand. 'I

resented the abominable invasion of privacy. And Kuhlmann agreed for another reason.'

'I decided,' Kuhlmann explained, 'that psychologically
it was another move which would confuse the man direc-
ting the kidnappers. What you call a carrot and stick
monoeuvre. The carrot was Westendorf resigning all his
posts – demanded by the rat who phoned him after the
kidnap. Then the stick was my ripping out all the listening
devices I had spotted – installed when the villa was
empty.'

'Any idea where they were made?' Tweed enquired.

'Hong Kong.'

Paula noticed the night had changed as they stepped into
Westendorf's stretched black Mercedes limo. It was a
damp cold now, the stars had disappeared and wisps of
mist were drifting towards the villa across the grounds.
She also saw the dragon's-teeth chain had been temporarily removed as they moved down the drive.

At Tweed's request, they stopped outside the entrance
and he got out to have a word with Marler sitting behind
the wheel of the Mercedes 600. A plain-clothes man was
stationed close by under a tree, armed with a sub-
machine-gun.

'We're driving to Blankense for a meeting aboard a
yacht Westendorf has moored in the harbour,' Tweed
told him.

'I'll follow at a discreet difference. Don't argue,' Marler said amiably. 'I've got a feeling you might just need
some back-up . . .'

Westendorf had taken the wheel with Tweed beside
him: in the back Paula revelled in warm comfort with
Newman next to her. As they drove past more villas the
mist thickened. On both sides they were passing through
what – in good weather – would be scenic parkland.

'We are now entering Blankenese,' Westendorf said. 'Once it was a small fishing port – now no fishing is permitted any more because the River Elbe is polluted. We pay a high price for the amenities of our modern civilization.'

'A society,' commented Kuhlmann, sitting between Paula and Newman, 'which that flood of refugees waiting east of our frontiers would give their right arms to enjoy.'

'Which is one subject I want us to discuss,' Westendorf remarked, and then concentrated on his driving.

He was driving slowly down a steep hill along a narrow tarred road. Paula had the impression Blankenese was a small town huddled on a series of hills. Peering out of the window she saw, as the mist drifted, villas perched high up and reached by flights of ancient stone staircases. They had left the High Street – deserted – behind and Westendorf drove very slowly as the downward gradient increased.

Blankenese, Paula decided, was now a labyrinth of narrow cobbled streets twisting and sheering up on either side in a way that recalled mountaineering. Frequently, instead of these alley-like streets there were *treppes* – endless stone staircases mounting up out of sight. By the blurred light of a street lamp she saw the name of one – *Becker's Treppe*. They had reached the riverside level when she saw another street name briefly under the faint glow of a street lamp. *Strandweg*.

As Westendorf stopped the car Paula found her nerves were twanging. The mist had become a fog. As they stepped out into it she heard the distant moan of a foghorn and shivered. The atmosphere was so like that night she had stood on the edge of the Lymington marina – waiting for Harvey Boyd to come home.

Following Westendorf's limo at a distance, Marler was bothered. From out of nowhere a bloody great brown

Cadillac had appeared. There were two men in the front of the great battlewagon of a car. He had little doubt they were tailing the limo.

Reaching the river level, the Cadillac turned left along the Strandweg, crawling. It stopped suddenly, Marler braked instantly. The Cadillac was a blurred shadow and he didn't think they had seen him: they were too intent on watching the limo. The fog parted for a moment and he saw the rear of the vehicle, a long radio aerial elevating automatically. They were reporting to someone.

Marler waited. The fog had closed in again, blotting out all sight of the Cadillac. He reached under his seat for the Armalite he had assembled while waiting outside *Schloss Tannenberg*. Locking the car quietly, he walked along slowly to where the car had parked. It was gone.

'Sorry about the fog,' Westendorf said, leading the way to the harbour. 'The met forecast got it wrong.'

The fog lifted again and Paula saw a small oblong basin fenced off from the Elbe by a jetty wall which ran out a short distance, turned at right angles, continued parallel to the silent river.

It was crammed with yachts. Most of them were co-cooned for winter in protective blue-plastic covers. Westendorf had reached the end of the short wall, had turned left along the main rampart. He looked back at Paula.

'The *Holsten V* is moored by the outer wall. No room in the harbour when I brought her back in.'

Tweed followed close behind Paula while Kuhlmann and Newman brought up the rear. Westendorf took Paula's hand to help her aboard a large luxurious motor yacht. He showed her the way with a torch beam, unlocked a door, ran down a flight of companionway steps, opened a second door. He switched on lights and they were inside a well-furnished saloon. Gleaming brass rails, the wood polished so she could see her face in it.

'Sit yourselves down,' he invited. 'Anyone like a drink to drive out the cold?'

Paula didn't sit. She stood near a window, peering out at the fog which was now a solid grey curtain drawn across the glass. Westendorf sensed her restlessness. He took her by the arm.

'You might find it interesting on the bridge. I'll switch on the radar.'

Another companionway at the far end of the saloon led up to the compact bridge. Westendorf pointed to a screen, turned on the radar. She gazed at the screen. Blank.

'Nothing will be out on the river tonight,' Westendorf remarked. 'Not in this fog. I will leave the door open so you can hear us. Come back into the saloon when you feel like it . . .'

He went back down the steps, took a bottle of Laurent Perrier champagne from the fridge. Tweed was relaxing on a comfortable leather banquette next to Kuhlmann. Newman was gazing out of a window. Westendorf handed round glasses, took one to Paula.

'It stimulates the brain cells,' he said when he returned. 'At least, that is my excuse. *Prost!*'

'You made a reference to refugees,' Tweed began. 'Have you ever met a Dr Wand?'

'Once.' Westendorf sat down, crossed his long legs. 'A curious man. I didn't like him. He has established a branch of his organization in Germany, another in Denmark. He said he was anxious that only talented refugees who would be an asset to the West should be allowed in. My impression was that he was lying. I said nothing. He went away. End of story.'

'But not end of the refugee story,' Tweed persisted. 'I remember you held strong views as Minister when you attended a meeting of INCOMSIN in London.'

'That is so. There are literally millions of refugees from all over the East – including gypsy hordes – who are waiting on the other side of the Oder–Neisse frontier ready to swarm in on us. They see Western Europe as a treasure-house of good things and if this tidal wave was to come they would destroy Europe's economy. I proposed taking a leaf out of the old Soviet Union's book – when they stopped their citizens fleeing here. They, of course, were very different, more civilized people.'

'Exactly how would it have worked?'

'To put it bluntly, I wanted to create a new death belt from the Baltic to the Adriatic. The refugee masses would be warned illegal crossing was *verboten* – would be lethal. I wanted a half-mile zone of no passage. Watch-towers on our side with guards armed with swivel-mounted machine-guns. Armed patrols with fierce dogs. And the lacing of the zone with anti-personnel mines. Also warships would patrol the coasts, checking any vessel from the East night and day. I would have saved Europe – but many illegals are now in our midst.'

'Did it occur to you,' Tweed asked, 'that a hostile power might smuggle in saboteurs and spies among the refugees?'

'It did.'

Tweed produced a copy of the photograph of the German coast, the islands, and the River Elbe including Hamburg. Showing it first to Kuhlmann, he then handed it to Westendorf.

'Does that cross marking a location downriver mean anything to you? A village, perhaps?'

'Oh, this must be Neustadt-Something – I forget the exact name. A new colony of houses. Inhabited, so I hear, by macho young executive types who drive Porsches and similar expensive cars. They keep very much to themselves.'

'How recently was the place occupied? The houses sold?'

'A few months ago. I'm not sure when. But recently.'

'I think Otto should have that photo.' Tweed turned to Kuhlmann. 'May I suggest you go nowhere near the place until I give you the signal. Then you raid it before dawn. I know of a similar colony on the south coast of Britain and another near Ghent in Belgium. It will be very important that we all synchronize the raids – to give no time for one lot to warn another.'

'There is a similar and larger development near the west coast of Denmark,' Westendorf commented. 'In Jutland – between the port of Esbjerg and the German frontier. A lonely area – especially in winter.'

'You mean about here,' Tweed suggested, producing another photograph. 'But how do you know about it?'

'Yes, apparently about there where the cross is marked. How do I know? Andover tracked it down. He travelled a lot, posing as a bird-watcher. He was very clever. At my most recent meeting with him in Liège he said this new development in Jutland was still unoccupied, although all the houses had been sold and furnished. He said because it faced the open sea – and Denmark is such a peaceful country – that the headquarters of a frightening subversive organization would be established there soon.'

'I have grim news,' Tweed said. 'Andover is dead – murdered in Liège. And the body of Delvaux's wife, Lucie, was discovered the other day floating in the Meuse. The attack on our way of life is accelerating.'

When he found the Cadillac had disappeared Marler moved fast. The fog lifted long enough over the harbour for him to see Tweed and the others boarding a ship. To his left – beyond the harbour – a stone wall bordered a wide footpath off from a steep green slope.

He ran past the harbour, the Armalite looped over his shoulder. Hoisting himself over the wall, he dropped on to deep soggy grass. He climbed the slope a short distance, turned round, leaning against the trunk of a tree. He was just in time to see the exact position of the motor yacht. Raising the rifle equipped with a night scope, he aimed it above the deck, which then vanished.

Marler settled down to wait, a task he was well accustomed to.

'I am shocked and appalled at this news,' Westendorf said to Tweed. 'Andover was one of the few first-class brains we had in the West. He saw the world globally.'

'And this is a global organization we are up against,' Tweed replied. 'A woman called Hilary Vane was murdered as she had disembarked from a transatlantic flight from Washington. Which could only mean someone at Dulles Airport in Washington had seen her board the flight, had relayed the news to London. One of my own people was nearly killed when an aircraft left Bangkok and blew up in mid-air. Fortunately I warned him to fly a different route at the last moment. Global,' he repeated. 'Worldwide.'

Paula was still on the bridge, sipping her champagne. Her eyes were glued alternately to the blank radar screen and the fog hanging over the invisible Elbe.

Only half listening to the conversation in the saloon, she was tense, keyed up. She began concentrating on the fogbound river. She frowned, leaned forward. The fog was swirling, creating strange shapes. Then she saw a vague outline, a faint shape coming towards the *Holsten V*.

She hammered her glass down on a ledge, turned, and ran down the steps into the saloon.

'Leave this ship!' she shouted. 'Now! Don't hesitate! Move, damn you . . .!'

Westendorf reacted instantly. He grabbed her round the waist with one arm, used the other to lift up her legs, ran up the exit companionway, stepped swiftly ashore as the cold clammy fog hit him, continued running along the jetty.

Behind them as he carried her up the companionway Paula heard Tweed shouting something, the clatter of footsteps rushing up on deck. Westendorf reached the shore, put her down as the others – Tweed, Kuhlmann and Newman – arrived, breathing hard.

'What the hell . . .!' Newman began.

He never completed his sentence. There was the sound of a brief, shattering crash. The jetty wall Newman had one foot perched on shuddered under the massive impact. The fog lifted again briefly. In time for them to see the *Holsten V* submerging with terrifying swiftness. No sign of any other vessel.

On the hill slope Marler saw their shadowy forms leave the vessel, counted, knew they were all ashore. He heard the menacing sound of collision. He had his Armalite rested against his shoulder. As the *Holsten* began to sink he fired blind – at a point a few feet above where the dying vessel had been moored – fired two shots.

Then he heard a muffled scream. Followed by silence. A moment later he heard in the heavy silence a splash of something hitting water. Then more silence.

37

On the inside of the harbour basin Tweed grabbed hold of
Kuhlmann by the arm. He spoke quietly but urgently.

'That was a Stealth ship which sunk Westendorf's
motor yacht . . .'

'Stealth?' the German asked, mystified.

'Listen to me, Otto! Like the Stealth bombers the
Americans built. You've heard of them? Good. There are
ships now built of similar materials – invisible to normal
radar. Paula saw nothing on the screen just before she ran
down into the saloon. Believe me, I know what I'm
talking about . . .'

'You normally do. An *invisible* ship?'

'Invisible to all present forms of radar,' Tweed stressed.

'Then I'll contact the river police. And the Coastguard.
This fog extends to the sea . . .'

This fog was lifting onshore. Kuhlmann ran up to the
entrance to a three-storey hotel as the others followed.
An old building of character, it had white plaster walls.
As the others followed him, entering a garden past a
beech hedge covered with dead leaves, Paula noticed a
turret at one corner and the date of its construction on the
side wall. 1902.

Marler joined Tweed and Paula, the Armalite concealed inside his hold-all. His trouser legs were sodden
with damp. He spoke quickly.

'I hit someone when I fired, heard his body splash into
the water . . .'

'Tell Kuhlmann quickly . . .'

Marler ran after the police chief as he mounted a flight of steps to the building. The Strandhotel. There was a brief consultation between the two men and Kuhlmann ran inside the hotel. Marler walked back down the path to join the others as Westendorf arrived.

'Paula is shivering with the cold. Let us go back to my car and wait for Kuhlmann,' the German suggested.

'I'll wait inside my own car, parked not far behind yours,' Marler decided.

He was careful not to report the incident of the man he was sure he had shot. He wasn't sure how much Tweed wanted Westendorf to know.

'That's better,' said Paula, settled in the rear of the limo and taking off her gloves to rub her hands. Already the heaters Westendorf had switched on were filling the interior with welcome warmth. And Westendorf had been tactful, attributing her shudders to the cold: she sensed he realized she was suffering from delayed reaction.

'What about your son, Franz?' Tweed enquired, seated in the front beside their host.

'He is being kept in a Bremen clinic overnight for a medical check-up. He will be back with me in the morning. I talked with him over the phone and he was quite indignant at being kept there while doctors "messed him about", as he put it. He sounded in very good shape, I'm relieved to say. Now, what happened back there at the harbour?'

Tweed explained quickly about Stealth, about the drama at Lymington when Paula had waited at the marina. He looked over his shoulder.

'All along I have trusted your eyesight. Now we've had further proof how good it is. Had you not acted so swiftly we would all be dead.'

'I did see something coming for the *Holsten*,' Paula responded. 'I couldn't be a hundred per cent certain at the Lymington marina, but this time I was. And the radar was blank – I glanced at it before I flew down the steps.'

'Andover and Delvaux told me about Stealth ships while I was in Liège,' Westendorf mused. 'I didn't believe them. Now I do. They add a terrifying dimension to the menace which faces Europe and – ultimately – America. We'll never even see the enemy coming. Andover told me a lot when I visited Liège.'

'Which enemy is that?' Tweed asked.

'The People's Republic of China, the citadel of Communism. He foresaw an army of twenty million sweeping across Asia, like the old Mongol hordes, but at much greater speed with modern tanks. He said he had talked with a Russian called Voronov in Hong Kong.'

'Not Viktor Voronov, the administrator of the KGB archives in Brezhnev's time?'

'The same. He was an old man when he sought out Andover to warn him.'

Westendorf stopped speaking. He was staring towards the harbour as though stunned by what had happened.

'Warn Andover about what?' Tweed pressed.

'By then Voronov was disillusioned with the whole system. Had been for a long time, apparently, which is why he slipped across the border into China and then Hong Kong. He told Andover the Chinese were in close touch with the old Soviet hardliners – in Kazakhstan, Russia, and Ukraine. As soon as the Chinese hordes arrive they'll install the hardliners as puppet rulers – so they'll just sweep over the old Soviet Union with no opposition and on into Europe. What puzzles me is these weird colonies of executives you mentioned.'

'I quote Andover's historical research from memory – "*Ogdai Khan swept his hosts across Asia to Russia in 1235 . . . Poland was ravaged, and a mixed army of Poles and Germans was annihilated at the battle of Liegnitz in Lower Silesia in 1241 . . . the Mongols embarked upon the enterprise with full knowledge of the situation of Hungary and*

372

the condition of Poland – they had taken care to inform themselves by a well-organized system of spies." ' Tweed paused. 'I draw your attention to the last few words. History is repeating itself.'

'You mean—' Westendorf began.

'That these so-called executives in Britain, Belgium, Germany – and soon to arrive, I suspect, in force in Denmark – are spies trained in the East, probably in China. They may well be the advance guard, the élite who will control more to come – across the Oder–Neisse frontier with other refugees.'

'You sound convinced,' Westendorf commented.

'Well, that's the way I'd organize it . . .'

He stopped speaking as Kuhlmann appeared, tapped on the window, and gestured for Tweed to join him. Outside the limo Tweed followed the police chief, who paused near to Marler's car.

'I have alerted everyone. Reinforcements of police will arrive shortly to search the shore. Ah, I think they are arriving already.'

Patrol cars were appearing as dim shapes, parking along the Strandweg. Uniformed men jumped out, went across a stretch of grass to the edge of the Elbe. Others ran back out of sight parallel to the river.

'Radio in patrol cars can speed things up,' Kuhlmann commented.

'Searching the shore for what?' Tweed asked.

'The body of the man Marler shot – and heard hit the water. The tide is beginning to recede. With a lot of luck the body may be washed up on one of the little sandy beaches further down the river. A long shot but—'

Kuhlmann broke off as a uniformed man ran back towards him. He stopped, panting for breath.

'Chief Inspector, we have discovered the corpse of a man lying on a beach . . .'

*   *   *

373

'To Berliner Tor!'

Kuhlmann gave the order to the police driver who had taken over the wheel of Marler's Mercedes 600. It was night. They had left Blankenese, had escorted Westendorf, driving his limo, to *Schloss Tannenberg*. A plain-clothes detective had materialized out of nowhere, had removed the dragon's teeth chain across the open entrance. Through his window Westerndorf gave Tweed a little salute, disappeared down his drive.

'What's the idea of that chain which was removed just before we left the villa?' Tweed asked Kuhlmann.

Marler sat in front beside the driver, who knew the way. In the roomy rear Tweed sat next to Kuhlmann, who had Paula on his left and Newman beyond.

'I feared the kidnappers – when they realized I was on their tails – might resort to attacking the villa, to kidnapping Westerndorf himself. There are three chains along the drive – just in case an armoured car was used to break in. Even such a vehicle would have been stopped.'

'And it will be possible for me to contact Inspector Nielsen in Copenhagen? On scrambler?'

'Why do you think we are going to Berliner Tor? A clever man, Nielsen. No wonder he is chief of police intelligence. You think the climax of all this grim business will take place in Copenhagen?'

'In Denmark,' Tweed said cryptically.

'I shouldn't have asked!'

'Mind you, I am guessing – gambling on a great scale. I am trying to out-think the swine behind all this villainy.'

'You usually guess right. You looked surprised when I asked Marler for his Armalite. I want it for ballistics at Berliner Tor – to check the bullet in the skull of the body we found on the beach. Something strange about him. No hint of his identity was found in his sodden pockets. Dressed like a seaman. I've never known a seaman with nothing in his pockets – no money, no photo of a girl friend. Just nothing. The pathologist may be able to tell me more about his origins. And I also phoned the harbour master. He'll report to me in the morning as to whether any vessel was moving on the Elbe in the fog. He doubts it.'

'You've been busy,' Tweed replied. 'Could I ask you to add one more task to your list? Check whether a Lear jet, owner Dr Wand, is waiting at Hamburg Airport? If so, has the pilot filed a flight plan? And if he has – the destination.'

'I'll send out an officer to have a word with the security chief. Discreetly. Wand carries a lot of clout.'

'Here? Why?'

'A strange man. He has this refugee aid outfit. That gives him influence. But mainly he has money. He is renting a villa out at Othmarschen – that's a wealthy district you pass before you reach Nienstedten, which is where Westendorf lives. Wand is on dining-out terms with several cabinet ministers in Bonn I won't name. They enjoy being taken out to expensive restaurants, served the finest wines.'

'The same technique Dr Wand uses in Belgium,' Tweed remarked. 'How long has he rented this villa?'

'No idea. The German owner has a place in California he prefers – or rather his new young wife prefers.'

Newman was staring out of the window. He had his bearings now. He leaned across Paula to speak to Kuhlmann.

'Could you drop me close to the Four Seasons? I have some people there I'd like to have a word with.'

'Brought the whole brigade with you?' Kuhlmann asked, looking at Tweed. 'You're treating this as a major operation?'

'It's serious,' Tweed said, and left it at that as the car stopped to let out Newman at the corner of Jungfernstieg and Neuer Jungfernstieg. He waved and walked towards the hotel as the Mercedes moved off.

* * *

Dr Wand sat at a desk in his large room at the Four Seasons. His confidant, Starmberg, the Luxemburger, was seated on a couch, watching his chief. Wand was studying the list of eminent Europeans pencilled in his slim notebook. He took a sadistic pleasure in crossing out one name. Tweed .

'That really was the most excellent news we had from Karl out at Blankenese,' he said, peering at Starmberg over the rims of his pince-nez. 'The opposition – which was really beginning to make a perfect nuisance of itself – must now be floating down the Elbe.'

'It was clever of you to foresee Westendorf might decide to visit the *Holsten V*,' Starmberg reminded him, knowing how much his chief appreciated flattery. 'I would never have predicted it myself.'

'Oh, simple psychology, my dear Starmberg. A knowledge of human nature – and the ability to step inside another man's shoes. Westendorf had been cooped up in his villa for weeks, he was an enthusiastic yachtsman. So what would be more natural – after his son had been rescued – than for him to wish to spend a little time in entirely different surroundings? And that reminds me.'

Turning back to his notebook, he carefully drew a line through another name. Westendorf. He took satisfaction from contemplating his list. The first four names deleted. Andover and Delvaux, also. Reports reaching him had informed him Delvaux, a shattered man, had recently been transferred to a clinic. Everything was going so well – in preparation for the vital Denmark operation. He checked his Rolex watch.

'I think, if I may say so, it is probably time we partook of a late dinner in the Grill Room here. And why, may I enquire, are you looking disappointed?'

'I had worked out a foolproof plan for grabbing Paula Grey. It is a very original idea, I had obtained the equipment and taught the team how to use it.'

'Well, well, do not feel your esteemed efforts have been wasted. You may well find you can put into practice your plan. After all,' Wand smiled, 'it is a very long list.'

'Incidentally, why are we staying here instead of out at the villa?'

'Dear me, you know I do dislike being asked questions. But on this occasion I will satisfy your overweening curiosity. I wish to talk to Vulcan, who is staying at this hotel. I thought it safer to do so in the discreet surroundings of this most excellent hotel. Especially when Tweed was alive. Now he is dead . . . Let us not dwell on the unpleasant side of life. Instead, let us make our way to the Grill Room . . .'

They used the stairs. Wand avoided elevators whenever he could: he had once been trapped inside an elevator for ten minutes and had never forgotten the experience.

At that moment Newman was mounting the first flight, his hand on the banister rail. Entering the hotel he had seen the backs of Brigadier Burgoyne and Willie Fanshawe walking into the only elevator available at that moment.

He looked up and saw two men descending towards him – Dr Wand on the far side, and Jules, the butler who had opened the door during his visit with Tweed to the villa at Waterloo. A heavy-set man with dark hair, Jules. An ugly customer, Newman thought, but the staring eyes were intelligent. He continued to climb as they walked down towards him. Jules' thick lips tightened and Newman knew he had been recognized.

The Luxemburger continued to walk alongside Wand, leaving little or no space for Newman to pass them. Jules's well-padded shoulder collided with Newman's as they met. He would have toppled the Englishman down the stairs but Newman was expecting some such aggressive act. With his hand gripping the banister firmly to maintain his balance, Newman stiffened his shoulder, took the impact and shoved. Jules staggered against Wand, who stood like a rock.

'You clumsy oaf,' Jules snarled in German.

'You gave me no room to pass,' Newman observed calmly. He looked at Wand. 'This is a five-star hotel. Do you think it wise to bring your pit-bull terrier in here?'

'You . . .!'

Jules's face was contorted into an expression of manic fury. Wand laid a restraining hand on his arm. He smiled at Newman.

'What a pleasant surprise to see you again so soon, Mr Newman. As I believe they say in England, it is a small world. Please excuse any display of unfriendliness on the part of Mr Starmberg. He has been working very hard and has had no sleep for days. Fatigue can upset the balance. Would you be so kind as to accept my humble apologies?'

'Just so long as we don't have a repeat performance . . .'

On this note Newman continued upstairs. Behind him the two men strolled towards the Grill Room. Starmberg whispered his comment.

'A great pity he didn't go down with the *Holsten*.'

'Now, now,' Wand chided, 'no need to be vindictive. There were other people in the party which boarded the ship with Tweed and Westendorf, but our Cadillac team wasn't able to see the others clearly. Be content with the evening's work. And now, kindly relax yourself. It would be a pity to spoil a first-rate meal with indigestion . . .'

Newman was thoughtful as he went on up the stairs. When he had collided with Jules Starmberg his hip had contacted something hard on the Luxemburger's hip under his jacket – something like a sheathed knife. He had also noticed a tell-tale bulge near the shoulder under

378

the jacket. Starmberg was carrying a gun. And he had paused at the top of the first flight, turning in time to see the two men heading for the Grill Room. Was it usual to go to dinner accompanied by your butler? Newman didn't think so.

He was starting the long walk along a wide corridor to his room when a familiar figure came towards him. Willie Fanshawe, swinging his room key. Willie, moving with the agility Newman had often noticed in plump men, hurried forward, beaming with pleasure.

'I say! First Brussels, now Hamburg. Never thought I'd have such luck. The Brigadier's here, too. Which really is why I'm here! He seems to hate travelling without an entourage of friends. But he's a bit tetchy this evening. Rather a trial, you know.' He lowered his booming voice. 'Strictly between the two of us, I don't think his business deal is going all that well. Well, I said to him, you can't expect to win 'em all. Didn't like that one little bit. I made myself scarce, made an excuse to leave him alone in his room a few moments ago. Best to let him be on his own when he's in that mood. I should know! Living next door to the blighter. How about a drink? In the Sambri bar off the lobby. They do a generous glass of champers . . .'

'I'm afraid . . .'

'And Helen is here, of course,' Willie tumbled on. He dug Newman playfully in the ribs. 'She rather fancies you. I know she'll jump for joy when she hears you're under the same roof. Now, about that drink . . .'

'Sorry, Willie, but I can't. Not just now. I have to keep an appointment. Maybe later in the evening?'

'Jolly good! You'll find me in the Sambri. Bet I'm three glasses ahead of you. Now don't forget . . .'

As Willie found all the elevators were in use and headed down the stairs Newman changed his mind. He waited – to give Willie time to settle in the bar – then stepped inside an elevator a couple had just left. It was time to warn Tweed.

38

Berliner Tor.

Police headquarters in Hamburg. A slim twenty-storey building sheering up into the night, ablaze with lights. Tweed remembered it well: it stood in splendid isolation, the only edifice of any height almost as far as the eye could see.

'Follow me!'

Kuhlmann led them into a vast tall entrance hall, waved his pass at the duty officer, hurried on to the bank of elevators, pressed the button for the fifteenth floor. While they waited he turned to Tweed.

'They've given me a large office on the fifteenth floor and all facilities. Scrambler phones, the lot. You want to call Nielsen now?'

'It's urgent. Yes. If he's in, but he works all hours . . .'

Paula and Marler were escorted to another room when they stepped out on the fifteenth floor. Kuhlmann said he was sending someone along.

'Coffee. Food. No alcohol, I'm afraid . . .'

He showed Tweed into a large office with a view of the moonlit Aussen Alster – the larger of the two lakes in the middle of Hamburg. Showing Tweed to a desk, he pointed to a phone, reminded him to press the red button for scrambler.

'I'm taking Marler straight along to ballistics. Back in a few minutes. You've complete privacy for your call – that instrument isn't linked to a recorder. Good luck . . .'

He left with Marler, who was carrying the hold-all

containing the Armalite. Kuhlmann never wastes a minute, Tweed thought, as he settled himself in a chair. Taking out a notebook, he checked Nielsen's number, pressed the red button, and dialled. Using the Dane's private number, he got straight through.

'Where are you calling from, you old scoundrel?' Nielsen greeted him jovially.

'Hamburg. Police HQ. On scrambler. Are you?'

'Always on this number. You usually bring trouble. Tell me the worst.'

'First, can you put someone to watch Kastrup Airport round the clock. For the arrival of a Lear jet. I have details here . . .' He checked what Marler had written down in his notebook, relayed them to Nielsen. 'And if it does land I think later it will go elsewhere. Vital I know where.'

'So we obtain the pilot's flight plan. Without letting him know he's under surveillance,' Nielsen promised in his precise manner. 'How do I get the data back to you?'

'Via your old friend, Chief Inspector Kuhlmann, here at Berliner Tor. In an emergency – if Otto isn't available – try and contact me at the Four Seasons Hotel, Room 311.'

'All clear so far. You wouldn't like to give me a hint as to what this is about? Even a hint?'

'Haven't finished. The danger zone is Jutland. What's the weather like?'

'In Jutland? Forecast of heavy fog along the whole of the west coat. Can you pinpoint the area?'

'Somewhere south of Esbjerg – between there and the German frontier. Probably on a lonely stretch of the coast.'

'Very dense fog there,' Nielsen warned. 'No sign of it shifting.'

'I have a big favour to ask you.'

'Here it comes. Unorthodox and illegal. Go ahead.'

Tweed thanked God that the Dane was always so co-operative. But would he wear this one!

'I may want to use an SAS team in the area. Are you still there, Henrik?'

There was a pause as though Henrik Nielsen was recovering from a state of shock. He cleared his throat.

'You don't ask for much, do you? I'll have to contact a Minister.'

'Do so. Give me his name. And I'll get our PM to talk to him.'

'As high-level as that?' Nielsen sounded impressed. 'In that case leave it to me. We are both in NATO, after all.'

'Exactly. But I will see you first – in Copenhagen. And soon. Take care . . .'

Tweed had hardly put down the phone when it rang. A girl operator informed him a Mr Robert Newman was on the line. Tweed asked her to put him through.

'I'm calling from a public phone box,' Newman opened, talking rapidly. 'I thought you ought to know that the tribe is here in force – Messrs Fanshawe and Burgoyne, with their women. Also – wait for it – Dr Wand, staying at the Four Seasons . . .'

He described tersely his encounter with Wand and Jules Starmberg on the staircase. Tweed thanked him for the information, adding he was not too surprised and would be back at the Four Seasons shortly.

As he put down the phone for the second time Kuhlmann came into the room. He was carrying a tray with coffee and a selection of sandwich rolls.

'I have news for you,' the German said as he sat opposite Tweed. 'There was a patrol car at the airport. Luckily one of the men was a sergeant I know – and a friend of the airport security officer. He radioed back just two minutes ago. About that Lear jet.'

'Any positive data?'

'Yes. The machine is being kept on stand-by twenty-four hours a day – with a three-crew roster. A flight plan has been filed. For Copenhagen.'

382

Tweed, suddenly realizing he was ravenous, had sunk his teeth into a ham roll. He nodded, swallowed, then told the police chief about his conversation with Henrik Nielsen. He went on to relay Newman's account of his confrontation with Jules Starmberg and asked if the name rang any bells.

'Deafening cathedral bells,' Kuhlmann replied. 'So Jules Starmberg is back in Hamburg. A Luxemburger and a very ugly piece of work. His wife was battered brutally to death in an apartment at Altona two years ago. Starmberg is the only man I never broke under interrogation. That is, a man I knew was guilty of a hideous crime.'

'What went wrong?'

'An unbreakable alibi for the time of the murder. He was supposed to be drinking in a bar on the waterfront at the relevant time. Three of his pals swore he was there.' Kuhlmann looked grim. 'But my main problem was Starmberg refused to answer one single question. He remained silent during the whole interrogation. His crook of a lawyer told me about the alibi. Starmberg is a man of teak.'

'That's how he struck me when I met him briefly in Brussels. He's now staying at the Four Seasons with Dr Wand.'

'In that case Dr Wand keeps very bad company.'

'That does not surprise me,' Tweed commented, drinking some coffee, then attacking another roll.

'I have more news for you,' Kuhlmann continued. 'In the morning the river police are using a barge equipped with lifting tackle to hoist up the remains of the *Holsten V*. Westerndorf is calling for you at the hotel tomorrow morning at nine o'clock to take you to Blankenese. If that is convenient.'

'I'll make it convenient. I want to see the state of the vessel. You're moving very fast, Otto.'

'I was just about to say that you are—'

Kuhlmann broke off as the phone started ringing. Raising his thick eyebrows, he answered. Listening, Tweed ate another roll. Paula opened the door, said she was going back to the hotel in a police car, waved to Tweed as she left.

Kuhlmann put down the phone, put his large hand to his head in mock amazement.

'That I have never known before. Normally I wait hours – days – while a pathologist takes his time. He has just made a cursory examination of the seaman's corpse. Well, now we know where he came from – and we don't.'

'What does that mean?' Tweed enquired.

'The fillings in the teeth. No dentist in Western Europe attended to him. He comes from the East. How far east? I asked. You know what he said? Maybe from Bulgaria, maybe from Romania, maybe from one of the old Soviet republics. Very precise – even if very prompt.'

'It fits in with the picture I'm building up of what is happening.'

'And you wouldn't care to sketch in that picture?'

'Too early yet.' Tweed stood up. 'Thanks for the food, for all your co-operation. I'd better get back to the hotel now.'

'I'll get you an unmarked car to take you there. See you in the morning – at Blankenese. I wonder what they will haul up out of the depths of the Elbe?'

Tweed thanked the driver, stepped out of the car. About to climb the flight of steps into the hotel he paused. Walking towards him was Paula. He advanced on her.

'What the devil are you doing out on your own?'

'Don't I count?'

Newman emerged out of the shadows where he had stopped for a second to glance in a shop window. He grinned at Tweed's discomfiture.

'We *are* looking after her, as you see.'

'Thank heaven for that. Sorry, Paula. I was worried. It is cold – the temperature has dropped suddenly. Let's get into the warmth.'

They mounted the steps with Tweed in the middle. As they entered the lobby Tweed stood quite still, motioned with his hands for Paula and Newman to do the same. Straight ahead of them extended an arm of the lobby where the toilets were situated. Hanging from the walls of the extended arm were several tapestries.

An imposing figure, clad in a smoking jacket, expensive blue trousers, a white shirt, and a red bow-tie, stood examining the tapestries. Dr Wand. Alongside him stood Jules Starmberg. The two men turned, began walking towards the lobby. They saw Tweed and his companions at the same moment.

Dr Wand stopped, motionless, staring at Tweed. He was so still he might have been a statue. Gazing at them through his pince-nez, his expression froze – showed no trace of emotion whatsoever. Starmberger lacked his chief's iron self-control. Astonishment, disbelief, fury – his reaction was clearly written on his brutish face.

Wand was the first to recover. Smiling his twisted smile, he came forward, his eyes gleaming.

'My dear Tweed, what an amazing coincidence. Of all the cities in Europe, this wonderful continent of such infinite variety, how extraordinary that we—'

'Good-night,' Tweed said, and led the way to the Haerlin restaurant.

Dr Hyde slowly climbed the hill behind the *hafen* – the harbour on the River Elbe in Hamburg. He had just enjoyed the company of an obliging lady he had met on the waterfront. Her fee had seemed rather exorbitant compared with Liège, but then he reminded himself that the quality of her entertainment had been rather higher.

He moved slowly because the fog made everything seem different. The last thing he wanted to do was to lose his way to the modest *gasthof* which he had made his temporary home. He sighed with relief as he saw the blurred neon sign indicating vacancies.

His attempt to use the key his landlady had lent him and enter unseen was a fiasco. As he crept towards the stairs she opened the door of her living-room. A scrawny woman with greedy eyes, her expression was one of unpleasant amusement as she greeted him in German.

'Not a night to linger on the waterfront. You must have had a long walk. You've been out over two hours.'

'And what concern is that of yours?' he snapped in his pidgin German.

'I thought perhaps you had found some company. There is a good selection of that on the waterfront.'

'Shut your trap, you old—'

His face had twisted into a glare of sheer malevolence – a mistake he tried to correct immediately. He gave her his best bedside manner smile, thankful he had stopped himself fom calling her a hag. That would have drawn a lot of attention to himself permanently.

'Please do excuse me, Frau, but I drank a little wine and it has upset my stomach. I hope you will accept my deep apologies . . .'

She pursed her lips, shrugged her thin shoulders, slammed the door shut in his face. Perturbed, he climbed the stairs, unlocked the door of his sparsely furnished room, heard the phone ringing, hurried to pick up the receiver.

Dr Wand sat at the desk in his room at the Four Seasons, drumming his thick fingers on its surface. Starmberg was waiting anxiously for his reaction. It came fast enough.

'What I would like to know, my dear Jules, is how in

the name of Heaven could Tweed have survived?'

'The Cadillac team reported over my car radio that the main consignment was aboard. That must have meant Tweed. I don't understand what went wrong.'

'Miss Paula Grey must enjoy our company,' Wand decided. 'You said you had a plan?'

'It is foolproof,' Starmberg assured him.

'Then will you be so good as to reactivate this marvellous plan? And I must phone Dr Hyde. This time we will wait only three days after Miss Grey has sampled our hospitality. Three days for Tweed to eat his soul out. Then we will send him a piece of Miss Grey to remind him he must remain in retirement.'

Wand checked the number of the *gasthof* Dr Hyde had phoned to him while Wand was still at his Waterloo villa. Dialling the number, he bit his thin lips as the ringing went on and on. Was the corrupt swine out spending his money on worthless women again?

'Who is calling?'

Dr Hyde's distinctive grovelling voice. He sounded short of breath.

'You know who is speaking,' Wand began. 'A patient will be needing urgent treatment. So kindly listen carefully. Your case is packed? Excellent. Leave at once for the railway station. Catch the first possible train to Flensburg on the German–Danish border. As soon as you arrive a car will be waiting outside to take you across the frontier into Jutland – Denmark. The driver will identify himself as Johnny from Tinglev. I will spell that name . . . Repeat it, please. Good . . .'

'Could I not catch another train to Tinglev—'

'My dear sir' – Wand's tone was pure acid – 'when I make a suggestion I have a reason for doing so. At that hour it is most unlikely there will be a connection. If, by chance, when you arrive at Flensburg station Johnny is not there, you wait for him. When he picks you up he will drive you to your ultimate destination. I will arrange for a nurse to be in attendance . . .'

'The patient—' Dr Hyde began.

'I would much appreciate it if you would refrain from interrupting me. I was about to tell you the patient needing treatment is a female. Now, ask the woman who runs that place to phone for a taxi. Immediately, I suggest.'

Dr Wand broke the connection. His face was flushed with annoyance. He gave the order to Starmberg.

'You heard what I said. Phone Clausen after checking the train arrival time at Flensburg. And the sooner you put into operation your plan to obtain the company of Miss Grey the better. You know where she is to be transported to, after hearing the name Tinglev.'

'For operational reasons the Miss Grey abduction will have to be carried out tomorrow evening.'

'That is your responsibility.' Wand's face expressed disapproval. 'I do wish you would not use such crude terms as abduction. She will be our guest.'

Tweed had just ordered from the menu in the Haerlin restaurant when he stiffened. 'Damn!' he muttered under his breath.

'Something wrong?' Newman enquired.

'Yes – with me. I've forgotten a vital task for Kuhlmann. Is that public phone box far away?'

'Only a few minutes' walk. I'll come with you.'

'Don't leave the restaurant,' Tweed warned Paula. 'We'll be back before the food arrives . . .'

Collecting their coats, which had been taken from them by the head waiter, they dashed into the bitterly cold night. Newman waited outside while Tweed called Berliner Tor, asked for Kuhlmann, who came on the line swiftly.

'One important request I forgot to make, Otto. There may well be a Dr Hyde, an evil man, in Hamburg. Can you send a courier to the Haerlin restaurant? I will give him a large number of duplicate photos of this creature. And I suspect he may frequent prostitutes.'

'A plain-clothes courier will come immediately on a motorcycle. Meantime I will alert patrol cars to converge on the waterfront area. That's where these girls hang out. The search will be under way within thirty minutes . . .'

39

No one had felt like sleep: tension gripped them all as they sensed the battle against Dr Wand was moving towards a climax.

They were assembled in Tweed's room – Paula, Newman, Marler, Butler, and Nield, plus a sixth man. It was after midnight and the surprise arrival of the newcomer had happened a few minutes earlier.

There had been a discreet tapping on the door. Newman, his Smith & Wesson concealed in his right hand, unlocked the door with his left hand, turned the handle suddenly, and jerked the door open a few inches. 'Good God!' he had whispered. 'Come in quickly.'

Philip Cardon had walked in, wearing a business suit of German cut. The small man Paula had nicknamed 'the Squirrel' looked round as Newman closed and relocked the door. Cardon smiled impishly as they stared at him in astonishment.

'Good morning, everyone. I knew you'd never do the job without me.' He looked at Tweed. 'What is the job?'

'Sit down, Philip. Have a good rest? For this time of night you look amazingly fresh.'

'I'm a night bird.' Cardon winked at Paula, sat beside her as she patted the couch. 'I wake up when the rest of the world is sleeping. The best time to catch the opposition off guard.' He looked at Tweed again. 'Who exactly is the opposition?'

'I was just about to sum up the present situation, Philip. Briefly, we are faced with the most sadistic, ruthless, and cunning enemy we've ever confronted. The body count so far shows that – all murdered.' He counted them off on his fingers. 'Hilary Vane, Irene Andover, a cab driver in Brussels, Sir Gerald Andover, Lucie Delvaux, Joseph Mordaunt – which makes six.'

'Don't forget old Mrs Garnett at Moor's Landing, who vanished,' Newman reminded him. 'I doubt we'll ever see her alive again.'

'I agree,' Tweed said. 'I do have an idea where to look for her – but that will have to wait until we get home. I now come to data which is top secret . . .'

'Has this room been checked out?' Cardon asked quickly.

'Thanks to Butler, it has.'

Earlier, when Butler had been one of the first to arrive, he had insisted on using an instrument he always carried to 'flash' the room – to check it for listening devices. In his thorough way, he had taken thirty minutes searching for any planted devices. Then he had nodded to Tweed.

'Clean as a whistle . . .'

For the next quarter of an hour Tweed gave Cardon a terse account of events, starting with Paula's experience at the Lymington marina and ending with his encounter with Dr Wand in the lobby of the Four Seasons. He had just finished when the phone rang. Paula answered it, looked at Tweed.

'Otto Kuhlmann for you . . .'

'We missed your good friend, Hyde, by no more than half an hour,' Kuhlmann reported. 'He had been staying at a *gasthof* behind the waterfront. The old horror who runs the place positively identified him from one of your photos my man was carrying. He had stayed there for several days and suddenly departed this evening after receiving a phone call.'

'He keeps slipping out of my hands. An elusive villain,' Tweed commented.

'Wait! There's more. Hyde told the old bag he was flying to Düsseldorf, then going on to Belgium later. Too much detail. I didn't believe it. I sent patrol cars to the rail station. They had orders to show his photo to all ticket clerks. One had unfortunately gone off duty. An officer got his address in Altona and drove out there. This ticket clerk remembered Hyde well. Hyde was in a bad temper, abused the clerk for not giving him his ticket to Flensburg fast enough.'

'Flensburg? That's close to the Danish border.'

'It is. I alerted the Flensburg police but they were just too late. The train from Hamburg had arrived ten minutes earlier.'

'Checkmate, then . . .'

'No! I am like a bulldog with a bone. I never let go – you know that. I phoned a friend who is a member of the Danish frontier control – not that it amounts to much these days. I described Dr Hyde with the photo in front of me. He has a distinctive face. My friend remembered a car arriving at the frontier – with Hyde as a passenger in the back. He knows where the driver comes from. A small Danish town called Tinglev – not too far inside Jutland.'

'You really are a bulldog. I can't thank you enough. I may well have the last link in the chain I have been constructing.'

'My pleasure. Any time. Why not get some sleep? Come to that, why don't I . . .'

Tweed put down the phone, his expression grim. He faced his audience, told them what Kuhlmann had said.

'Denmark,' he concluded. 'I think I guessed right. Denmark is the key. To be precise, the lonely stretch of the west coast of Jutland between Esbjerg and the border with Germany. Denmark,' he repeated once more.

'Why Denmark?' Cardon queried.

'Point one, Westendorf told me Andover thought that part of Jutland was important. Point two, Dr Wand's pilot of his stand-by Lear jet has filed a flight plan for Copenhagen. Point three, Dr Hyde, Wand's creature, is now somewhere in the region of Tinglev, a small town in the south of Jutland and not too far from that coast, which in winter is almost deserted.'

'Adds up,' Cardon agreed laconically. 'So what do we do next?'

'We mobilize our forces – at the strategic points in Denmark. Marler, you have a hired car. Tomorrow I want you to drive to this place, Tinglev. Take Butler and Nield with you – and you are in charge of the team. You have photos of Dr Hyde. Locate him, then tail him if he moves.'

'How can I contact you?' Marler asked.

'Probably late tomorrow I'll be flying to Copenhagen. I'll stay at the Hotel d'Angleterre. If I'm not there, call me here.'

'Weapons?' Butler asked.

'Kuhlmann has agreed to supply them – in return for those you purchased from your friend on the waterfront. He says those guns may have been used earlier for criminal purposes.'

'What about my Armalite?' Marler enquired. 'It's in perfect condition.'

'Kuhlmann is sending another one for you.'

'What about the rest of us?' Newman asked. 'We're not going to this Tinglev?'

'No. I'm dividing my forces into a pincer movement. Paula, you and Cardon will fly to Copenhagen with me. So both of you will have to give up your weapons – airport security.' He turned to Marler. 'You won't have any trouble with your weapons – driving over the frontier.'

'I'll tape them under the chassis. Not that we'll look at all suspect. We're three businessmen selling marine equipment.'

'You've built up a strong case for Denmark,' Newman commented, 'but you're still guessing.'

'Point four,' Tweed hammered home, 'one of those crosses marked on General Li Yun's war maps in Lop Nor is in the same area of Jutland . . .'

'It certainly is,' Cardon agreed amiably. 'Don't be so sceptical, Newman. I saw it with my own eyes before I took those photographs.'

'It does look like Denmark,' Newman assented.

'Plus the fact,' Tweed reminded him, 'that Andover said that in Jutland there is a new colony of houses, bought and furnished, but not yet occupied. I think Dr Wand is soon on his way to Denmark to supervise the arrival of a big team of so-called executives. Saboteurs and spies. We want to be waiting for them.'

Someone tapped on the door. Everyone except Tweed froze. He accompanied Newman to the door.

'That will probably be the second courier from Kuhlmann – the one with the weapons . . .'

Tweed peered out. He recognized one of the plainclothes policemen Kuhlmann had introduced him to just before he had left Berliner Tor. He was carrying a large shabby hold-all, which Tweed took off him.

'Could you please come back in five minutes? Thank you.'

He opened the hold-all, took out an Armalite with spare ammo, and exchanged it for Marler's weapon. There were also two 7.65mm Walther automatics with spare magazines. He handed one each to Butler and Nield. Collecting Newman's .38 Smith & Wesson and Paula's Browning, he put them into the hold-all with the spare ammo, zipped up the hold-all. When the courier returned he handed it to him and apologized in German for keeping him up all hours. The detective grinned, handed him permits for the weapons.

'My chief doesn't think clocks exist . . .'

'What next?' Newman enquired, suppressing a yawn.

'In the morning Westendorf is calling for us here at nine o'clock. Now, you all get some sleep, and that's an order. Lord knows what tomorrow will bring.'

It was a remark he was to recall with horror later.

At nine o'clock on the dot that morning the black Mercedes, with Westendorf at the wheel, pulled up outside the Four Seasons. Tweed sat next to the German while Newman and Paula climbed into the back. The fog had gone.

'How is Franz?' Tweed asked, as they moved into heavy traffic.

'He was brought home early. He's very fit – mentally and physically, shows no signs of his ordeal. We talked nonstop for an hour, then he fell fast asleep.'

'He's guarded at the villa?'

'The inside and the grounds are swarming with concealed and heavily armed police. Kuhlmann insisted on it.'

'But what about yourself? Shouldn't you also be guarded?'

'I am – against my protests.' Westendorf glanced in the rear-view mirror. 'Not far behind us are two unmarked police cars. Kuhlmann's work, I'm sure.'

'Very wise . . .'

Paula looked out as the car moved through the suburbs

which gave way to the wealthy districts. By daylight – and with the sun shining – she could see clearly the magnificent villas in their generous grounds. Tweed gestured towards them.

'You have friends here, I suppose?'

'Not really.' Westendorf smiled. 'These rich – very rich – people keep to themselves. Many go back for generations. Some are in shipping, others own large breweries founded ages ago. They form a select club and mix only with each other. Nothing wrong with that. They have a right to preserve their own way of life.' He smiled again. 'But if one of their daughters tries to marry outside their class all hell breaks loose. I do not expect Franz to find his fiancée round here . . .'

He fell silent, concentrated on his driving. Paula realized they were taking a different route from the previous evening. They climbed and then Westendorf pulled up at the edge of a grassy slope. He waved a hand.

'The Süllberg, the highest point in Blankenese. If you don't mind a short walk we can look down and see what is going on. Then we drive down to the harbour.'

They climbed a wide flight of steps leading to a restaurant at the summit. Westendorf opened a door and they followed him inside. Westendorf greeted a waiter carrying a tray piled high with clean dishes.

'They know me here,' he explained, 'so they won't mind us looking at the view.'

He led the way to a glassed-in terrace and Paula almost gasped at the extent of the panorama. It was a beautiful morning and the air was clear to the horizon. On the far side of the Elbe, which lay below, open countryside stretched away. Tweed pointed downwards.

At the edge of the harbour was anchored an enormous barge. Standing on its decks was a massive lifting crane, the chain disappearing below the water. Paula shook her head to clear her mind. It seemed unreal – the wonderful view and the nightmare of the previous evening. Westendorf pointed to the far shore.

'Over there they grow the largest cherries you will find anywhere in Germany. But perhaps we had better drive down now . . .'

There were crowds of sightseers held back a distance from the harbour by uniformed police. Several patrol cars were parked – cream Volvos with a blue trim and the word *Politi* in black on their fronts and sides.

Tweed was pleased there was a crowd. He had delayed the departure of Marler and his team for Denmark so they could check for signs of the opposition. As Kuhlmann, smoking a cigar, approached, Newman slipped away, donning a cloth cap he had taken from his trench coat pocket and a pair of glasses with plain lenses.

'Come with me,' Kuhlmann said. 'Whatever is down there is making its appearance shortly.'

Paula followed, puzzled by Newman's swift departure. She had already noticed that one of the unmarked cars had stopped, that plain-clothes detectives leaving the car were close to Westendorf. She had also seen Marler on the edge of the crowd and Cardon, in his German suit, walking round behind the sightseers.

Kuhlmann led them to the end of the shorter jetty, held up his hand, and waited. The lift crane was straining at something, like a fisherman hauling in a giant fish. The chain was taut, made a clanking sound as it slowly ascended. The crowd had gone quiet.

Two frogmen appeared from below the surface of the Elbe and climbed up steps along the jetty wall. They stood still while water dripped off them, staring at the water which was churning now, creating small waves which lapped against the wall. The crane's catch emerged suddenly. Paula sucked in her breath.

'My God!' growled Kuhlmann. 'What the hell could have done that?'

Shedding a small Niagara of water, the claw of the crane's lifting device appeared, clutching the prow, the bridge, and a section aft of the bridge of the *Holsten*. Half the hull and the stern were still at the bottom of the Elbe. But it was the clean-cut break in the vessel which had caused Kuhlmann's outburst.

There was not a loose splinter of wood visible. It was as though an immense axe had sliced straight through the vessel amidships. Holding on to Tweed's arm, Paula peered over the edge of the jetty. The stone wall had a deep fissure where something had rammed it with tremendous impact. She told Tweed what she had seen.

'I'm not too surprised,' he said.

'Why not?'

'I remember what Commander Noble said in London when he was listing the ships which have disappeared all over the world. His story about a crewman dropped from a helicopter with a cradle – when they found the relic of a small vessel belonging to a German fisherman called Vogel. Only the bow remained – sliced clean off with Vogel's decapitated head jammed in that relic.'

'How many of these Stealth ships do you think there are?'

He didn't reply because Kuhlmann came back to them. He looked grim.

'The frogmen – and one is ex-Navy – say they've never seen anything like this. What's your guess?'

'A ship with a knife-edged prow made of some sort of steel.' Tweed shrugged. 'And that is only a guess. Were there any ships moving on the Elbe last night?'

'No!' Kuhlmann was emphatic. 'I've been in touch with the Harbour Master. The fog was so dense nothing left its berth. A tanker was due to sail downriver but cancelled its departure. And the Coastguard reported the fog was dense at the mouth until dawn. No ship was at sea – their radar would have picked it up.'

'No, it wouldn't – they don't have the right equipment.'

'If you say so. I have to get back over there. You'll keep in touch?'

'Of course.' Tweed waited until Kuhlmann had gone before he answered Paula's question. 'How many Stealth ships? A lot, I suspect. And maybe with vastly different tonnages. The one that sank the *Holsten* – and hoped to sink us – may well have been testing its skill in navigating up a major European river. It just happened to be handy and in radio contact with some of Dr Wand's thugs . . .'

He stopped speaking as Newman, who had removed his cloth cap and glasses, appeared by their side. He dropped his voice.

'Don't stare round, but I spotted our friend, Jules Starmberg, mingling with the crowd. Marler has photographed him three times with that second camera he always carries, the one that develops and prints automatically. And Starmberg hasn't a clue his ugly mug has been recorded. Paula, you haven't seen him – here is one of the prints.'

'Ugly mug is the right description,' she commented.

'Interesting,' Tweed said, 'that Wand's so-called butler is down here watching. Wand was pole-axed yesterday evening when I appeared alive and kicking. Keep quiet now . . .'

Westendorf, who had walked along the riverside jetty to get a closer look, returned. Like Kuhlmann's, his expression was grim.

'That really is awesome. Paula, we owe our lives to your swift action. I personally am in your debt for ever.'

'Nonsense.' She dismissed the subject with a smile. But she had flushed with pleasure at the eminent German's compliment. 'I just saw something in the nick of time.'

'And the radar screen you said was blank.' Westendorf

shook his head as he looked at Tweed. 'This Stealth development is hideous. Now, if you're all ready, I'll drop you back at the hotel.'

'That would suit me admirably,' Tweed replied.

'You sound as though there's someone at the Four Seasons you want to interview,' Paula suggested as they followed Westendorf and Newman.

'Vulcan. When I can I'm going to talk to both Fanshawe and Burgoyne. And I want Newman to chat up Helen Claybourne.'

'You sound as though you know who Vulcan is.'

'I don't. But the field has narrowed,' Tweed replied.

40

'Paula Grey was at Blankenese this morning with Tweed,' reported Starmberg. 'One of my men watching the Four Seasons confirmed they returned to the hotel.'

'I would much appreciate it, Jules, if you could guarnatee this second attempt to obtain the company of Miss Grey will be successful.'

Dr Wand sat in the large study of his villa at Othmarschen, the district which adjoined Nienstedten where Hugo Westendorf lived. As at Waterloo, even though it was daytime, all the curtains were closed. The same applied to every other room in the villa, both downstairs and upstairs. The furniture was swathed in dust sheets. There were six of Starmberg's men in the villa but from the outside it appeared unoccupied.

'This new plan is so original it will succeed,' Starmberg assured his chief. He ran a hand over his thick well-groomed hair. 'It is organized for execution some time this evening. Well before midnight Miss Grey will be our guest in Denmark.'

'I would hope so.' Wand peered at Starmberg over his pince-nez. The Luxemburger stirred uneasily under the piercing stare. 'And,' Wand went on, 'I have finally decided I will let Tweed enjoy three sleepless nights.'

'And then?' Starmberg checked.

'Then? Why, Mr Tweed will receive a part of Miss Grey as a keepsake. Prior to that you will tell him he must resign his position immediately if he ever wishes to see Grey alive again. Our contacts in London will tell us if he has obeyed our demand.'

'So, we will scoop up Miss Grey within a matter of hours.'

'And I will call Dr Hyde. He will have preparations to make for the treatment.'

Near the bleak stretch of coast in southern Jutland Dr Hyde was returning from a short walk by himself. He had not enjoyed it – the area was deserted and the monotonous scrubland stretching to the beach and the sea beyond depressed him. Even more depressing was the eternal wind blowing off the sea, causing wispy sand to fly in the air. He might be on the moon, he thought – except for the house.

An ancient gabled two-storey structure built of wood, it stood on its own and at one time must have looked picturesque. But it had remained empty for a long time before Dr Wand had bought it through a holding company.

The once bright red paint of the main façade and the white trim round the windows was peeling away, eroded by the salt air. It still had a derelict, unoccupied look. With his long neck poked out of his stiff collar Dr Hyde

400

resembled some vile bird. He cast one look back before inserting the key: a mournful desert where nothing grew except tussocks of stubby grass amid the powdered sand.

He heard the phone ringing as he closed the door, hurried to the back room. The caller could only be one person and Hyde knew he would be rebuked.

'If I may be so bold as to enquire, where have you been? It seems unlikely you would find any feminine company in that part of the world,' Wand commented sarcastically.

'I have been for a brief walk. I have to keep fit for my work,' Hyde responded waspishly.

'How very commendable of you. I should apologize for what always appears to be my ill-timed calls.'

'I am at your service,' Hyde replied in an oily tone, regretting his outburst.

'Excellent! You will not be idle for long. A patient, a lady, will arrive soon. I foresee that treatment will be required within three days. Not before, you understand. Now, this is what I suggest, subject to your own diagnosis . . .'

Wand put down the phone as soon as he had completed his instructions. They had been phrased carefully in words Hyde understood but so their sinister significance would mean nothing if an operator had listened in. Starmberg, who had left the study, returned at the moment the call had ended.

'Eight more of my men have arrived,' he reported. 'The whole team is ready to carry out this evening's operation.'

'I trust there was no chance that the vehicles were seen entering the grounds?'

'None at all. The same method was used as when we came in. A vehicle parks near the entrance, waits until no other traffic is about, the gates are opened, the vehicle races down the drive, the gates are closed behind it. I was wondering – what do we do now about Westendorf?'

'Nothing. And you really must, if I may suggest it, rid yourself of this habit of wondering. As you have raised the matter I will explain briefly. Westendorf was not a complete success and for some months he will undoubtedly be heavily guarded. After some time has passed we may eliminate him.' Wand leaned forward into the light thrown by his desk lamp, the sole illumination. His expression was unpleasant but he spoke in his normal detached tone.

'Concentrate your mind now, Jules, on Miss Grey. I will not tolerate another fiasco. She must be in Denmark before midnight – I repeat, *before* midnight.'

Before leaving Blankenese Tweed had given Marler orders via Newman to drive immediately with his team across the Danish frontier. That left him only Paula, Newman, and Cardon to accompany him to Copenhagen. He felt sure it would be more than enough.

He had a stroke of luck when they arrived back at the Four Seasons. Saying goodbye to Westendorf, who drove off in his limo, he climbed the steps and the first person he saw was Willie Fanshawe.

'Leave me alone with him,' he whispered to Paula and Newman.

'I say! Am I glad to see you,' Willie began. 'Hate being on my own. Look, we're only three paces from the Sambri bar. Be a good chap. Join me in a glass of champers. Bit early for a sundowner, but what the hell. Oh, your friends have gone off. They'd have been more than welcome . . .'

'They had an appointment,' Tweed said, edging his way into the flood of words which went on.

'Well, we can have just a man-to-man conversation. I love the ladies, God bless 'em, but sometimes it makes a change to have a nice chat on our own. Champers, of course!'

Tweed reluctantly agreed. They were already inside the

empty bar under Wilie's enthusiastic impetus. He ordered two glasses from the barman and they sat down on the banquette furthest from the door.

'What's happened to Brigadier Burgoyne?' Tweed asked casually as he raised his glass, took a sip, put down the glass.

'Oh, the Brig.'s off haggling over some little deal, I'm sure. He loves it. Always on parade, is his motto. What he doesn't love is the present state of England.'

'Indeed? What's wrong with it?'

'Everything . . .' Willie became emphatic. 'According to the Brig. No self-discipline any more. Morale has collapsed. The welfare state has undermined the strong fibre we were once noted for. Everyone's holding their hands out for a freebie. They have a slight headache and rush to the doctor because it's supposed to be something for nothing. According to the Brig., that is. Half the country wants to be nannied. The young, instead of struggling to make a career on their own, want it all handed to them on a plate. And now the cranks want to break up the old UK into separate bits. A good dose of iron government is what is needed – so the Brig. thinks. Shock treatment is the only answer, he keeps saying.'

'I suppose it's his military background,' Tweed suggested.

'That's another thing! Conscription should be introduced again. That would instil some discipline into these louts who bang old ladies over the head to grab a few pounds. And often for what? To finance their beastly drug habit. Very hot on that, is the Brig.'

'And what do you think?' Tweed enquired.

Willie beamed. 'Have another glass. I'm going to . . .'

'I haven't finished my present drink, thank you.'

Tweed felt sure this was Willie's second visit to the Sambri bar this morning. His face was even more flushed than usual as he ordered a fresh glass for himself.

'My view?' Willie pursed his wide mouth. 'The Brig. does rather go over the top. Up Guards and at 'em. But he was a brilliant soldier, so I just listen. Not much choice once he gets going. A real martinet. But there's never a dull moment when he's around.'

'He's staying on in Hamburg for a while?'

'Never can tell with him. He's like the proverbial grass-hopper. We could be off to Vienna at the drop of a hat. The Brig.'s hat.' Willie chuckled, drank some more champagne. 'What about you?'

'My programme is vague. Depends on how events unfold. I hope you'll excuse me. I also have an appointment . . .'

It was a very thoughtful Tweed who went up to his room.

'There's your chance, Bob,' Paula said after they had left Tweed and wandered into the lobby. 'Tweed said get next to Helen – and there she is. Looking this way and prac-tically sending out a siren call to you. I'm going to get a bath. Have fun . . .'

Helen Claybourne, seated on a couch, was writing in a notebook with her large elegant fountain-pen. She tucked the cap over the nib and gave Newman her cool smile as he sat beside her.

'Unless you're busy,' he suggested.

'Very glad not to be.' She'd closed her notebook with a snap. 'Willie has the wildest schemes for making money. I spend half my time persuading him not to invest in some hare-brained scheme. He's a sucker for con-men – unlike Maurice. You wouldn't get a penny out of the Brigadier until he'd interrogated you into the ground.'

Helen looked smart as paint, as always. She wore a grey pleated skirt which ended just above her shapely knees. A well-cut grey jacket hugged her figure and underneath she was clad in a white blouse with a high-necked collar.

Perched in a corner of the couch, she tucked her legs under her like a cat and turned to face Newman. She flicked a speck of cigarette ash off his lapel and stared straight at him with appraising eyes as she asked the question.

'Just what are you up to, Mr Newman? You seem to be on the go most of the time. I saw you leave earlier about nine with Paula and Tweed. Are you after a juicy story? Or shouldn't I ask?' she teased him.

'We've been exploring Hamburg, taking in one business call. You're staying on here?'

'God knows. Maurice is talking of moving on to Copenhagen. Do you know a decent hotel there?'

'The d'Angleterre,' Newman said promptly.

'Maybe we could have lunch?' she suggested, her eyes still holding his. 'I suppose you do know nowadays it's not thought too forward for the woman to chase the man?'

'We might do that – have lunch. If we can avoid Willie and the Brigadier.'

'Talk of the devil, here comes Maurice. Save me from a fate worse than death.'

Burgoyne, spruce in a check sports jacket, navy blue trousers, hand-made brogues, and with a crimson cravat at his neck, pulled up a chair. Sitting in it very erect he tugged at his moustache and gazed at both of them.

'Hope I'm not intruding – or are you beginning to start an affair?'

'I live in hope,' Newman replied in a neutral tone.

Helen's reaction was savage. She straightened up, leaned forward. Her grey eyes blazed and her tone was venomous.

'That's an outrageous suggestion. You'd do well to watch your tongue. You're not in the Army now. Bad manners in the officers' mess don't go down well in these surroundings.'

'Did I drop a great big boulder in the pond?' Burgoyne asked ironically. 'It was a joke. You do know the word, Helen? Spelt j-o-k-e.'

'In the worst possible taste,' Helen fumed.

'Anyone for coffee?' Burgoyne enquired, quite unperturbed.

'I thought you were going to say anyone for tennis,' Helen continued her onslaught. 'You do realize that half the time you talk like old China hands back in Hong Kong – language thirty years out of date?'

Newman noticed a flash of fury in Burgoyne's eyes at the phrase 'old China hands'. It lasted only for a second. Burgoyne continued to be anything but conciliatory.

'I suspect I touched a raw nerve with my use of the word affair. You really must learn to conduct these things more circumspectly.'

'And you,' Helen told him, 'might learn not to butt in where you're not wanted. Half the time, back in the New Forest, you're dragging Willie and I off somewhere we don't want to go. Or hadn't you caught on?'

'Willie,' Burgoyne observed, 'will tag on to go anywhere – provided someone else is paying for the drinks, food, and accommodation.'

'For a pseudo-Brigadier you have a crude way of expressing yourself,' Helen rapped back. She looked at Newman. 'I'm feeling peckish, Bob.'

'Then let's try the Grill Room.'

As they stood up Helen threw one more verbal javelin, glaring at Burgoyne.

'If you're having lunch here too, I can recommend the Haerlin restaurant . . .'

Tweed and Paula stepped out of the elevator and immediately Paula spotted Burgoyne, who was still sitting with a cup of coffee in front of him. She nudged Tweed.

'I've seen him. Let's go and have a little chat with our eminent soldier.'

To her surprise the Brigadier smiled as though he welcomed their company. She was even more surprised when he jumped up, offered her a chair.

'Miss Grey, you are looking positively radiant. I like your suit. Very chic.'

'Thank you.' She sat down slightly dazed at the absence of Burgoyne's normal brusque manner. Tweed chose a seat placing him between them. 'They've left you on your own?' Paula suggested.

'I'm afraid so,' he replied, sitting down next to her. 'I don't appear to be very popular. Would you do me the honour of joining me in an aperitif?'

Paula stared, taken aback by the politeness. 'A glass of dry French white would go down nicely.' Burgoyne glanced at Tweed, who chose mineral water.

Burgoyne raised a hand, beckoned with his index finger to a waiter. Oh dear, Paula thought, reverting to type – dealing with the peasants. She had a further surprise.

'Could you be good enough to fetch us a glass of French wine, mineral water, and I'd be grateful for a double Scotch?'

'I hope we're not spoiling a few minutes on your own while you ruminated on a business problem,' Tweed remarked.

'On the contrary, it's a change to enjoy pleasant company. I've just had a vicious duel of words with Helen Claybourne. She's gone to lunch with your Robert Newman. She banned me from taking my own lunch in the Grill Room.'

'Doesn't sound like the Helen I've met,' Paula commented. 'I wonder what was wrong?'

'Ah! You don't know the real Helen. That outward coolness fools everybody. Underneath she's a ruthless tigress.'

407

'That's interesting,' Tweed interjected. 'It sounds very much as though she's taken a dislike to you. If so, why on earth does she travel with you?'

'Willie . . .' He paid the waiter, added a generous tip, and sighed. 'Willie,' he repeated. 'She appears to feel her job involves looking after him. Which is amusing. Master Willie is only too capable of looking after Number One.'

'He seems so indecisive,' Paula said.

'That is the impression he creates, I agree. In business, as well as earlier in the Army . . .' He paused and looked at Tweed. 'I learned never to take people at face value. You can come badly unstuck if you do. But I'm sure the insurance game has taught you that . . .'

They chatted for a while and then Tweed said he was taking Paula out for a breath of fresh air. They put on their coats they had propped over chairs, thanked Burgoyne for his hospitality. Again it was a thoughtful Tweed who left the hotel with Paula at his side.

'He seemed to be making a show of pointing the finger at Willie,' Paula observed as they crossed the road towards the lakeside walk.

'And very adroitly done,' Tweed agreed.

The white Volvo pulled up behind them with a screech of burning rubber. Tweed grabbed Paula round the waist, ready to shove her ahead of him and tell her to run.

'No need to call the police,' a familiar voice growled.

They swung round and Kuhlmann was stepping out of the front passenger seat, leaving his driver behind the wheel. He removed the unlit cigar from his mouth and jiggled it up and down like a conductor's baton to emphasize what he was saying.

'A fresh development. Didn't think it wise to talk over the phone when you're so close to Berliner Tor.'

'What's happened?' Tweed asked.

'Thirty minutes ago Dr Wand took off in his Lear jet from Hamburg bound for Kastrup Airport, Copenhagen.'

'That's very satisfactory. Thank you, Otto. Things seem to be working out as I foresaw. By the way, did Wand take Jules Starmberg with him?'

'No, definitely not. I dug out old photos of that villainous Luxemburger from the time when his wife was murdered. Gave them to the men watching the Lear.'

No alarm bells rang for Tweed at this information. He was too absorbed in racing over in his mind the precautions he had taken.

'And your present plan?' Kuhlmann asked.

'We are flying to Copenhagen ourselves this evening, and your co-operation has been invaluable. I've had two intriguing conversations recently.'

'Which you won't tell me about. Play it your own way. You always do.'

'Something's just struck me – I must contact Nielsen at Copenhagen police headquarters . . .'

'I've already done it.' Kuhlmann grinned. 'By now he will have plain-clothes men waiting at Kastrup for the Lear to land. They'll follow Wand, find out where he holes up. I'd say that wraps it up for now.'

'You think of everything. Thank you again . . .'

Tweed and Paula resumed their walk along the footpath by the Binnen Alster lake. They were walking through a parkland of green grassy slopes and trees. The sound of the traffic was muffled. For Paula it was dreamlike after her experience at Blankenese harbour. No one else was about as they wandered on in the chill air and the sunlight.

'It's a beautiful city,' Paula enthused. 'I love the green roofs of those magnificent old buildings across the lake. I suppose the roofs were once copper and have turned that colour with exposure to the elements.'

'I imagine so,' agreed Tweed.

'It's such a green city. And I love those mansard roof-tops – they're so elegant. We hardly ever see them back home.'

The path curved, following the lake, and they walked under a small bridge arch. Ahead of them was a marina and an even vaster stretch of water. As Paula slipped her arm in his Tweed nodded towards the new lake.

'This is the Aussen Alster, the larger of the two lakes. You can walk for miles but I think we'd better turn back.'

'Lord, I'm revelling in the peace,' she said as they returned along the silent footpath while a breeze trawled shoals of water towards the bank.

Newman, Tweed, and Paula had an incredibly early one-course dinner in the Grill Room. Newman was always insistent on allowing plenty of time to catch a flight. Tweed would have left it to the last minute – to avoid hanging about Hamburg Airport waiting for the Copenhagen flight.

Even at that early hour they had company at a nearby table. Burgoyne and Lee, Willie and Helen, were eating a leisurely meal. Burgoyne sent over a bottle of Laurent Perrier with his compliments.

'Nice of him,' Paula commented. 'Can't think what's got into him – he's become so human.'

'Camouflage,' Newman decided. 'Incidentally, I had a chat with Helen in the lounge area before I took her here to lunch . . .'

He described the scene between Helen and Burgoyne. Tweed, drinking mineral water, listened with interest. Newman and Paula demolished the bottle of champagne together. It was near the end of their meal when Lee, wearing another of her off-the-shoulder dresses, wandered towards them, holding a glass of red wine.

410

'I'd say phsycially Lee was very strong,' Paula remarked.

'And she's as high as a kite,' Newman added.

'Dear Mr Tweed' – Lee leant over him, her bare arm round his shoulders – 'I need some stimulating company. Take me out for a drink later? Please!'

'I'm sorry, but we're—' Tweed began.

That was when Lee tilted her glass and a cascade of red wine poured over his suit jacket. Lee was appalled. She grabbed a napkin and began dabbing at the cloth as she babbled on.

'I'm so dreadfully sorry. Red wine is the worst . . .'

'It's all right,' Tweed said standing up, 'but I'd better go to my room and change.' He looked at Newman. 'If you could handle paying all our bills? Good. And we do have loads of time . . .'

Newman called for the bill as Paula stood up. She felt a little woozy. Too much champagne after a long day.

'I'll go up and pack my sponge bag,' she told him.

She walked out of the Grill Room into the lobby.

PART THREE

By Stealth

41

Paula paused at the hotel exit. Something seemed to be going on outside. A uniformed doorman she hadn't seen before came up to her, all excited.

'They are making a film outside, using the hotel as a background. I don't know who the star is.'

I might as well get a breath of fresh air, clear my head, Paula thought. She vaguely noticed the doorman's uniform didn't fit him too well. She walked down the steps carefully and the doorman ran ahead of her to open the doors.

'Does this often happen?' she asked.

'First time I have ever known it to happen. It will be good publicity for the Four Seasons.'

The night air was cold, welcome and refreshing. Raising a hand, she shielded her eyes from the glare of the arc lights. Several white vans were parked alongside the kerb. Each carried the legend INTER-VISION TV UND RADIO GMBH.

Two cameras on tripods were aimed at a point at the edge of the parkland opposite. A couple, a man and woman, were embracing each other. Paula counted about a dozen men in white coats and wearing white gloves. A man she presumed was the director carried a bullhorn.

A generator thumped away on a pavement near the open doors of one of the vans. Beyond the open doors of the nearest van she could see a small amount of equipment and another stockily built man in the shadows inside who also wore a white coat.

She wandered a few feet along the pavement to get a closer view. The activity was frenetic. Was it really necessary or did TV crews think that was the way they were supposed to act? She paused by the open doors of the nearest van.

The next moment she felt two pairs of hands grasp her, lifting her off her feet and propelling her inside the van. She opened her mouth to scream her head off. A hand clamped over her mouth. She bit the fingers almost to the bone. A snarling voice yelled 'Bitch!' and she was hurled towards the shadowy figure deep inside. She broke the momentum by forcing herself sideways, crashing into the wall of the vehicle. The glare of an arc-light was projected into the interior.

'This is crazy! Bastards!' she shouted.

One of the two assailants who had grabbed her from behind came at her, hands clawed to grasp her throat. She whipped out the canister of hair spray from her shoulder bag, aimed it at his eyes, pressed the button as she half-shut her own eyes. Her attacker squealed, clapped both hands hard over his eyes. She moved closer, kneed him between the legs. He squealed again, bent over double, his hands still covering his eyes. Pressing her back against the side of the van, she kicked his head, and he staggered back against the opposite side of the van.

The second assailant reached her. Too close to use the spray again. She dug her fingers deep into his greasy hair, took a firm grip, pulled him towards her. As she'd expected, he tried to jerk his head away. She suddenly pushed with all her strength, still holding on, driving him across the van. She heard his skull crack against the van's wall. Dazed, his legs sagged, he slumped to the floor.

Glancing towards her escape route, the open doors at the rear, she was astonished to see a camera apparently recording the scene while the arc-light continued to glare into the interior. Then she slipped on a spool of film tape

416

and tumbled on top of both her attackers.

She made herself jump to her feet. That was when Starmberg came up behind her, pressed a soft pad over her nose and mouth. She smelt the deadly aroma of ether and rammed her clenched fist behind her, aiming for the kidneys. She heard an agonized grunt, the world blurred, and she sank into a pit of endless depth and darkness.

Colonel Winterton and his wife, Edith, an elderly couple, had emerged from the Four Seasons, muffled against the cold. They watched the violent struggle inside the van. The white-coated man holding a bullhorn walked up to them. He noted their very English style of dress and smiled.

'It's the opening scene of our new thriller. You have to grab the audience from the word go.'

'It's cold, John,' his wife, Edith, snapped. 'And we will be late for drinks with the Reuters.'

'Of course, my dear . . .'

The man with the bullhorn watched them walk away, turned round, and slammed the doors shut on the van. He ran to the driver and called out in German.

'Your cargo is aboard. Get this bloody van moving.'

The vehicle moved off. Within five minutes his team had packed all their kit inside the other vans, which promptly drove off. Peace and quiet returned to the Neuer Jungfernstieg outside the Four Seasons.

'Where on earth can Paula be?' Tweed looked at Newman and checked his watch. 'We shall soon be cutting it a bit fine.'

'She's the most prompt woman I've ever met,' said Cardon.

The man Paula called 'the Squirrel' had brought his bag

417

to Tweed's room after receiving a brief phone call to his own room from Tweed. Up to that moment he had kept away from the others as though they were strangers.

'I'm going to go along and knock on her door,' Newman said impatiently. 'As far as I'm concerned, we've probably missed the flight already.'

'Cool it,' Cardon advised and grinned.

Almost as soon as he had finished speaking the phone rang. Tweed snatched up the receiver. His tone was normal as he asked who it was. A woman's muffled voice answered.

'This is Paula. It's a pretty lousy connection. I hope you can hear me?'

'Yes, I can. What's happened?'

'I saw someone leaving the hotel. No names over the phone. A taxi was cruising past so I flagged it down and followed a car. I expect to be back at the Four Seasons . . . Can you hear me? This really is a lousy connection. Don't worry. Back soon . . .'

The line went dead. Tweed stood rather still. Then he told the others the gist of the brief conversation. Newman reacted first.

'Are you sure it was Paula?'

'No, I'm not.'

'Has she ever done this before?' Cardon asked. 'Dashed off on her own without telling you? And what was she wearing?'

'She has a lot of initiative,' Tweed said slowly. 'To answer your first question, occasionally she has – when she saw something and would have lost it if she'd waited to consult me. You know from your own experience I give my people a lot of loose rein. Why the question about how she was clad?'

'She was wearing her blue suit when I last saw her,' Newman intervened.

'I asked,' Cardon went on, 'because it's a very chilly

night. But if she grabbed a taxi the weather wouldn't have bothered her.'

'One thing's for sure,' Newman decided. 'I'm cancelling our flight reservations right now.'

'Yes, do that,' Tweed agreed with a faraway look.

Paula woke up feeling terrible. She gritted her teeth as a wave of nausea swept over her, fought it down, kept her eyes closed. The van had been moving at speed and then it slowed. She peered through half-opened eyes, saw the back of Starmberg perched on a flap seat.

She was stretched out along a leather seat at the front of the vehicle, her head rested on a hard pillow. Moving her right hand very slowly, she found it was pinioned at the wrist with what felt like a strap. Same with the left hand.

She wriggled her feet very cautiously, found that they also were imprisoned by straps. The van was slowing down even more, then stopped. Starmberg glanced round suddenly, realized she was awake. He pressed his large hand over her mouth. With his free hand he produced a wide strip of sticky plaster, plastered it roughly over her mouth, gagging her. She listened.

Conversation outside the van and from the direction of the driver's cab. It was very quiet otherwise. She listened hard. The two voices engaged in conversation sounded to be talking in some Scandinavian language. She thought about hammering her head against the rear of the driver's cab, knew it was hopeless.

Starmberg stood over her, his stance tense. At the first sign of movement on her part he'd probably apply more of the ether. A second dose she could do without. The voices continued, sounded to be joking. There was laughter as the engine was switched on. It began to move forward again.

After a few minutes it accelerated. God, she thought – where the hell are they taking me? How long, roughly, have I been unconscious? She couldn't even guess at the time span. What worried her most was that her captor had not used a blindfold, had let her see his face, so she'd have been able to identify him. What that suggested was chilling.

'I'm going downstairs to have a word with the doorman,' Newman said.

'We should have thought of that before,' Tweed agreed.

It was quite some time after he had received the call from the woman with the muffled voice who might have been Paula. Left alone with Cardon, who sat silently on a couch in the bedroom, Tweed stood gazing out of the window. He stared at the illuminated fountain in the lake Paula had admired.

He stood very still, hands clasped behind his back, showing none of the mounting anxiety he was feeling. He had thought of contacting Kuhlmann, but Newman had objected.

'We have no proof yet that anything has happened to her,' he pointed out. 'No solid proof Kuhlmann would need. And you'd have to tell him about the phone call – and go on to tell him Paula has acted on her own initiative before.'

'I suppose so,' Tweed had said. 'You're right. We must wait a little longer.'

Inside, the waiting was killing him. His sixth sense told him something was dreadfully wrong. He recalled the earlier attempt in Brussels to kidnap her when she had been saved by the intervention of Newman and Nield. But he still couldn't imagine the circumstances under which she might have been tricked. The atmosphere in the room was hellish.

In the lobby downstairs Newman found a different doorman was on duty, standing on the steps. He walked down as the doorman ran outside to open a taxi door and a young German couple entered the hotel. The night air seemed even more biting.

'Just come on duty, have you?' Newman asked casually.

'Well, Mr Newman, I'm not supposed to be on duty at all. One of our men has disappeared – the man who was supposed to be on duty. He has vanished. A complete mystery.'

'When did this happen?'

'Quite some time ago. And Edgar is always reliable.'

He opened the door again to admit an elderly couple. The husband looked a military type, Newman thought. His wife appeared displeased.

'Really, John, it was hardly worth venturing into the cold. The Reuters seemed to be in a bad mood tonight. And I see that television film lot have gone. Those awful lights . . .'

'Excuse me,' Newman said, 'but when did you see the television crew?'

'You're Robert Newman,' the husband said. 'The foreign correspondent chappie. Often seen your picture in the newspapers. Not so much recently.'

Normally it would have irritated Newman to be recognized. Now he seized on this familiarity to press his questions.

'This could be very important. How long ago was it when you saw these TV people?'

'I'm Colonel Winterton. My wife, Edith. Oh, it was quite a while ago when we went out. Inter-Vision and Radio. I remember the name on the sides of their vans. In German of course. They were filming a rather violent scene – a girl being dragged into one of the vans. The producer was pleased with himself – said it was the opening shot and you had to grab the audience from the word go.'

'I prefer musicals,' Edith sniffed.

'Can you describe the girl?' Newman requested. 'Colour of her hair, roughly her age, how she was dressed?'

'Rather attractive – to a man of your age,' Edith broke in, darting a glance at her husband. 'Late twenties, early thirties. What they call raven-black hair. Slim. She wore a navy blue suit. A calf-level hem – not one of those disgusting miniskirts which makes girls nowadays look undressed. I must say she's a very good actress – it was a frighteningly convincing fight she put up with the two men she was struggling with. Her face had good bone structure.'

'How did you see all this so clearly?' Newman queried. 'I must say your description was very precise.' His old reporter's scepticism prompted the question.

'Well!' Edith reared up. 'They had one of those beastly lights shining inside the van and a camera filming the scene. I could see her as clearly as I can see you. Nothing wrong with my eyesight!'

'I'm sure there isn't, and I'm very grateful to you.' He turned to Colonel Winterton. 'Would you mind repeating the name you saw on the sides of the vans?'

'Inter-Vision TV und Radio GmbH – to give it to you in German. Is something wrong?'

'I don't think so.' Newman smiled. 'But I've heard they are working on a secret project and there might be a good story in it. I do a piece occasionally – to keep my hand in. Thanks a lot.'

Edith tugged at her husband's arm. 'I'm tired, John. I want to go to our room. The central heating seems to be efficient here . . .'

Newman waited until they had disappeared into the lobby. The doorman looked at him.

'There is something wrong, isn't there? All this – and Edgar disappearing.'

'I don't think there is for a moment. And there might be a story in it for me.' He handed the doorman a generous tip. 'Good-night . . .'

'You'd better brace yourself,' Newman said grimly to Tweed as he closed the bedroom door. 'I've just been talking—'

He stopped speaking as the phone rang. Tweed walked swiftly to the phone. He reached out to grab it, then made himself wait while it rang several more times before he lifted the receiver.

'Mr Tweed?' a man's voice asked.

'Speaking. Who is—'

'Shut up and listen! We have Miss Grey—'

'I can't hear you properly. Wait a second . . .'

Tweed covered the mouthpiece. He looked at Newman, nodded towards the phone.

'Quick! What is it, Bob?'

'They've got Paula. No doubt about it.'

Tweed removed his hand. He banged the mouthpiece against the desktop.

'That's better. Who is this? What did you say—'

'I said shut your bloody trap!' Speaking in English, the voice had a guttural accent. 'We have Miss Grey. If you ever want to see her again resign your public position tonight. You have two hours. If you don't resign you will get her back. In four pieces . . .'

'I need proof of life. She could be—'

'Resign, I said! Or you'll get proof of death. And don't contact the police. If you do, the result will be the same. We'll know if you've obeyed our instructions. Retire! Now! That's it. Two hours . . .'

'Listen. I must first have . . .'

423

The line had gone dead. Tweed replaced the receiver with care. He told Newman and Cardon what had been said. Newman tersely told him what he had learned from the Wintertons. Tweed sighed, sat down on the couch next to Cardon.

'They have been very clever this time. And it's obvious she is in their filthy hands. I have no option.'

He stood up, went back to the phone, dialled the Park Crescent number he knew so well. Monica answered, sounded so pleased to hear his voice.

'Is Howard still in the building – or has he upped and offed to his club?'

'No, he's still here. He's been working all hours since you left London . . .'

'Put him on the phone to me immediately, please.'

'Can't I help—'

'I said put Howard on the phone immediately. This is an emergency.'

'I'll transfer you right away . . .'

Monica sounded hurt at his abrupt order. But in less than thirty seconds Howard came on the line. His normal pompous manner was absent as he asked the question.

'What emergency? Where are you?'

'Hamburg. Four Seasons Hotel. Don't phone me. As of now I am resigning my position. It is to take effect at once. I will send written confirmation by courier.'

'You sound tense,' Howard commented. 'This action is really necessary?'

'It is. Don't try to argue me out of it. I have resigned. As of now. I am retiring. Immediately.'

'This is an emergency situation?'

'It is. I'm offering no explanation. Just do it.'

'I accept your resignation. I will be here all night so as to attend to the formalities. I regret this more than I can convey.'

'Thank you . . .'

Tweed put down the phone and his forehead was beaded with perspiration. He sat down again on the couch next to Cardon. He used a handkerchief to mop his forehead. Newman came and sat on the other side of him. Tweed looked at him and ran a hand over his face.

'It is the only thing which may save Paula's life for a few days.' He lowered his voice. 'Go to that public phone box you use. Call Kuhlmann – drag him out of bed if necessary, although my bet is he's still at Berliner Tor. Tell him what's happened. Give him the name of that TV outfit. Above all, tell him the kidnapping must be kept secret.'

'I'm on my way,' was all Newman said.

42

Sprawled out on the leather seat, Paula was being rocked from side to side as the van moved over rough ground. They had obviously turned off a made-up road a moment ago. She felt sick, had a thumping headache, but the tape over her mouth had come loose and been removed.

As the van slowed down Starmberg stood up from his flap seat. Unfastening the strap pinioning her right hand, he clamped a steel handcuff over her wrist. He released the strap holding her other hand, forced her to sit up, and clamped the twin handcuff over her wrist. Her arms were now held firmly behind her back.

'You'll end up with terrible punishment for this,' she snapped.

'If you don't shut your bloody mouth I'll shut it for you.'

He released the straps binding her ankles one by one

and closed a second pair of handcuffs over the ankles. The van had stopped. Outside there was an eerie silence which jangled her already taut nerves.

Starmberg moved behind her and suddenly inserted a tight gag of twisted cloth over her mouth. She sensed the physical strength in the brute and felt completely helpless.

'You've arrived at your new home,' he said sarcastically. 'There's a very nice man waiting to greet you.'

The driver, who had left his cab, opened the doors at the rear but she couldn't see him clearly. It was a pitch black night and bitterly cold. Siberian air flowed into the van.

'Don't struggle or I'll knock your teeth out,' Starmberg informed her.

He hauled Paula over his shoulder like the proverbial sack of potatoes, stooped to clear the roof of the van, walked to the rear and stepped down into the night. Immediately a raw wind blew sand particles into her eyes. She was carted, head down, across scrubland and inside a house.

Her eyes saw only a scruffy wood-block floor passing below her, a floor with several blocks loose and which hadn't seen a smear of polish for ages. Starmberg, one hand holding her roughly round the neck, used the other to open a door. She blinked as bright fluorescent light hit her.

Starmberg descended a flight of wood-plank steps in the basement area. Against one wall was a long leather seat. He dumped her without care on the seat, stretched her out. He began talking to someone she couldn't see as he removed the handcuffs from her hands and replaced them with leather thongs and then performed the same action with her ankles. Remembering something Butler had said during the tough training course, she compelled herself to relax as the thongs were applied. The gag was removed.

'Well, Dr Hyde,' Starmberg stated in his guttural English, 'this is your new patient, Miss Grey. You will be operating on her.'

'I have the most precise instructions,' an oily voice replied. 'It is only a question of timing.'

'You will be told when. It will be within three days. I leave her in your tender hands . . .'

Sounds of heavy feet tramping back up the plank stairs, a door opening, slamming shut. At the last sound Paula's morale sank. And that macabre sentence. *You will be operating on her*.

'Now, my dear Miss Grey, are you comfortable?' the oily voice enquired and the speaker came into view, staring down at her.

Clean shaven, he wore rimless glasses, had a high forehead and thinning brown hair. Smiling down at her, he exposed a perfect set of large teeth. The smile was as phoney as a con-man's but she thought she detected in the smile a streak of sadism.

'What the blazes do you mean by asking if I'm comfortable?' she burst out. 'And do you know the penalty for kidnapping? The crime took place in Germany so you'll be tried there. And while we're on the subject, where am I?'

'Oh, dear me . . .' The hideous smile became pronounced, reminding Paula of a shark's open mouth. 'You must calm yourself,' Hyde rebuked her. 'If you become hysterical I will have to give you something to put you to sleep. Lie still, I have to complete my examination of your condition.'

He leaned further over her and she saw he was a large man, heavily built and with a paunch. He wore a white jacket like those used by surgeons. His fingers were long, slim and sensitive, like talons. They pulled her jacket off her right shoulder and paused.

'You will be supplied with good food and plenty of

427

liquid. It is essential you do drink a lot of liquid. One hand will be freed at meal-times. Are you left- or right-handed?'

'Right-handed,' Paula said without thinking.

'Wrong shoulder.'

Hyde's fingers pulled her jacket back into place, turned their probing attention to her left shoulder. Removing her jacket, he pulled her blouse free, slid the shoulder strap of her slip down her left arm. His fingers felt, prodded her left shoulder, grasped its bareness, squeezed it.

Paula stopped herself shuddering with revulsion under his searching touch. Then it flashed into her mind that Irene Andover's left arm had been severed close to the shoulder. She fought back a feeling of faintness. You loathsome pervert, she said to herself. She made herself speak in a controlled tone.

'If you spare me it will be taken into account at your trial.'

'You stupid bitch!'

As he spat out the venomous words his fingers dug savagely into her flesh. She gritted her teeth to stop screaming with the pain. The smile had gone. He stood up and used one finger to push his rimless glasses higher up his nose, which was slightly hooked. He disappeared out of view for a few moments. Then she felt a hand grasp her right wrist. At that moment the door into the basement was opened, closed, and she heard clumsy elephantine footsteps treading down the planks.

'Ilena, come here,' Hyde called out. He looked down at Paula. 'Ilena is the nurse who will help me when your time comes. Meantime she will attend to your needs – so, Ilena, come and meet our latest patient.'

A nurse? Looking up Paula saw a woman, also wearing a white hospital-like coat, leaning over her. A short and stocky woman whose arms bulged like tree trunks under the sleeves. Her face was slab-like, Slavic, Paula guessed.

A Romanian? Certainly from Eastern Europe. Hard eyes without humanity stared down at her. She was built like an ox. With a feeling of despair Paula realized she'd be no match for this peasant-like horror if it came to a struggle between them. The woman's hair was dark, trimmed very short.

'Does she speak one single word of English?' Paula burst out again. 'She's going to be a hell of a lot of use.'

'Ilena speaks a little English – enough to understand what you have just said,' Hyde remarked in his worst bedside manner.

He handed the hypodermic he had been going to use himself to the woman.

'You might as well practise on the patient now – so you give her the injection.'

Ilena seized Paula's wrist in an iron grip. Without any consideration she rammed the hypodermic home, pressed the plunger. Paula stifled a scream of agony. The world blurred again. *I mustn't go under this time*, she told herself. But the whole world faded away into nothing.

Kuhlmann, still at Berliner Tor, reacted with great speed and energy after listening to Newman's phone call. A small group of detectives, dressed in jeans and anoraks, was driven in a plain van and deposited in a side street near the Four Seasons.

Waving empty beer bottles, they staggered into the Neuer Jungfernstieg opposite the Four Seasons Hotel and started a mock fight. Patrol cars with uniformed police appeared, battled with the pseudo-punks, eventually 'arrested' them.

While this was going on an unmarked police car stopped at the entrance to the hotel. A plain-clothes detective went inside and straight into an elevator up to Tweed's room. He showed his identity card, produced a floppy-brimmed hat of German make and a German trench coat.

'Put these on please, sir. I'm taking you to Berliner Tor. It's a precaution – in case the opposition is watching the hotel . . .'

Inside the vehicle, with Tweed beside him as he drove at speed round the lake, he explained.

'This is a very special car. All the windows are one-way glass. We can see out, no one outside can see in. And Mr Newman has taken a taxi to Berliner Tor. He told Chief Inspector Kuhlmann he could disguise himself with a cap and some glasses he was carrying . . .'

Arriving at Berliner Tor, he drove the car to a rear entrance, escorted Tweed inside the building, took him in an elevator to the large office Tweed had used to phone Inspector Nielsen in Copenhagen. Newman was smoking, pacing the office while Kuhlmann spoke on the phone. Finishing his call, Kuhlmann jumped up as Tweed removed the hat and coat.

'No one will know you have been here. Sit down. I have a lot to tell you.' He glared at Newman, waved his cigar at him. 'And you sit down now. I know you're worried – so listen. Wheels are turning at top speed.'

'Paula *has* been kidnapped,' Tweed said quietly as he sat down.

'I'm afraid so,' Kuhlmann agreed. 'I know this will have hit you hard – you do have all my sympathy. But action is the order of the day.'

'Absolutely right.' Tweed stiffened himself. 'What do you know so far?'

'I phoned a friend of mine at Inter-Vision TV. They work late too. He told me no film was being made on any location within miles of the Four Seasons. He has also checked his transport and no Inter-Vision vehicle has been stolen. Obviously the kidnap gang plastered similar white vans with stickers printed with the company's

430

name. They'll have peeled them off hours ago. It was an audacious ploy. We are dealing with someone very clever.'

'Any trace of one of those vans?' Tweed asked.

'Not yet. Let me go on. I staged my own play act outside your hotel, organized a mock punk fight – which gave me a plausible reason for sending patrol cars into the area. One of the guests at that hotel may be keeping a watch. We found the doorman they grabbed to use his uniform – all tied up with a blanket thrown over him and shoved beneath some undergrowth near the lakeside walk opposite. Edgar, his name is. He's in hospital with a severe chill.'

Tweed looked at Newman who was listening intently.

'Tell us briefly again about the last time you saw her.'

'I've already told Kuhlmann. After you left the Grill Room to change your suit I waited to sign the bill before paying for everything at reception. Paula said she was going upstairs to pack her sponge bag. I haven't seen her since. I feel responsible . . .'

'No regrets!' Tweed's tone was suddenly decisive. 'It looks as though a fake doorman, dressed in Edgar's uniform, lured her into the street . . .'

'We've already concluded that,' Kuhlmann interjected.

'No point in setting up road-blocks, I imagine?' Tweed suggested.

'Too late. They've already had several hours to get clear. I've got men watching the airport for the morning flights. Anyone taken aboard in a stretcher will be checked. But I don't think they'll go that route. Same with the railway stations. And the river police – they are systematically searching every vessel due to move by daylight. Kohler, the Hamburg police chief, is a good friend – he's given me a quarter of his entire force. Plain-clothes men who will use great discretion to keep it quiet.'

'Thank you again,' Tweed said. 'You seem to have covered the waterfront, as we say.'

'I haven't even started! Just listen. You remember you asked me to trace a Dr Hyde? I got lucky when I called a Danish frontier post – from my description the Danish officer told me a driver from Tinglev had taken him as a passenger across into Jutland – Denmark. I called him again a few minutes ago. A white van which transports a special sort of cake Germans like returned after midnight. The officer thought it was a strange hour for him to be coming back. He said his van had broken down, was delayed while it was repaired. They joked about the amount of the cake the Germans eat. Later the officer wished he'd had the van opened up – something rang phoney about the driver's manner.'

'Jutland. Again. Always Jutland,' Tweed said aloud but really talking to himself. He looked at Kuhlmann. 'I'd appreciate the use of your scrambler again. Mind if I make the call on my own? It's a difficult one.'

'I have other things to check in the communications room down the corridor . . .'

Newman remained silent as Tweed dialled the Park Crescent number. He was more tactful with Monica when she came on the phone.

'I need to speak to Howard again, if he's still there. I will ask him to give you certain instructions after I've finished the call. Instructions which are vital, and I know you'll do a perfect job. He's there? Good. Put him on the line, please . . .

'Howard, this time I'm on scrambler at police HQ in Hamburg. So I can talk more frankly. I'll get Kuhlmann to send one of his couriers with my resignation by the first flight in the morning. Written on Four Seasons letterhead, dated and with the time.'

432

'Do you have to take this drastic action?'

'Yes. And I can't tell you why. What is terribly important is that Monica spreads the news immediately through our network of contacts here and overseas. She'll know who to get in touch with.'

Howard's voice changed, became businesslike. 'It will be done. You're faced with some appalling emergency. I can guess, but I'm not going to.'

'Howard, this is equally vital. Strictly between you and me. Don't even tell Monica – and while I remember, put a strong guard on her. She might just be grabbed to check on the story of my resignation.'

'This gets grimmer. Go on.'

'I want to retain control of all the men I have over here. And that's most secret . . .'

'You have control.' There was a pause. 'I do have my own bit of bad news. The PM won't sanction use the SAS team from Hereford without knowing more about the operation.'

'Forget the SAS then. We'll have to manage with what we've got. And one man I do need the support of – Commander Noble of Naval Intelligence. I want to phone him as soon as I can.'

'He called me only a few minutes ago to speak to you. He's working through the night at the Admiralty. I'll not risk the phone – I'm jumping into my car and driving over to tell him personally. With no traffic at this hour the job will be done within fifteen minutes from ending this call.'

'Let's end it then.'

'Tweed, good luck . . .'

'Why did you have to resign?' Newman asked while they were still alone. 'I know you think it might give us three days to find her, but let's face it – Wand is so inhuman

433

Paula may be dead already.' He looked so downcast that Tweed rallied.

'Yes,' he said, standing up and pacing, 'that is one reason. And a top priority is to save her. But another priority is to throw Wand off guard. When the news of my resignation reaches him he'll think all opposition to him has faded away. I'm pretty sure I know now how his evil mind works.'

'So, what next?'

'I have been worrying that our forces were split in the wrong way. Now I realize I've got it exactly right. One task force – Marler, Nield, and Butler – is heading for Jutland. The sordid Dr Hyde is in that area, as Kuhlmann discovered. It may not be a pleasant thought, but I'm sure that wherever the sordid Dr Hyde is, Paula is being held. Marler won't let the grass grow under his feet. And you and I will go to Copenhagen later tonight with Cardon . . .' He paused. 'How tired are you? If Kuhlmann will lend us a car I propose we drive to the Danish capital through the night. Otherwise I could drive . . .'

'No! I can go two nights without sleep. I'm fresh as a daisy. And I suspect you're still in a state of shock, running on automatic pilot . . .'

The door opened, Kuhlmann thrust his head inside, spoke quickly to Tweed.

'There's a man called Cardon on the line. Wants to talk to you urgently.'

'He's one of mine . . .'

Tweed was lifting the receiver as Kuhlmann disappeared. He asked who was speaking.

'Cardon, Chief. From Newman's favourite public phone box. Marler came on the line, asked for me when they couldn't get you at the Four Seasons. Can I talk?'

'I'm on scrambler. Tell me about Marler.'

'He's reached Denmark. He played it clever, knowing he was going through an operator. He said, "I'm having a

434

super holiday. I'm at a place called Tønder." He gave me his hotel name – I gather it's a small place – and the number. Here it is . . .'

Tweed noted down the details on a notepad already lying on the table in front of him.

'Philip, is your case packed?'

'Yes. I'm ready to leave at a moment's notice.'

'Do just that. Your bill is paid. Give the hotel some plausible excuse for leaving at this hour. Damned if I can think of one.'

'I'm moving to the Atlantic,' Cardon said instantly. 'Why? Because my girl friend's staying there and I want to be closer to her. I'll watch the clerk's expression, see if he can preserve the dignified "the client is always right" this place is noted for. What do I do then?'

'Get well clear of the Four Seasons. Find a cruising taxi. There are always some in Hamburg. Get the driver to take you to the Hotel Berlin, pay him off. Then look round – I'm at Berliner Tor and it's the only twenty-storey-high building in sight. Ask for me – I'm on the fifteenth floor . . .'

'You smiled at something he said,' Newman observed.

'He said something funny. He always cheers me up. He'll be here soon.'

He had just finished speaking when Kuhlmann entered the office like a whirlwind, sank into a chair facing Tweed.

'Something I forgot to tell you. Dr Wand landed at Kastrup Airport a few hours ago. Inspector Nielsen called me. A limousine met him – he arrived alone. The limo drove him to the Gentofte area north of Copenhagen – a wealthy district with some expensive villas . . .'

'That's Dr Wand,' Tweed said cynically. 'All financed by his refugee aid organization. You have an address?'

Kuhlmann took out a piece of folded paper, pushed it across the desk.

'That's it. Near some posh hotel called Jaegersborg,' Nielsen said. 'His men are watching Wand's villa.' He held up a hand as Tweed opened his mouth to speak. 'Don't worry – Nielsen's men are being very discreet, conducting their surveillance from a distance with special equipment.'

'Could you do me a favour?' Tweed produced the envelope addressed to Howard containing his written resignation. 'I badly need a courier to fly with this to London urgently tomorrow – no, today. He is to go to Park Crescent and deliver this envelope into Howard's hands personally. No one else but Howard.'

'That's easy.' Kuhlmann took the envelope. 'Any of the local detectives welcome a trip to London. Kohler will choose someone reliable. He'll be aboard the first flight.'

'Another favour. Can you provide us with a good car to drive to Copenhagen? There are no flights at this hour and I want to be at the Puttgarden ferry terminal to cross the Baltic to Denmark as early as possible. I think I can outmanoeuvre the insidious Dr Wand.'

'A Mercedes, if possible,' Newman chipped in. 'Without police plates.'

'Not wasting time, are we?' Kuhlmann commented. 'I'll go and arrange for a car now. Be back soon . . .'

Thirty minutes later he opened the door again.

'A friend of yours. See you . . .'

Philip Cardon walked into the room, winked at Newman, sat down on a couch with his case by his side.

'Has Marler a chance in hell of tracing Dr Hyde?' Newman asked anxiously.

'I'm convinced Starmberg is in Jutland with them,' Tweed told him. 'And Marler has pictures of that gentleman he took at Blankenese yesterday morning – you showed one to Paula. He gave me copies.'

Opening the case he had brought from the Four Seasons, Tweed extracted a plastic wallet packed with prints. He handed Newman several of Starmberg. Walking over to Cardon, he selected more prints, spread them on the couch.

'That one is Dr Wand – taken by Marler at London Airport. This one is Dr Hyde. And these three are Jules Starmberg.' Standing up, he felt the fatigue, sat down at the table again.

'When Kuhlmann provides the car I suggest we leave at once, driving through the night to Puttgarden. It's the direct route to Copenhagen.'

'And I suppose,' Newman mused, 'we mustn't forget Stealth – especially after our experiences at Blankenese harbour with the *Holsten*.'

'Stealth ships are in the forefront of my mind,' Tweed assured him. 'Especially with Wand dashing off to Denmark – and that large colony of unoccupied but furnished houses waiting for occupants in Jutland.'

43

Latitude 57.45N. Longitude 20.0W. The *Mao III*, with the *Yenan* close behind it, was proceeding at less than top speed over two hundred miles west of the tiny island of Rockall. The two vessels, still avoiding the main shipping lanes as far as possible, were well out in the Atlantic.

Kim had ordered Captain Welensky to reduce speed because they had made such good time from the Cape of Good Hope – and it was essential they arrived at the rendezvous at the agreed time. Not before.

It was dead of night as Welensky's massive figure stood on the bridge, arms folded, while the diminutive form of

Kim stood beside him. Welensky hoped the Chinese would remain silent, a false hope.

'You will, I assume, continue on course before we make the big turn south-east,' Kim remarked.

'It is my job to maintain the course, to arrive on schedule,' Welensky snapped. 'And what about your problems? I have heard the Scandinavian passengers we are carrying and also those aboard the *Yenan* are getting restless.'

'No more,' Kim purred. 'When strong mugs of coffee were being prepared for them I personally ground up a small portion of the sleeping drug Soneryl. This was added to their coffee. They are all now very quiet – not asleep, you understand, but extremely passive.'

'When we do turn south-east between the Shetland Islands and Norway, heading for the southern coast of Jutland, I'll need all my concentration. There is plenty of shipping in that area – to say nothing of small vessels supplying the oil rigs.'

He hoped to God Kim would take the hint. It was another futile hope.

'I will, of course, be standing by your side in case of an emergency. And it is vital that we reach the Jutland coast in the middle of the night. That is essential. You have a met forecast yet for that part of the world?'

'Fog. Dense fog.'

'Splendid.' Kim almost smiled. 'We might have ordered it.'

Paula woke up suddenly. Very alert. She was still sprawled on the leather couch, hands and ankles imprisoned with the leather thongs. It was the middle of the night. Thank God they switched off that bloody fluorescent strip. She was aching, every limb stiff from being kept in one position for hours except for the short periods when she was given food and water by Ilena.

She frowned as she heard a noise she'd detected before – a sound like distant breakers crashing on a shore. Was it the sea or pure imagination? She remembered two things Butler had taught her during the refresher training course out at the country house.

'If you're ever held prisoner in solitary confinement by the opposition, concentrate your mind on a problem – to keep your brain active . . .'

He had also instructed her in what he had called the Houdini technique. She began to practise what she had learnt – as she had done earlier when the light went out and Ilena had slammed the door closed. Letting her right hand and fingers go limp, she began to revolve her wrist inside the thong. To start with she seemed to be getting nowhere, then she sensed a looseness. She persisted, stopped immediately she heard a fresh sound.

A banging, flapping noise which repeated itself at regular intervals. Faint light appeared from the outside world. She realized a shutter closed over the semi-basement window was being whipped back and forth. A fresh sound: the key inserted into the lock on the outside of the door. She shut her eyes.

The door opened, the dazzling fluorescent light came on, and Ilena's deliberate thumping footsteps descended the plank staircase. Reaching the bottom she walked over to the couch and shook Paula by the shoulder.

'I know you not sleep. You want toilet?'

'No. Thank you very much.'

She was careful not to provoke the unpredictable peasant. A trip to the toilet was humiliating. Ilena produced an ancient 7.63 mm Mauser pistol with a long barrel. Had she brought it with her from Romania – or wherever she had come from? Aiming the muzzle at Paula, she unfastened the straps, stood back. Paula then had to push open the door in the basement which led to little more than a cupboard. Inside was an Elsan toilet. While she attended to her needs Ilena stood watching, the gun pointed at her. She was then returned to the couch, the straps reapplied.

'Then I prepare operating table. Dr Hyde very clean man . . .'

Ilena turned her back on Paula who twisted her head to see what was going on. To her horror she saw Ilena had brought with her a plastic bucket of hot soapy water and a scrubbing brush. She proceeded to scrub every inch of a long wooden table.

Paula had a reaction of terror and fury. Terror at what the preparation forecast for her. Fury that this pig of a woman had woken her up – so she must have assumed before entering – to do this foul job in the middle of the night.

Staring at the broad girth of Ilena's back, Paula realized again she would be no match for this ox-like creature if it came to a hand-to-hand struggle. Ilena finished her task, stood back to admire her work.

'That is good – no infection as doctor say when operation is made.'

She then perched the single wooden chair under the window. As she stood on it the chair groaned under the punishment. *Break your flaming back!* Paula said under her breath. The woman fiddled with the catch of the shutter, and Paula saw she had to reach through bars to grasp it. No escape that way. The job completed, Ilena lowered her bulk to the floor and turned round. As she picked up the bucket with the brush inside it she made one final remark before climbing the steps, switching off the light, slamming and relocking the door, a remark which chilled Paula's blood.

'Operation soon now.'

*   *   *

440

Earlier, when Marler, with Butler and Nield as his passengers, reached the Danish frontier post north of Flensburg, he had his British passport in his hand. The Control officer, a man in his fifties with very Nordic features, didn't take any interest in the passport.

'Business or pleasure?' he enquired.

'Very much business,' Marler replied.

'Sounds official,' the Dane commented.

Marler took a lightning decision, a big chance. He abandoned his story about selling marine equipment. Instead he took out a photo of Dr Hyde, handed it to the officer.

'Have you by any chance seen this man pass through during the evening? A few hours ago, possibly.'

The Dane examined the photo by the light of the torch he had shone into the Mercedes. He took his time, glanced at Marler again, then returned his attention to the photo. Marler had the impression he was intrigued by his question, by the photograph.

'Where are you from?' the officer asked eventually.

'We've just driven hell-for-leather up from Hamburg.' Marler smiled drily.

'Of course. From Hamburg, you say? You know someone important there?'

Marler chanced his arm again. He sensed he was on to a winning streak.

'Yes. Chief Inspector Otto Kuhlmann of the Criminal Police from Wiesbaden.'

'I see.' The Dane paused as though taking a decision. 'I find this an intriguing coincidence. You know Kuhlmann well?'

'I've known – and worked with him – for years,' Marler replied. His tone was friendly but his manner that of a man on official business. 'Otto is always very co-operative with us.'

The Dane was tactful enough not to enquire who 'us'

441

might be. He fingered the photo, looked again at Marler.

'The coincidence is Kuhlmann phoned me earlier, gave a word description of a man. It corresponds exactly with this picture.'

'I know,' Marler assured him. 'He wanted to know if he had crossed the frontier into Denmark. You are observant – you told him you had seen that man travelling as a passenger in the back of a car. You know the man who was driving that car?'

'Yes. His passenger was an unpleasant-looking character. Very conceited, was my impression.'

Marler waited, hands relaxed on the wheel, betraying none of the tension inside him. Would the Dane come across with the information he so vitally needed?

'Your journey is concerned with the phone call I had from Kuhlmann?' the officer enquired.

'Definitely.'

Marler left it at that. Don't disturb the mood of confidence he had built up by saying too much.

'So it would be useful if you knew the name and address of the car's driver? He lives in Tinglev. Again, not one of the most pleasant of human beings. He cheats at cards.'

'A bad sign. He may cheat at other things,' Marler commented.

'We are talking about Johnny Clausen, a man with a glib tongue.'

'It would be most helpful if we knew his address,' Marler told him. 'It might prevent a major crime. We are racing against time.'

'So serious?' The Dane was writing on a notepad he had picked up, writing laboriously in capital letters. He tore off the sheet, handed it to Marler. 'That is where Johnny Clausen lives in Tinglev – on the edge of the town. I wish you luck.'

'And thank you for your invaluable help. We are indebted to you. Now, if you don't mind, we must move fast . . .'

'We are going straight to Tinglev?' Butler asked from the back of the car when they were clear of the frontier post.

'Not at this hour.'

Marler had stopped the car in the middle of nowhere. He gave the piece of paper with Clausen's address to Butler. Then he handed Nield a photo of Dr Hyde.

'I've checked the map,' Marler explained. 'We should be noticed if we turned up in Tinglev in the middle of the night. We're going to find separate accommodation for each of us in Tønder – it's about fifteen miles west of Tinglev. We don't know each other.'

'And in the morning?' Butler pressed.

'You won't get much sleep. Rise at dawn. Find someone who will loan you a car – tell them your own has broken down and is being repaired in a garage. For a generous sum of money – you have plenty of kroner – you should get a vehicle. Drive to Tinglev and track down Johnny Clausen. How you get him to talk is your business, but do it. Where he took Dr Hyde is what we're after.

'Pete,' he went on, addressing Nield, 'in the morning find yourself a car. Then show Hyde's picture to the locals – officially you owe him money for an operation he carried out on your ankle. That makes you sound honest – and the Danes appreciate honesty. When we get to Tønder give me the phone number of wherever we find accommodation for both of you. Tell them I lost my way in Schleswig-Holstein before crossing into Denmark. Hence our arriving in the middle of the night. No questions? Good. We must keep moving . . .'

*   *   *

443

Later in the early morning Paula cursed to herself as she was woken again by someone opening the door, switching on the glaring light, walking down the staircase. But these footsteps were different, were not Ilena's coming back to bother her yet again. She opened her eyes and stared.

A well-built man with ruffled black hair, shirt sticking out of the back of his hastily donned trousers, stood looking at her. Jules Starmberg. It was the first time she'd realized he was staying in the house. Then she heard the same sound she had heard earlier – the slow flapping and banging of the loose shutter.

'That stupid cow,' Starmberg fulminated. 'She can't even fix a loose shutter. Disturbed your beauty sleep, has it?'

'Could you sleep with that row going on?' Paula snapped.

'The lady has guts.'

As Starmberg hauled the same chair under the window she heard another sound between the banging. The sound of a powerful car's engine labouring over the rough ground. Then, for a brief moment, headlights swung over the open window. Starmberg swore, climbed on to the chair, put his hand through the bars, and pulled the shutter towards him.

He fiddled with the catch, taking his time. Outside Paula heard the car driving away and despair overwhelmed her. For a brief moment she thought someone was calling at the house. Satisfied that he'd done the job properly, Starmberg stepped down, pushed the chair back to its original position against the wall. He looked at her again.

'The lady is going to need those guts. Tweed has poked his nose into where it doesn't belong once too often. And you are the sacrificial lamb.'

*   *   *

444

When Marler had found accommodation for Butler and Nield in Tønder – and a room for himself – he decided night was a good time to explore the area. Since he had paid the landlady at his own lodgings for a week's stay, he had no difficulty in persuading her to give him the front-door key.

'I need some fresh air,' he explained to Mrs Pedersen, a grey-haired old lady dressed in a pristine warm padded housecoat. 'I've been driving for hours in the over-heated car. Even at this hour I fancy the smell of the sea.'

'Have you a map?' she asked anxiously. 'There will be no one about in the middle of the night.'

'A very good map of the area,' he assured her.

Outside he glanced up at his first-floor window over-looking the narrow cobbled street. All the houses were old steep-gabled edifices built of red brick and with red tiles on the roofs. Some had plaster walls painted in yellow or white. The silent, deserted street had a fairy-tale atmosphere. He climbed behind the wheel, drove slowly so as not to wake the inhabitants.

On the outskirts he studied the map again and decided to head west for the small town of Hojer. The land was flat and reaching Hojer he turned north along a road running roughly parallel to the sea. He met no traffic, saw not a single human soul, not a light in the few houses he drove past. His night vision was excellent and he could make out to the west the dykes protecting the land from the fury of the sea. Arriving at a lonely intersection, on a whim he turned west again. He was crossing a wilderness of scrubby grass and sand.

The wind increased in force, scooping up powdered sand, hurling it against his windscreen. Off the road stood an isolated house. Switching on his wipers to clear sand from the windscreen, he swung the car off the road, bumping over rough ground. Despite the fact that the windows were closed, particles of sand were penetrating

445

the car, and now he could hear the thunderous boom of great rollers crashing on the nearby shore.

He had driven past the house, which looked derelict, and now he drove about twenty yards from the front entrance. Definitely an abandoned property. Red paint peeled off its façade, white paint off the trim round the windows. He frowned as he suddenly saw a light appear in a semi-basement window. Odd. He swung his headlights over the two-storey building. The light disappeared. Had he imagined seeing it?

He drove on over as bleak a heathland as he had seen so far. Braking, he stepped out. The boom of the sea became a roar. Surf caught by the ferocious wind landed a few feet away from his car. He half closed his eyes to protect them against the fine sand as the wind threatened to blow him over.

I've had enough of this, he thought, as he climbed back behind the wheel. It took all his strength to pull the heavy door shut. Back to Tønder and a warm bed. Tomorrow was another day. The real search for Paula would begin then.

44

'Tweed has already cracked up, as I predicted.'

Inside the large villa, set back from Jaegersborg Allé with a large front garden screened by a hedge, Dr Wand rubbed his hands with satisfaction. He sat behind a Regency desk in a room at the back of the building. The curtains were shut over the windows and again the desk lamp was the only illumination.

The villa was located at Jaegersborg Allé 988 in the Gentofte district north of Copenhagen. The only other occupant was the gaunt Mrs Kramer, dressed as always in black, a tall, thin woman whose face might have been carved out of stone.

Wand had phoned her from Hamburg, telling her to fly direct to Copenhagen, to prepare the villa for his arrival. His instructions had been precise. 'The villa, as you know, dear lady, has an unoccupied appearance. I would be most grateful if you would preserve that illusion. Leave The Boltons, please, at the earliest possible moment, to catch a Copenhagen flight.'

'You are sure this Tweed has been broken?' Mrs Kramer now enquired.

'I had the news this morning. He has resigned. Retired. I took the precaution of phoning the Four Seasons Hotel. They informed me he had checked out. He is now, I am sure, on his way back to London. He will no longer be present to interfere with my very important activities. A cup of black coffee would be most welcome . . .'

Left alone, Wand checked his watch. 11.30 a.m. Earlier he had phoned a senior civil servant in London who always knew what was going on. He had confirmed positively that he had heard Tweed had resigned from public life.

Wand knew he could rely on his informant – after all, he had loaned the man a large sum of money for a mortgage on a property in the English countryside. And he had no intention of letting Mrs Kramer know his source. Keep everyone in watertight compartments.

Wand operated a cell system. In Jutland he had twenty men awaiting the arrival of the *Mao III* and the *Yenan*. None of them knew the two Stealth ships were due to land their human cargo on the remote South Jutland shore. They would be given their instructions by Starmberg at the last moment.

'Goodbye, Mr Tweed,' Wand said to himself.

It was a relief to hear he had permanently immobilized the Englishman. The cargo of trained men who would be put ashore was the most important consignment of agents Wand had ever handled. They would be the leaders of the entire underground apparatus Wand was planting strategically in Europe – including Britain, the most important objective.

Thoughts of Tweed reminded him he must phone Dr Hyde. He dialled the number of the old house in Jutland, prepared for a long wait. To his surprise Hyde answered at once.

'My dear sir,' Wand began, 'I trust your new patient has been delivered to you and is in your competent hands?'

'She is here, yes. Everything is ready,' the oily voice assured him.

'I said we would wait three days before you carried out the operation. It is possible you may decide to complete the treatment earlier. If you would be so kind, please wait for my next call.'

'Everything is ready,' Hyde repeated. 'I can carry out the operation at any time—'

Hyde realized the connection had been broken, that Dr Wand had replaced the receiver. 'Arrogant swine,' he muttered.

A short distance away from the villa a large white van was parked on the opposite side of the road in Jaegersborg Allé. Painted on the outside was the name of an interior decoration firm: just the sort of vehicle which might be parked in this wealthy district while a team refurbished one of the elegant rooms inside a villa.

A rather different team occupied the interior of the van. Equipped with large windows made of one-way glass, very unusual equipment for an interior decorator was arranged inside. Long-distance video cameras were aimed at the entrance to No. 988.

They had already recorded the arrival of Dr Wand earlier, driving his own limo. One camera had taken close-up pictures as Wand's heavily built figure had climbed out to open the gate, prior to driving the limo down the short distance into a garage with electronic doors operated by remote control.

Ulf Kilde, leader of the three-man Police Intelligence undercover team, used a high-powered transmitter to report back to Inspector Nielsen at intervals. In case Wand left the villa to drive to a fresh destination Kilde had a back-up vehicle parked in a nearby side street.

This vehicle was quite a contrast to the gleaming white van. It was battered old Fiat with a souped-up engine. Kilde was in touch with the waiting driver by radio.

'Still no sign of activity,' Kilde reported to HQ. 'The villa looks unoccupied – all the shutters are closed. But our friend is definitely inside . . .'

During the early morning of that day Newman, behind the wheel of a black Mercedes supplied by Kuhlmann, had driven north from Hamburg through pleasant countryside towards the ancient Hanseatic town of Lübeck. His ultimate objective was to board one of the huge car ferries at the Puttgarden terminal on the edge of the Baltic.

'Tweed has fallen asleep,' remarked Cardon, referring to their passenger in the back.

'Thank God for that,' Newman replied. 'He's exhausted with worrying about Paula. I can understand that.'

Both men could not have been more wrong. Tweed had his eyes closed but his brain was racing. Mentally he checked over what he must do when he reached Nielsen's HQ in Copenhagen.

Nielsen would have a scrambler. The first priority was to contact Commander Noble at the Admiralty in London. Tweed hoped to heaven Noble had managed to dispatch one of Delvaux's advanced radar systems to Tug Wilson, commander of the missile-armed frigate *Minotaur* patrolling the North Sea.

Perhaps an equal priority was to try and call Marler at the Tønder phone number he'd transmitted to them at Berliner Tor. What were the chances that Marler's team could trace the unspeakable Dr Hyde in time? He coughed so as not to startle Newman.

'Bob, did you say Helen Claybourne told you the Burgoyne Quartet, as Paula nicknamed them, might be moving on to Copenhagen?'

'Yes. And I told her we'd be staying at the d'Angleterre. I hope I did the right thing?'

'You did. If those four turn up again I will be pleased beyond expression.'

'Why? They're a peculiar crowd.'

'Why?' Tweed repeated. 'Because among other targets I want to get my hands on Vulcan.'

'And you think either Fanshawe or Burgoyne is Vulcan?'

'I don't *think*. I'm convinced of it. And that devil is a key figure in Wand's plans – according to what you told us, Philip.'

'He is,' Cardon confirmed. 'My source was a mint one.'

'Wake me when we're coming into Lübeck for breakfast,' requested Tweed.

He closed his eyes again but sleep wouldn't come. He kept recalling what Fieldway, the MOD officer, had told him about Burgoyne. The Brigadier had disappeared for some four months while fighting on the battlefield in Korea. *Vanished off the face of the earth*, was the phrase Fieldway had used. Then Burgoyne had suddenly reappeared. An odd business, that.

Tweed's mind changed gear. He was also convinced that either Helen Claybourne or Lee Holmes was a professional assassin. He had witnessed the first killing of Hilary Vane, coming off the Washington flight at London Airport. Cyanosis.

The same woman – whoever it was – had killed a cab driver in Brussels to steal his cab. Cyanosis. And the smell of a perfume. Guerlain Samsara. The same woman had driven down Sir Gerald Andover in Liège. And had probably killed Joseph Mordaunt. Cyanosis. Yes, he hoped that the Burgoyne Quartet turned up at the d'Angleterre.

At the tip of the German island of Fehmarn, at Puttgarden, Newman drove the Mercedes inside the giant maw of the huge ferry. Arriving early, he had positioned himself at the head of the vehicle queue. Parking next to the side of the lowest deck, he switched off the engine.

'I think I'll stay with the Merc.,' Cardon said. 'Then I can make sure no one tampers with it. I'll tuck myself inside that alcove . . .'

Thirty minutes later, Tweed stood alongside Newman on the main deck near the prow. He had taken a Dramamine after eating breakfast in ancient Lübeck, a town he loved out of season. The massive ferry moved out into the Baltic in the face of a strong wind. Large surf-tipped waves rolled towards them.

'You usually stay inside,' Newman commented. 'It's going to be a rough crossing.'

'I need the fresh air to keep my brain moving . . .'

Sunk deep in thought, the passage seemed over in a flash to Tweed. They drove off at Rødby and were in Denmark.

Still sunk deep in thought, the car drive to Copenhagen also passed in a flash for Tweed. They drove past the old pre-First World War railway station and into a part of Copenhagen few tourists ever visited.

Following Tweed's instructions, they drove past the grim and grey triangular building which is police head-quarters. They turned on to Hambrosgade, a long wide anonymous street running past one side of the triangular building. Newman stared when Tweed pointed to a collection of single-storey wooden cabins.

'Nielsen works here. Park.'

Newman gazed at a very long cabin built of wooden planks and painted bright red. The legend on the side read KRIMINAL POLITIET. Cardon said again he would stay with the Merc. as Newman followed Tweed, who walked up to the door, pressed the bell. Inspector Lars Nielsen, Chief of Police Intelligence, opened the door himself.

'Welcome to Copenhagen, Tweed. And I recognize you,' he said, studying Newman. 'The foreign correspondent. Come inside. Everything is happening.'

Nielsen was a small thin-faced Dane with strong features and alert blue eyes which seemed to look inside you. The office he led them into was comfortably furnished, to Newman's surprise.

'How did you come to be expecting me?' Tweed asked after a warm shaking of hands.

'Otto Kuhlmann phoned me, estimated very accurately when you would arrive. You have to phone him urgently. That phone is scrambler. You'd both like coffee? Good. Have you eaten? Good. I'll be back. Make your call . . .'

'Kuhlmann here. Ah, Tweed. Where are you speaking from? You've arrived at Nielsen's log cabin? Marler called me. You should call him now. You have the number? Do it now. Call me back whenever I can help . . .'

Tweed dialled the number in Tønder. He prepared

452

himself to speak carefully to the hotel proprietor. Marler came straight on to the line.

'I'm speaking from my lodging house,' he warned.

Marler had no reason to think his landlady, Mrs Pedersen, now working behind a closed door in the kitchen, was listening in. But he was still going to be careful what he said.

'I'm with Nielsen in Copenhagen,' Tweed replied. 'Have you discovered any sign of our missing package?'

Tweed held his breath. Package wasn't a very flattering way of referring to Paula, but he also was being cautious.

'No,' Marler told him bluntly. 'And we've had a delay over finding transport for Butler and Nield. I had to drive them to Avis in Esbjerg – the locals call it Espay, something like that. Both Nield and Butler are trying to locate our friendly doctor. Butler is the one likely to do the job.'

'There isn't much time left,' Tweed reminded him. 'From now on you can get in touch with me either through Nielsen or at the Hotel d'Angleterre in Copenhagen. As soon as events dictate, I expect to arrive in Jutland myself.'

'That's it then for the moment. I'd better get out on the road myself . . .'

In the old house at Tønder Marler put down the phone. He felt relieved that Tweed had arrived in Denmark. But, by God, they had to track down Hyde soon. Time was *not* on their side.

Tweed was frantically but purposefully active during the next half-hour. He phoned Commander Noble at Admiralty.

'I'm sleeping on a camp bed here while this operation is in progress,' Noble said after being assured Tweed was on scrambler from Copenhagen. 'The *Minotaur* has the new radar system. Tug wants to know which area to patrol.'

'First tell me, have any more ships vanished?' Tweed asked. 'If so, that will give us some idea whereabouts the Stealth vessels I'm convinced are coming have reached.'

'A small oil-rig supply vessel has gone missing. North-east of the Shetlands. Between the islands and Norway.'

'Tug should patrol roughly twenty to thirty miles along the Jutland coast north of the Danish–German frontier,' Tweed suggested.

That was approximately the position of the cross on a map print Cardon had brought back from Lop Nor in War Room West.

'He's close to there now. And he's sent a small boat on a so-called courtesy visit to the port of Esbjerg. Equipped with a transmitter that can contact the *Minotaur*. Can you go to Esbjerg when the crisis is near?'

'I can. I will. Within the next twenty-four hours would be my guess, or maybe forty-eight. The mastermind behind all this is in Denmark,' Tweed said.

'Keep in touch. Take care . . .'

Tweed had earlier had confirmed to him by Nielsen the data previously passed to Kuhlmann: that Dr Wand had arrived by Lear jet at Kastrup Airport. Also the fact that from Kastrup he had driven himself in a limo to a villa outside Copenhagen.

'I had my best men watching Kastrup,' Nielsen had told him. 'They followed him in a van to Gentofte. The discreet but thorough surveillance continues. Dr Wand is still there.'

'Lars, I need to know urgently if Wand leaves that villa. And, if possible, where he's gone to . . .'

Nielsen had promised this would be done. Now, still alone with Newman, Tweed phoned three other key men. First, the Special Branch officer in London he had warned earlier about Moor's Landing. While travelling to Copenhagen in the Mercedes Tweed had worked out what three o'clock in the morning would be in different countries –

bearing in mind the different clock times.

'Tweed here. It doesn't matter where I'm calling from . . .'

'Howard came to see me,' the officer told him, phrasing his words carefully. 'I know about your official resignation. I'm listening.'

'The time is approaching for your raid on Moor's Landing. I want the place sealed off, then turned over at three a.m. All the inhabitants must be arrested as illegal immigrants. I'm synchronizing this when the time comes with three other raids on the continent. Timing is vital.'

'I'll send a large team to hide in the Southampton area at once.'

'Good. And don't forget to grab Mrs Goshawk at April Lodge in Brockenhurst.'

'Already noted.'

'When I call you to act I may be short of time. The code-word for the operation is Landslide.'

'Landslide it will be . . .'

Tweed next phoned Benoit, gave him similar instructions to raid Vieux-Fontaine, the colony of new houses Paula and Marler had discovered outside Ghent. He gave him the same code-word, Benoit gave him a similar reaction.

'A team of heavily armed men will be prepared at once. I will lead the raid myself. We'll drag the bastards out of bed, search the houses from top to bottom. I await your call . . .'

The third call was to Otto Kuhlmann at Berliner Tor. The German listened, also said he would organize a strike force to stand by. Objective: Neustadt-Something, the colony of new houses west of Blankenese.

'We'll overwhelm the thugs,' he promised.

Nielsen came back into the office as Tweed put down the phone. He suggested similar action to be taken at the right moment. Extracting one of Cardon's map prints, he showed the Dane the cross marked on the coast of Jutland.

'That's the place.'

'I know it. A settlement of twenty-eight new bungalows built behind the dunes. There's some mystery about it – a holding company based in Luxemburg financed this odd development. It is rumoured a European conglomerate will be using it for a holiday-cum-training course for executives. The bungalows have been furnished and waiting for occupation for some time.'

'I couldn't get permission to use the SAS, Lars. So you'll not have to argue the point with your Minister.'

'We do have our own élite anti-terrorist squad. We haven't advertised the fact. They are at your disposal.'

'Could you move them at once to Esbjerg? And let me know how I can get in touch with their leader?'

'Anton Norlin. A very tough character. I will airlift them to a military training camp just south of Esbjerg. Here is the phone number. Ask for Norlin, use your own name.'

Tweed tucked the folded piece of paper inside his wallet, stood up, stretched the aches out of his arms. He shook hands with Nielsen.

'I can't thank you enough . . .'

'Don't try.'

'So now we'll drive to the d'Angleterre. There may be a few interesting people waiting for us when we arrive . . .'

45

Paula braced herself for the worst. Dr Hyde had arrived in the basement room with Ilena. Both wore white coats and Hyde carried a large old-fashioned doctor's bag. He

456

placed it on the table as Ilena pulled down Paula's left sleeve over her arm.

'What are you doing now?' Paula snapped.

Hyde turned slowly round, smiled, exposing his teeth. He pushed his rimless glasses further up his hooked nose and smiled again. It was like the smile of a crocodile which has spotted its prey.

'Just relax, please. Let Ilena do her work.'

The Slav-faced woman was unbuttoning Paula's blouse, pulling it down to reveal her bare shoulders and forearm. Her thick fingers removed the shoulder strap, dropping her slip. Paula was revolted by the touch of Ilena's clumsy, ugly fingers.

Hyde took out a thick roll of cloth, unfastened the knot, opened the roll, and laid it on the scrubbed table. He laid out a row of gleaming scalpels, lovingly felt them with his hands protected with surgical gloves. Paula was chilled with fear. Hyde looked round at her again.

'The tools of my profession. You have nothing to worry about. I am one of the most skilled surgeons in the world.'

'You're going to carve me up, you swine!' Paula spat out.

'Now that is not polite.' A flash of venom appeared for a second in his soulless eyes. 'It is really most important that you relax. Of course, you will be given an anaesthetic. You will feel no pain.'

'You will when my friends catch up with you,' she flashed back. 'You'll wish you'd never been bloody born.'

'Dear me, the patient is so agitated. Ilena, are you satisfied you know what you have to do?'

'I am very OK. I know the work I do.'

'So, when we operate everything will go smoothly,' remarked Hyde.

Ilena was lifting her shoulder strap back into place, then she buttoned up the blouse and roughly lifted the sleeve back up over the forearm and shoulder from

457

Paula's hand pinioned by the leather strap. Standing up, she stared down at Paula, her trunk-like arms akimbo.

Hyde was replacing the scalpels neatly across the cloth and rolling it up with care. Refastening the knot, he slipped the heavy roll back inside his bag. Turning round, he gave Paula an even more ghastly smile.

'That was merely a rehearsal. I said you had nothing to worry about. You must learn to trust me, to have confidence in my abilities. Give her some more soup for lunch, Ilena. We must keep up her strength.'

Followed by Ilena, Hyde climbed the stairs, opened the door and disappeared. As usual, Ilena slammed the door shut. Paula heard the key turn in the lock. Her reaction was a mixture of relief and murderous fury.

A rehearsal! The sadistic bastard. She was bathed from head to toe in sweat. She'd have given anything for a bath, a change of clothes. As sweat dripped off her she suddenly thought the liquid might help.

Once again she began slowly twisting her damp wrists under the straps. They felt looser. Careful not to hurry, she went on working her wrists from side to side. Then she relaxed her fingers and pulled her arm upwards. This time her hand came half-free from the strap. Only the width of her knuckles held her prisoner. She began again, working her wrists from side to side.

'Are we getting anywhere at all tracing this Johnny Clausen?' Marler asked Butler.

They were standing on the south-eastern outskirts of Tinglev. The countryside was level with monotonous fields and a track leading across them away from the town. Marler's Mercedes was parked by the roadside behind the Volvo Butler had hired in Esbjerg.

'I've found out where Johnny lives. In a small cul-de-sac not far from here,' Butler replied. 'He's out on a job with his car, taking a passenger to Bolderslev – that's a short distance north of here. I'll be waiting for him when he gets back.'

'You have to make him talk,' Marler insisted. 'How are you going to go about it? Every minute counts.'

'In the back of my car on the floor is a long loop of rope. Bought it from a ship's chandler. Follow me . . .'

He led Marler along the track. No one else was about. A few cows grazed in a nearby field. The track curved behind a large clump of trees and the landscape changed. Marler stared at a treacherous-looking stretch of marshland. Dark water stood still amid large tufts of acid-green grass. Under the water he detected a bed of slime and mud.

'Johnny Clausen must talk,' Marler emphasized. 'Must tell us where he took Dr Hyde.'

'Leave it to me. Johnny will talk,' Butler said. 'I guarantee it.'

Pete Nield climbed out of his own hired Volvo. Carrying a photo of Dr Hyde, he walked into a small bar furnished with dark oak. The counter, the ceiling beams, the woodblock floor all oak. No one else was in the place as he approached the barman, ordered a glass of Coke.

'I'm looking for a friend who was supposed to be staying round here,' he began and smiled. 'I owe him some money. Here's a picture I once took of him. Have you by any chance seen someone like this recently?'

He placed the photo on the scrupulously clean bartop. It was the tenth place Nield had visited that day up and down the coast and inland. The florid-faced barman, polishing a glass which was already gleaming, stared at the photo for longer than Nield would have expected. Then he looked up at his customer.

'Did you say this man was a friend?'

Sensitive to people's reactions, Nield heard alarm bells ringing. He fingered his trim moustache.

'I was being polite. Frankly I don't much like him. So that is another reason I want to pay back the loan with interest. Then I'm rid of him.'

'He was in here yesterday. He had three double gins. I had one other customer, a young attractive girl. He was making suggestions to her she didn't like. When he asked for another double gin I told him he'd had enough. He swore at me before he staggered out to his car.'

'To his Volvo?' Nield suggested.

'No. It was a blue Fiat. I went to the door to watch him drive off. The Fiat seemed to be a drunk as he was.'

'He is staying here in Tønder?'

'No idea. Never seen him before. Never want to see him again. I spent twelve months in London once serving behind bars – and never saw such an unpleasant type.'

Nield thanked the barman and went out. He sat behind the wheel of his Volvo, drumming his fingers on the rim.

'Sighted in Tønder.'

He must report that to Marler urgently.

Tweed and Newman walked into the reception hall of the Hotel d'Angleterre while Cardon paid off the cab driver.

Newman had decided not to advertise the fact of his Mercedes' existence. He had left it in a car park near the Rådhuspladsen – the Town Hall Square. Danish words were jaw-breakers. The three men had then taken a taxi to the hotel.

Tweed sat in a chair facing a receptionist across a desk, registered for three separate rooms. Lifting his case, he walked up the steps to an interior lounge area. Unlike the Four Seasons, this sitting area had no windows on the outside world. The chairs were comfortable but lighting was dim. A few groups of people were scattered round the room.

Lee Holmes, wearing a black off-the-shoulder dress, jumped up. She walked straight towards Tweed, with a slight but graceful swing of her hips.

'I don't believe it,' she began. She kissed him on the cheek. 'You're following me.' She lowered her voice. 'At least I hope you are. I know a night club where we could have a lot of fun. A bit noisy but lively. Will you escort a lady this evening?'

'Not sure of my plans. Let's decide later.'

He was watching over her shoulder. Helen Claybourne had stood up from where she had been sitting with Lee and Willie. She strode over, very erect, held out her hand.

'Welcome to Copenhagen, Mr Tweed.' Her cool grey eyes gazed into his. 'Could we have a chat somewhere quiet?'

'He's mine,' Lee informed her.

Willie had trotted after them. Beaming all over his face, he clasped Tweed round the shoulder.

'My dear chap. How about a drink? Celebrate our reunion. It's a small world, or has that been said before? Never mind. A drink . . .'

'Not just now, thank you. We've only just arrived. I don't see the Brigadier.'

'Better look behind you. Creeps up on you like a cat.'

'I heard that remark,' a familiar voice growled.

Tweed glanced over his shoulder. Burgoyne had come from the direction of the old-fashioned elevator leading to the upper floors. Dressed in cavalry twill trousers, a navy blue blazer with gold buttons, and a cravat at his neck, he didn't look pleased to see Tweed.

461

'Can't shake you off, can we?'

'I thought it might be the other way round. Newman told Helen we'd stay at this hotel.'

'Helen keeps herself to herself. Interesting to hear she is on such close terms with Newman . . .'

'Drop dead!' Helen told him savagely, her eyes blazing.

Tweed nodded, joined Newman and Cardon who had been watching and listening with amusement. He led them to the old-fashioned elevator and pressed the bell.

'There's a bank of elevators over there,' Newman remarked.

'More room in here with our luggage,' said Tweed, who had used the hotel before. As the elevator began to ascend he spoke again. 'Come to my room, both of you. Didn't take us long to bump into the Burgoyne Quartet. Significant.'

Inside the villa at Gentofte, Mrs Kramer entered Dr Wand's room at the rear of the house. Wand, studying a map of the coast of South Jutland, closed the map.

'What is it?' he snapped with unusual brusqueness.

'A woman calling herself Anne-Marie is on the phone.'

'Leave me alone so I can concentrate.' He picked up the receiver on his desk. He had been careful to conceal from Mrs Kramer that Anne-Marie was a code-name. 'Yes, my dear,' he said, 'I am sure you are calling from a public phone box. There has been a development? Please be good enough to bring me up to date.'

'Tweed,' a woman's voice reported. 'Tweed arrived at the Hotel d'Angleterre here in Copenhagen within the past hour.'

Dr Wand's hand gripped the receiver like a vice. He could not speak for a few moments. His mouth twisted into an expression of disbelief, then of the utmost cruelty.

'Are you still there?' the woman's voice asked anxiously.

'I am here.' Another long pause. 'Thank you for calling me . . .'

He replaced the receiver before she could reply. Pressing a button under his desk, he summoned Mrs Kramer. When she entered the room his huge fist crashed down on the desk – with such force that a glass ornament toppled off, broke into pieces on the wood block floor.

'Leave that alone!' he screamed as she rushed to clear up the mess. 'The Lear jet is on stand-by at Kastrup with a crew waiting, I trust?'

'Yes, it is . . .'

Mrs Kramer, a woman of no emotion, was terrified. Standing quite still, she stared at Wand who gazed at her with a penetrating glare.

'I shall be leaving very shortly,' Wand rasped. 'Shut up the villa and return to London—'

'I will deal with it immediately—'

'Don't interrupt me!' he shouted. 'There is a special instruction you have to carry out first. This is what you must do . . .'

The call from Marler to Tweed came through minutes after he had arrived in his room with Newman and Cardon. Marler chose his words carefully, knowing he was speaking through a hotel switchboard.

'I have to tell you that so far we have not traced the package – the missing package. We are continuing our efforts non-stop. As soon as we have succeeded I'll let you know. Excuse me if I go now.'

'Yes, don't waste time . . .'

Tweed put down the phone: Marler had gone off the line. He told Newman and Cardon the gist of the message. While he was pacing the room Newman phoned room service, ordered a meal for three. Tweed had not eaten for hours and Newman agreed with Napoleon – *an army marches on its stomach*.

They had almost finished their meal when there was another tapping on the door. Newman opened it, his Smith & Wesson in his other hand. A youngster wearing a white peaked cap and white jacket and trousers was holding a long box wrapped with blue ribbon.

'Who is this from?' Newman demanded.

'Probably a note inside.'

The young man was gone as Newman closed the door. Tweed stared at the oblong shape of the delivery. Newman looked at him.

'It feels very cold.'

'Give it to me.'

Grim-faced, Tweed placed the ice-cold box on a table. His blood was chilled as he felt the temperature. Taking a deep breath, remembering what Paula had found inside Andover's fridge in the New Forest – the severed arm – he stripped off the ribbon. Without hesitation he lifted the lid and stared at the contents. A plastic carton filled with ice. Placed under chunks of ice was a red rose.

Newman exploded. 'I don't care what you want to do next. I am flying to Esbjerg to help Marler. I thought that damned box contained a piece of Paula – her hand, her arm.'

'So did I,' Tweed said quietly. 'Go out now, find a phone box, call Nielsen, ask him the quickest way we can reach Esbjerg, and could we have a car waiting at Esbjerg Airport to take us to Anton Norlin's unit . . .'

Newman had hardly left the room when the phone rang. Tweed heard Nielsen's voice at the other end. The Dane was also cautious how he worded his information.

'I thought you ought to know our friend has returned to Kastrup. The pilot of his jet has filed a flight plan. For Esbjerg.'

'Newman will be phoning you shortly. Thank you, Lars . . .'

Tweed told Cardon what he had just heard. The Squirrel nodded, said it was fortunate they hadn't unpacked a thing.

'And I paid for the rooms for a week in advance,' Tweed reminded him. 'So we can slip quietly out of the hotel when Newman gets back. It means I can be at the scene of the final crisis which – with Wand leaving for Jutland – I'm sure is very close.'

To Tweed, it seemed for ever before Newman came back. In fact he had only been away for three quarters of an hour. He flopped in a chair, mopped his damp forehead despite the bitter cold outside.

'After phoning Nielsen, I couldn't find a taxi. I ran all the way down the Walking Street. I've handed in the hired Mercedes, then caught a taxi back here.'

'But what did Lars suggest?' Tweed asked impatiently.

'No flights to Esbjerg at this time of day. He's fixed up for us to fly there in a small Piper Archer plane from Kastrup. An unmarked car will be waiting for us on the other side of the square – at this end of the Nyhavn. The driver will be wearing a yellow carnation in his buttonhole and smoking a cheroot for identification.'

'Sounds a natty dresser,' Cardon observed. 'When does our chariot await?'

Tweed was staring out of the window in Room 209, which overlooked Kongens Nytorv square. Beyond the bare skeletal branches of trees he thought he saw a car parked on the far side.

'The driver should be waiting for us now,' said Newman.

'Then we leave at once,' Tweed ordered. 'Philip, go first, ring us from the lobby if none of those four people I talked to are about.'

The phone rang two minutes later. Cardon reported the

coast was clear. As Tweed left the hotel with Newman, walked into the arctic temperature, he made the comment to him.

'That was a frightening package delivered to us – as it was meant to be. But Wand committed a strategic blunder. The only person who could have informed him of my arrival is one of the Burgoyne Quartet. The question is – which one?'

Before boarding his Lear jet, Dr Wand made a phone call from inside the Kastrup Airport concourse. He dialled Dr Hyde's number. Again the connection was quick.

'You know who this is,' Wand said brusquely.

'I do. I have stayed in so as to . . .'

'Just listen, if you would be so kind,' Wand said sarcastically. 'The operation on your patient must be carried out earlier – this evening. I want to smash someone's morale into the ground . . .'

He slammed down the phone so savagely he nearly broke the instrument. Then he hurried to the waiting jet.

46

'Hello, Johnny.'

Butler had climbed out of his Volvo, which was parked across the stretch of lonely road from Bolderslev to Tinglev. His right arm hung limply by his side, his left hand clutched a thick wad of kroner banknotes.

Butler had decided it was time to speed things up. Earlier he had talked to a neighbour of Johnny Clausen's in Tinglev. He had explained he needed a driver urgently, that he was willing to pay well for the service.

'I gather he's taken a passenger to Bolderslev,' Butler had continued. 'If you could tell me the make of his car and registration number I'll try and meet him on his way back. I've had too much to drink for the long drive I have to make.' He had breathed fumes over the neighbour, fumes manufactured from smearing his lips with gin from a bottle he had bought.

The neighbour, a jolly-looking Dane, had nodded in understanding. Which is how Butler had learned Clausen drove a blue Saab and its number.

Now he walked unsteadily towards Johnny Clausen who had climbed out of his Saab and walked towards Butler. With a toss of his head Clausen reacted aggressively.

'What the hell do you mean by blocking the road?'

Clausen was a weasel-like man with shifty eyes. Then his manner changed when he caught sight of the wad of money. Dressed in a soiled anorak and denims ripped at the sides, he put his thin hands on his hips.

'What do you want?'

'I need someone to drive me to Esbjerg. Too much to drink. I'll pay well.'

'Let me see . . .'

He never finished his sentence. Butler's limp right arm suddenly came alive. There was a blur of movement inside his unzipped windcheater and Johnny stared into the muzzle of a 7.65mm automatic. Butler pocketed the banknotes.

'You get the money if you do exactly what I say. Or you get your head blown off. First job, get back behind the wheel of your Saab. I'll sit beside you . . .'

Under Butler's brusque instructions Johnny drove his Saab off the road deep inside a copse of evergreen trees. He then got out and, with Butler close behind, walked back to the Volvo.

'Same act,' Butler snapped. 'Get behind the wheel and follow my instructions. If we meet a patrol car don't play clever. This gun will be rammed into your guts . . .'

He directed Johnny to drive towards Tinglev, then take a quiet road which practically bypassed the town. They came to the track Butler had led Marler up earlier.

'Turn off here. Drive up that track. Someone we have to pick up.'

The Volvo bumped over the track and Butler told Johnny to drive it behind the copse of trees he'd seen on his first visit. Obeying Butler, Johnny switched off the engine, climbed out of the car. Butler ran round the front, still aiming the automatic. They stood close to the verge of the marsh. Butler had his automatic jabbed into his prisoner's back.

'I need to know where you took a passenger you brought in from Germany.' He thrust the photo of Dr Hyde in front of Johnny's face. 'Where did you take him?'

'I've never seen this man before.'

'He paid you that much to keep your trap shut? Here is your money . . .'

As Johnny turned round Butler slammed a haymaker into his jaw. The Dane collapsed and Butler got busy. He spread the body face down, fetched the rope already looped into a wide noose from the rear of the Volvo. It took him no time at all to slip the noose over the out-spread arms and down the body to the waist. At this point Butler tightened the slip-knot. He had been careful not to hit Johnny too hard, using only half his strength. In a few minutes the prone figure began to stir.

Dazed, he looked up at Butler. Waiting a few more minutes, Butler asked his question again.

'Where did you take that passenger to?'

'I've never seen him . . .'

'Oh dear.' Butler sounded regretful. 'You want it the hard way. Because you'll end up dead if you don't talk.'

Tucking a rolled end of the rope inside his belt, Butler stooped, lifted Johnny bodily, carried him to the edge of the marsh and threw him forward. The Dane landed in a pool of filthy water with a splash. His legs went down first, sucked under into the ooze. He struggled futilely, waving his arms, calling out for help.

Butler took the roll of rope from his belt, pulled it tight and for a moment Johnny's downward progress into the marsh was arrested. Then Butler played out more rope. The waist sank under the gurgling slime. It crept up his chest. He screamed for mercy. Butler paid out more rope and the mud rose to Johnny's shoulders. His arms were trapped under the marsh. Only his neck, his terrified face were visible.

At Kastrup Airport in a remote part of the complex Tweed, Newman and Cardon boarded the small Piper Archer plane. They first stepped on to the wing and then entered through a door like that of a car.

The interior reminded Tweed of a car. There was the pilot's seat with another alongside, which Tweed sat in. Behind were two more seats occupied by Newman and Cardon. They sat with their cases in their laps. Tweed glanced over his shoulder at Newman.

'This plane, Bob, has only one propeller,' he teased.

'If we have to fly to Jutland on a wing and a prayer that's OK by me,' Newman snapped. 'Just so long as we get there fast.'

'Agreed,' said Tweed.

When they had strapped themselves into their seats the pilot supplied by Nielsen started up the engine. It was icy cold and fortunately they all wore heavy overcoats. The sky was clear as the plane moved forward, left the ground, climbed.

'We fly to Esbjerg at a maximum altitude of three

thousand feet,' the pilot told Tweed. 'The met forecast is for this weather all the way so you'll have a unique view of Denmark.'

'What about tonight?' Tweed enquired.

'A major weather change – especially in Jutland. Heavy fog along the whole coast. You're not thinking of enjoying a sailing trip, I hope?'

'I never enjoy a sailing trip,' said Tweed with vehemence.

They flew over the large island of Sjaelland, which Copenhagen sits on. The pilot had been right, Tweed thought, as he gazed down. From that height he could even see people walking, tiny figures. The landscape was something most tourists never saw. Beautiful rolling grassy hill slopes, some of them wooded. The isolated lake which gleamed like a sapphire. Cosy-looking single-storey homes tucked away amid trees at the end of twisting drives. It was like passing over paradise.

'We're flying due west?' Tweed checked with the pilot.

'Not quite, at the moment. We've been routed more north-west for the moment. We're passing over the Farum area down there. Soon we turn south and then due west.'

They flew over a stretch of sparkling sea which the pilot said was the Store Belt. Ships cruising north and south were crystal clear with their pure white wakes. They crossed another large island, Funen, then a brief stretch of narrow sea and land reappeared. The pilot said they were now over Jutland.

'Thank God!' said Newman. 'As soon as we arrive I'm hiring a car from Avis. They have an outfit in Esbjerg. Then I'm driving immediately south to contact Marler. I want to know if he's had any success.'

'I agree,' Tweed replied. 'You have the phone number of my hotel. Also Anton Norlin's number. I insist you keep me up to date. That's a direct order.'

Newman then realized Tweed was as worried about Paula as he was. Studying the landscape had been a way of distracting his mind from this extreme anxiety. But would they be able to find Paula in time?

Marler was searching for Butler. He drove through Tinglev and headed for the track where he had last seen him. As he turned on to the track and drove past the copse of trees an extraordinary sight opened up. He parked, jumped out of his car.

Butler was hauling a thin, scrawny man attached to a rope out of the marshes. The apparition was coated with slime up to his throat. Giving one mighty heave, Butler hauled the man on to firm ground, dropped the rope, turned to Marler.

'I made him talk. He nearly went right under, the bloody fool.'

'He knows where she is?' Marler asked quickly.

'No, but he's told us where he dropped Dr Hyde, haven't you, Johnny?' he asked, addressing the sorry figure lying on the ground.

'Yes . . . I told you . . . for God's sake . . .'

'For God's sake get out of those clothes,' Butler retorted. 'I have a new outfit you can put on. Too large, but it's clean.'

Butler ran to the Volvo, returned with a pair of denims, a flannel shirt, and a windcheater. He threw them down next to Clausen together with a box of paper tissues. The Dane clambered to his feet, stared at his muddy hands.

'Clean them up as fast as you can, get into those fresh clothes. You've got two minutes.'

Butler waved the Walther towards him. Clausen, shivering in the cold wind, performed a quick-change act. Butler gathered up the discarded clothes, rolled them into a bundle and threw them into the marsh. He took out a map.

'Now, show my friend where you dropped Dr Hyde.'

'Here.' Clausen pointed with a grubby finger. Butler marked the spot with a cross. 'In the middle of nowhere,' he continued. 'A green Renault was parked further up the road. My passenger stood in the wind until I'd almost driven out of sight back towards Tønder. Then, in the rear-view mirror, I saw him walking to the Renault, which had another man behind the wheel.'

'You're doing well, Johnny,' Butler said ironically while Clausen used tissues to wipe mud off his neck. 'But you took your time.'

'You nearly killed me. Another few seconds and I'd have gone under that bloody swamp.'

'You would,' Butler assured him. Normally laconic, he was speaking fast. He moved closer, touched the side of the Dane's head with the muzzle of the Walther. Clausen froze. Butler's next words were delivered in a grim tone.

'One more thing. You don't tell anyone about what happened here. Not anyone. Not for three weeks. We have reliable informants in the area. I hear you've dropped one wrong word and I'll be back. You'll get a bullet in the back of the neck.'

'The money—' Clausen began.

'Oh, you get that at the end of the three weeks. If you are still alive. When we've gone, wait five minutes, then drive home. Those clothes are a lousy fit. And you've still got mud on your face, neck, and God knows where else. Your story is you were out here with a girl. You were drunk, fell into the marsh. This will back up your story.'

Butler produced the bottle of gin he'd used earlier on himself. He poured a small quantity down the front of Clausen's outsize windcheater.

472

'And, Johnny, don't have second thoughts,' Butler warned menacingly. 'They could be the last ones you ever have . . .'

He agreed to follow Marler back off the track, got behind the wheel of his own Volvo, drove slowly as Marler reversed on to the road. They were approaching the outskirts of Tønder when Marler signalled to park at the roadside while they were still in open country.

Butler left his car, joined Marler in the front passenger seat. Marler had driven fast and now he spoke fast.

'Let me look at that map you marked with a cross where your Johnny dropped Dr Hyde. I only peeked over your shoulder.'

'This is interesting,' he commented. 'I drove through Hojer and turned north. Then I turned west at an intersection in the wilderness. Johnny dropped Hyde close to that some intersection. I couldn't find anything. We'll drive back to my lodging house at Tønder – in case there's a message. I just hope Paula is still all right . . .'

47

'She is asleep, Ilena. That is helpful. We can make our final preparations now.'

'You want bowl of hot water?'

'Not yet.' Hyde sounded testy. 'I will tell you what is required when it is required. Clean this floor again with that vacuum cleaner. Sand has penetrated from outside.'

Paula, stretched out on the couch, had her eyes shut but was wide awake. She compelled her whole body to remain relaxed, to give no indication that she was fully conscious. Listening but not seeing was a horrible experience. Her imagination worked overtime.

She heard the purr of the vacuum cleaner as Ilena obeyed Hyde's instruction. She heard the familiar snap as he opened his bag. A minute or so later there was a tinkle. He was carefully laying out his scalpels in the correct sequence.

She'd had her eyes wide open just before the sound of the key being inserted in the door behind the wooden platform at the top of the steps. The platform had a single wooden rail, thigh high to guard against someone falling over the edge.

It was still daylight but the light was fading. The wind was still blowing and as Hyde continued arranging his instruments there was a banging sound. The shutter had come loose again. They had switched on the fluorescent strip when they entered – and this made keeping her closed eyes still more difficult. Hyde swore foully.

'You stupid cow! You still haven't fixed that damned shutter. Do I have to do everything for myself?'

Obviously, Paula thought vaguely, Hyde had forgotten that Starmberg was the one who had most recently attended to the closing of the shutter. As the vacuum went on purring she heard the scape of the chair across the floor. Hyde was about to stand on it to fasten it once more.

'Your clumsy fingers!' Hyde railed as Paula heard again the chair creaking, protesting under the weight of a human being standing on it. Human being? she thought. That was a misnomer if ever there was one – Hyde was a monster.

There was another bang as Hyde pulled the shutter closed, then the scraping of metal as he struggled with the catch. Hearing – not seeing – was becoming unbearable. Paula gritted her teeth, heard the chair being pushed back into its position against the wall.

The purring of the vacuum cleaner stopped. There was

a forbidding silence. She might have been alone for a few brief seconds. Then Hyde spoke.

'Take that thing away. Prepare the bowl of hot water. It must be boiling hot for sterilization of my instruments.'

The heavy clump of Ilena's elephantine footsteps mounting the stairs. The door opening, closing again. She was now alone with Hyde. Thin talon-like fingers grasped her by one arm, shook her vigorously. She opened her eyes slowly. Dr Hyde was smiling down at her.

'As you will see, Miss Grey, the operating table is ready. Now there is nothing to worry about. I am going to give you an injection which will put you to sleep. Then I will move you on to the table . . .'

With Butler following close behind in his own Volvo, Marler had driven at speed to Tønder. The sky was a sea of grey clouds scudding above him in the wind. He arrived, driving slowly now, in the cobbled street where his lodging house was situated.

To his surprise he saw a grey BMW parked on the opposite side of the street facing his temporary home. Then he saw Newman, smoking a cigarette, striding up and down with obvious impatience. Second surprise. As he parked, Newman opened the passenger seat door and sat beside him.

'Don't turn off the engine,' Newman snapped.

'If you say so,' Marler replied calmly.

'Have you got a lead to where they're holding Paula?' Newman demanded.

Butler had left his own car, was leaning outside the open window, listening.

'Not yet,' Marler admitted reluctantly. 'But we have some sort of a lead as to where that cab driver dropped Dr Hyde,' he added quickly.

Newman's manner and expression was bleak. He

475

seemed on the verge of explosion point.

'Far from here? Tell me quickly.'

Tersely, Marler recalled the information Butler had extracted from Johnny Clausen. He also explained how he knew the area from his drive beyond Hoger the previous night. Butler produced his map, showed Newman the cross marking the point where Clausen had dropped Hyde.

'Leave your car here,' Newman ordered Marler. 'We'll drive there in my BMW.' He looked at Butler. 'You keep up with us in your Volvo. Come on! Every minute could count.' He paused, half-way out of the car. 'Are you both armed?'

'I am,' Butler said. 'Walther.' He patted his hip.

'And that hold-all on the floor in the back contains my Armalite,' Marler informed him.

'Bring it with you. And better switch off your engine . . .'

Marler sat beside Newman as they accelerated once outside Tønder. Newman gestured with his head towards the windscreen, which was smeared with gritty sand.

'Tønder is a gem. Coming down the coast road through the South Jutland area is pure hell. God, what a wasteland! Like Macbeth's blasted heath. Miserable scrubland. Nothing but sand and weedy tufts of grass. Then the wind blows up the blasted sand all the time. It's a nightmare.'

'I have found Dr Wand's colony of twenty-eight new bungalows, all furnished and waiting for occupation. In a remote spot close to the sea, hidden behind sand dunes. And it is in the area marked on one of those maps brought back from Lop Nor by Cardon. Where is Cardon? And Tweed?' Marler asked.

'Cardon is doing his own thing. Tweed stopped off at some closely guarded military encampment south of

Esbjerg. He thinks Stealth is due tonight. But Paula is our priority.'

'Agreed.'

Marler kept quiet for a while, sensing Newman's mood of fury and frustration. It was Newman who broke the silence when they were north of Hoger, approaching the intersection where Marler had turned west heading straight for the sea.

'You must have driven around a lot – searching. Sure that you haven't seen a likely place where they might be holding Paula? Something odd that caught your attention?'

Marler snapped his fingers. Newman's phrasing had triggered off a recollection. He was still guiding him.

'Slow down, we're coming to a side road off to the left. Not much of a road, but take it . . .'

'Why?'

'Stop asking bloody fool questions. Slow down. We turn off *here* to the left,' Marler snapped.

Newman swung the wheel and they drove more slowly down a strip of road. Marler spoke as he leaned forward to see more clearly while the wipers whipped madly to clear the sand.

'A remote house. Sizeable, but derelict, I thought. The light was just about as it is now. Fading. Driving past the front twenty yards or so away – across sand off the road – I saw a light in a semi-basement window. When it vanished, I thought I'd imagined it. Now I don't think I did. There it is. Get ready to turn off the road, drive over the sand when I say so. *And don't ask why!*'

'A green Renault? That was the car parked by the road where that cab driver dropped Hyde?'

'A green Renault, yes.'

'There's some sort of shed at the back which could serve as a garage . . .'

'Turn on to the sand. Now!'

*　　*　　*

After waking Paula, Hyde walked away to the operating table, picked up a hypodermic out of an enamel tray where his instruments were neatly laid out. He took his time. Never rush things.

Behind him Paula slid her hands out from under the straps. She had struggled for hours to achieve freedom of movement. Once her hands had been freed, she had loosened the straps round her ankles. Left alone, she had exercised her aching legs, bending her knees time and again, flexing her wrists, gripping the fingers of one hand with the other.

Would her legs hold her up? Hyde had his enamel tray at the far end of the long table. She whipped her legs on to the wooden floor. It was a one-to-one duel – but only before Ilena, the ox-like horror, returned.

She felt unsteady but forced herself to move to her end of the table. At that moment Dr Hyde turned round, hypodermic grasped in his right hand, saw her. His eyes widened with surprise, then with manic fury. He moved towards her and she waited. When he was close she made her legs run down the far side of the table – so they had a barrier between them.

Her right hand grasped a scalpel as he came after her. A moment later he was close. Her other hand picked up a small glass containing a blue liquid. She threw whatever the contents were into his face. He stopped, blinked, put his left hand up to his glasses. Still unsteady, Paula lurched forward. Remembering something else Butler had taught her on the training course, she aimed the scalpel for a point between his ribs. Hit the ribs and it would glance off. She put all her strength behind the thrust, felt the scalpel sink in through the cloth of his coat and well beyond. Like a knife going into butter, she thought viciously. No mercy for this bastard. She rammed the scalpel in deep, let go, stood back.

Expressions flitted across Hyde's face as he stood

stock-still. Surprise, amazement, fear. The hand holding the hypodermic flopped gently on the table, releasing the hypodermic with its deadly needle point. A patch of red welled up over his white coat where the scalpel had penetrated. He took two steps towards the foot of the staircase, then slumped face-down to the floor.

He wriggled, rolled over on to his back, his legs flapping on the floor, then there was less motion and he let out a deep groan of pain.

Paula, more hard-faced than anyone had ever seen her, picked up the hypodermic. Ilena would be back soon with her bowl of boiling water. Paula was not confident she could successfully eliminate the stocky nurse. And as soon as she entered the basement she'd see Hyde lying on the floor.

Paula, her strength growing with every movement, climbed the stairs and stood on the platform. She held the hypodermic ready and prayed. That was when she heard the key being inserted in the lock, but it was not turned. In the hall someone was hammering on the outer door.

After pressing the bell and hearing nothing inside, Newman used his fist to hammer on the heavy front door of the house. They had found a green Renault inside the makeshift garage at the back. This was the place. He heard sounds of bolts being withdrawn, a clumsy key being turned. He had a smile on his face as the door swung slowly inwards.

A squat, slab-faced woman with very short hair, wearing a white coat, faced him. She held a long-barrelled Mauser in her hand, aimed at his stomach. He frowned, raised his hands.

'No need for that. I've lost my way.'

He backed away slowly, step by step. She followed him.

'How you get there?'

The barrel of the gun emerged beyond the doorway, then the thick hand holding it. Pressed against the side of the house, Marler brought down the barrel of his Armalite with savage force on her wrist. She dropped the gun and grunted like a wild boar. As she retreated back into the house her other hand produced a wicked wide-bladed knife, doubled-edged. She held it in front of her as she continued back and Newman followed.

'Where is the girl?' Newman snapped.

'Girl die if you come in . . .'

Newman continued to advance, followed by Marler and Butler. She reached the door to the basement. Despite Marler's ferocious blow, her right hand turned the key and she backed on to the platform inside the basement area.

She saw Paula and started to swing her huge knife round. Two things happened at the same moment. Paula plunged the hypodermic into her thick wrist, depressed the plunger. Newman's right leg shot up and kicked her in the stomach. It was like kicking a tree trunk but Ilena was rammed back against the rail. The wood refused to take the strain. With the hypodermic still in her wrist, her eyes rolling, she fell backwards ten feet to the wood floor. Her obese body lay still, her head oddly twisted to one side.

'Oh, thank God!'

Paula threw herself into Newman's arms. He hugged, kissed her as she clung to him, then straightened up. She spoke as Butler, Walther in hand, began to search the rest of the house upstairs. Marler checked the ground floor.

'Lord, I need a wash,' Paula said.

'Try the kitchen at the back,' advised Marler, who heard her as he returned from his swift scrutiny. 'There's a sink with taps.'

480

When she had gone Newman and Marler went down the steps into the basement. Newman checked Ilena's pulse. Nothing. He looked up at Marler.

'Dead as a doornail. Her neck's broken.'

'This thing's alive,' Marler reported, pointing to Hyde. 'What do you think?'

'If he faces a trial, he'll get X number of years. Then some shrink will testify he's normal and they'll release him. I'm not in favour.'

'Join the club.'

Using his knuckles to avoid leaving fingerprints, Marler heaved over the table. Hyde screamed as it landed on his knees, pinning him down. His precious scalpels scattered all round him.

'He'll bleed to death before he's found,' Newman commented.

'Which is the object of the exercise,' Marler replied.

Paula freshened herself up under the tap of cold water. Butler had found her shoulder-bag thrown on a couch in a front room. To her surprise the contents were intact – including her .32 Browning.

'No one and nothing else in the house,' Butler remarked. 'Except an oil lamp burning in the front room.'

Newman disappeared inside the front room. He closed the door, knocked the oil lamp on to the wooden floor, went back into the hall, again shutting the door.

Paula had walked out into the fresh sea air, took in deep gulps. Then she stiffened. The wind had dropped suddenly. As night fell the air was still. No more sandstorms. Only an uncanny silence. She had stiffened because of what she saw creeping in from the sea. A dense mist. Growing denser every minute.

48

'It really was a trifle disconcerting,' Dr Wand remarked to Starmberg as the Luxemburger drove him away from Esbjerg Airport. 'We were held in a holding pattern while some stupid light aircraft was permitted to land. I gather it was lost and they wanted to get it on the ground before we landed.'

The two men were inside a limousine with tinted glass windows. Wand had no idea that Inspector Nielsen had phoned the Esbjerg traffic controller.

'When a Piper Aircraft, call sign Kalundborg, comes within your orbit, could you please give it top priority over all other planes?' he had requested.

'Request granted,' the traffic controller had agreed.

Earlier, at Kastrup Airport, Nielsen had arranged for the take-off of the Lear jet to be delayed. He had guessed Tweed would want to arrive first. Nielsen was staying in his office all night if necessary – at least until he had heard from Tweed.

Starmberg wore his chauffeur's uniform and dark glasses as he bypassed Esbjerg and drove south on Route 11. He was heading for South Jutland by the direct route. Wand, completely relaxed, glanced at the Luxemburger.

'There will be two Stealth vessels coming in tonight – a powerful missile-armed vessel leading the way, with *Yenan*, the smaller ship, following it. All the top operatives are aboard the *Yenan* . . .'

'Why is that?' enquired Starmberg.

Wand sighed. 'Again I am asked questions, which you know I dislike . . .'

'My humble apologies . . .'

'Just keep quiet and your question will be answered. The lead vessel, the *Mao III*, has as its main task the protection of the *Yenan*. There are also operatives aboard *Mao III*, but they are far less important. I am happy to say that as soon as the *Yenan* team has landed and occupied the bungalows waiting for them, my whole European apparatus will be established in place.'

'Most satisfactory. You have planned this so well,' Starmberg replied with grovelling enthusiasm. Wand preferred top subordinates who looked up to him. 'Everything is now ready in Jutland for their reception.'

'Kindly assure me that the escorts are in position.'

'Twenty armed men will now have hidden themselves behind the dunes.'

'And the dinghies, I trust, have been placed in a strategic situation? The *Mao* and the *Yenan* will have to stand offshore while the operatives are landed on the beach.'

'The dinghies are also concealed behind the dunes. Trucks delivered them an hour ago.'

There was silence for some time as Starmberg drove steadily south. Wand appeared to have sunk into one of his trances. They had reached the wilderness in South Jutland now. Wind blew a veritable storm of powdered sand over the windscreen. Starmberg had turned on the wipers at top speed but still a film of sand coated the screen.

'You have checked the met forecast, I trust?' Wand asked suddenly.

'Wind due to die at dusk. Then dense fog along this coast.'

'It is dusk now . . .'

Wand had just made the remark when the wind

dropped, went away. A few minutes later, glancing to the west, Wand saw in the fading light a turgid grey mist creeping in from the sea. His mouth twisted into a smile of pleasure.

'You haven't asked me about our good friend, Tweed.'

'You don't like me to ask questions,' Starmberg reminded him respectfully.

'Good. Very good indeed. You might like to know Tweed is due to receive a memento of his cherished Miss Grey. Namely her severed arm. That will break him finally.'

'A pleasure for him, I'm sure,' Starmberg replied with relish. 'We have nearly reached the bungalows. Inside the one which will be your headquarters a powerful transmitter has been installed.'

'I would hope so. That is my means of communication with the *Mao* . . .'

Both men were so absorbed in what lay ahead of them they had never even glanced behind them. Even if they had, it was doubtful if they'd have seen the scruffy Ford Sierra which had followed them all the way from the airport. Behind the wheel Philip Cardon slowed down, driving with great skill with only his sidelights on.

While the Piper Archer was in midair, and soon after its take off from Kastrup, Tweed had – at Cardon's suggestion – asked the pilot to transmit a message to Nielsen over his radio.

The pilot had immediately picked up his microphone and had spoken to Nielsen on the prearranged frequency. He had asked for an anonymous car – equipped with a powerful transmitter – to be obtained in Esbjerg and kept waiting for their arrival. As usual, Inspector Nielsen had delivered.

On landing at Esbjerg the security chief had led the

three passengers to two vehicles parked in a secluded area. One was a much-used Ford Sierra disfigured with smears of mud.

'This is the one with the transmitter,' the security chief had informed them. 'Tuned to the correct waveband – and this bit of paper gives you the call sign to reach someone called Anton Norlin.'

'That's mine,' Cardon had said.

He had waited at the airport until Wand's Lear jet had landed. Nielsen had radioed the Piper Archer *en route*, telling Tweed about the strategem he'd used to delay the Lear jet. Cardon had been behind the wheel of the worn-looking Ford Sierra when Wand had appeared, had climbed into the front passenger seat while the uniformed chauffeur held the door open for him. He had watched cynically as the heavily built man with the ponderous walk had disappeared inside the limousine.

Know you're the big cheese, you do, Cardon had thought.

Later, driving after them into South Jutland, he had found his souped-up engine was taking him too close. He had slowed down as the gritty sandstorm raged all round him.

He only stopped when he saw the limousine swing west off the road towards the sea and a range of rolling sand dunes. Approaching the dunes on foot, he had seen they concealed a large colony of bungalows. The limousine was parked outside one bungalow where a tall aerial was automatically elevating.

He had immediately returned to the Sierra, settled again behind the wheel, reached for the radio telephone.

Earlier, walking outside Esbjerg Airport, escorted by the security officer, Tweed and Newman had been led to an Opel Omega. A plain-clothes driver had ushered them inside the rear of the vehicle.

485

'I understand I have to drive you to Anton Norlin at the military encampment,' he said over his shoulder.

'Not yet,' Tweed replied. 'First, can you drop my friend at the Avis car-hire outfit in Ebsjerg? He has to drive somewhere very urgently. Then I must go to the harbour – I have to visit a vessel waiting there.'

'Avis first, then the harbour, then Anton Norlin,' confirmed the driver tersely.

He dropped off Newman outside Avis and drove on with Tweed.

The town was pleasant, busy, but without a strong character. As they reached the harbour in the Byparken the driver pointed out a red-brick crenellated water tower. The harbour was crammed with fishing boats. Stepping out, Tweed spotted a large launch with an ample deckhouse from which the Red Ensign flew. Leaning against the wind, he hurried along the waterfront as waves splashed against the wall and a forest of masts swayed drunkenly.

At the gangway leading to the launch – thank God it had rails on either side – Tweed was met by a tall, clean-shaven man in his thirties. Clad in a white roll-neck sweater and immaculate navy blue trousers, he wore a peaked seaman's cap at a jaunty angle.

'I'm Tweed.'

'Dave Lane. Welcome aboard.'

With a tight mouth Tweed descended the gangplank, which was rising and falling, gripping the handrail. Lane escorted him inside a comfortable saloon, closed the door, turned to his visitor.

'Identification, please, sir. Regulations . . .'

Tweed produced his passport, carefully avoiding gazing out of the windows. Lane examined it with care, returned it.

'You want to contact Commander Wilson?'

'Where is the *Minotaur* now?' Tweed asked quickly.

'Out there.' Lane waved a hand towards the open sea. 'He is patrolling off the South Jutland coast.' He sat down in front of a transmitter hidden from the outside world by heavy net curtains drawn over the windows. 'Radio contact may be a bit crackly. Let's see, shall we?'

A minute later he handed the phone to Tweed who sat in the chair Lane had vacated.

'Tweed here. Repeat, Tweed here . . .'

'Heard you the first time. Tug Wilson at this end. We met at a bash at the Admiralty two years ago. Remember you well. How many targets are expected?'

By 'targets' he meant Stealth vessels. Tweed now recalled the cheerful weatherbeaten face of Tug Wilson. And he was being careful – talking on an open line.

'I have no idea,' Tweed confessed.

'Are they armed?'

'Again. Haven't a clue.'

'You're a mine of information!' Wilson chuckled. There was no crackle and the communication was crystal-clear. 'But I understand you're the one who sent me my Christmas present. Most acceptable. My thanks.'

'I shall need to communicate with you from now on from a landbase,' Tweed warned. 'That should be possible – they have excellent equipment, I'm sure.'

'Ask Lane for the data. Put him on again, please. Glad to have you aboard . . .'

Tweed handed the phone back to Dave Lane, walked swiftly to another chair, sat down. The large launch was rocking merrily and he hadn't had the foresight to take a Dramamine. But despite a growing queasiness Tweed felt relieved: Tug Wilson was a good man to have on your side. That last reference to being glad to have you aboard was a great compliment, coming from the tough Navy commander.

He happened to look up at a moment when the launch was heeling towards the sea. He hastily averted his eyes as a fleet of large waves rolled into the harbour. Tweed thanked Heaven he was *not* aboard the *Minotaur*. The relief vanished when the thought of Paula flashed into his mind. A deep depression enveloped him. Lane had finished talking to Wilson. He wrote swiftly on a pad, tore off the sheet, folded it, and handed it to Tweed.

'That is top secret. It gives the waveband you can contact the *Minotaur* on, and the code-word. As you'll see, both are changed every three hours on the hour.'

'I appreciate the excellent security. It's only right you should know the transmitter I'll be using will be operated from a military base. A rather special one. And now, if I may ask, I expect you're returning to the *Minotaur*?'

'No fear!' Lane grinned boyishly. 'The Commander agreed that I should leave harbour immediately – if that suited you. I'm heading down the coast for South Jutland. You think there'll be a rough house?' he asked eagerly.

'I think that today there will be the deadliest and strangest duel ever fought.'

49

'We'll drive north fast and investigate that weird colony of bungalows you found,' Newman decided.

'Suits me,' Marler drawled. 'I did locate them.'

'Paula,' Newman urged, putting his arm round her shoulders, 'I think you ought to go back to Tønder and get a real rest after what you've been through . . .'

They had driven away from the house of death, leaving behind Ilena and the infamous Dr Hyde. Only when they reached the road and the house had vanished in the fog had Newman stopped his BMW with Paula beside him.

Marler had followed in his Volvo while Butler brought up the rear in his own Volvo. Now they were all standing outside the BMW. For ten minutes Paula had been striding up and down the road, exercising her limbs, bringing herself both physically and mentally back to normal. She gently removed Newman's arm.

'You think you're going to pack me off to bed when the real climax could be near? I appreciate your sympathy, but I am staying with you.'

'Newman could be right,' Marler suggested.

Paula flared up. 'You can both stick it!' She stood, hands on her hips, glaring at them. 'Stick it, I said!'

Butler, who normally used words as though they were money to be spent frugally, stepped forward.

'The lady is fit again. Didn't you hear what she told you to do with your idea of treating her as an invalid?'

'And I wish to God,' Paula continued, 'there was some way we could let Tweed know I'm OK.'

'Facilities for communication are a bit scarce on the ground in this part of the world,' Marler warned.

'Then let's bloody well get moving! We're all armed. Drive north. Stop hanging about,' she stormed. 'Bob, I'll travel with you. We'll lead the attack column . . .'

Fog. Dense fog was rolling in like a poison-gas cloud from the sea. Paula hid from Newman the emotions which welled up inside her. Fog spelt the horror at Lymington marina on the south coast of Britain – when Harvey Boyd had failed to come back alive.

Fog spelt the nightmare on the Elbe at Blankense harbour – the terror of the *Holsten* being split in two and sinking barely seconds after they'd rushed ashore.

Fog spelt the unknown, fear, menace. She slipped her hand inside her shoulder-bag, gripped the butt of her

Browning for comfort. At that moment Marler drew alongside them, waved his hand for them to stop.

As Newman and Paula climbed out Marler leant in, switched off the BMW's lights. Paula glanced back. No lights any more on Marler's car, on Butler's. She spoke first.

'What's happening? Where are we?'

'Very close to those dunes over to the left,' Marler said sombrely. 'And I saw lights – beams from flashlights. A lot of them. If each is held by one man there must be up to twenty of them.'

'So, we're outnumbered – if they're armed,' Paula commented.

'Oh, they'll be armed,' Newman said. 'I think I caught a glimpse of a range of dunes when the fog drifted a moment ago.'

'You did,' Marler confirmed grimly. 'The road from here on is pretty straight. I suggest we drive further north half a mile or so, get away from this place while we think what to do next.'

'Agreed,' replied Newman.

Getting back inside their cars, still led by Newman, they crawled without lights. Soon Newman's night vision showed faint pinpoints of light moving about among the dunes. He continued moving north and then saw a small ridge towards the sea. Checking his rear-view mirror to make sure that Marler was close behind, he turned off the road.

'Where are you going now?' Paula asked.

'That ridge should be a good vantage point to spy on what's going on.' He descended into a small dip, parked the BMW and got out as the other two cars pulled up behind him. His right hand flashed inside his windcheater, withdrew the Smith & Wesson. A small figure was coming towards them.

'Mr Robert Newman, I presume?' Philip Cardon called out.

'What the devil are you doing here?'

'Surveying the enemy—' He broke off. 'Paula! Thank God! Are you OK?'

'Very OK. Now,' she added. Briefly she told him of her ordeal without making a big thing of it. Cardon took her by the arm, followed by Newman. 'Tweed will be desperate to hear you're alive. I've got a radio transmitter in the car behind that hummock. Come and talk to him . . .'

Several hours earlier, Tweed had left the harbour and was driven to the military encampment south of Esbjerg. He was again impressed by the security. Dropped by the driver at the entrance, he was escorted by a uniformed Danish officer inside the guardhouse.

The wide-spread complex, behind a twelve-foot wire fence he suspected was electrified, comprised single-storey huts like giant portacabins. He had to show the officer not only his passport but also his SIS card.

'Anton Norlin is expecting me.'

'He *is* expecting you, sir. Please follow me . . .'

The officer led the way between two rows of huts to the largest edifice. Perched on its roof was an array of aerials and a large satellite dish which revolved slowly. Tweed had a slight shock as the officer opened the door, ushered him inside, closed it without entering. Back in the guardhouse he had briefly used a phone, speaking in Danish, not a word of which Tweed had understood.

The shock came when a tall, sturdily built figure stood up from behind a desk and turned round. His face was hidden by a Balaclava helmet. Penetrating eyes stared at him as he came forward and shook hands.

'We are most glad to see you, Mr Tweed. I am Anton Norlin, although that is not my real name.'

It was exactly like meeting a commander of the British SAS. As they were shaking hands Tweed observed the large hut was divided into two sections. Half-way down the long room a glass wall with a closed door cut them off from the far end. Norlin must have noted his quick glance.

'Behind the glass wall is the sophisticated communications section. That will be at your service if needed.'

'It will be needed . . .'

Sitting down, as Norlin poured coffee from a percolator, he saw all the men beyond the glass wall also wore Balaclavas. Norlin brought his chair round from the other side of the desk to sit close to Tweed.

'Is there anything I should know?' he enquired.

'A great deal . . .'

Norlin listened attentively without saying a word while Tweed told him about his conviction that secret hostile vessels would be approaching the South Jutland coast, about the weird colony of bungalows – he showed Norlin the map marked with a cross – about the *Minotaur* patrolling off the coast. He put the Dane completely in the picture. Norlin nodded when he had finished, thought for a moment.

'Inspector Nielsen has been in touch with me. I have ready a large team of heavily armed men. They can be transported swiftly to this objective marked on the map. Either by a fleet of helicopters or by trucks.'

'I suggest the main body is moved south by truck,' Tweed urged. 'The arrival of choppers would alert the men who I am certain will be ashore waiting to receive the human cargo from those ships.'

'Trucks, then. These men waiting there – we expect them to be armed?'

'I'd assume they will be. It's rather a complex operation. Subject to the safety of your own troops, I don't give a damn how many already ashore are wiped out. But if possible I'd like to take alive for questioning all those men who are being brought ashore from the ship – or ships.'

Norlin picked up the phone, spoke rapidly in Danish. Tweed had the impression he was issuing orders at machine-gun speed. Without having seen his face, he was already very impressed by Norlin. The Dane exuded competence, resolution. He put down the phone.

'I have just arranged for large dinghies with outboard motors to be transported aboard the trucks. Also grappling equipment – in case we have to board the ships while at sea.'

'A very sound idea,' Tweed agreed. 'The trouble is I don't know what we shall be facing.'

'So, we prepare for all contingencies . . .'

He picked up the phone, which had started ringing. A brief stream of Danish. Norlin replaced the receiver, stood up.

'Please come with me into the communications room. There is a message for you from a man called Philip Cardon . . .'

'Tweed here. Any news of Paula? Found anything, Philip?'

'Answering your first question, I'm entirely on my own at present. Newman and the others could be on their way to me now. We have a tough team searching for Paula,' he reassured Tweed. 'I can answer your second query positively. At the spot marked X there are twenty-eight bungalows well hidden behind sand dunes. Close to the coast. Only a rough estimate, but I'd say there are between fifteen and twenty thugs gathered for the party. Your favourite person is also present, ready to wave his magic *wand*. You can hear me clearly?'

'Perfectly. All understood. Anything more?'

Cardon had been speaking at rapid-fire rate. He never had trusted radio communication.

'Yes. They have been practising with dinghies with

outboards. Launching them into the sea, going out a few hundred yards, returning to the beach. That's it so far.'

'Good. Very good. Keep in touch . . .'

Tweed swivelled round in the chair in front of the transmitter. He told Norlin what Cardon had said.

'Good job I arranged for us to take our own dinghies . . .'

Norlin had made his remark and they were leaving the communications room when the soldier who had slipped back into the chair took another message. He called out to Norlin in Danish.

'Tweed, you're wanted again on the phone,' Norlin told him. 'Inspector Nielsen from Copenhagen.'

'Tweed speaking.'

'I owe you an apology,' Nielsen's distinctive voice began. 'I have been compelled to inform Danish Military Intelligence . . .'

'Yes?'

The line crackled, went dead. The operator took over and tried time and again to bring Nielsen back on the line. Eventually he stopped, spoke to Norlin again.

'This happens, Tweed,' Norlin explained. 'Something in the atmosphere. You find you can't get through.'

'Could that happen in the middle of the operation – between here and South Jutland?' Tweed asked anxiously.

'No. It's a question of range. Copenhagen is a far greater distance away. From here to the operational area in South Jutland is no more than thirty miles, or even less. We'll have contact with this base without any trouble at all.'

'That's a relief.'

Returning to the other section of the hut, Tweed sat down while Norlin poured more coffee. He was bothered by the reference Nielsen had made to Danish Military Intelligence. He simply couldn't imagine what Nielsen had been trying to warn him about. But he took grim satisfaction from the news that Dr Wand was at the scene of the coming operation. It also confirmed that something big and important was about to take place. Those furnished but unoccupied bungalows *were* a new Moor's Landing. The black dog which still sat on his shoulder was the fate of Paula.

Night had fallen on the military encampment. Tweed had compelled himself to eat some of the excellent meal laid before him. It has his duty to keep up his strength.

Outside the wind had vanished. In its place a sinister fog was rolling in across that part of Denmark. Tweed got up and paced backwards and forwards. Norlin remained perfectly motionless in his chair. Iron nerves, but he hadn't got on his mind the worry which was eating up Tweed.

The glass door opened from the communications section. The operator called out urgently in Danish. Norlin jumped up as Tweed ran for the door.

'It's a Commander Wilson calling,' Norlin reported as he caught up with Tweed.

Grim-faced, Tweed picked up the phone. Why the hell hadn't he heard from Newman?

'Tweed here.' He gave the code-word. 'Any development?'

'You are a genius,' Wilson's voice boomed. 'Two targets in sight. One large, one smaller. Like a mother ship bringing in baby. Not a flicker on our normal radar, but blips as clear as the nose on my face on your Christmas present. About twenty miles off shore. Coming in on a course which, if maintained, will make their landfall north of a place called Hojer. When do I challenge – then intercept if necessary?'

'Not until they're stationary very close to the coast – if that action is practical.'

495

'It is. Incredible – two *Marie Celeste*s coming home. Will keep reporting their position.'

'Thank you, Tug. This is it . . .'

Again Tweed was leaving the communications room when he was called back. Among the Danish the operator spoke as he vacated the chair Tweed caught the words 'Robert Newman'. He grabbed the phone.

'Tweed?' Newman's voice came over clear as a bell. 'Hold on. I've got someone here who'd like a word with you.'

'This is Paula. I'm OK. Absolutely OK . . .' Tweed nearly choked when he heard her buoyant voice. 'Tweed, are you still there?'

'Yes, I'm here. How are you? Did they . . .'

'No, they didn't. I'll say it again. I'm OK! OK! OK! Got it? Wonderful to hear your voice. This lot tried to send me to bed. Would you believe it? I won't repeat over this line what I told them to do. Any news about you know what?'

'Yes, Paula, there is. And it's wonderful to hear your voice. But we're short of time. Better put Bob back on the line.'

'Here is the mastermind . . .'

'Bob, keep everyone under cover. Friends are coming down to help. Professionals. Wait until we reach you. That is an order. We'll be proceeding by stealth.'

'Understood,' Newman said crisply. 'Get your skates on . . .'

50

'I'm in touch with the *Mao*,' Starmberg reported. 'Both of the ships are very close. Only about twenty miles off shore.'

'Tell them we are ready to offload their passengers, if you please,' Dr Wand ordered.

They were seated inside the spacious living-room of the bungalow equipped with an aerial which could be elevated and retracted automatically. Starmberg, wearing a headset, repeated his chief's message. Wand sat behind a desk in an executive chair.

The curtains were closed over the one-way-glass windows. A few minutes earlier Wand had pulled aside a curtain, noted with satisfaction the fog drifting over a nearby dune. The weather was ideal for the operation. He gave his new order when Starmberg had completed contacting the *Mao*.

'No, be so kind as to go outside and rehearse our teams again in launching the dinghies.'

'We have already carried out a major rehearsal,' Starmberg reminded him.

'Dear me, you know how I dislike having to give an instruction twice. They must be ready to land our guests swiftly. Last time they were launching the dinghies into a stormy sea. Now it is like a millpond.'

'Of course, sir!' Starmberg jumped up out of his chair.

Before running out into the night he snatched one of the two Uzi machine-pistols looped from a hook on the wall. It was expected that there would be no interference, but Dr Wand always worked on the basis of preparing for trouble. He called out again as Starmberg grasped the door handle.

'I have decided I will personally travel out in the largest dinghy to congratulate the expedition commander on a new successful enterprise.'

'May I suggest that could be hazardous, sir?' Starmberg ventured.

'I am under the impression you just did. When I want your advice you may be sure I shall not hesitate to consult you.'

Starmberg flushed at the sarcastic rebuke. He must remember Wand was an autocrat, had the manners of a brusque military commander.

'I will have the largest dinghy ready for your departure. May I enquire – have we any idea when the ships will stand off shore?'

'About two o'clock tomorrow morning. As you know, at the moment they are now stationary out at sea. Two o'clock is the hour of my triumph.'

At the military encampment the assault teams aboard trucks had been put on stand-by. Tweed had received a new message from the *Minotaur*.

'Both targets are now stationary. About twenty miles off shore. Well outside the territorial water limit. Will continue to keep you informed . . .'

Tweed asked Norlin the question when they had once again returned to the Dane's desk in the other section.

'Should your men be moved closer south now?'

'Not necessary. We might be seen. The two ships are lying twenty miles off shore. Your frigate commander friend seems very efficient at keeping us in touch. I shall drive the first truck of the convoy when the time comes.'

'There is dense fog,' Tweed warned.

'Makes no difference. I know that road like the back of my hand. My truck – and those following me – will have their red tail-lights on. So each truck, keeping close, will be guided by the red lights on the truck in front. We wait for the ships to move in.'

'I think I'd like to join my people there as soon as it can be arranged.'

'Now, if you like. A car equipped with a transmitter and a driver who knows the road as well as I do.'

'Another favour, if possible. You seem to have an excellent canteen here. I'd like to take my people – six of them – some warm food and drink. Could your chef produce a large quantity of vegetable soup, some rolls, a thermos of coffee, and a large apple cake?'

'Consider it done. For six people.' Norlin picked up the phone, rattled off a stream of Danish, put the phone down. 'Ready in thirty minutes at the outside. The chef is now preparing a similar meal for the men aboard the trucks. Are you armed? No? Would it not be wiser to carry some weapon?'

Tweed hesitated. It was rare for him to use firearms. But this could turn into a vicious dogfight.

'A 7.65mm Walther automatic, if available.'

'Hey presto! As I believe you used to say in England.' Norlin unlocked a deep drawer, produced a Walther and a generous supply of spare mags. 'Will that be OK?'

'Very.' Ejecting the magazine, Tweed checked the mechanism. 'In first-rate condition.'

He pocketed the weapon inside his trench coat thrown over the back of a chair. Then he nodded towards the communications room.

'One more vital task. Does your operator speak English, will he be on duty all night, and what is his name?'

'Very good English. Came on duty just before you arrived. Will be here all night. Name – Erik.'

'I have another continent-wide operation which must

499

be triggered off as soon as those ships start landing their human cargo.' From memory he wrote on a pad the names and phone numbers of Kuhlmann, Benoit, and the Special Branch officer in London. 'Clear?'

'Perfectly.'

'I need to phone these people to tell them it will be Erik who calls them – only when he hears me contact him and use the code-word, Landslide.'

Tweed called all three men who were still at their desks – would be there all night long. Then he instructed Erik.

'It has to be rapid. Identify yourself by your name when you're sure you're speaking to the right man. Then repeat the code-word three times. Landslide. Once you've done that get off the line fast. They'll want to move like the wind.'

'Seems clear enough,' Erik replied from behind his Balaclava. 'Just wait for you to call me with the code-word . . .'

'You seem well organized,' Norlin commented approvingly as they sat by his desk. 'Now all we can do is wait – something I am very accustomed to.'

Tweed checked his watch. Coming up close to midnight.

'Not much longer to wait before the balloon goes up,' he observed.

Wand, clad in gumboots, stepped ashore from the large dinghy. It had taken him with Starmberg a quarter of a mile out to sea – a sea which was calm as a lake of oil. They were walking up the beach towards the bungalow when they heard the plane coming.

Starmberg, realizing it was approaching from the north, raised his Uzi machine-pistol. Wand used his fist to slam down the muzzle.

'You bloody fool. You want to confirm there is activity here? Stand still and wait . . .'

The machine, a light aircraft, appeared as a dim shape as the fog thinned briefly. It was flying no more than fifty feet above the beach. Its silhouette flashed past, flew on south, the engine sound vanishing almost at once, muffled by the fog. Wand pointed a finger at one of the men patrolling the beach, an automatic weapon looped over his shoulder.

'You. Is it unusual for light aircraft to fly over this area?'

'No, sir. There is a flying club at Esbjerg. They fly down the coast which gives them guidance. I think that one had lost its bearings.'

'I don't like it,' Starmberg commented.

'Who asked you to like it?' Wand demanded.

He stared at the Luxemburger who had his head cocked to one side. He was staring out to sea. Wand slapped his hands together: it was very raw and cold.

'What are you doing now, Jules?'

'I could have sworn I heard that machine flying back out to sea.'

'So get your ears tested when this is all over.' Wand checked his watch. 'We must get back to the transmitter. Call up the *Mao*. It should be starting to come in soon now . . .'

'We are very close to that area marked with a cross on your map,' the driver told Tweed who sat beside him. 'That is why I am now crawling along.'

It was the same driver who had brought Tweed from Esbjerg Airport earlier to the harbour and then on to the military base. His name was Langhorn and he was the only man whose face Tweed had seen. They were travelling without lights and how he had kept the Opel Omega

501

on the road was beyond Tweed's understanding. To his right Tweed could just make out in the distance a range of sand dunes as Langhorn stopped the car at the summit of a small ridge. He lowered his window, letting in a current of freezing air. Yes, he had been right: he could hear a small aircraft flying further west. He frowned as the machine's engine faded.

Had Norlin blundered – sent an aircraft to spy out the land? The grave danger was that it would alert Dr Wand. Then he dismissed the idea: Norlin was too shrewd. Still . . . something cold and metallic was pressed against his skull from outside the open window.

'Tell the driver to remove his keys from the ignition or you'll both get a bullet,' a familiar voice threatened.

'That's a friendly welcome to South Jutland, Bob, I must say,' Tweed remarked.

'God! I'm sorry. I didn't recognize you in that hat,' Newman said, removing the Smith & Wesson.

'What's happening?' Tweed snapped as he climbed out into the swirling fog, which was growing denser.

Another figure appeared, ran forward. Paula flung her arms round Tweed, hugged him and kissed him on the cheek. Her windcheater felt damp from exposure to the drifting fog. He embraced her warmly, looked at Newman.

'Nice that someone is glad to see me. Which means I can well do without a hug from you.' He looked at Paula as she released him. 'I can't tell you how relieved I am to see you. Are you really all right? I suspect you've had a grim ordeal.'

'No time to talk about that now. Too much happening here.'

'The first thing is to get this car off the road into a dip in the ground,' Newman said crisply. 'Paula, fetch Butler and Nield from behind the ridge.' He looked at the driver as she rushed off. 'Get ready to be pushed by hand. Can't risk the bandits behind those dunes hearing your engine. Luckily that plane drowned its sound as you came so close . . .'

Butler and Nield appeared and, with Newman's help, pushed the Opel off the road as Langhorn turned the wheel, across a belt of scrubland and down into the gulley where the other cars were parked. Tweed had followed with Paula and was about to ask again what the position was when Langhorn picked up the phone, which was bleeping. He listened, replied in Danish, called out to Tweed.

'It's Norlin. For you . . .'

'Message just received from Commander Wilson,' Norlin said tersely. 'Targets are moving inshore. We're on our way.'

Crouched down behind the ridge, Paula served the hot soup out of a large thermos Tweed had hauled out of the back of the Opel. Norlin had handed Tweed a large picnic basket and Paula crooned over its contents when she checked them with a pencil torch.

Besides the large thermos of vegetable soup there were plastic mugs, spoons, knives, plates, a generous supply of rolls, another thermos with coffee, more mugs and plates, paper napkins, and the biggest apple cake she'd ever seen.

Her mouth watering, she insisted on supplying the others, including Marler who lay prone with his Armalite, before she helped herself. Tweed realized they were all ravenous. While they were eating and drinking he borrowed a pair of night glasses from Paula, adjusted the focus, scanned the colony scattered amid the dunes. His mouth tightened.

'I've counted fifteen men patrolling along the beach and they are all armed.'

'Sensible to supply plastic cutlery,' Pala remarked to lighten the atmosphere. 'No danger of clinking cutlery made of metal.'

'Which is why Norlin supplied them,' Tweed whispered back. 'He doesn't miss a trick. Everyone feeling a bit better?'

Heads nodded. 'Then I'll give you the news which was just passed to me by Norlin. Two Stealth ships, one a big job, are now on the move – heading for this very point on the coast, I'm sure. Tug Wilson, whom I know, is commander of the frigate *Minotaur*, which is shadowing them. He's keeping in close touch with me. And now you've all finished your meal you've got to put these on – Norlin said he'd prefer not to gun down any of us.'

From a canvas bag he'd carried from the Opel he produced seven Balaclava helmets – a smaller one for Paula. He also showed them a collection of wide elasticized armbands.

'You all wear these as additional recognition – one on each arm. Put them on now.'

When Paula had slipped a helmet over her head, adjusted it so her mouth and eyes were level with the openings, Tweed slid a green fluorescent band up over each of her forearms. He had just donned his own gear when he remembered his next priority.

'Back in a minute. Have to check something with base . . .'

Crouching low, he ran back to the Opel. Langhorn was just getting out, stopped when he saw Tweed, opened the front passenger door.

'I have to contact Erik urgently,' Tweed said.

'First, I was coming to tell you. Another message from Wilson. The two ships he's shadowing are less than ten miles off shore and moving in fast.'

'Thank you.' Tweed checked his watch. 2 a.m. 'Now get me Erik . . .

'Erik,' Tweed began, after giving the code-word, 'can you hear me clearly? Good. I expect soon to be giving you the signal to make those three phone calls.'

'Standing by, Mr Tweed. A fresh message from Wilson – the targets are five miles off shore and moving very fast.'

'Then I'll be calling you again very soon . . .'

Aboard the *Minotaur* Commander Tug Wilson, a stocky figure with ice-blue eyes and his cap rammed carelessly over his dark hair, stood in the communications room. He was staring at the screen on Gaston Delvaux's device. Two blips stood out clearly.

'Amazing,' he commented gruffly to the operator.

'Uncanny, sir,' the junior officer agreed. 'Look at our own screen.'

Wilson glanced at the other screen. Blank. Not a trace of a vessel within miles.

'How far off shore now?' he rapped out.

'Four miles at the moment. They're still moving in fast.'

'Keep me informed minute by minute.'

Wilson returned to the bridge. Dense fog everywhere. A curl of mist rolled over the prow. This wasn't going to lift. Confrontation was imminent. He gave the order.

'Missile section. Action stations. I may press the button at any minute. Aim for larger target . . .'

Tweed ran back from the Opel, flopped between Newman and Marler behind the ridge. Marler was squinting through his night scope, following a man patrolling the beach and holding an automatic weapon.

'Our friends – with Norlin in command – will arrive at any moment. Don't let them startle you. Any idea of how they'll proceed down there?'

'Yes,' Newman said briskly but quietly. 'They've been

practising launching those dinghies lined up by the sea on the beach. They're going out to meet the Stealth ships when they arrive. Obviously the Stealth vessels will have to unload their passengers into those dinghies well off shore. I say we go after one of the last of the dinghies to be launched, grab it, get in amongst them.'

'An excellent tactic . . .'

Despite Tweed's warning, Newman nearly jumped out of his skin as the voice spoke quietly behind him. He was swivelling his Smith & Wesson when Tweed's hand clamped down on his wrist. He had recognized Anton Norlin's voice.

Slowly they all turned round. Paula suppressed a gasp. She couldn't count the number of menacing figures which had crept up, unheard, behind them. All wearing Balaclavas and a neutral-coloured one-piece uniform which merged with the background.

51

'Erik . . . Landslide! Landslide! Landslide . . .'

'Roger.'

Satisfied that his message had got through, Tweed ran back from the Opel to the ridge where rows of men lay prone on the ground. Again he flopped between Newman and Marler. Norlin was still holding a restraining hand on Newman's shoulder.

Earlier, the final message from Tug Wilson had arrived.

'Targets stationary half a mile off shore. Moving in to intercept.'

Norlin had been crawling among his men, who

appeared to be divided into sections with separate tasks. He had whispered orders, then had returned to lie down behind Newman. Tweed whispered his own order to Paula who lay next to Newman.

'You stay ashore. That's an order.'

'I heard you,' was all she replied.

Tweed had borrowed Marler's night-glasses, had them now focused on a familiar tall, heavily built figure wearing gumboots and striding towards the last but one dinghy putting out to sea. He could even see the pince-nez at that short range as the figure climbed inside a large dinghy held steady by four other men.

'Dr Wand – I want you.'

Although said under his breath Paula heard the words and was startled. She had never heard such cold ferocity in Tweed's voice. His right hand gripped his Walther. He had taken a Dramamine thirty minutes before: this was one occasion when he didn't want to feel queasy.

The dinghy's outboard motor burst into life, the remaining three men jumped aboard as Dr Wand sat at the prow. The dinghy moved straight out to sea, was swallowed up in the fog, the red light at its stern vanishing. Norlin pressed his hand firmer on Newman's shoulder, an action which caused Paula to smile to herself. The Dane knew who was straining at the leash. She slipped her Browning out of her shoulder-bag, a slow movement to ensure Tweed wouldn't see her action.

A final large dinghy was being hauled down to the edge of the sea by five men, all with automatic weapons looped over their shoulders. Newman stiffened, turned to glare at the unseen face of Norlin.

'That's the one we're supposed to grab, for Christ's sake.'

'Have patience. The strategy has been carefully worked out. And pass this message to your friends. *Our* dinghies will have green lights. *Green . . .*'

Newman passed the message to Paula on his right as Tweed repeated the instruction to Marler who, in turn, told Butler and Nield. It was then when Tweed saw the point of Norlin's holding Newman back. As the five men went on hauling their dinghy seawards, six men wearing Balaclavas appeared like magic from behind a nearby dune.

'My men,' Norlin whispered.

Fascinated, Tweed watched through his glasses. The six men moved with such speed and so silently they were on top of Wand's thugs in seconds. Four of them were felled instantly with savage blows from hand-gun barrels on their skulls. They slumped to the beach. One thug had time to tear his automatic weapon from his shoulders. A knife flashed up in the hand of a Balaclava man, flashed down, and was thrust up to the hilt into the thug's chest. He fell back into the water.

More Balaclava-clad men appeared carrying large stretchers. By the time they arrived the unconscious men had their wrists handcuffed behind their backs, gags plastered over their mouths. Without ceremony they were lifted, dumped into the stretchers. The thug who had fought sprawled motionless on a stretcher, the knife handle still protruding. As the stretchers were carried swiftly away to one of the bungalows another man appeared, flashed a torch three times.

'All clear,' Norlin said in a normal voice. 'One section was told to check the bungalows. Any men inside could have shot us in the back. Bungalows empty.' He took his hand off Newman's shoulder. 'Go, boy!'

Newman took off like a greyhound, Smith & Wesson in hand as he ran down the south-west slope, followed by Marler, Tweed, Butler and Nield. Tweed showed surprising agility as he slithered and hurtled towards the beach, overtaking Marler.

They reached the dinghy as Norlin drew level with

Tweed. The Dane switched off the red light at the stern, removed the bulb, replaced it by another, switched it on. Green light. The others were aboard as he attached a small metallic disc with rubber suckers to the side of the craft well away from the outboard.

'A bleeper,' he explained quickly. 'Range twenty miles. You won't hear it, but we will if we have to come looking for you. As you'll see, there will be plenty of us to keep you company.'

Tweed, seated on a plank at the prow, glanced back. The beach was crowded with Balaclava men carrying a fleet of dinghies to the water's edge. Marler fired the outboard motor. As it burst into life a sixth figure climbed aboard and they were moving. Tweed glanced back again and swore under his breath. Seated on the rearmost plank next to Marler was Paula. She lifted her left hand and waggled it, giving him a little wave.

On the bridge of the *Mao III* Kim stood beside Captain Welensky, who for the first time sensed nervousness in the Chinese, although his face remained impassive. They were hardly moving and behind them the *Yenan* was also nearly motionless.

'Well,' the captain told Kim with unconcealed satisfaction, 'we have made our correct landfall. The radio messages from the shore prove it.'

'No more than what I would have expected,' snapped Kim.

'You sound tired,' Welensky ribbed him.

'I sense danger.' Again Kim snapped.

Welensky followed as Kim moved towards the weapons-control complex. Kim gave the order over the fixed microphone.

'Prepare missiles for launching. Red alert.'

Standing in front of a console, Kim inserted a key. The

metal lid slid out of sight. A row of inset buttons, each a different colour, appeared. He only had to pass one and a missile would be launched.

When he had given the order two flaps near the prow had opened back, exposing the mouths of the slim silos housing twelve missiles. Kim remained by the console, hands clasped behind his back.

'Are you crazy?' Welensky roared. 'We are just off the coast of Denmark – not out in the middle of the bloody Pacific.'

'Has the retractable staircase been dropped?' Kim asked, his voice now calm. 'It must be in place for General Chang to come aboard. I will receive him. Kindly leave the bridge.'

'I am the skipper of this vessel,' Welensky said quietly. 'So long as I am, I remain on the bridge.'

'If you insist.'

Kim decided it was pointless having a confrontation with Welensky at this critical moment. Kim was quite capable of taking control of the ship. They would cut Welensky's throat, weight him, and throw him overboard on the return journey to Cam Ranh Bay in Vietnam.

Peering out of the narrow window almost flush with the curved deck, Kim saw a large man mounting the staircase over the hull. He opened a door and bowed low as Dr Wand came on to the bridge.

'Welcome aboard my most humble ship, General.'

Seated at the rear of the dinghy alongside Marler, who had one hand on the tiller, Paula gripped the underside of the plank tightly. The nightmare was starting all over again.

She recalled her lonely vigil at Lymington marina. Dense drifting fog. The terrifying incident aboard the *Holsten*. Again, dense swirling fog on the Elbe. As the dinghy moved straight out to sea the same atmosphere overwhelmed her – more fog, drifting slowly, assuming horrific shapes. She peered into it, convinced that something was close – and not one of Norlin's dinghies.

The fog cleared away briefly. She heard the chug-chug of a ship's engine on the starboard bow, stiffened. Marler whipped up his rifle. Tweed was the first to see clearly the launch, slowing down: the tall figure wearing a roll-necked white sweater. Dave Lane. He shouted at Marler.

'Lower that blasted rifle. These are friends.'

'Care to come aboard?' Lane enquired. 'Told you I would be coming south from the harbour to join the party.'

'Yes, we would indeed,' Tweed said with feeling. 'Get us out of this damned toy boat . . .'

He was the first on the launch's deck and helped Paula to come aboard. The others followed and then helped Lane and two of his crew to haul the dinghy aboard. Tweed became very active.

'We have to replace that light of yours with our green light. Immediately! It identifies us to a swarm of Danish marksmen floating around in dinghies.' While Lane removed the green bulb and substituted it for his own light, Tweed forced the beeper device off the side of the dinghy, wetted the suckers in the sea, attached it to the hull of the launch.

'A powerboat is roaring around somewhere in the fog,' reported Lane. 'One of your Danish friends' boats?'

'No. Certainly not as far as I'm aware.'

Tweed found the news disturbing. The launch was under way again as he asked his question.

'Did you hear a light aircraft flying down the coast?'

'Yes, I did. I assumed it was checking out the lie of the land. Again, belonging to the Danish lot.'

'Norlin – the head of the strike force – decided not to fly in choppers until later so as not to alert the opposition.

I'm sure he wouldn't risk a light aircraft. It flew about fifty feet above the colony of bungalows – where we expect the Stealth ships to land more saboteurs.'

'So, a mystery powerboat, preceded by mystery plane. A weird business,' Lane reflected. 'And I think one of your people has seen something . . .'

Tweed swung round. Paula had positioned herself at the prow of the launch. She was alternately pointing to something in the fog, looking over her shoulder to beckon to Tweed. He ran forward with Marler at his heels.

'There's something large and very close.' She saw the sceptical expression on the face of Lane who had joined them. 'Don't look at me like that! Use your bloody eyes . . .'

The fog drifted away. A huge grey shape like that of a half-submerged giant whale appeared. Standing on the curved hull Dr Wand stared down at them. He snatched an automatic weapon from a man close to him, aimed it point-blank at Tweed.

Everything happened like a film running fast. The sound of a powerboat roaring in on the port side, stopping suddenly. A second before Wand sprayed them with a hail of bullets, Tweed fired his Walther, gripped in both hands, twice. Wand's right arm fell limp, the weapon tumbled to the deck. The shots flew harmlessly into the air. There were two more shots fired from the direction where the powerboat had stopped. Wand was hurled backwards against the low-profile bridge.

'That was a .45 gun,' said Newman, now behind them.

The powerboat's engine started up. As Tweed glanced to his left it disappeared into the fog, only its wake visible as it headed towards the shore. Lane grasped Tweed's arm.

'Look! To starboard. The *Minotaur* . . .'

The frigate was less than a quarter of a mile away where the fog had temporarily cleared. It was racing forward as they heard Wilson's order to the Stealth ship magnified over a powerful tannoy.

'Lane, stand well clear. Now!' The launch was under way at high speed in seconds. At the prow they hung on to the rail to avoid being flung overboard. The tannoy blast was addressing the Stealth vessels now in Wilson's commaning voice. 'Heave to. We are coming aboard. Any hostile act will receive a hundred-fold retaliation . . .'

Inside the bridge of the *Mao III* Welensky was shouting at Kim, who stood in front of the console.

'It's over. Keep away from that goddamn console.'

'Prepare to fire,' Kim ordered.

The *Minotaur*, which had been broadside on to the *Mao*, was turning swiftly, presenting now only the smallest possible target, its prow. Kim jabbed his thick thumb down to press the button. Welensky's weighty bulk collided against him, knocking him away from the control panel. It only took seconds. A knife appeared in Kim's hand, was rammed deep into Welensky's side. He staggered away. Kim jabbed his thumb down on the button – but it *was* seconds later. The missile soared out of its silo, sped towards its pre-selected target, a target which had now moved its position.

The missile exploded under the sea, fifty yards or so away from the *Minotaur*. Tug Wilson didn't hestitate. In a calm brisk voice he gave the order.

'Fire!'

A single missile whooshed through the foggy air, landed on the prow of the *Mao*. A perfect hit. On top of the bank of missile silos. There was a tremendous explosion. The shockwave swept across the sea, shaking the launch where Paula was hurrying back to the stern, gripping the handrail, followed by Tweed and Marler. Butler and Nield had already arrived there.

During the frantic struggle with Welensky, Kim had forgotten Wand was still outside, perched on the hull. Despite four bullets hitting him, he was hauling his way back to the door leading to the bridge as the missile landed.

The explosion shattered the whole Stealth vessel aft of the bridge. As Paula stared through her Balaclava she saw Wand caught in the ferocious spearhead of flames shooting skywards. He staggered, alight from the feet up to his waist. Waving his powerful arms frantically, he pirouetted with the searing pain. Losing all sense of direction, he staggered into the inferno, vanished.

'Burnt out,' Newman commented. 'And a damn good job too.'

The section of the *Mao* aft of the bridge broke off, sank between the waves. There was a sinister hissing sound as the sea quenched fire with a temperature of over one thousand degrees. The whole vessel began to turn turtle. Several of Norlin's dinghies full of armed men, ready to board, had turned away, speeding across the sea. Behind them the *Mao*'s bridge went down first, hoisting the stern high above the water. Then the entire vessel plunged into the depths like a rocket diving. The sea boiled and large waves spread out in all directions. Then it was suddenly quiet as the sea settled again. Quiet, but only for a moment.

The titanic explosion had dissipated the fog and now the smaller Stealth vessel appeared. The *Minotaur* was moving at high speed, taking up a position behind the ship. The bullhorn voice of Tug Wilson boomed out over the tannoy again, hard and demanding.

'Continue on your present course. East. At top speed.'

Another missile was fired, aimed deliberately to miss the Stealth vessel, landing in the water well clear of its port bow. Inside the low-profile bridge the *Yenan* was skippered by a Balt. The Chinese commissar who had stood by his side was below decks, trying to pacify his panic-stricken passengers.

The Balt didn't hesitate. Witnessing the destruction of the *Mao III* was enough encouragement. The missile added to his terror. He screamed the order to the engine room.

'Full speed ahead! Now!'

It never occurred to him where this action would take him to. Aboard the launch Tweed blessed Tug Wilson. He had remembered his request for prisoners. The *Yenan* shot forward, slicing its way through the calm sea. In only a short time the Balt looked ahead and a fresh fear gripped him as he saw where he was going.

Before the battle started Tweed had given Philip Cardon special instructions. He must stay ashore, remain on the ridge where he had an overall view of the beach.

The Squirrel had not waited idly. Taking out a capacious handkerchief, he had scooped up handfuls of sand, dropped them on the cloth, and had then tied it up by the corners.

Completing this task, he had settled down to wait. He had heard the terrific detonation out at sea – so strong it had dispersed the fog and blown up curtains of sand along the beach. It was minutes later when he saw the dinghy racing ashore. He lifted the glasses Tweed had left him, focused them. From a photograph he recognized the sole occupant – Jules Starmberg.

Realizing it was all over, Starmberg had thrown overboard the two other occupants of the dinghy and had headed for the shore – for escape. He jumped out of the dinghy as it hit the beach and ran up the side of the ridge about ten yards to the left of where Cardon lay. The Squirrel ran along the top of the ridge in a crouch. He arrived just in time to see Starmberg standing by a Volvo hidden in a similar gulley to the one where Newman and the others had parked their own cars.

Starmberg held car keys in his hand, was inserting one when he heard Cardon behind him. He swung round as Cardon socked him on the back of the head with his makeshift sandbag. The Luxemburger collapsed. Within five minutes Cardon had Starmberg slumped on the floor of his Ford Sierra behind the front seats. He stared down at the unconscious figure, wrists handcuffed behind his back, a gag inserted into his mouth.

'Justice, mate,' Cardon said aloud. 'You did that to our Paula. Enjoy yourself . . .'

He was back in his old position, lying behind the top of the ridge when he saw a sight which made him wonder if he could believe his own eyes. The *Yenan* – its engines so silent he had no warning of what was coming – raced ashore at full speed, its momentum carrying it through the shallows and half-way up the beach.

Smaller than the *Mao*, it was still a large vessel. Cardon stared as the huge whale-like shape, its prow carving a deep fissure in the sand, rocketed ashore. For a moment it remained upright – half on the beach, half in the sea. Then it keeled over to port with an earth-shaking smack and lay still.

A fleet of dinghies with green lights and full of men with Balaclavas landed on either side. Norlin's troops stood waiting and as dazed passengers emerged they were handcuffed. Any resistance was discouraged with a tap on the head with a gun barrel.

Tweed's launch appeared, paused off shore. Tweed and the others were so anxious to reach land they stepped into the sea and trudged the last few yards on to the beach. Cardon ran to greet Tweed who had Paula clutching his arm.

'I have Starmberg trussed up like a Christmas turkey.'

'Christmas has come early this year,' Tweed replied.

516

'Landslide . . .'

Otto Kuhlmann had acted swiftly, ruthlessly, on receiving the codeword. In the middle of the night his teams of armed men surrounded the new colony of houses to the west of Blankenese.

They had arrested twenty men aged between twenty-five and forty and two women. A huge cache of arms and explosives had been found – together with aerial photos of Hamburg and Frankfurt airports. Their papers had been checked and found to be excellent forgeries.

'You are charged with being accessories to the attempted murder of Hugo Westendorf and others,' Kuhlmann had informed them.

'That should hold them behind bars for a very long time,' he had told an aide with relish.

'Landslide . . .'

Benoit in Brussels had acted with equal speed once he had been given the codeword. At the same hour chosen by Kuhlmann armed detectives in convoys of cars had sealed off the new village of Vieux-Fontaine outside Ghent.

Twenty-five people, including three women, had been hauled out of bed. After they were taken away in police vans the houses had been turned over. More weapons, more explosives had been found – again with detailed aerial photographs of Zaventem and Liège airports, so detailed they gave the lengths of individual runways.

'Sabotage and terrorism are the charges,' Benoit had

told his prisoners. 'You will be our guests for an eternity.'

'Landslide . . .'

A large force of Special Branch officers had raided Moor's Landing at 3 a.m. Ironically, the assault team had come up the Beaulieu River and ashore at the landing stage – the route Tweed was convinced had been used by Stealth ships to bring in the infiltrators. Before dawn twenty-eight adults, including two women, aged between thirty and thirty-five, were taken aboard a fleet of vehicles driven in by road and disguised as tradesmen's vans. Detailed plans of London Airport, Gatwick, and Standstead were found, plus bombs with timer mechanisms and weapons.

The Special Branch officer in command made no comment.

53

'Well, that cleans up that,' Newman remarked.

'No, it doesn't,' Tweed contradicted him. 'We still have to unmask the identity of Vulcan – probably Wand's most dangerous agent in Europe. Also we have to detect the assassin – the woman who injects cyanide without a second thought.'

They had driven through the night after the climax on the Danish beach – driving south across the Danish border back into Germany. In the early hours of the morning they had arrived back at the Four Seasons in Hamburg.

Paula, Newman, Butler, Nield and Cardon were now assembled in Tweed's old room overlooking the Binnen

Alster. It was noon and the only person who seemed fresh was Tweed, who had got up early.

'I went to Berliner Tor,' he told them. 'Thanked Otto and phoned Inspector Nielsen, Benoit and the Special Branch in London. Also Commander Noble at the Admiralty. He has flown a team of experts to examine the *Yenan*. The Danes have been very co-operative. A huge lifting dock is on its way across the North Sea to collect the *Yenan*.'

'The energy of the man,' commented Paula, who had dark circles under her eyes.

'Now you've eaten' – Tweed waved to the relics of a room service meal on several trolley tables – 'we must leave at once for the airport. We have a flight to catch home.'

'Where maybe we can get a rest?' Marler suggested.

'Suit yourself,' Tweed told him. 'I've phoned London Airport and there will be cars waiting to take us straight down to the New Forest.'

'Why there?' Paula enquired.

'Because I also phoned Copenhagen and spoke to reception at the d'Angleterre Hotel. They confirmed the Burgoyne Quartet checked out yesterday afternoon. Special Branch told me *Leopard's Leap* and *The Last Haven* – Burgoyne and Fanshawe's homes – have people at home. That is where we will expose Vulcan. And find our murderess. Not a pleasant woman.'

A December chill gripped the New Forest. Paula noted that as darkness fell mist trails crept among the bare trees. She shivered as Tweed drove along the drive of *The Last Haven*. There were lights in the Scandinavian-style house.

In the rear of the car sat Butler and Nield. They had all surrendered their weapons to Tweed at the Four Seasons on arrival. He had taken them to Berliner Tor, had handed them over to Kuhlmann. He had also arranged for fresh weapons to be supplied to everyone – except himself – as they drove away from London Airport. Paula, who sat beside Tweed, asked her question as they proceeded up the drive.

'Where are Newman, Marler and Cardon going to now?'

'Why, to the Brigadier's residence next door. I've issued an invitation for him to join us. With the glamorous Lee Holmes, of course.'

'Of course,' she replied acidly.

'Had to hold our little tête-à-tête at one of the houses,' Tweed continued in buoyant mood as he pulled up.

'You think you know who Vulcan is?' she asked.

'Yes, I do.'

'And the murderess?'

'Again, yes.'

Paula restrained her cat-like curiosity. In any case, she was sure Tweed wouldn't tell her anything at this stage. As he reached out to press the bell the door swung inward. Willie Fanshawe stood there in a smart but rumpled navy blue blazer and grey slacks. With his figure, Paula was thinking, he'd never look immaculate. He beamed with pleasure, stepped forward and kissed Paula on the cheek. 'I say! What a bit of luck. Completed the circle, haven't we? Eh, Tweed? You met us here. Then we hopped all round Europe. Now, back again to base! Must say I'm entranced to see you. Bit of a flattener – getting back to the New Forest. Wonder why they call it that? It's an old forest! Do come in. What about your two chaps out there?'

Butler and Nield had climbed out of the car. They made no move towards the house. They'd received their instructions from Tweed – patrol the grounds behind the house.

'I think they'd sooner get a breath of fresh air,' Tweed replied. 'They've been driving for hours,' he lied.

'Then come on in you two.' Willie took Paula by the arm. Beyond the heavy front door they walked straight into the L-shaped living-room furnished in Scandinavian style. To Paula it seemed years since they had last entered this house. 'Sit yourself down on the couch,' Willie urged as he relieved her of her trench coat.

'Helen!' he called out. 'You'll never guess who has just turned up. Close your eyes and I'll give you three tries.'

The door from the kitchen opened and Helen strode in, her fountain-pen and a notebook in her hand. Clad in a grey cardigan half zipped up to the neck, she wore a white blouse underneath with a mandarin collar. Her slim slacks had a razor-edge crease and were also grey. She had her eyes wide open. The Grey Lady, Paula thought.

'Don't play silly games, Willie,' Helen chided him. Her cool eyes passed over Paula, fastened on Tweed. She went towards him, holding out her slim hand. 'How very nice to see you again. What would you like to drink?'

Tweed, who had refused Willie's offer to take his trench coat, saying they wouldn't be staying long, clasped her hand. It was firm and cool. With her back to the others, she gave him a secret smile, then turned and sat down by the side of Paula on the couch. She waved her pad and pen.

'Shopping list. Someone has to see there's food in the house.'

'I hope you don't mind,' Tweed said, addressing Willie, 'but I asked Bob Newman to bring Burgoyne and Lee Holmes round. A sort of reunion . . .'

The doorbell rang as he was speaking. Willie hurried to open the door and Tweed accompanied him.

'Capital idea,' Willie enthused. 'We've hardly seen the Brig. and his *femme fatale* since we got back.'

Outside Newman had swung round his Volvo so it

pointed back the way he had come. In the shadows of the house he noticed a Mercedes – smeared with mud – was parked. Tweed's Ford Escort stood out of the way in front of the door which now opened.

Burgoyne, dressed in country clothes, stepped out of the back of the Volvo as Lee alighted on the other side. He looked grim and not at all pleased. Before calling for them Newman had dropped Marler and Cardon on the road – they were now concealed among the trees facing the entrance to the drive.

'Tweed, darling!'

Lee, wearing a green off-the-shoulder creation, rushed forward, hugged and kissed him, her strong hands gripping his shoulders.

'How absolutely marvellous!' she told him. 'When we can, let's go off somewhere together for the weekend,' she whispered.

'It's something to think about,' Tweed replied.

She had an arm round his waist as they entered the living-room. Paula glanced at Helen seated next to her, saw her lips curl briefly. These two women are not all that fond of each other, she reflected.

'Double Scotch. Neat,' rapped out Burgoyne when asked what he'd drink.

'Why not champers for everyone?' Lee suggested, dragging a chair close to Paula. 'I could nip back for a bottle. This calls for a celebration.'

Burgoyne was sitting in a carver chair in a corner where he could see everyone. Newman perched on the arm of the couch between Paula and Lee. Tweed, still standing, thrust both hands into the pockets of his trench coat, the stance his old colleagues at Scotland Yard would have recognized.

'I am afraid this gathering is no cause for celebration, Lee,' he began. 'It is an investigation into the identity of a multiple murderess and a professional traitor.'

*   *   *

522

The atmosphere changed instantly, became tense, disturbing, menacing. Burgoyne was the first to react, his voice harsh as he gripped his glass of whisky.

'Tweed, what is all this bloody nonsense?'

'Don't you know?'

Tweed stared at the Brigadier, who glared back at him with an expression of ferocity. He drank half the contents of his glass, placed it on a side table, uncrossing his legs.

'No, I don't. I think you owe us an apology.'

'I think, instead, an explanation might be more useful.'

Tweed paused as Lee produced her jewelled holder. With trembling fingers she inserted a cigarette, then perched it at the corner of her full red-lipped mouth. She held it there with two fingers of her left hand.

'Let's take the identity of the multiple murderess first,' Tweed went on in a conversational tone. 'So far the following people have been murdered by the injection of cyanide. A girl called Hilary Vane as she disembarked at London Airport from a plane flying in from Washington. Still in England, Irene Andover was finished off with a cyanide injection – that came before the murder of Vane. Now, we move to Brussels. A cab driver was also killed by the same method – injection of cyanide with some sort of hypodermic. Vane and the cab driver were killed by a woman. The same woman then took the dead cab driver's vehicle to Liège where she drove down and killed Sir Gerald Andover. Later, I'm sure . . .'

'This is quite beastly,' Lee protested. There was a steely note in her voice. 'Do we have to go on?'

'We do,' Tweed continued relentlessly. 'Later, I am sure, the same woman finished off Lucie Delvaux with a cyanide injection after one hand had been amputated. Then a man called Joseph Mordaunt was murdered in the Parc d'Egmont. Again with a cyanide injection.'

Helen had been scribbling down the names with her fountain-pen on her pad. She counted.

'My God! You're talking about at least six murders,' she commented.

'Which is why I used the phrase multiple murderess. And I found it significant that two of them took place within a stone's throw of the Hilton – the cab driver in the Marolles, Mordaunt in the garden behind the hotel. Where both of you were staying.'

'Surely you are not suggesting that one of us—' Lee began.

'Not suggesting,' Tweed rapped back. 'I am accusing.' He turned his attention to Lee. 'The London Airport murder, that of the cab driver, and Mordaunt – all these suggest a very specially designed hypodermic was used. Something which outwardly was an everyday item. Lee, could I look at your cigarette holder?'

'Certainly not! The jewels fall out easily if carelessly handled.'

Paula felt her face with one hand, smoothing it over her complexion. A moment before Tweed had taken his left hand out of his pocket, rubbed the side of his nose with a finger, then shoved his hand back inside the pocket. The signal he had arranged with Paula.

'I need something to freshen myself up,' she said. 'If either of you could give me some Guerlain Samsara – my favourite perfume – I'm sure that would do the trick. Lee, I believe you use it. I caught a waft when you were playing cards in the Hilton.'

'I borrowed it from Helen.'

'I'll get you my bottle.'

Helen jumped up, left the room by another door close to the kitchen. She returned with the bottle and sat down again as she handed it to Paula. Thanking her, Paula applied a small quantity under her ears, then returned the bottle to Helen who placed it on a side table.

'That's what we were looking for,' Tweed told Helen. 'You see, when two policemen opened the closed cab containing the driver's body there was a strong aroma of perfume. Yours. Guerlain Samsara.'

'Very clever, Mr Tweed.'

As she spoke, Helen placed the cap on her pen, an action Tweed had seen before. But this time she then turned the cap, screwing it on tight. With her palm she pressed the end and a needle shot out. With her left hand she grabbed Paula's wrist.

'Anyone who moves towards me kills her,' she said in a cold voice, her grey eyes blank, devoid of any human emotion.

Paula whipped over her other hand, grasped Helen's hand holding the hypodermic. A tigerish struggle to the death began. Helen stood up and Paula jerked herself upright with her opponent. The side table went over, the bottle smashed on the floor. The two women were facing each other, fighting savagely, their bodies moving like two manic wrestlers.

Newman tried to intervene but the hypodermic was flailing about unpredictably. Paula was surprised by Helen's lithe strength. She hung on to the wrist, forcing it away from herself. Helen aimed a kick at Paula's right leg, but only grazed her. Steadily Helen forced down the needle nearer to Paula's body. Another side table went flying. The needle came closer still to Paula. Then Paula used her free hand to grasp Helen by the throat in a strangler's grip. She dug her nails into Helen's neck.

Helen made a supreme effort to thrust the needle into her antagonist. Paula diverted the thrust. The needle sank deep into Helen's chest and – involuntarily – Paula pressed the plunger. Helen's whole body stiffened. She stopped struggling, sagged over the back of the couch, lay quite still.

Tweed glanced at Burgoyne who now stood by, staring at the corpse.

'Cyanosis, Brigadier. You recognize the symptoms?'

54

'Helen! Of all people! I can't believe it.' Willie went to a double-doored wall cupboard, opened the left-hand panel. 'I need a pick-me-up. This is just too awful . . .'

He poured himself a glass of Cyprus sherry, perched the bottle back on the shelf, leaving the door half open as he stumbled back to a chair, sat heavily in it. He drank half the glass, looked round in dazed fashion.

'Sorry. Anyone else need a drink?'

Heads were shaken as Paula walked with stiff legs to a different couch. As she sat down Newman joined her, put his arm round her tense body. Her breasts were heaving with the effort.

'No,' Burgoyne said, seating himself again in the carver in the corner, 'I'm not familiar with the symptoms. At least I wasn't until now.'

Already Helen's lips were a bluish tinge and the same colour was spreading to her stiffened face. Willie flapped a hand.

'Can't just leave her like that. I'll move her . . .'

'*Don't!*'

It was Tweed's order. He still stood with hands inside his trench-coat pockets. A half-minute earlier he had run close to Paula, but, like the others, couldn't find a way to disentangle the flurry of arms which had waved about.

'Nothing must be touched until the police are called – but that can wait for a few minutes longer. Brigadier, ever heard of someone called Vulcan?' Tweed asked.

'I believe I have. In Hong Kong.'

'Ah, the Far East,' Tweed recalled. 'Where long ago you went missing for four months behind the Chinese lines in Korea. What did Mao's lot do when they captured you?'

'I say, hold on there!' Willie protested. 'We've just had a frightful tragedy. The Brig. doesn't like those days being recalled. Show some sensitivity.'

'Mao's crowd didn't do anything to me.' Burgoyne gazed straight at Tweed. 'Because I was never captured. Went to ground until I could get away. You seem to know a devil of a lot.'

Lee had collapsed back into her chair. Her teeth chattered. Tweed sensed she was on the verge of hysteria. She sat playing with her cigarette holder.

'They say it's rained non-stop while we were away. All the rivers are swollen.'

It was the sort of remark people sometimes make when they are excessively upset. She suddenly burst into tears and Paula hurried over, kneeling beside her. Tweed waited until she had quietened down, then swung round to look down at Willie.

'You have heard of Vulcan?'

'One of the old Roman or Greek gods. Made thunderbolts for Jove . . .'

'And you made them for Dr Wand.'

'Sorry. Not with you.'

'Willie, remember that chat we had in the Sambri bar at the Four Seasons? The topic of Brigadier Burgoyne came up. I listened while you told me that what he doesn't love is the present state of England. You went on about the welfare state, about the young wanting everything handed to them on a plate. A good dose of iron government is what is needed – the implication being Communist discipline . . .'

'Tommy-rot!' Burgoyne blazed.

'Let me finish. Willie remembered now and again to say

527

these were your views. But he'd had a lot to drink and really let his tongue run away. It sounded to me that Willie was expressing *his own* attitudes – camouflaging them as the Brigadier's. But, Willie, you were just a bit to *vehement* in expressing those views – which are your own. Because you are Vulcan.'

'I'm confused. Need another drop of the good stuff . . .'

He stood up, walked unsteadily towards the two-door cupboard. Reaching inside, he unlooped the Heckler and Koch sub-machine-gun concealed inside the left-hand door, turned round, suddenly alert, and aimed it point-blank at Paula.

'First person who moves and she gets the whole mag.'

Everyone froze. Especially Tweed. The stock of the sub-machine-gun was collapsed but the muzzle stayed aimed at Paula. The Heckler and Koch: its performance rattled through Tweed's mind.

A 9mm weapon, it had a rate of fire of six hundred and fifty rounds a minute. A range of almost five hundred feet. It would obliterate Paula. She stayed on her knees, staring over her shoulder.

'You are Vulcan,' Tweed said quietly.

'Key to the whole operation – which you've smashed. But don't worry, we'll be back. I have my contacts. And now I'm leaving. By the front door. Anyone who opens it within five minutes gets the full burst.'

His genial 'favourite uncle' face was etched as though in stone. Willie backed towards the front door, opened it, slipped outside, closed it. Newman, holding his Smith & Wesson, ran to the door, listened. He heard the engine of the Mercedes start up, speed off down the drive. He opened the door just in time to see the car turn left – towards Beaulieu. He ran to the Volvo, jumped inside, started the engine, his gun on the seat by his side, and raced down the drive.

*   *   *

Fanshawe saw the lights of the car pursuing him, pressed the button which automatically slid back the sun roof.

Drifts of mist and cold air flooded in but Fanshawe turned the heaters full on. An opportunity might come to ambush his pursuer. If so, he could stand on the seat, poke his head and shoulders out of the opening, and look down on his target. The sub-machine-gun lay on the seat beside him.

As they raced along the deserted winding road through the forest Newman became aware the temperature had nosedived. Ice was forming on his windscreen. He set his wipers going, turned his headlights full on. This was dangerous weather – one unnoticed patch of ice on the road and he'd end up against the trunk of a tree.

Fanshawe was driving like a maniac, increasing speed all the time. A heavy white frost crusted the dead bracken, coated the bare branches. They had left the forest behind and with a few hundred yards between them Newman passed Hatchet Pond. The moon had come out and he saw the surface of the small lake was coated with a sheet of ice. No weather for moving at such speeds.

Fanshawe reached the approaches to Beaulieu, tore down the hill. To Newman's horror he saw two boy cyclists on the diabolical bend where the road to Buckler's Hard turned off to the right up Bunker's Hill. Without reducing speed, Fanshawe skidded round, missing the cyclists by inches as he roared off up Bunker's Hill. The cyclists, unhurt but terrified, had fallen off on to the verge.

'Stupid cretins!' Fanshawe shouted, waving one clenched fist while he held the wheel with the other hand.

'Cold-blooded bastard!' Newman growled to himself.

He took the bend more slowly, accelerated as he climbed the curving hill. A minute later he was on the level stretch of lonely country road. Fanshawe's red tail-lights were disappearing as Newman rammed down his foot. He shot forward like a rocket, closely watching the road surface at the limit of his lights.

Fanshawe had turned down the private road to Buckler's Hard when Newman reached that point and also turned. He pressed his foot down harder, closing the gap. Ahead, Fanshawe was skidding round corners. Why was he heading for Buckler's Hard?

Newman controlled the wheel with one hand. With the other he held his Smith & Wesson, rested his arm on his open window, fired two shots over the roof of the Mercedes. As he'd hoped, Fanshawe panicked, drove even faster and Newman fired one more shot, again aimed over the roof.

Inside the Mercedes Fanshawe kept looking in his rear-view mirror, checking how close his pursuer was. His concentration on this fear made him forget the speed at which he was travelling. He arrived at the anchorage and only then stared ahead in horror.

Newman was reducing speed, swinging his Volvo to a stop by the boatyard when the Mercedes reached the ramp leading down to the river. *All the rivers are swollen.* Newman recalled Lee Holmes' words as he saw how high the water had reached and the speed of the current flowing down from Beaulieu upstream.

Fanshawe jammed on the brakes. Too late. He was on the downward-sloping ramp which was covered with shot ice. The Mercedes aquaplaned – rocketed forward at high speed into the river. It was half-submerged when Newman jumped out after grabbing a torch. He held that in his left hand and his Smith & Wesson in the other hand as he stood on the edge of the bank, switched on the powerful beam.

The car seemed to suspend itself as Newman directed his torch beam on to the vehicle. Fanshawe had climbed on to his seat, thrusting his wide shoulders up through the open roof, holding the sub-machine-gun. His mass of

530

white hair was dishevelled, his voice hoarse as he called out.

'Throw me a rope, Newman, or I'll gun you down.'

'You won't – then you'd have no hope of surviving. So drop that weapon.'

Fanshawe's nerveless hands let go of the machine-gun and it fell back inside the car. Waving his empty hands, Fanshawe began pleading.

'For God's sake throw me a rope. There are lifebelts on the shore.'

'I might consider rescuing you – provided you answer truthfully one question.'

'Hurry up, man! I'm going down . . .'

'The truth, remember. I'll know if you're lying. Did you pass on Dr Wand's orders at any time to kill the victims?'

'I had to,' Fanshawe gabbled. 'I was his deputy. I had no choice . . .'

'I see,' Newman replied in a hard voice. 'You were obeying orders. I seem to have heard that excuse before. I have now considered rescuing you – and decided not to.'

'I can't swim!' Fanshawe screeched. 'In the name of humanity . . .'

The Mercedes had propelled itself quite a distance. The rear was in the water, the front resting on dark muddy ooze, swamp-like. The car was tilted, its rear lower than its front. Then the front sank deeper and more rapidly into the slime. The Mercedes was now submerged almost to the rim of the roof.

Newman stood quite still, his torch beam still shining on Fanshawe who was screaming a mixture of obscenities and pleas. The anchorage was deserted on that eerie December night. Near by a power boat was tied up – Fanshawe's intended means of escape. Vertical trails of motionless ice mist hung over the anchorage.

Newman made no response to the desperate cries for

531

help. This sadist had been instrumental in murdering innocent men and women. The entire vehicle sank lower, watery mud creeping over the roof, sliding down inside the opening. The last sight Newman had of Fanshawe was hands waving as the mud deluged inside the vehicle. The hands, the crown of white hair vanished a moment after Fanshawe let out a fearful gurgle of pure terror. Bubbles appeared where the car had gone down and swiftly disappeared, caught up in the flow of the river heading for the Solent. The silence was total.

Epilogue

'First, how did you realize Helen – and not Lee – was the murderess?' asked Paula.

Monica, Newman, Marler, Butler, Nield, and Cardon were all assembled in Tweed's office at Park Crescent several days later. They listened, drinking the coffee supplied by Monica as she turned up the central heating. It was an arctic December day outside.

'Temperament. That was the first clue,' Tweed explained as he relaxed in his swivel chair. 'To kill at least six people – three of them women – by injecting them with cyanide took someone pretty cold-blooded. I know both women had briefly been actresses, but the more I got to know Lee the more she seemed genuinely a fun person, as she called herself.'

'Whereas Helen was cool as ice,' Paula commented.

'Exactly. Then there was the puzzle of the everyday instrument which was a disguised hypodermic – designed back in Hong Kong, I imagine. It could have been Lee's jewelled cigarette holder, but she was too *obvious* with it.'

'Obvious?' Paula queried.

'Yes – always waving it about, drawing attention to her precious possession. Again it was a process of elimination. Whereas Helen Claybourne only used her fat fountain-pen now and again.'

'And what about Vulcan?' Newman asked. 'I thought it was Burgoyne.'

'So did I for a while. Two factors made me doubtful. At the MOD an officer called Fieldway rather overdid hinting that he was a suspect character. When the Burgoyne Quartet boarded the same plane as we did for Brussels how did the Brigadier know we'd be taking that flight?'

'Well, how did he?' Paula asked impatiently.

'He could only have known because someone at London Airport had been pressured by the MOD to inform them when I booked a flight. That someone had to be Jim Corcoran, the chief security officer. I noticed Corcoran seemed embarrassed when I arrived – even tried to avoid me. I detected the same kind of discomfort in his attitude which Fieldway had shown.'

'Was that conclusive?' Marler enquired.

'No. But as I explained when we were in the New Forest recently, Willie was a little too vehement in his anti-British views. Belatedly he attributed them to Burgoyne to put me off the track.'

'And what part did Burgoyne himself play?' Marler persisted.

'After Newman drove off in pursuit of Willie I had a chat with Burgoyne on his own at *Leopard's Leap*. He has been working for Military Intelligence for years – trying to trap Dr Wand. Hence the MOD's co-operation with him. He decided I seemed to be having better luck, so he attached himself to us. Hence the Burgoyne Quartet's repeat appearances wherever we went.'

'But what about that mysterious light aircraft and then the powerboat which appeared later when we were tackling the *Mao* in Jutland?' asked Newman.

'That was Burgoyne. Again, he'd used his muscle to get Nielsen to tell him where I'd gone. Nielsen tried to warn me, but the radio connection broke down. Burgoyne can fly, hired a plane at Esbjerg Airport, flew down over the beach to do a recce. I told him off about that and he had the grace to apologize.'

'And the powerboat?' Newman asked again.

'That also had Burgoyne aboard. He is convinced Dr Wand was a General Chang, Chief of Staff to Cardon's General Li Yun at Lop Nor. After tracking Wand for all those years he was determined to kill him. He fired the two shots after I'd fired at Wand. A .45 you said, Bob, and you were right. The Brigadier takes some satisfaction from having put two bullets into him. Although Dr Wand would have been burnt to a crisp anyway. Talking about burning – Nielsen phoned to say the house where Paula was held had been totally destroyed by fire. The remains of two bodies – one of them presumably Dr Hyde – were found in the ashes of the basement. A real cremation.'

'You do have a graphic way of expressing yourself,' Paula commented.

'They were evil men. Wand's entire apparatus – which might not have been activated for years – has been eliminated. The Moonglow organizations have also been closed down all over Europe and in Hong Kong. And Jules Starmberg is singing like the proverbial bird.'

'At least there was no problem in getting him through security at Hamburg and London airports,' Paula recalled.

'Kuhlmann was again co-operative – escorting us so we bypassed all normal checks. Jim Corcoran seemed only too glad to perform the same service at London

Airport. I think he was relieved to make up for tricking me earlier. Not that he had any choice.'

'And any news of Mrs Garnett, late of Moor's Landing?' Newman asked.

'Yes. I advised Stanstead, the Chief Constable, to check all the local graveyards. Sure enough one had been disturbed – a grave, I mean. They dug up a few feet of soil and found the poor old soul lying face-down on top of a coffin. Her skull had been split. Barton, the phoney estate agent, and the other Moor's Landing occupants are being charged as accomplices to murder. I don't think they wanted a fresh body floating in the Solent.'

'Moonglow was some sort of cover organization then?' Paula queried.

'It was exactly that. Accounts going through the books have already found Moonglow was laundering huge sums of money.' Tweed looked grim. 'It was a vile business. Under the pretence of aiding refugees the Chinese army was using vast profits from the drug trade to finance setting up the apparatus ready for their ultimate invasion of the West.'

'And Stealth,' Newman remarked, 'is now capable of being defeated?'

'Absolutely.' Tweed was cleaning his glasses. 'That huge floating dock with giant lifting cranes will soon reach Jutland. It will take on board the intact *Yenan* and bring it back here for examination by experts. On top of that, poor Gaston Delvaux's new radar system has given us the means of easily detecting any such vessels or planes.'

'And you've withdrawn your resignation. End of story,' Newman said.

'Of that story, yes. The East will never now invade us by stealth.'

Addendum

WAR OF WORDS OVER 'INVISIBLE' SHIPS AND PLANES

All branches of the US Armed Forces plan to incorporate Stealth features . . . The US Navy is working on designs for Stealth cruisers and destroyers which would have no bridge and no decks and be commanded from a main interior control room, as happens on submarines.

Masts and antennae, all of which contribute to a ship's large radar cross-section, would vanish below decks. The aim, eventually, would be to produce frigates and destroyers that did not need air cover . . .

Daily Telegraph, Monday, November 28, 1988.